MW00623702

SEEDS
OF
WAR

THE SMOKESMITHS
Book One

JOÃO F. SILVA

Copyright © 2023 by João F. Silva

First paperback edition May 2023

Edited by Sarah Chorn

Proofread by Ed Crocker

Cover Design by MIBLART

Interior Illustrations by CyberOni Arts

ISBN 979-8-8299-6383-5 (paperback)

Published by João F. Silva

www.joaofsilva.net

To my wife, W, without whom I would never have the strength.
To anyone struggling beneath the surface.

This book is for you

CONTENTS

Ainusian
Ocean

Adla

Ainis

Vaerg

Enoris   Lim

Mosend

Mungir Bay

Alarkan

eon Erialast Fajar

THE BARREN WOT
◆ Samor The
Seven
Peaks

Ultfaest The Slop

BENAVEN
MOUNTAIN

◆ Benaven

THE THOUSAND HILLS Noha

n Gasho Raebur ◆

Mevon

Abirad
◆

Ledal ◆ Seirgrave

hari

Gloomwood
◊

Sirestir

Capo ◆ Ushar
Tec

Yab

◆ Yabish

WORLD

Shadesgrowl

Marcruncher

Bloodsleuth

Hearthspear

Mossback

ONE

VISITORS

GIMLORE

P *lease have mercy. I cannot recall. My memories fade and I am nothing
but weak. Old things haunt my dreams.*

—From *Mother's Memories*

By the time she was ten, Gimlore had already lost her parents to the war,
escaped the King's smokesmiths, and learned to survive. Selling a product
nobody else had should be easy by comparison. Yet, there was something
off about this whole ordeal. The door creaked open and Edmir stormed
in, bringing with him the stuffy humidity from outside the tavern. The
bald, stocky man walked towards Gimlore, twirling his moustache as he
approached the counter. He wore a stained, short-sleeved shirt revealing
veiny arms marked by scars. "They're almost here, boss."

Gimlore swallowed. "How close are they?"

"They're reaching town, but they ride at a snail's pace."

"Good. Is our contingency plan prepared?"

Edmir nodded.

"Let's go, then," she said, walking towards the door.

Outside her tavern, clouds obscured the sun, but the moist air continued to press on everyone. Beads of sweat made her shirt stick to her back, and she wiped her damp forehead with her sleeve. To make matters worse, the main street was still filthy with mud after the night's heavy downpour.

"Tell Nork and Nosema to keep the kitchen knives sharp," Gimlore said. "The visitors are going to arrive tired, hungry, and smelling like shit."

"I'll make sure it's all prepared," Edmir said. "Don't worry about nothing, boss."

Moments later, she was waving a welcome from the middle of the street.

"Shitheads came riding shadesgrowls to the marshes," Gimlore whispered as the eight feet tall, furry grey beasts with antlers struggled in the heat. Their flat hooves made it hard to stay balanced in the mud without slipping. Those were creatures of cooler climates.

Riding them was a group of men wearing strange apparel. Their long silk robes of varied bright colours contrasted with the earthy tones of the town. Especially in a street filled with mud, soot, and dung. The clothes were embroidered with intricate designs of flowers, trees, and picturesque scenery. They were all inlaid with small gemstones.

People nearby stopped what they were doing and stared, their loud voices turned to murmuring. Sweaty merchants in ratty clothes stopped loading their rustic wagons. A gang of shoeless children stopped pestering the adults. Carpenters and apprentices dropped their tools.

One man wearing a loose blue robe jumped off the shadesgrowl and almost slipped on the mud but found his feet. A shorter man struggled with his robes in the muddy street. After a while, he gave up on trying to keep his apparel clean. There were chuckles and muffled laughs from the gathered crowd.

"Worry not, good sir. I'll have your robes washed for you," Gimlore said. "They'll look like new."

The man gazed at her. He had a pointy nose and a bony, sharply shaved face. "These silks are only available in Sirestir. You cannot wash them," he said with a continental accent. "Are you the one in charge?"

"I wouldn't say *in charge*," Gimlore lied.

"What do you mean?"

"Heleronde is a new little township, you see. We've only been around for ten years, since the end of the Crimson Wars. Here, everybody is welcome but no one is *in charge*. We help each other out. I'm Gimlore."

"I am the interpreter for Herald Basa Akan, envoy from the Kingdom of Sirestir," the man said, tidying his robe and wiping sweat from his forehead.

Two of the Herald's bodyguards helped the large, tree-like man off his mount. They all had neatly groomed, silky dark hair and brown skin—lighter than hers—and wore cheaper green robes under studded chest armour.

"We've travelled on orders from His Majesty, King Doemus of Sirestir," the translator continued.

"What an honour to welcome such a venerable guest to our insignificant town. Let me know if something isn't your style. Please forgive anything rude my comrades might do or say. We're a little rougher than esteemed individuals such as yourselves."

The translator murmured her words back to Herald Akan and he responded in a baritone voice.

"The Herald thanks you for the hospitality. He says he is eager to discuss the matters that brought him here. But first, he needs a wash, a good meal, and some wine."

Gimlore bowed again. "Certainly! Please follow me to my humble establishment. I believe my people are already preparing lodging and a bath for everyone. Of course, you're welcome to stay as long as you want."

Gimlore walked into the Maiden's Hall, now nearly empty. The damned tavern had taken years to build, and she loved every creaking piece of the solid oak floorboard, every greasy spot on the counter, and the dusty bottles stored behind it. She even loved the dung splatter on the door. It was dirty but it was *her* dirt. After so many years bushwhacking, she finally owned something.

Her children got up from their chairs, smiling and waving at the Sirestine entourage in a rare moment of innocence.

Good kids, Gimlore thought, almost breaking into a chuckle. When she was their age, she still couldn't put on a show like that.

"These are Tinko and Thata," Gimlore said. She urged the entourage to the stairs that led to the rooms above the tavern. "They're wonderful children. They'd never hurt a fly."

....

A few hours later, the Maiden's Hall was closed to other customers. Gimlore sat opposite Herald Akan, who ate his supper in silence. Was he bothered by how poor or dirty the Maiden's Hall was? Or perhaps unhappy about having to eat the Bastard's Stew? It was a bestseller among her clients. It looked nasty, but it wasn't good to waste food, including deep-fried lizards, calf liver, heart, bone marrow, and brain. Delicious.

"The spices make you sweat," she said, trying her best to entertain them.

She tapped her foot on the floor as Edmir pretended to dry the glasses and plates. Nork and Nosema were on alert. They had come a long way since the Crimson Wars. The first had adjusted well enough to his new job as a hand but he still relied on his twin for some of the kitchen work. Everything she was doing here—all her business dealings—was for them. And Edmir. And her kids. By looking after her own interests, she was taking care of those around her. She might as well get down to business, then. A little smooth talk first.

"If I may?" Gimlore asked the Herald as she grabbed a pitcher of cerro wine when no one responded. "I'm told the Sirestine like their wine."

The Herald didn't need a translation and nodded for Gimlore to go ahead. The maroon liquor was the potent and fruity kind that left a bittersweet aftertaste, like cerro berries.

Gimlore filled his glass as the man spoke, followed by the translator. "The Herald says Sirestir has the best wine on the continent. Other countries have similar claims, but Sirestir has the greatest. He asks, is this wine produced here?"

"I'm afraid it's imported," she said.

More like smuggled.

"What do you produce?"

Gimlore feigned a light chuckle.

"I'm not a farmer. I'm just a businesswoman and a landowner. I enable the farmers to produce. I can take you to the farmlands and show you. I'm sure the Herald would love to see them. We have plenty of time before it's dark."

"The Herald would like that," he said.

Gimlore whistled and told Edmir to prepare for a ride.

············

Gimlore rode a hearthspear as slowly as the restless creature allowed. The Herald and the translator rode similar beasts. A burnt yellow coloured their scales, and their long, athletic legs were unlike those of any other creature. Pronounced spikes covered its back, thighs, and tail, making for an uncomfortable ride if not for the saddle. The creature roared, exposing its teeth.

"What do you think about our mounts? You don't have these on the old continent, do you?" she asked, tapping the animal on its thick, long neck, feeling its cold scales. "We call them hearthspears."

"Impressive," the interpreter said as Gimlore petted her mount over its muzzled maw.

"They can gallop through our marshes like a shadesgrowl on land. A remarkable creature, as you can see. I'll sell you a few if you wish."

The translator seemed confused but talked to the Herald, who nodded as he tried to slap away mosquitoes. "We can discuss business after the visit to the farmland."

"Oh, my mistake. I should have been clearer. Everything you see here *is* farmland," she said, waving an arm to encompass the landscape.

Dense, bushy trees hid the sky, and mud, ponds, and thick vegetation covered the ground. Her workers had carved trails through the canopy to make the transit easier both on foot and riding, though the marshlands were still largely unexplored.

Gimlore looked at the translator, and he stared back at her. "Is this a joke?"

It was easy to see why he would ask that.

"Absolutely not. This is our farmland," she said, and the translator whispered to the Herald. "Maybe we can stop here."

Once everyone dismounted, Gimlore walked through the bush to a large creek and knelt.

"Make no mistake," she said, eyeing the Herald to gauge his reaction. "Alarkan is a swampy wasteland. It's too hot, and it has too many insects. In the ten years since it rose from the ocean, it has become full of petty criminals, exiles, and war refugees. That's who we are. I'm a mix of all of those myself, depending on who you ask."

She withdrew a dead mouse from the pouch tied to her belt and shook it in the air.

"We discovered that a very interesting creature lives here. It's a carnivore, but it attacks nothing larger than the mouse I have in my hand."

The water moved first. Then three heads surfaced and the six-legged creatures walked onto the shore with their eyes fixed on the mouse. Their reptilian scales were red, but they had thick grey and green fur on their backs. The foreigners flinched and grimaced at the sight and the bodyguards unsheathed their short swords.

Gimlore dropped the rodent and the creatures lunged for it. They snarled and fought, each trying to win the food.

"We call them mossbacks. These are small, still wild, but we can domesticate them."

The Sirestine retainers couldn't look away, but despite their raised brows, their mouths were twisted in disgust, as though they were looking at a creature from the underworld.

"You may ask yourself what this has to do with farming. Well... we farm *them*."

The translator seemed incredulous, but he completed his duty without masking his contempt. "The Herald asks what you use them for."

"We use their fur for clothes. We harvest their eggs, their skin, and their meat."

And their liver elixir, but you don't need to know that...

The Sirestine nodded, exchanging looks until the translator spoke again. "We also heard about an... elixir... Is it related?"

Ah! Wouldn't you like to know?

Gimlore opened her pouch and produced a small vial with transparent liquid inside and held it for the Herald to see. "You mean this? I'm afraid I can't reveal its secrets, gentlemen."

The strangers leaned forward, their eyes sparkling as if they had found buried treasure.

They had come for this. She had to be careful.

"Perhaps the Herald would be interested in buying a few crates of elixir for King Doemus? It's a very rare product, and I'm taking bids from royal buyers before I hear merchants."

And I'm jacking up the damn price for you.

The translator looked at the Herald. "A demonstration would be good. How does it work?"

"I've never tried the elixir myself. I'll never try it, may the gods help me. I don't want to get addicted. But my men have tried it and I'm going to let them show you. Edmir?"

The man nodded and moved forward.

"Edmir drank some elixir a few minutes ago. It takes a while for its effect to kick in. But when it does..."

Edmir roared and flexed his muscles, his veins swelling. Edmir approached a boulder that was probably four feet wide and hugged it. He strained but lifted it and threw it at least two dozen feet.

The translator gaped at Edmir.

Edmir formed a fist in his right hand and crashed it into an enormous tree trunk. When he pulled his bloodied hand back, he exposed a massive crater in the wood.

"Strength, bravery, and fast healing. That's what my elixir provides to those who partake. Who wouldn't want their soldiers to possess such attributes?" The translator spoke with the Herald with urgent words. Gimlore waited, knowing this had almost certainly warranted her a new client.

They seemed excited, like fish swimming to a worm.

And they bit the hook, so it was time to reel them in.

Two

Out of Luck

Gimlore

I've made mistakes. My eyes got used to darkness. Everyone I knew was lost and forgotten.

— From *Mother's Memories*

Gimlore smiled as Nosema poured a stronger brand of cerro wine for the Sirestine bastards and a virgin version for herself. She suppressed a sigh upon realising her henchman was still wearing the red bandana that made him stand out like a peacock. At least she could trust him to read the hand signals and the way she placed the cutlery on the table.

With the guests loosened by the liquor, it was time to talk business. Tinko and Thata pretended to play with wooden toys by the window and Nork and Nosema continued to serve the big table.

She would squeeze every penny from the Herald and improve her elixir trade with the mainland after the first batch sold to Noha had already left her coffers half-full. They would realise how valuable her elixir could be and offer her the world in exchange. It wasn't personal, but she hadn't spent all those years cheating death to now be kind to these people. The war was over, but this was business, no feelings involved. She had two mouths to feed. Many more if she counted the rest of Heleronde.

"Gentlemen, may I have your attention?" She cleared her throat. "I don't want you to go back to your homeland thinking we are simpletons. I wanted to treat you to our special events, so I arranged one especially for you."

This piqued their attention.

Gimlore took the foreigners to the next room where a wide, square cage with steel bars dominated the space.

"We give spectators a chance to bet on who they think will win. Edmir, bring in the fighters."

Gimlore sat next to the Herald, and Edmir soon returned with two tall, bulky, shirtless men who had their fists wrapped. The long-haired Foloi was one of hers.

"Would the Herald place a wager? People enjoy doing so."

"The Herald does not engage in such lowly affairs," the interpreter said.

"Let's talk about the reason you came here, then."

"Our business."

"Our business." Gimlore nodded.

The fight began. Foloi took his time with the opponent, whom Gimlore had never seen. This was Gimlore's deception. Keep them drunk and focused on the fight and they'd pay triple or request an exclusive supply of the elixir. Then, she could use the gold to expand the town, take on more refugees. Give these people a better life. In peace.

Foloi picked his opponent apart with jabs and hooks. Each blow landed as his fists smacked the opponent in his mouth. The fighters' sweat flew and they grunted as they chased each other inside the cage.

Gimlore turned to her guests. "I'd like to start by asking you something, if you don't mind."

The translator nodded.

"Why do you need the elixir? The war ended ten years ago."

The translator applauded one of Foloi's right hooks, connecting with the opponent's left ear. Then, he spoke, "Do you care to guess?"

"You wouldn't waste the Herald's time on barren land. You want insurance. Something for your kingdom. Something that can elevate it over your enemies. An edge."

"You are correct. King Doemus is looking to set up colonies on this continent. We are exploring other... recruitment options. This elixir is very interesting. The fundamental question is how many crates you'd be willing to sell."

Gimlore drew a breath and waited. For a moment, it was as if only the fighters existed—their heavy breathing, punches landing on others' faces. How she wished that was the case.

"I'm open to offers, if the Herald has any."

"We are interested in the elixir, of course, but the land is what His Majesty requires. The King doesn't want to waste resources and lose months deforesting, however. You've cleared yours already. If we buy the land from you, the farmers would be able to stay and pay us a levy. It will be but a change of hands."

The damned translator was speaking with the eloquence of someone sober. She hid a hand signal, telling Edmir to pour more drinks, and he filled the translator's glass. *Land? They want the fucking land?*

Inside the cage, Foloi mauled his opponent with right crosses and jabs. The man's nose dripped blood though Foloi remained composed, as if he was sparring.

"Very well, I'm open to offers," Gimlore said. *This shit doesn't feel right.*

It seemed the Herald had given his translator the trust to negotiate, which was odd, but perhaps this was how they did business.

"We'd like to buy six lots for now. We know you own over twenty-five. His Majesty wants to pay you five malleans of gold."

Who do these fuckers think they are?

Foloi finished his bulky opponent with a powerful knee kick to the chin. The man dropped, unconscious and the Sirestine entourage applauded, as did Gimlore.

"You'll pardon my response," she said, taking a deep breath. "That doesn't sound like a reasonable offer."

"Care to counter?"

Her head pounded as she struggled to tame her anger. "You've seen my lands. They are not barren. They are worth at least *twenty-five* malleans per lot, and I wouldn't sell at that price since the value will go up once your neighbouring kingdoms come knocking on my door asking about the elixir, which only *I* have."

The translator sighed. "I would recommend you take the offer."

"Why is that?"

The fellow stared at her with an intensity she didn't expect. Then he smirked.

"If we're being honest, Madam Gimlore, you're alone in this wilderness, aren't you? You are a landowner, but what's stopping other kingdoms from seizing your land? I see no army, no political leaders, no generals, and no protective walls surrounding your town. You have no power. You're an exiled woman who was lucky enough to stumble upon something precious. It's only a matter of time until others discover the source of your elixir. Why would we pay for what we can... take?" The man paused, sipped his drink, and continued. "Look, all you have to do is sell it at the price I offered. You should take it now before you lose the land *and* the gold."

She drew in a breath, trying to contain herself. Her hands trembled in rage as she wiped her mouth. "If you'll excuse me, I need to freshen up."

She took off, not looking to see if the Herald would approve of her leaving in highly unusual fashion. She hurried to the next room, then to the stairs that led to the second floor, before stopping halfway, breathing hard. It was as though the air had vanished and she was choking in fear and anxiety. As though she was a cornered animal.

You are all alone...

Those words tore at her as if peeling off bandages covering deeper wounds. How many times had she heard that? Those words took her back, reviving memories that had no business being unburied. The Sirestine were no longer playing by business rules. It would have been one thing to outsmart her in business terms, but they had come for her livelihood and for everything she had.

Gimlore couldn't let them do as they pleased.

She sat on the stairs, her hands gripping her legs and teeth gritted. Her right hand slipped to the sheath attached to the ankle and she grabbed the dagger that brought back memories good and bad, just as the translators' words had. She observed the immaculate, thin blade, gifted by Madame Mazi. "What should I do about these bastards?" she whispered.

Madame Mazi, the previous owner of the dagger, would probably tell her never to cry, to keep her emotions in check, and to never let anyone take advantage of her. She had owned the clandestine orphanage where Gimlore spent most of her youth.

Like any other orphan children in Mosendel, Gimlore had been property of the crown. And if the crown had it their way, she should have been shoved into a smoke chamber to see if she could become a smokesmith or die in the attempt. If she could, they would have turned her into a killing machine and groomed her for complete loyalty. If she couldn't, she would be another dead urchin who could no longer cause trouble. Madame Mazi found her before the King's smokesmiths did. Before they could turn her into one of them.

To the rest of society, the madame was an old bourgeois maiden, but she outlived an abusive husband without help and dedicated her life to helping young girls in secret. She taught Gimlore to lie, cheat, steal and, most importantly, survive in a rotten world.

You are like me, child. A survivor, she always said. *Women don't live long in this world. Not if we cave to the fear and whims of men who are, by all accounts, inferior.*

"A survivor," she whispered.

Gimlore controlled her breath, remembering the exact words the old maiden had used to get her to stop crying when she had killed the gross, burly man who had pinched her bottom. The first man she'd ever killed.

Sometimes, it feels like our world is in flames. They trapped you in pressure, in heat, so how can you not react? You inhale the fire if you must. You will be tired, scared, sad, angry... But then you continue to breathe. Doubt always seeps in, but I'd be more worried if you felt nothing after taking someone's life.

Clasping the hilt of the dagger, it dawned on Gimlore she had been away for a while now, so she got up and walked back to the cage room.

She was no longer the little lady who liked to play with knives. She was a mother. A war veteran. They needed her elixir more than she needed their gold. How dare they come to *her* house and issue ill-concealed threats?

She stood and composed herself, taking a deep breath before she walked back to the Herald and his translator, giving her crew a few covert hand signals.

"I'm so terribly sorry about the delay, gentlemen. You know how it is with us women. There's always something that needs fixing."

The translator sighed and rolled his eyes. "The Herald would like to retire. You don't have to give us an answer now. We can continue tomorrow."

What would she do—let them bully her? Threaten her livelihood? *I'd rather die.*

"I don't think so," Gimlore said and whistled.

Nork, Nosema, and Edmir stabbed the Sirestine retainers in the gaps of their studded armours and her children threw a pair of knives at the Herald's face. Eyes wide, the soldiers saw their shouts muffled by Gimlore's henchmen with hands over their mouths. The soldiers fought back, but in vain as blood squirted from their open necks until they had no more fight in them. With blades deep inside his brain, the Herald let out a faint yelp as his body hit the floor with a loud thump. They all crumpled in pools of blood except for the astonished translator, who had Edmir's dagger kissing his throat.

"You *made me* do this. Now, if you scream or make any loud noises, your throat will be opened in less than a minute."

"What's this? You're violating guest protocol!" he snarled, trembling under the blue robe. There was genuine fear in his eyes. All the smugness vanished.

"What guest protocol? You're not here on a diplomatic visit. You're in my fucking town and we don't answer to any kingdom. We're free."

"You killed the Herald!" the translator squealed. "King Doemus will send his army after you, woman. Unless you let me live, that is. Only I can deter him from coming after you. Now, you must free me."

Gimlore sighed at the predictable try at negotiation, unconvinced by the man's request.

"You can stop the farce," she said. "Something has bugged me all day. It was always you doing the talking, and I wondered why. You know, people come to my tavern to drink and talk their asses off, so I get to hear their stories. I remember one about how certain diplomats use body doubles to avoid assassinations. So, all along... you're the actual Herald, aren't you?"

The man's face adopted a snarl.

"I shouldn't have come here. A savage is what you are. They warned me not to meet with the Viper. I listened to the stories about you and your little crew. The things you did during the Crimson Wars just to stay alive, with no allegiance to any king or queen."

"I thought about keeping you alive so you could warn the King that this place is not for the likes of him or any other dynastic asshole. To tell him to pay up fivefold if he wants the elixir. To tell him I won't let him bully me. But if I did that, they'd come after me, which would be bad for business.

So, the reason I kept you alive was to let you know you didn't have me fooled with your pathetic game of doubles."

"Foolish woman..." The real Herald smirked. "You thought you could keep selling samples of that elixir to the Nohani and no one would wonder where it was coming from? My King knows all about you and your covert operation. Sooner or later, we will know how to produce the elixir. He sent me in good faith, hoping you would see reason. As we speak, hundreds of soldiers and settlers are on their way here. If they don't find me alive when they arrive, they will destroy everything you have. They will kill everyone you care about, take it all for themselves. No one will remember you. Do you think the townspeople care about you? They're used to kings and queens. They won't miss you as long as they can keep their bellies full. You're a taverner who dreamt too big. It's time to wake from your fantasy."

Gimlore hesitated, every word like a knife thrust into her stomach, fear settling low. *Is he bluffing?*

"You know I'm right," the Herald said with unusual confidence, considering he had a knife at his throat. "Kill me and you'll die too."

She sensed no lie and no bluff. If she were to let him live, he would make sure his King would steal or destroy everything she had. They'd have no reason to leave her alive unless she was to bend the knee to them. Killing him might not solve that problem either. Heck, it would probably create more problems—she swallowed just thinking about it—but at least she would wipe that pathetic grin off the bastard's face.

"Your death would be undoubtedly well deserved. And you see... I've always had a softness for the neck."

She nodded. Edmir slit the Herald's throat and let the body drop.

There was only mild relief.

"Come on," she said to her crew. "What are you looking at? There's a lot of blood to scrub off the floor. I want this place smelling like a god's arse tomorrow morning when the drunkards come."

"W-what about the bodies, boss?"

"Give them to Pinesy. And take that damned bandana off, Nosema."

"And their mounts?" Nork asked.

"Handle them."

She started climbing the stairs, each step like a mountain of nerves and questions to answer. She got to her room, closed the door, and lay in bed, clasping her hands to stop the shaking.

Instinct told her the Herald hadn't been bluffing, that she had been a fool to kill him. They would come for her, for her town, for her elixir. On the other side, she had the memories of Madame Mazi raising her with a dagger in hand. *It's meant to be used,* the old woman used to say. *So, use it!*

She punched the wall, her arm trembling.

What have I done?

The seeds of war were being planted again. The very thing she had avoided at all costs. She had run away then, in the Crimson Wars, but she couldn't run now. Not when all she had was here. Her children. Her friends. Her tavern.

She had been too naïve, thinking she could turn into an innkeeper and spend the second half of her life swimming in gold and drowning her demons from the war in liquor. She had been foolish to think this was a time of peace, that monarchs would come, listen to her offers and open their purses.

They would come for her even though she had been careful not to show them how the elixir is extracted and from where. And when they arrived, they wouldn't have their necks so exposed.

THREE

GOD HIMSELF

ORBERESIS

*T*he Pawn of Fate, the Old One, invoked the ones who trampled. The ones who crawled upon the earth.

— From *Mother's Memories*

Being a god was almost more trouble than it was worth.

Orberesis reached inside his white silk robe and found the heavy silver chain that hung around his neck. It supported a red crystal orb, the source of his power. Had it really been ten years since his miracle? That moment when the earth shook. Four nations cleared of the creatures that plagued them. The day when the land swallowed cities. He had done what no soldier or army could do. In mere moments, he ended the Crimson Wars and lifted a continent from the depths of the Southern Ocean.

Yet he couldn't remember how he'd done it.

They had been riding for weeks, and every day more pilgrims joined the procession. Over five hundred people were now following him and his

Order of the Red Orb. It was a testament to the success of his priests who preached about him and his miracle.

Even now, dressed in their dark robes despite the heat, they preached to both the farmers and those who held the whips to make them work.

Every soul was a potential follower.

Orberesis held on to the red orb with a tight grip and tried his best to remember how he had managed his miracle so he could do it again. His followers hungered for more miracles. Why wouldn't the orb bless him with power again?

He saw the changes to the landscape he'd caused. Cracks and fissures tore the earth open and forced rivers to flow in different courses. Farmers had abandoned their lands and settled elsewhere. Volcanoes had risen and swallowed towns, blending them into hills and mountains. Those were necessary changes that brought balance and a much-needed respite from the beast hordes.

Orberesis was sweating under the blistering sun and his near-constant migraine flared to new heights when his caravan crossed the borderlands of the kingdom of Sirestir. The problem of posing as a god or someone holy was that people expected perfection and divinity. He, on the other hand, was a ball of headaches, migraines, and nightmares he couldn't shake off. That meant he had to hide the pain. No grimaces and no complaints. At first, pretending to be a god had been a fun idea. Spread some lies, collect people's gold tributes. He'd performed a miracle, after all. Saved the world. But then he realised he could also exploit that to try to find a cure for the pain. Gold was good, but a painless existence was better. Much better. He'd scoured the world searching for something—anything—that would ease his migraines or stop the nightmares, but nothing had worked. He had already exhausted the cures available to the common folk. Now it was time to get access to remedies of kings and lords.

The farmland reminded him of the sweat province where he grew up, where fields of crops grew taller than children and painted the plains and the hills with berry crimson.

The worship leaders led the way to Ushar, and the pilgrims followed on foot. Orberesis rode in the heart of the convoy, alone, about fifty paces between him and his followers. Only a few had permission to approach him.

The farmers in the crimson fields took a break to appreciate the rare sight of a religious leader, and he waved at them. A tanned man in ratty clothes fell to his knees and removed the straw hat that shielded him from the smouldering sun. Others were braver and came closer.

Orberesis had no problem with people approaching. He revelled in being among commoners, devout followers or not. Of course, devout was better.

An elderly woman approached. Her front teeth had fallen out and her dark skin looked wrinkled as a raisin.

"Is it really you, God Himself?" she asked, as she did her best to keep up with the caravan. Two worship leaders tried to push her away, but Orberesis stayed their hands.

"That is what they call me," he said, gathering himself into a regal posture.

"I believe you, Highest One," the woman said. "I believe you are. They say you're returning home. Are you from Sirestir? Are you one of us?"

Memories of fire, mud, and soot flooded his mind. The awful stench of smoke, ashes, and dung, worse than his nightmares. He shook it off and kept his composure.

"Born and raised in the Gloomwoods," he said, swallowing. "This is where I belong. I don't want to be anywhere else. This is my land."

"This is your land," she repeated, then looked at the farmers scattered across the fields. "God Himself is here! He rid us of the wretched beasts! He put an end to the Crimson Wars and now He returns! Yet He rides a shadesgrowl like the common folk. He has nothing left to prove! Thank God Himself for His power and His kindness!"

The woman knelt and pressed her face to the ground.

"Bless you, kind woman," Orberesis said.

These famished bastards were desperate but fooling the poor was the first step in fooling the rich. And he would not ruin ten years of hard work building this persona and enduring migraines and cursed dreams for the sake of honesty or pity.

Next to him, Solvi tucked her light blonde hair behind her ears and let the bright sun illuminate her pale face as she approached the peasant woman. Beads of sweat formed on her forehead, but she still insisted on wearing the dark robe of the Order. Orberesis' eyes lingered on her figure and their gazes met for a charged second before Solvi broke off contact. Her thin nose and freckled cheeks gave her an allure he had a hard time not studying. If he wasn't such an ill bastard, he might even make a move.

"Rise, woman," Solvi said. "God Himself, has blessed you. Let's spread His word now. Or join us and march to the capital."

Orberesis called Solvi close and whispered in her ear, "Good job. I'm pleased with you."

Her face brightened. She curled the hair behind her ears again and lowered her head, flushing. "I'm not worthy, Highest Lord."

"You are."

Solvi was the reason for the growth of his cult. She was a force to be reckoned with. He had shown her humanity and love when she was reeling from the atrocities of the Crimson Wars. Now she was on his side. And what an asset she was. He wished she could continue to be that, or perhaps something more. But he needed to get healthier first.

"How many folks have followed our caravan since our journey started?"

"Too many to count, Highest Lord. Hundreds for certain."

"And you are confident many more will follow by the time we reach Ushar?"

"Yes, Highest Lord. Even the King is a follower."

"I'm humbled to hear that," Orberesis said and excused her.

It was the third time Solvi had told him King Doemus of Sirestir was a follower. The son of the now-deceased Queen Bitch, who had ruled with ruthlessness and set her smokesmiths upon his entire sweat province. The one who had ordered everyone there to be executed for the crime of being poor and hungry. She was dead now, but her legacy remained with her pathetic son.

The caravan progressed and the red fields of cerro berries gave way to small forests and little towns. Hundreds more peasants had joined the parade. Such a following would impress any decent king. Orberesis might even enjoy the landscape if his head didn't pound like a giant gong, reverberating through his heartbeats, affecting his hearing and blurring his vision.

They continued towards the capital after three breaks and he noticed how few soldiers kept the roads to Ushar safe—another sign of a weak ruler's fragile grip over his kingdom.

Orberesis could almost see his legend grow in every town he passed as he travelled east; the chatter among the peasants, the declarations of faith and the jealous lords who could not force their subjects to love them the same way they loved him. But talking to his followers was hard when the headache seemed like it would never leave him. He wished he could spend time conversing with them, telling lies and leaving them with gaped mouths, perhaps persuading them to donate some more funds to the Order of the Red Orb. But the bloody headaches...

Pound.

Pound.

Pound.

How could he maintain a conversation like that? How could he charm them as he knew he could? He clasped his hands hard on his mount's reins and tightened his jaw. It was pure misery and he couldn't even express it without leaving them second-guessing his divinity.

His oldest friend steered the reins of his shadesgrowl towards Orberesis. His greasy hair dripped sweat onto his face and uniform. Orberesis contained a laugh as Tavanar tried to mimic the appearance of a nobleman or a royal guard, holding the hilt of his sword as if he knew how to use it.

"What are you doing here?" Orberesis whispered. "You're supposed to be commanding the pace, not dropping by for a chat."

Tavanar raised his hands, also careful not to be overheard. "I'm doing my part. Just wondering if our plan will work. It seems... too bold to put our lives on the line like this. The idea was mine, but I never thought you'd go along with it."

"Keep your mouth shut," Orberesis whispered, trying not to show a smile. "They'll hear you."

"It's fine, Doi. They're not close enough."

Orberesis froze upon hearing the name he had long abandoned. It no longer defined who he had become. He had locked away his past self.

"Everything alright, Highest Lord?" Solvi shouted from a hundred paces away.

"Ah, yes, yes. General Tavanar and I are discussing logistics."

Solvi bowed and pulled the reins of her shadesgrowl away. Tavanar locked his eyes on her figure, spurring anger in Orberesis.

"You've got to keep your urges to yourself or they'll wonder why God Himself lounges with such perverse figures."

"You're worried I'll make you look ungodly?"

Orberesis sighed. "Yes." And Solvi wasn't for the likes of him either.

Tavanar chuckled and Orberesis almost felt like laughing too. He missed it—the jests, the laughs, and the heists. But now he needed to focus on a cure for his incapacitating headaches. For years, nothing had worked.

"If you had ten minutes with Solvi, she'd skewer you in less than five. Unless I ordered her not to kill you," Orberesis said. Then he allowed himself to relax. "Solvi is not too fond of men."

"Gods are alright, though, I assume."

"Only this God."

"Is she powerful?" Tavanar asked.

"She is a smokesmith. What do you think?"

Tavanar scowled. "You only say that because she is dying to kiss your stinky feet. Speaking of which, when are we stopping for a wash?"

"I planned to wash in a palace tonight, but we might need to stop soon," Orberesis said.

"Why don't you use your godly powers to get us there faster?"

"It doesn't work like that, arsehole."

Orberesis didn't really know how the power of the orb worked either, but Tavanar didn't need to know *he* didn't know. It was always best if he seemed in control, at least to a certain extent. Truth be told, the Miracle had been a fluke. He'd tried to get the orb to work for ten straight years, to no avail. A little spurt of power would be enough to get his followers amazed, but no. Nothing. Right now, he was living on reputation, the appearance of divinity, and the fools he managed to swindle, which had been enough so far.

Tavanar shot him an apologetic smile. "How do you feel about returning to Ushar? I wonder how much has changed..."

Orberesis shrugged, shoving away memories of the last time he and Tavanar had been inside the city's walls.

"The kingdom is a mess. Do you see the people here? They are sick and starved, even worse than they used to be. They're defeated. Remember how quickly they joined my cult after the worship leaders offered the slightest comfort? The King seems to care more about his ancient tomes than he does about governing."

Tavanar sighed and grimaced. "It doesn't matter how long you're away. Some things never change."

Orberesis nodded.

"Speaking of never changing... How has it been? Your illness, I mean?"

Orberesis swallowed. It wasn't easy to talk about, even with Tavanar. He didn't even know what illness it was, though it was clearly something malign. "The paralysis is rare, but the nightmares and the migraines are constant."

"What if the elixir doesn't work? They said it heals people faster and strengthens them, but that doesn't mean—"

"I know, Tav, but what choice do I have?"

They had heard rumours spreading of a miraculous elixir. There wasn't much information about its effects yet. The reports had mentioned super strength, which he didn't care about, but also fast healing. That got him excited. The problem was nobody knew where one could find this elixir. That's why he needed to go to Ushar. To the palace. If there was something rare and valuable in the world, Ushar would probably have it.

Tavanar's face dropped. "We'll get the elixir, don't worry. Rest, now. You have a big day tomorrow."

Orberesis nodded. Oh, how he wished Tavanar was right. "Tell the worship leaders to set up camp," he said. "Let's spend the night here."

Tavanar smiled and nodded, the same smile Orberesis had grown used to seeing. The same smile that kept Orberesis sane and grounded. It comforted him to have someone around who knew he wasn't a god, even if Tav thought he had control over the powers. Even if Tav had a heart sometimes too tender for his own good and for what needed to be done.

The moon shone above the Gloomwoods on that muggy summer night. Festive decorations covered the trees; the anglers brought giant wickplates to shore and Doi watched them strip the meat they were going to grill. His mouth watered and he smiled. His favourite part of the festival was that they allowed him to stay up all night too, just like everyone else.

Most of the adults danced and drank. His father sat on a rock next to the bonfire. Amid the commotion, Doi and the other children from the Gloomwoods gathered, and his father warmed his hands over the fire.

Doi chose a spot as close to his father as possible. He loved listening to his dad's stories. He could picture them well and imagine himself in them. Perhaps one day he would have stories of his own.

His father told of when he was arrested for stealing a necklace, and by a miracle ended up living to tell the tale.

"You have something on your mind, Doi. What is it?"

Doi hesitated. He was no longer that young and he wasn't stupid. But he still didn't understand what the story was about. "This story was different. It was... specific. Ushar, the Gloomwoods. You talked about places we all know."

"So, what is your question?"

"How did you do it? You were in bonds with a rope around your neck!"

His father's smile widened.

"I can tell you, but you've got to use that head of yours. You'll go places, Doi. I know you will. But these invisible mental walls limit your thinking. You can do great things when you tear them down."

For hours, his dad told the story within the story. Nothing had been what it seemed. He had thought it was just a story, and it was really true. His father was a thief. A criminal. Someone who had stolen a lady's expensive necklace.

"You look disappointed," his father said.

"I am."

"Doi, there are always two sides to every story and those things you are talking about don't exist. Goodness... Innocence... What makes the lady

innocent and the thief guilty? She was rich, was she not? She had dozens of other necklaces. Maybe the lady still went to sleep in silky sheets, soldiers posted outside her door while your old man slept in the mud. I merely dared to tip the scales in my favour. Just a tiny bit. Sometimes you must trick people and do bad things for good reasons. You get it? That is life."

Doi nodded. He thought he glimpsed something in his father's eyes. A passion he seldom saw. "Then where is the necklace, Father?" he asked.

Father smiled and produced something from his pocket. He looked around, and when he made sure no one was glancing, he showed Doi a precious white pearl before hiding it again.

Doi's eyes widened upon seeing the precious stone. It made sense now. "Y-you... Why did you...?"

"Look around, Doi. Look at your neighbours. All of them. Singing, dancing, and eating proper food for the first time all year. Don't they look happy? Don't they deserve it after the year we've had? Shouldn't they be happy?"

A necklace stolen. Sold in exchange for food and drinks.

Happy. Happy. Happy.

Everything turned into an unnatural blur.

The Queen's smokesmiths sent after his dad, the thief. The Gloomwoods turned to flames. Columns of smoke painted the sky dark. Screams of pain amplified. Flames burning one hundred feet tall. Smokesmiths roping people to the trees and burning them. Father, in the middle of the crowd, tied to a tree. The smokesmiths sticking dried leaves and bushes at his feet.

Happy. Happy. Happy.

Words hitting with the power of a whip.

"The Queen sentences you to death by fire. It would only be you, but they all enjoyed the spoils of the necklace you stole. So, they must pay."

The smokesmith's torch meeting the bushes, and Father screaming in pain but his eyes resting on Doi. A panic large enough to set off the wisest of men.

Doi needed to run.

But he was paralysed. He tried to run but his body wouldn't move. Doi looked back, a giant grey man chasing him. His face was a blur, he was as tall as the sky. His sole attention was on Doi.

Run! He needed to run. But he couldn't. He was paralysed. The giant man reached out his hand to him.

Run! He needed to run.

Run.

Orberesis woke covered in sweat and jumped out of his cot, but he struggled to stand, the paralysis of his dream still weighing on him. His last meal burned his throat and he let it out. For some reason, he found himself craving wickplate pie. He had always hated it, and yet now at this strange moment, the craving was strong.

That nightmare.

That damned nightmare cursing him, plaguing even his peaceful nights. Orberesis' eyes welled, and he sobbed like a child, not only for the memories it brought but for the torment he suffered. One would think that after years of experiencing the exact same nightmare, it would get easier, but it never did. It had been the worst day of his life, at first, when he'd lost his father to the Sirestine smokesmiths. Lost everything. But he never understood what that giant man was and where it came from.

He *needed* a cure for whatever illness he had and for that, he would do anything.

FOUR
THE BLIND KING

ORBERESIS

*W*hen I look inside, I don't have to hide. I tried hard. Now, chaos organises me.

— From *Mother's Memories*

The rest of the journey was gruesome. Orberesis wished he could open his white robe to cool off. The heat from the shadesgrowl he rode made it all the much worse. He wanted to scratch his balls, but God Himself couldn't do such a human thing in front of everyone.

He spotted the great walls of a city he never thought he would visit again. Ushar, capital of the Two Nations of Sirestir and Yab, rested atop a steep hill, looming over everything. Built by the Ancient Ones, it was a true marvel of craftsmanship. The Palace of Brilliance stood at the very top, guarded by giant barriers—a city within the city.

With the migraines miraculously subdued, nostalgia took over Orberesis and he found himself humming a tune he didn't recall knowing. Strange. Where was that from?

He shook that off and turned to Solvi. "You know what's impressive about Ushar?"

"I don't, Highest Lord."

I hope she finds me impressive.

"Look to the right." He pointed towards the part of the city that met the Southern Ocean.

"The ships, Highest Lord?"

"Not just any ships. The Floating City Fleet! Have you heard about it?" Solvi shook her head.

"I grew up hearing tales of it. My father sat me and all the other children down around the fire pit and talked about these gargantuan nine-mast vessels with red sails, four-hundred-feet long and two-hundred-feet wide. Five times bigger than any other ship ever built. It used to be my dream to visit these ships. In less than three years, the old queen built a fleet of sixty. I hear they have hundreds now, sailing across the world, trading between north and south, east, and west."

"It sounds incredible, Highest Lord."

"It is. Hundreds of giant ships challenging the oceans. Crews of tens of thousands of men and women living aboard them. It's a true floating city. When I was a child, I thought I'd end up in a crew."

"Maybe I should arrange for you to visit, Highest Lord."

"That won't be necessary. Those were the dreams of a child."

That story was true, but he left out the part where he and Tavanar tried to steal a vessel and were chased by the Queen Bitch's smokesmiths, forced to leave the city. Or the part where he'd failed to join the marines due to being too weak and undisciplined. Solvi didn't need to know any of that.

The closer Ushar was, the twitchier he became and his head started pounding him from the inside out again. More farmers and citizens followed them. Tavanar ordered for the standards to be raised and the red orbs painted over the large black flags that waved in the warm wind, leaving no doubt as to who all those people were.

The city gates were behemoths of wood and steel, as impenetrable as the giant stone walls. The Order of the Red Orb waited for the gates to be opened. With every passing moment, Orberesis' heart raced a little faster.

"If the gates don't open, the pilgrims will wonder what's going on," Tavanar whispered amid the lively chatter.

Orberesis scowled. "Solvi told me the King admires me. Can you imagine?"

"Kings are as dumb as peasants," Tavanar said. "And he is his mother's son, after all."

Dozens of guards lifted the heavy cast iron bars that protected the city while others kept it suspended with heavy chains in a pulley system.

Orberesis nodded permission for his standard bearers to go forward. The caravan marched at a slow pace into the city. He shook at each step, knowing very well God Himself couldn't show fear.

He forced a haughty posture and rode until he was inside the city walls. They were so tall that they covered a big part of the houses in shade. That wasn't always a bad thing in the scorching southeast.

Orberesis admired the sprawling capital city where he had learnt what survival meant. Ushar was immense in every sense of the word. The rooftiles spread all the way towards the Palace of Brilliance and narrow alleyways carved the residential quarters, splitting the city into sections. He remembered well which rooftops would make a better escape route for scoundrels like him.

On the streets, cheering crowds drew his attention. In his years away, Ushar had changed for the worse. The Two Nation's capital was grimier than he remembered it. Filth covered the cobblestones, and peasants no longer cared to wipe the soot or grime off their faces. The air held a hint of smoke that almost masked the stench of rotten fish and piss emanating from the narrow alleys.

He didn't remember everyone being *that* poor.

"Are you from here?" a toothless city-dweller asked, forcing him out of his thoughts. Dirt and grime covered the man's face, but his eyes sparkled.

Orberesis put on his best impression of a regal face. As much as his migraine allowed. "I am," he said with a slow nod. "Would you join my procession?"

"Me? Join you? Of course, Highest One. I pray to you day and night and I'm going to send my child to learn the ways of the Order."

"I'm honoured."

He often found humility and simplicity worked best with the simple folk. They didn't care for big words. It was all about presence. He wondered if they would still follow him if he one day decided to admit he was a farce.

"Long live God Himself!" the man hailed. "Long live the Highest Lord!"

Such chants should please him, though it was still hard to believe anyone would consider him a god. In Ushar, he and his cult had no say, though. He was at the King's mercy. And being stuck inside a massive, gated city was not ideal if those in charge were not on his side.

Others repeated the chants. Shopkeepers, shoe shiners, merchants, and even slaves. They came to see him. *Poor bastards have no idea I'm as ill as they are.*

"Solvi," he called, unable to muster the appropriate cheerfulness. "They are so supportive."

"Don't be so humble, Highest One. The people love you. And these are *your* people."

"Yes, I guess they are. Are we being taken to King Doemus?"

"Yes. As a religious Order, we have full clerical access to the palace and the King. The people would revolt if their King denied you welcome."

"They love me that much…" he reflected, resting his eyes on the crowd. "I hope the King is as devout."

"Oh, he is. You'll see," she said with a courteous smile.

The journey to the Palace of Brilliance was slow. The cobblestone walk-way was slippery, and shadesgrowls had a hard time hiking the steep slope. The palace sent servants with chairs and had Orberesis sit in a large one carried by four strong slaves.

That was a good sign.

The palace gates were open and his caravan remained outside as Or-beresis, Tavanar, Solvi, and his personal aides walked into the courtyard. Dozens of elite warriors stood motionless, bowing their heads to him as he passed. Their uniforms were pristine, of fine cut too. A decade ago, he wouldn't have minded stealing one of those.

The chief servant ushered them inside without looking at Orberesis' face. "His Majesty King Doemus is expecting you, Miraculous One," he said.

An invisible weight continued to wear on Orberesis. Doubt seeping into his mind. What if they discovered he was a farce? What if the pain became too much to bear and he started to slide away from the expected behaviour of a god? He must be crazy to put himself in that situation, but he couldn't think of another way to find a cure—any cure.

He peered at Tavanar. His friend did a good job of pretending not to break a sweat, but the back of his shirt and his palms would reveal it to anyone watching. Orberesis looked for any unwanted attention, but none of the servants looked at those they served. Orberesis saw a bit of himself in them. They all looked like him, with their brown skin, thin frames, and long, dark hair.

The chief servant guided them through the wide halls of the palace, un-derneath the ancient archways, towards the Ceremonial Room. Triangular banners covered the walls. Each one had a crest of an anchor and a shield, representing the alliance between Sirestir and Yab.

Father, would you believe I'm here?

A polished wooden floor led them straight to where King Doemus sat in the distance. His advisors sat on either side while aides and servants stood with their eyes glued to the floor. They knelt when they noticed Orberesis' arrival.

"Your Majesty, I bring the Highest One. The Miraculous One. God Himself," the chief servant announced. "He is a child of the land, born and raised in this very kingdom. He saved humanity from the wretched beasts that plagued it, allowing peace to replace the Crimson Wars. He raised a continent from the ocean and became Creator and the bearer of the red orb. Orberesis!"

The crowd erupted into cheers and chants. Higher lords, diplomats, and prominent merchants filled the reception room and they were... hailing him. Bowing and applauding. Orberesis couldn't help but wonder how genuine this support was.

"May your grace bless us!" they chanted. "May God Himself live forever!"

Orberesis lost his composure for a moment. It was surreal. He had expected the peasants to fall for his scheme... but nobles? And merchants?

King Doemus stood from his throne, which had been encrusted with precious pearls captured during the Floating City Fleet's western journeys.

"You are most welcome to every lot, castle, or abode within our realm," he said.

The resolve in his voice did not match his frail physique. His natural slouch betrayed the countless hours spent leaning over scriptures and tomes.

Next to the King, Queen Thura intertwined her arm in his. Her dark hair was wavy and long. She couldn't be younger than Doemus, but her smooth, luscious skin shone under the sunlight that streamed through the windows. She wore a long, burgundy dress displaying a daring amount of cleavage.

Orberesis pushed his nervousness down and forced a sympathetic smile.

"I am humbled by the reception."

Doemus knelt and extended his hands towards Orberesis. His dark complexion highlighted the white of the pupils.

"Highest One, I'm pleased to meet you and to have you here before me. I've prayed to you every night. Did my prayers reach you?"

"They did," Orberesis lied after a brief hesitation. If Orberesis didn't know what Doemus' family had done for decades, he might even regret lying. "I'm sorry about your eyes."

"It's not about the eyes, Highest One," the king confessed, caressing the Queen's arm that intertwined in his. "I am how I am. I can't change my blindness, as long as I adapt to it. But I don't think a life without being able to read is worth living. The pleasure is in reading, not having someone do it for me. I wish I could still read on my own."

"Don't say that!" The Queen's grasp on Doemus' arm tightened. Her harsh words echoed louder than Orberesis had expected. "I'll always read for you."

Orberesis swallowed, trying the waters. "Perhaps I can help you develop a system to read with your hands instead of your eyes."

Doemus' mouth gaped. "Oh, Highest One! That would truly be a divine gift. What would it take?"

First, I need to heal myself. Perhaps I could test his faith for now.

"Faith is always the solution. The worship leaders from my Order tell me you are one of my staunchest followers. I couldn't believe it at first. Would you say you are a true believer?"

The King smiled. "If I don't believe a miracle maker, then who am I to believe? I worship you with all my strength, Highest One. With all my heart. And I pray at least three times a day."

There was truth in his words. Orberesis wasn't sure about Queen Thura, but maybe she'd come around. Fooled like the peasants.

If only he could go back to his father and show him this moment, when a king bowed. How the Queen Bitch's son now asked for his help.

Orberesis looked for Tavanar. His best friend sported a modest smirk. This was the perfect moment. There was no time for doubt. No time to waste. He summoned all the calm and confidence he could muster, bottling up his nerves.

"Miracles don't happen overnight. They take time. They are difficult to carry out. Even for me. You must have nothing but patience in your heart. I will know it, then. I would love to be your greatest help. Your spatial and spiritual guide. Your closest confidant."

"I'd love nothing less, Highest One!"

There it was. His chance. "Then perhaps I could have a place at your side? A physical seat on the governing council?"

Silence followed gasps. The King's face went blank for a second. A second during which Orberesis nearly shat himself with anxiety and fear, mixed in with the chronic drum pounding in his head.

"I believe so, Highest One," the King said. "Nothing would make me happier. In fact, I often wonder why it is that monarchs often reject spiritual counsel..." he trailed off.

"Y-Your Majesty," an older man with an elaborate moustache said. "This is a grand ask. The greatest ask! There is no precedent for this. All the members of the governing council are there for a reason. Some by blood of the Two Nations' founding fathers and others by the value and prosperity they bring via their trade and development. You must ponder with the utmost care and think about the traditions of our realm. Many people believe in Orberesis as God Himself but having him take a seat on the governing council would undermine the integrity of the realm as we know it."

The man stood close to Doemus, implying a high status. A senior advisor? His long robe was blue and red with gold overlays, a sign that he was wealthy enough not to be challenged often. Thick rings around each of his fingers clinked as he moved.

A hint of fear threaded through Orberesis, though he remained tall and proud on the surface. This had every chance to go sideways. He and Tavanar must have lost their minds. But why not try to get close to the King? He had quite the following now, numbering in the tens of thousands. Hundreds alone stood outside the palace. Even the King was a worshipper. He had the Order behind him and hundreds of pilgrims crossing the world to see him. By being close to the King, he could first access the best healers and medicines in the Known World and then take everything away from the stupid King, like the Queen Bitch had taken his father and burned his village. He would need to watch out for the advisors and factions in court, but he had Solvi to protect him.

"Enough of that nonsense, Taishay," King Doemus said. He motioned for the man to leave before he answered. "I *am* the realm. And I say we need a spiritual counsel to shape our way of government. You coddle me like a child because of my eyes. Yes, I'm blind now, but I'm not *blind*! I am a bloody king, capable of making decisions to keep our nation prospering. My wishes are not to be ignored or countered at every instance. God Himself is a confirmed miracle-maker and I say we should be honoured he chose us among every kingdom in the world. Enough of this."

"Calm down, dear..." Queen Thura said. "They're saying this isn't a light decision to make. It would change things."

"No, Thura!" Doemus pointed fingers at his advisors. "My mother always believed we need to listen to the gods. Now here is God Himself and everybody claims to be devout. How can you say that if you fail to commit? Isn't faith about believing? Being willing to do what is necessary? How could I refuse help from God Himself?"

"Help is welcome, Your Majesty, but giving him a seat on the governing council..." another advisor said. This particular one seemed keen to copy Taishay's apparel to the tee.

The King's face turned sour and he spoke with gritted teeth. "Do you believe you're more deserving than God Himself?"

"My King, we meant no disrespect. I beg you, take a few days to think about it, at the very least," Taishay said.

Doemus pondered this and fell back into his chair with a sigh, exhausted and defeated. "Fine. We'll meet here tomorrow at the same time. Is that alright, Highest One?"

"But of course! As long as the decision is *yours* alone, not anybody else's."

....

The following day, Orberesis entered the ceremonial room followed by Solvi, Tavanar, and three worship leaders. He walked towards the King, who sat in his chair with his arms folded. The room looked unchanged from the previous day, but his migraine pounded with every step and blurred his vision. Sometimes he wondered if this pain came as a price to pay for all the lies he'd told. If it was, the worst was yet to come. He could barely focus on the nobles and the merchants staring at him, like daggers piercing his back.

Believers my arse. Orberesis wondered if the royal subjects could tell how anxious he was about the King's decision. Or how much pain the migraine caused. Tension grew, wrapped in silence, making his skin prickle. The underlying uneasiness mixed with his fear of failure, of not seeing his maladies cured and the miserable life that awaited him if he failed. This would be the last resort. He doubted he'd ever have access to royal healers and cures otherwise. Even those were not a guarantee, but he couldn't live with the pain anymore. It was no life as long as his head pounded, and his nightmares were filled with the giant man. He glanced to both sides of the room. Soldiers hid behind ridiculous lords and merchants, their disdain clear in their snarls. Smokesmiths were surely among them.

The thought made him swallow.

He had hoped for a quick decision due to the King's faith, but Taishay and the other court nobles had the evening to poison the King's mind while Orberesis was away.

"Thank you for waiting, Highest One," the King said. To his right sat Queen Thura. Taishay stood to the King's left. Their nervous faces revealed no knowledge of his decision.

Orberesis nodded and smiled, allowing the King to speak. He held himself despite the anxiety gnawing at him.

Shit...

"I will say a few words before I announce my decision," Doemus said. "I think you know me rather well, though perhaps not as well as you think. As you know, I was a younger sibling. I was not groomed to be king. Instead, I had tutors who prepared me to be a scholar. I studied poetry, scripture, history, sciences, and arts."

Orberesis stole a glance at the audience. Some were swallowing, shuffling in their feet and others scratched their necks around collared shirts. *They look no more at ease than I am.*

"My family prepared my brother to be king after my mother. The crown should have been his. His cunning and bravery would have made him a great leader. He should be king now. In fact, he *would* be king if it hadn't been for his... appetite for adventure."

Orberesis had heard about the Prince's fate. He embarked on a ship to capture wickplates but ended up finding none. Instead, a line from a fishing net caught him and pulled him overboard to his ultimate end at the bottom of the Wickplate Ocean.

"Of course, his bravery would have made him an excellent king. I, on the other hand, am mediocre. I have no physical qualities," Doemus paused. His gaze dropped to the floor before he continued. "You'll appreciate my honesty when I say I care little for politics. To make matters worse, I haven't produced an heir. I'm a far worse king than my brother would be."

Gasps and murmuring overtook the room, but he remained focused.

"But I'm not incapable. I'm not lazy or looking to have others do my job for me. You can be sure that I can prove myself. I can elevate the Two Nations higher than they've ever been. My eyes might not work, but I make up for it with the great people surrounding me. The governing council cannot be limited to the old military and business minds of the present. We all need spiritual guidance, and that includes me. As a man of faith, how can I not consider the Highest One's request? He has already proven what he can do with his miracle ten years ago. He can help me connect the Two Nations with the empire of the heavens. People are nothing without faith or passion. So, how can I deny my subjects the closeness of God Himself, who they follow?" There was conviction in Doemus' voice and Orberesis let out a breath he had been holding.

"This was no easy decision, but I intend to dedicate my life to serving God Himself in any way I can, just as he helps me rule the Two Nations. God Himself shall have a permanent seat on the governing council. I signed the decree this morning. It is done."

"But Your Majesty, you are..." Taishay said.

"Mind your words, Taishay. I was very clear."

The Queen had a look of concern as she leaned forward to hold his arm. Orberesis noticed she had red eyes, a puffy nose, and dark rings around her eyes. "My dear, think about what your mother would have done."

"Don't bring my mother into this, Thura!" Doemus hissed.

"Never!" a pompous merchant shouted as he stepped forward. He wore shiny rings on each finger and was wreathed in blue robes with gold inlays. He raised his finger, pointing at Doemus. "Ship merchants like my father and his father before him built the Two Nations with their blood and sweat. Your mother understood that and rewarded it. That's why we prospered. I will not let our home become a theocratic cesspool!"

Orberesis did not recall seeing any prosperity as a child. He only recalled the Two Nations being a *mercantile* cesspool. There wasn't much difference.

About twenty of the merchant's retainers stepped forward, adopting fighting stances and gripping their halberds. The King's guards stepped in to protect His Majesty. No one moved.

"You dare challenge my resolve, Kene? Betray your nation? Raise arms against me? Don't you ever forget who *made* your family." Doemus bellowed at the merchant.

"*You* are the one who betrays the nation," Kene said with a snarl. "And you are allowing the kingdom to be poisoned by this slimy cult leader! I have given everything for this realm in the form of riches and tariffs collected by the palace. What has *he* paid to get a seat on the governing council? I will not have it!"

If only the bastard knew how much Orberesis and his family had paid in blood.

"Hear, hear!" other merchants said, as their retainers also got into fighting stances.

"I'm willing to let this impostor be around, but I will not allow him a seat on the governing council! Not as an equal!" Kene said.

"Hear, hear!"

"*Impostor*? Have some respect," King Doemus spat. "The Highest One saved the world and ended the Crimson Wars which allowed your trade to prosper. Your wealth of the past ten years is partly due to him!"

Orberesis swallowed, struggling to contain his migraine at the worst of times. He wouldn't fare well if the merchants staged an uprising before he could get friendly with the King.

Kene shook his head at the King and turned to address the nobles and merchants. "Friends and rivals, we must put our differences aside and install a governing chamber over the Two Nations. We can no longer trust this so-called *king* to keep the kingdom safe. The safety and prosperity of

our citizens must come first! Unless he reverts his decree, the king can stay
in his quarters and the chamber will do all the governing. We can vote on
the members. Agreed?"

"Agreed!"

"Yes, indeed!"

The Queen's eyes were wide, shuffling between her husband and the
insurgents. She was scared for her life. "Dear, perhaps you should recon-
sider?"

"I'd rather die than give up the throne! Arrest these traitors!"

"Get the King!" Kene said.

It all happened fast. Kene's retainers made the first move, charging the
King's men. Chaos ensued in a flurry of swords and halberds flailing in
every direction in a storm of metal clanging as weapons collided. The
soldiers grunted as they stabbed at each other on behalf of their masters,
breaking long-lasting allegiances.

Orberesis took cover behind Tavanar and three worship leaders, who
took him to safety in a corner. He hated how vulnerable he was. God
Himself should be able to flaunt his power, and yet the orb refused to work
even when he begged it.

More of the King's guards blasted through the doors to fight off the
traitors, but several of them had already fallen, their bodies sprawled across
the floor, blood staining the carpet.

"I won't let them touch you, Highest Lord," Solvi whispered.

She removed a handful of herbs from her pouch and doused them
with belleaf oil. The herbs burned and she inhaled the smoke. After a
deep breath, Solvi jumped to the centre of the fray, a trail of white smoke
following her, circling her like a shadow. Enhanced by the smoke, Solvi
took inhumanly long, quick, strides and aided the King's army.

Orberesis was glad he had her at his side, though it was hard to keep
track of her. She'd explained her abilities to him once. Somehow, the smoke
shrouded her for seconds at a time, allowing her to disappear from every-

one's sight and appear somewhere else moments later. Temporary invisibility she called it and used it to perfection, disappearing in the smoke and appearing behind a soldier to slit their throat. Solvi wasted no time, fighting Kene's retainers one by one, using her speed and temporary invisibility to prevent them from getting to her. Every movement was precise and riddled with murderous intent. There was no hesitation.

Orberesis didn't like watching smokesmiths fight. It reminded him of his childhood. Of him, Tavanar, and the other kids being chased through the city and rounded up. He had been lucky not to see the inside of a dreadful smoke chamber, but Solvi hadn't. The few who survived with the herbal smoke in their lungs, like Solvi, went on to become smokesmiths. Where else would they go?

Solvi jumped under a cloak of smoke, invisible for a moment. But it was enough to land behind a guard unseen and place a hand over his mouth before sliding her dagger across his throat. The soldier collapsed with a thud. Other soldiers flinched as they saw her semi-visible figure. Even guards were afraid of smokesmiths, as they should be. But not every smokesmith had abilities like hers. The smoke enhanced them, made them stronger and faster, but the invisibility was unique to Solvi, she had said. What good were swords and halberds against an enemy they couldn't see?

Solvi appeared again and slashed two men. She was already onto other guards, no time wasted. The smoke flowed and danced around her, playing chase, catching up to her unbelievable speed. She jumped at another group of guards, disappeared in mid-air, and slashed their throats before she became visible again.

That was not the work of an amateur, Orberesis knew. She had done this hundreds, perhaps thousands of times, since she was a little girl.

She was smoke and she was air.

It was as if her body held no weight and she was free to move as she desired, leaving behind a trail of dead guards. Solvi struck again as the bravest retainers brandished their halberds and tried to reach her, wherever she was. Her dagger appeared and disappeared in precise motions, reaping death. Her strikes were firm and precise, performed with no hesitation.

Orberesis watched Solvi do what she did best but wondered how long she could keep this up with the smoke raging inside her, flaring up her lungs. The smoke gave but it also took away. Smokesmiths borrowed their power from the herbal smoke, but not without a cost. Coughing blood, struggling to breathe, and respiratory issues were common. Not even smokesmiths could keep going for long without collapsing in pain. The more smoke Solvi inhaled, the worse the pain she would be in afterwards.

Kene's retainers made room for a woman and seemed to keep their distance from her. She was tall and had thin, long arms and a dark complexion. Her dark hair was tightly wrapped in a long braid, and she wore a white two-piece combat garb that contrasted with the silk worn by the nobles and merchants. Her attention was on Solvi, eyes fixated on her with not a hint of fear. Orberesis noticed a cloud of white smoke dancing above her head as well.

She's a smokesmith too.

The woman didn't wait for Solvi to charge and took a deep breath of her own white smoke. Just as Orberesis was confident that regular smokesmiths could never beat Solvi's abilities, the newcomer grew taller, almost too tall for the high ceilings of the King's main room.

Shit. She has an ability too.

Orberesis couldn't tell what the ability was, but her arms and legs elongated far beyond normal. His skin prickled. That's why he had always hated smokesmiths. They were powerful, yes, but also unpredictable. When he thought he knew what the bastards were capable of doing, they pulled a strange ability that no one had seen yet.

The newcomer's arms and legs brightened in yellow hues underneath her skin, like a lit candle, and the woman charged. Solvi became invisible in a curtain of smoke and avoided the dangerous blow.

Orberesis sighed with relief.

The long-limbed woman spun to catch Solvi with her outstretched arm in a spinning back fist. Solvi leapt into the air to avoid the blow and zipped out of Long-limbs' way. The brute smokesmith continued to attack Solvi with punches and hammer fists and elbows. It was incredible how someone with such long, unnaturally changed limbs could remain so nimble. That was a good ability. With long limbs, she could strike at her opponents without being in the enemy's striking range. Solvi bit on an obvious feint strike and Long-limbs struck her in the face with a heavy punch, forcing her to spit blood.

Orberesis swallowed. He'd never seen Solvi suffer from a direct blow like that.

Long-limbs kept attacking Solvi relentlessly with punches and elbow strikes, like a giant prayer mantis and as deadly as one. Someone with that power and speed did not need to use blades.

Solvi roared and struck back with her dagger. Orberesis saw the anger in her eyes, as though she was mad at herself for letting Long-limbs hit her. She shrouded herself in smoke and appeared just behind Long-limbs, landing with her feet on the opponent's head. Long-limbs flailed and shook her head, but Solvi held on, dagger set between her teeth. Solvi grabbed the blade and slashed at the back of Long-limbs' neck.

The woman cried in pain and her arms and legs shrank to their normal human size. Solvi didn't wait for the transformation to subside. She picked up the dagger and shoved it into Long-limbs' right ear. Orberesis grimaced at the bloody sight.

Long-limbs was dead but fighting like that didn't leave Solvi much to spare. She leaned against a wall to catch her breath, panting, and spitting blood. She had sacrificed her lungs but won the scuffle. The retainers' bodies littered the floor. Most of the lords had already fled. Only Kene and two others remained.

Sensing no further danger, Orberesis stood and walked towards King Doemus, who was still shielding himself from the traitorous merchants. "Are you alright, Your Majesty?"

Doemus had the look of a man experienced in bittersweet victories. He'd squashed a rebellion's first spurt, but it would flare up again. There would be more traitors, more insurgents. The King glanced at Kene and the other lord merchants. "Arrest these traitors at once. These conspirators. They'll answer for this."

Paralysed, Kene looked at the King, then at Orberesis and snarled, a dozen halberds pointed at him. He spat towards Orberesis.

"One day *you* will answer for all of this, you fiend," Kene said. One of the King's guards hit him with the hilt of his sword and two others took him away, along with the other conspirators.

Silence was once again restored to the ceremonial room as bodies of soldiers littered the floor. Orberesis patted the King's shoulder. "Rise, Your Majesty. I promise your faith in me will not be misguided," he said. "Though I fear I put a target on your back. Perhaps I shouldn't have—"

"No, Highest One," Doemus said. He gestured for Orberesis to accompany him as he took his seat on the bejewelled throne. "You mustn't pay for the mistakes of your subjects. You kindly offered your counsel and I eagerly took it. I'm still the king, though sometimes men forget I'm not just here as a puppet whose strings they pull. If I decide something, it *will* be done. I'll deal with the traitors. From now on, you shall sit by my side."

"Thank you, Your Majesty," Orberesis said, struggling to stay composed. The stress from the scuffle had left him with a headache much worse than normal, as though the bones of his skull had turned to mush, and his brain was sensitive with air. Fuck, it hurt. But the King couldn't see him like that lest his faith waver. He had to push against the migraines and offer to help. "Perhaps my worship leaders can... assist with handling the insurgents."

He considered Kene and the other lords, surely being taken to the catacombs, others planning a coup. Not many of them had been too happy with his presence. Taishay, the main one. There was something about the man Orberesis didn't like. And Queen Thura had given him cold looks since the start. Her face looked frosty pale since the skirmish had broken off.

I will have to keep my eyes open and my ears even more so.

He was no longer fooling peasants and city-dwellers. He was now deep in the lion's den and there was nothing but sharp fangs everywhere he looked.

FIVE
WHISPERS OF GRIEF

REDNOW

I could see the chaos before me. They knelt for their Old One.

— From *Mother's Memories*

High in the mountains, the air was fresh and thin. Rednow was used to it. He headed towards the nearest summit, jumping over creeks and rocks, and hiking up a hill. It took him a long time, but he reached the top before midday. Birds chirped and leaves rustled in the wind. He rubbed more tallow on his face and hands to cover up his scent from enemy scouts and moved through the rocks. He wasn't as nimble as he had once been, though he hadn't met anyone who still moved like him after having lived sixty winters.

Rednow found a clearing. Birches, junipers, blue pines, and bamboo gave way to a small half-frozen pond caught in a rare ray of sunlight. He spooked the dark birds that perched atop it but made his way further, crouching like a predator, blending in with the landscape until he reached a ridge. Carefully, he lay on the frozen grass and peered down, exposed to icy wind.

At least up there, with his brain nearly freezing, he could numb himself to the voice of his dead sister that muffled his every thought. She had been brave and kind. More than he could have ever asked for. But now she was dead. Yet she still spoke to him; plagued him with her words.

He shook his head and squinted, taking in as much as he could from what he saw below the ridge. Silence was key. The enemy had scouts, and he was getting too old for this. It was too cloudy, but the Nohani encampment had more than a few hundred tents and about five dozen bonfires issuing threads of smoke that blended into the grey clouds above.

"One day I'd like to understand why you do this," a voice startled Rednow.

He frowned and sighed as Merey dropped to the ground and lay next to him. Her dark hair was braided tightly to her scalp and, like him, she wore thick winter clothes made from marcruncher fur. "You're the leader of the Leeth, the Blood Collector! And here you are, risking your life to do the job of a scout. Why is that?"

His heart was still racing from the scare, so he took a deep breath. Risking his life was a little bit of an exaggeration, though her point stood. He couldn't tell Merey or the others that he was still hearing Rebma's voice in his mind. Not yet. They'd think him mad. "I needed to get some fresh air and a closer look at their ranks."

"Oh, really?" Merey whispered, a snarl forming in her face. She and Tellwoon were like daughters to him. He had raised them and all the other mercenaries since they were nothing but orphan children, victims of war and a twisted fate. "Next time cover your tracks better, old man. If I was a Nohani scout, I could have snuck up on you."

"Why are *you* here? Any new instructions from our *beloved* patron, King Caligo?"

Merey scoffed, eyes still peering over the enemy encampment. "That bastard? He doesn't want to get involved. Says that's why he's paying mercenaries to do the work."

Rednow could understand that. And King Caligo of Gasho was paying him handsomely. The Leeth wasn't just any mercenary army—they were the best and most coveted one. Rednow had started the Leeth forty years ago as a small warband to defend himself and other refugees up in the mountains, but he soon realised he could turn it into a way of feeding orphan children hurt by the wars and rescue more of them over the years. He trained them, fed them, and sent them out into the world to be decent members of society. When someone hired the Leeth for a job, Rednow would call upon them and they would answer the call to arms. That arrangement allowed him to fight wars anywhere in the Known World and take in new children from all corners of the world to be turned into lethal soldiers. All of that came with a hefty price not all monarchs were willing to pay.

"Are you alright?" Merey eyed him with a frown. "You look thoughtful. Remember what you told me once?"

"You can't travel far with your thoughts pursuing you. Yes, I remember."

"So?"

Rednow sighed, dreading the lack of solitude. "It's nothing. Let's go back to camp."

....

As Rednow and Merey arrived at the Leeth's base camp, the mountain wind howled and the shielded flames grew ten feet tall. He thought he could see Rebma's bright red hair flowing freely, but it was just the campfire. Next to his tent, there were hundreds of others, insulated with thick marcruncher fur. Training grounds and several utility areas for tanners, blacksmiths, and cooks spanned beyond. The young recruits were feeding dry pinewood to the fire and the heat soothed the pain in his soul as he walked to the command tent.

You're too stubborn, Rebma's voice echoed in his mind, startling him. *After all these years, you still want to prove yourself.*

Rednow ignored the voice, shaking his head as though that helped. It never did.

Merey stole another glance at him. "Are you sure you're alright?"

"I said I am." He'd sounded more serious than intended. She looked away and he hurried to wipe his watery eyes as his right hand reached the messenger bag Rebma had left him, with all the poems and songs she was writing before she passed. The bag he always had with him now. He hadn't had the courage to open it yet. Maybe he never would.

Merey was still eyeing him. "If you say so."

He sighed. "I'd promised Rebma I was going to retire. This was supposed to be my last job. She had been begging me for it."

"Oh."

Sometimes, I dream of us when we were young, brother. We're running on a beach and you're showing me how fast you can run. It's so warm there that the rain doesn't even matter. And we were so happy. Do you remember?

For the Gods, that voice was unbearable, tearing into his hard shell. He couldn't imagine any curse worse than this—being forced to listen to the voice of a departed loved one. Every day. Rednow didn't dream of a beach, or the warm summers spent as a child. Darkness filled his dreams now. He dreamt of Rebma's bloody body on the ground, impaled by a spear, and of the words she had uttered when she passed.

The Essence flows in me, she had said in her dying breath.

He still didn't understand the meaning of those words. Was she hallucinating then, or seeing the white path to the underworld widening in front of her eyes? He shook those thoughts from his mind.

"And are you?" Merey asked.

"Am I what?" He'd forgotten he was walking with Merey.

"Going to retire?"

The question hung in the air for a moment as they walked towards the command tent. The first winter snow of the year would soon arrive and when it did, hunting would stop, but the warriors would still need to eat. And so did the blacksmiths, the tanners, and everybody else. He clenched his fists. It was a lot of responsibility; he just wasn't sure his generals could replace him. At the same time, he had made a promise. He was meant to have been Rebma's rock. Her haven. The protective older brother. And she had wanted to go somewhere warm where she could forget about war. Where blissful memories and the ghosts of the past wouldn't haunt her. Instead, her voice haunted him now.

"I'm thinking about it," he said.

"Where would you go?"

"Somewhere warm. That's what she wanted."

"Hmm," Merey said, leaving it at that.

The northern icy wind caressed his face. He didn't find the southern foothills of the Benaven Mountains as cold as the Leeth's base camp just north, in the Seven Peaks, but the scenery sure looked similar. The land between him and the Seven Peaks was wild, full of rough terrain and even rougher beasts. No man was insane enough to settle there since the high altitude didn't allow for farming, but that patch of land happened to be on the border of the kingdoms of Gasho and Noha. Both kingdoms claimed it belonged to them and had been feuding over it for centuries.

Now at midday, groups of the Leeth's hunters and scavengers were returning to the Leeth's war camp, bringing meat, bags of winter seed, leaves, and berries with them. Rednow kept pace alongside Merey as loud chatter could be heard from inside the tents, where squad leaders educated their younger trainees on battle tactics and strategy, healers patched up the wounded, and smithies hammered the anvil day and night. Soldiers bowed to them as they made their way to the command tent. Rednow had taught them not to bow to anyone, but they still did.

They would have bowed to Rebma more, he thought.

They continued through one of the practice grounds where the captains had divided inexperienced children into groups of ten to complete several drills involving carrying heavy logs and chopping them with axes. They weren't battle ready yet. Leeth warriors could only fight and start earning pay once they had proven themselves against the elements, combat, and death. When their training was complete, they would return to civilisation and the Leeth could call them for battle when needed.

Rednow pulled the flap to enter the command tent and was greeted by the welcoming heat of the coals that burned inside. The captains were already there and a group of pineheads huddled together for warmth. They looked like human children, except their hair was thick and wiry, clumping together in chunks that resembled the brown scales of an open pinecone, making them look as though their heads were big pinecones with a human face and bright, spooky eyes just below.

"Blood Collector." Tellwoon gave him a nod as she finished combing her short dark hair. Merey sat next to her, and they exchanged looks. "Where have you been?"

Rednow sat on the rug and exhaled. "Surveying the enemy camp."

"So were our pinehead friends," Tellwoon said, biting her lip.

"Any news?"

Tellwoon hesitated. "Three more of ours didn't make it through the night. Their wounds were wicked, as you saw. Almost like they've been hurt by beasts, not soldiers."

"Troubling." Rednow had seen it and didn't like it one bit. Something was off with the enemy soldiers. The Leeth warriors were supposed to have sent the Nohani home with ease on first contact. Instead, they had gained ground and the Nohani soldiers had fought like savages. "What did the pineheads discover?"

"They are carrying crates. Glass clinking inside them."

"That explains the vials we saw scattered around the battlefield," he said. "You think they're taking a potion that... makes them stronger?"

Tellwoon nodded. "We heard rumours of such a thing existing, didn't we? We just didn't know these bastards had it."

Rednow pondered everything he knew and sipped water from a leather mug. The Leeth were a strong army. One of the strongest in the Known World. But if such a potion was real, he would need to take extra precautions. He couldn't allow any more of his soldiers to be careless.

"Tomorrow, before first light, prepare the east-north-west formation and march them before the usual time. It's crucial we get the terrain advantage. We need that hill," he said.

Merey and Tellwoon exchanged looks. "But that's too risky. Too dangerous."

Rednow shook his head as he saw fear in their eyes. It was always like this. They were formidable warriors and even better people, but how could he retire? They still needed him. "It will be alright. I'll take a closer look myself."

Merey grimaced. "Yes. It's too dangerous *for you*, old man. Smokesmith or not. You're our leader. There is no reason in the underworld why you should be in the front lines."

Still trying to prove yourself, Rednow. Always trying to prove yourself, Rebma's voice told him. For the gods, it sounded just like her.

"No. I'm going to be fine. I've been doing this all my life." *Maybe Rebma is right.*

Tellwoon shook her head. "That's what we mean. You've been doing it all your life and look at the state of you. Last time you tried to breathe the smoke you were coughing blood for days. Who knows what will happen next? Do you have a death wish?"

Rednow hesitated. "I'm thinking this will be the last job. One last time won't hurt. Not too much."

Tellwoon looked at him with her mouth agape and then at Merey. "Did you know about this?"

"He just told me."

"I haven't decided yet, but I had promised Rebma I would retire."

Merey sighed and turned to the rest of the captains and the pineheads. "Can you leave us?"

Everybody left the tent, and a freezing draft entered as Rednow was left with the two generals. Merey eyed the ground and Tellwoon cleared her throat.

"Merey had thought this moment would come," Tellwoon said. "But I didn't think it would be for another year or so. Why now?"

Rednow couldn't tell them about Rebma's voice, which he heard throughout the day. Her inflections, her accent. It was Rebma, all too real. They were all words she would say and that kept her alive in his mind. How could he grieve? And how could he lead warriors to battle again if he was always in a state of interrupted grief?

He picked the easy answer. "This is the last job in a while since it's almost winter. I haven't made up my mind."

"What's holding you back?"

Rednow swallowed. "I have not decided who my replacement would be."

He loved Merey and Tellwoon like the daughters he'd never had. He had raised them since children. They were kind and brave, and had the wits to lead, but every time he looked at them, he saw youth. Inexperience. No one could lead a mercenary army unless they had seen enough darkness. To make it worse, they weren't smokesmiths like him.

They exchanged glances, fully aware it would be one or the other. Rednow saw hints of fear and regret in their eyes. He was like their father, but the love these two shared wasn't a sisterly one. Their bond was stronger than he had ever been able to understand. If he made one the new leader of the Leeth and not the other, he was afraid it would become a thorn between them, ruin their relationship.

"Why can't we *both* lead?" Tellwoon asked.

Rednow shook his head. Perhaps it was just him being a stubborn old man, but mercenary warriors needed to know who they fought for. A single, undisputed soul responsible for them staying alive or being sent to the underworld. "Bipartisan leadership always leads to disagreements and even betrayal, even among family. Even among lovers. Don't think it wouldn't happen to you. No, it won't work."

Tellwoon swallowed, grabbed Merey's hand and looked at her, then back at Rednow.

"I wouldn't want to do that anyway," Merey said, still frowning. "If Tellwoon is the next leader, then that is it. I'll follow her. But I also want that opportunity. And if I become the new leader, I will not share the post with anyone. Even if I love them."

Tellwoon nodded. "I feel the same way."

Rednow smiled. It was nice to see their ambition. "Very well. We're marching for battle tomorrow. I'm going to be in the frontlines. This campaign has lasted much longer than it should have. It's an opportunity to *persuade* me you should take the leading role, so do your job well."

Foolishness isn't bravery, brother. You would do well to remember that.

Rednow bit his lip, wishing Rebma's voice would go away. That it would leave him alone just for once. He knew, though, this was a madness.

And madness only ever gets worse.

SIX

POWERFUL SMOKE

REDNOW

I'm *flesh and bone. I can't blame it on everything I've done. And now, there's no one else to love. I've got used to the darkness.*

— From *Mother's Memories*

Rednow patted his shadesgrowl in the flank and let the pinehead take the beast away. He walked to the top of the hill where the otherwise green valley below was speckled with brown and dark spots—the Leeth warriors. They had reached the hill before the enemy. Five hundred warriors or so stood banging their weapons on their shields and facing the bottom of the valley from where the enemy soldiers would have to come.

"Leeth," they bellowed. "Leeth! Leeth!"

Rednow turned around and a light count revealed another five hundred warriors behind him, hiding. To his right, another five hundred stood, hiding at the top of the hill.

You're going to breathe the smoke, aren't you? Rebma insisted on pestering him, even in the most important of moments. *Haven't you had enough?*

Rednow swallowed and lightly touched the satchel in his belt, where he kept his Ominous Kas herbs. "Not quite yet..." he whispered to the ghost.

The smoke had been the bane of his existence and the solution to his problems at the same time. He was a child when the crown smokesmiths of Shari first got hold of him. They had shoved him into a locked chamber along with other urchins and filled the room with the smoke of their burning herbs. Kingdoms always needed fewer urchins and more smoke-smiths, and the latter were always keen on turning others into what they were. Rednow still remembered well the other kids choking on the smoke, scratching the wood door to get out, screaming for help. In the end, they had all dropped dead on the stone floor, but Rednow had stayed on his feet having breathed the smoke and remained alive to tell the story. His triumph had the smokesmiths doing their best to make him one of them. With access to the King's deep pockets, they gave him riches, the best food, and the best wine. Most kids couldn't resist and by the time they were adults, they had bought into the entire system. Even as a child, Rednow had known he would always be a weapon to them, not a man, so he learned how to breathe the smoke safely, how to wield weapons, how to cultivate the herbs and when to burn them.

And then he escaped.

A smokesmith who didn't serve a king or a lord. The rogue, they called him. But he travelled far and wide without ever being caught, and his reputation took a darker turn. The Blood Collector. He trained day and night to protect himself and others like him. Now, the epitome of what he had done sprawled before him in those foothills. Thousands of soldiers at his command. But old men did not live long, especially not with their lungs rotted by all the years of smoke inhalation. Attempting to breathe it again could very well kill him, but it was a risk he had to take.

You've always loved risks, the voice said.

He shook his head, focusing on the battlefield. Everything was in place. Merey commanded the frontline, Tellwoon was in charge of the flank, and Zatak and his bloodsleuths hid behind on the eastern foothill.

It was midmorning when constant thumping echoed in the distance. These thuds became clearer and soon the first lines of the Nohani army appeared. The standard bearer carried the Nohani flag, coloured in dark with a silver half crescent in the middle. Thousands of soldiers poured through the valley and halted, maintaining distance. Without the eastern and southern garrisons in sight, the Leeth looked outnumbered, but Rednow wasn't concerned about that. He worried more about what potions these people were drinking that made them act like animals.

Once the Nohani soldiers were all lined up at the foothill, the Leeth warriors started banging their weapons into their shields again. "Leeth! Leeth! Leeth!"

A war horn echoed, and the enemy charged, soldiers bellowing. They carried spears and their heavier armour didn't allow for a fast charge. The muddy grass under their feet even less so. Rednow smiled. If he got what he wanted, they would be tired by the time they reached the Leeth's first line.

"Steady!" Merey shouted and held the last vowel. They didn't move an inch. "Spears!"

Those in the frontlines planted their feet and flexed their legs, holding their long spears forward, pointing right at the charging enemy. "Shield wall!" she bellowed.

The Leeth warriors got their shields stuck in the mud and hid behind them, leaving only the spears poking out. That should deter the fast charge.

The Nohani still marched with heavy feet, no longer shouting and the initial momentum lost. But there were many of them. Rednow just wanted to see it. The potion... He kept his eyes focused on the soldiers at the back of the line, in case there was any trick or unexpected play.

"Arrows!" A row of about thirty archers rose and pulled arrows into their bows, arms tense, waiting for the sign. "Release!"

A volley of arrows flew and landed on the Nohani soldiers who had been caught in the muddy grass. About a dozen of them fell dead; others suffered wounds. So far, the Leeth had been well-organised. How, then, had such average soldiers as the Nohani units been able to inflict such damage to his warriors in previous battles?

The Leeth's shield wall resisted as the Nohani tried to break through. Many of the soldiers got caught by the Leeth spears before they were able to reach the shields. It didn't feel like a real attempt at defeating the Leeth. It felt like...

They're stalling.

He glanced at the horizon and searched for signs of an ambush. There it was, on the western side. A group of Nohani soldiers, dressed in dark uniform, started engaging with one of the Leeth's hidden flanks.

Shit. "Tellwoon!" he bellowed.

Tellwoon saw it too. She quickly organised her units into a defensive formation, with shields and spears poking out, but there just wasn't enough time to do it right. Unlike the first batch, these Nohani bastards were not charging at a slow pace, and not uphill either. They raced with eagerness. There was something odd about them. Something that almost reminded Rednow of himself. He had to take a closer look.

He opened his herb satchel, removed the chords, and looked for a handful of his Ominous Kas herbs. He clamped the crushed leaves in his palm and opened his hands. He then doused the leaves with a drop of belleaf oil, blew on them and they started burning. The smoke that came from the herbs was different, and it followed Rednow instead of simply dissipating, searching for his nose, eager to be inhaled. Rednow allowed the smoke to engulf him.

One breath only, he thought.

He filled his chest with the foul smoke. It was tainting his lungs, eating at him. His eyes burned, turning red. But he still held the smoke. Only smokesmiths could do such a thing. He felt the smoke from the Ominous Kas increase his blood flow, as it rushed inside his veins. His heart pumped faster. He could sense his lungs expanding and drew even more of the smoke. Blood rushed madly through the veins and his bones, muscle, and skin all strengthened. Not all herbs gave smokesmiths the same powers, and everyone's bloodline reacted differently to the smoke, but he had found Ominous Kas to be his favourite.

Once he was in control of his new strength, he willed his transformation. His fingers grew into daggerlike claws and all his skin hardened. Thorns emerged from his back, ripping his clothes, turning him into a beast.

The Blood Collector.

Some smokesmiths became faster, others had special abilities, depending on their bloodlines and on which herbs they burned, but this one suited Rednow best. He ran towards the incoming Nohani soldiers. With no warning, Rednow's lungs ached, and he coughed in despair, unable to stop. His insides contracted and tortured him. He had used too much of the smoke and for too damn long. He felt blood on his tongue and spat it all out but kept going.

He ran like the monster he was. And the smoke followed.

Thrashing through the battlefield, he dwarfed both the Leeth warriors and the Nohani soldiers. He needed to get close and observe. Some of the enemies drank from a vial which they tossed onto the mud while their comrades were already charging, swords and spears in hand. Rednow was used to the enemy fleeing as they saw him in that form, but these did the opposite. With raging eyes and snarling faces, they charged him, as though only the moment mattered, not the future.

Something is off with them.

One of these strange Nohani struck, sending a Leeth warrior to the ground with ease. He looked just like a regular soldier, but he charged as though he was as large as Rednow, all confidence and bluster. It didn't help that there were a dozen more of these.

"Tellwoon, we have to strike first. Abandon the defensive position. Finish them before more of them drink the potion."

Tellwoon's eyes widened as she saw him in the monstrous form, but there was no time for fear or concern. She bellowed commands and the western flank warriors shuffled just before the Nohani struck with a force unlike any Rednow had ever seen from foot soldiers. Weapons slashed, helmets clashed, and shields flew.

Still followed by the tainted smoke, both curse and cure, Rednow jumped into the middle of the Nohani berserkers. It didn't matter that they looked human. Those were monsters, like him. Rednow tensed his fingers and used his claws, craving them deep in a berserker's neck. He kicked another. And another.

Tellwoon. He needed to protect her and her units. "Retreat! Cover Merey and I'll handle these."

Tellwoon hesitated but gave the order and her units fell back. The Nohani tried to give chase, but Rednow blocked their way. They weren't thinking. They were all snarls and hate. Their eyes were red, and their veins about to burst. Rednow would have wished for more time to analyse them and the potion, but this was war. And he was the Blood Collector. He could not lose.

He kicked at another berserker, his sword causing nothing but scratches on his hardened skin and bones. Rednow turned to face more. There were ten of them, now turned on him. He let them come. All at the same time. When they were close, he charged at one, grabbed his arms, and snapped them in half. He grabbed another's head—it fit neatly into his palm—and simply flicked his wrist, breaking his neck.

The berserkers kept on coming, as though seeing their comrades dying elicited no emotions. Rednow kept at them. He would end this without any more of the Leeth warriors getting injured.

Another whiff of the smoke.

His lungs burned as though they were being sliced open from the inside out, pain spreading inside his chest. A berserker jumped at his back and latched onto his neck, trying to find an opening to slit his throat. Rednow took hold of his head, pulled him down to the ground and squeezed his face until the bones popped and blood squirted out.

The battlefield was carnage and he wavered. He was too old for this. Too hurt. But Tellwoon needed his help. This was a job that needed done.

Three swords had hit him hard enough to remain attached to his skin, but Rednow barely felt them. He noticed the berserkers didn't seem to feel any pain either. Unless he hit them with a killing blow, they thrashed and slashed until their body no longer allowed. Another latched onto his leg, trying to slice his heel. He was a monster, yes. But he alone would not be able to defeat an entire army of men and women enhanced like this.

He kept fighting with punches and elbows. Piercing them with his claws. Stomping on them. While he had the smoke, he would thrive. The problem was afterwards. The burn in his lungs slowed his breathing. Only the gods knew when the Blood Collector was going to die, but he reckoned he was well past testing his luck.

A volley of arrows landed where he was. Three of them hit him. One on the shoulders. Two in the thigh. He looked around as the rest of the berserkers had been wiped out by the projectiles. With a look back, he saw Tellwoon and gave her a nod before he ripped the arrows from his skin. All around him, the rest of the Nohani formation was in tatters, others surrendering.

Tellwoon nodded back and held her arms in the air. One pointing at the sky and the other parallel with the earth. An L for Leeth. The Leeth was victorious.

Rednow willed his transformation back to his normal form but soon dropped to his knees, hand on his chest. There was no cure for this kind of pain. As he glanced at the floor, he picked up a vial that still looked full. It was small and a silver liquid flowed inside. Rednow grabbed it.

···········

The burn hadn't been as bad as last time. It hurt every time he breathed, but he had sustained only minor physical injuries. Just cuts and bruises, no medical attention needed. The same couldn't be said for his warriors. Some were being carted off, others had been laid on the grass in improvised graves.

He hurried back to the campaign camp, where the first batch of wounded were starting to arrive after they had won the border skirmish. The surviving Nohani troops had surrendered and were now being tied up and captured to be used by the Gashoine as leverage and prevent any further attempts from the Nohani to expand their border.

"Rednow!" A desperate man came running towards him. Rednow was in no condition to receive anyone, his clothes ripped, covered in sweat and blood, and smelling of smoke, but the man's panicked voice nearly kicked the soul out of his body. "Rednow!"

He rushed to the man, a blacksmith, who stood before him, panting. The man had high cheekbones and long hair in a top bun. He held a young man in his arms, unconscious.

"What happened to him?" Rednow asked, though the answer was clear enough.

The blacksmith's eyes welled, and fear choked him before he could muster a few words.

"He was caught by one of those berserkers. He's still alive, but barely. Can you heal him with the smoke?"

Rednow gestured at his tent. "Bring him in."

The blacksmith followed Rednow and laid the young man in the padded cot where they sat. Full of anticipation, his eyes shifted wildly between the boy and Rednow.

"He's dying," Rednow said. "Are you sure this is what you want?"

The blacksmith nodded. "If he's dying, there is nothing else to be done."

Rednow swallowed and focused on the child. Killing people as a smoke-smith was one thing. Easy enough. He had done it so often he had long lost count. Making sure they *lived* was something else, entirely up to luck. Just as Rednow had survived the smoke as a child, there was a small chance this young man could survive the smoke now. If he didn't, he would die anyway. But if he did... the smoke would keep him alive and he would eventually make a full recovery and potentially become a smokesmith, which was both a blessing and a curse. His lungs would hurt, but the bleeding would stop and the wounds would close.

It was worth trying.

Rednow wondered if any of the kingdoms in the Known World had realised this was possible—a last minute gambit to save someone's life.

He wiped sweat from his palms. Even if it was up to luck, it still required him to be careful. And patient, given the time it took. If he blasted the young man with smoke, the kid would probably die in a heartbeat. Not enough smoke and he could easily bleed out before the smoke had any effect. It was a combination of luck and manipulating the smoke well enough.

He pulled out his herbs and rubbed a bit of belleaf oil into them, creating a tiny flame that helped ignite them and produced a putrid smoke. Rednow grabbed the back of the boy's head and placed the herbs right under his nostrils, forcing him to inhale the smoke. It was a faint chance, but enough to attempt in terminal cases like these. Rednow continued to blow his smoke at the boy, burning his lungs further in the process.

Minutes passed. Perhaps hours.

Rednow didn't flinch in that state of near death. He kept blowing the smoke, hurting his lungs while at it, but it was as though the boy didn't want to be saved. *Shit.*

Rednow finally gave up and punched the ground, angry at the futility of it all, at his powerlessness, his flared lungs giving again.

The young man had stopped breathing.

Shit. He shook his head.

The blacksmith became frenzied, his pupils dilated as he faced Rednow, then he looked at the floor and dropped to his knees, wailing.

He was never going to live, brother. Just as I wasn't... It's not your fault. Rebma's voice tortured him further. *It's alright, brother. It's alright.*

Rednow hurt but this time it wasn't just the lungs. Right next to them, a big vacuum seemed to be swallowing him from the inside out. Tears flowed. Rebma was right. Retirement couldn't come soon enough.

This had to be goodbye.

SEVEN
CLEAN-UP DUTY

GIMLORE

I see the night. I see strange lands and stranger beings.

— From *Mother's Memories*

"Did you not sleep?" Gimlore asked.

Startled, Edmir stood, dropped the water bucket and the cloth he was using, and scratched his bald head.

"Oh, morning, boss. There's still a spot where the blood won't wash out."

Mission given was mission accomplished. Old habits were hard to break. Even those that kept them from falling asleep or haunted their nights. Edmir had aged a lot over the years and was perhaps a little less broken than he had been when she had found him in the steppes, shaking in manic shock.

"Take a break, Edmir."

The man smiled and nodded. "Yes, boss."

"Why don't you ask Nork and Nosema to do that last bit now? Tell them I asked for their asses to get in here," Gimlore said.

Edmir smiled again and went outside to call his underlings, which gave Gimlore more time to prepare and think about her next move. Shouting from the third floor interrupted her thoughts. She lightly banged her head against the counter as the ruckus intensified.

I should just pour myself a drink.

She had to dedicate more time to the children and give them a proper education. But who was she kidding? They would be scoundrels like her, anyway.

The shouting turned into banging, and a figure emerged from the staircase. Large, with broad shoulders and defined muscles, Foloi scratched his eyes. His long, blonde hair was in a bun and his shirt was so tight it looked like it might tear.

"You got to do something about your kids," he said as he sat in front of her, leaning on the counter.

"What happened?"

"Those kids are draining my sanity. I should teach them a lesson," he said.

"You will need to teach them hand-to-hand combat soon. They're of age. If they don't do something with all that energy, they'll end up killing each other."

Foloi nodded. "Believe me, I know. Speaking of killing each other, who were the offenders last night?"

"I don't know if I want to talk about it," she said.

"Come on."

"Spoiled diplomats from a faraway land."

"And what did they want?"

Gimlore grimaced. "What do you think, Foloi? They wanted the elixir and my land. All for half a coin. They threatened to bring an army if I refused."

Foloi raised his eyebrows. "That's not very nice of them. What are you going to do? Aren't you afraid they'll bring an army?"

Gimlore swallowed and nodded, pressure intensifying. But she had to seize control. "There's that."

With a little luck, it would take them time to travel. A few months at sea, or a few weeks before reaching Alarkan. Either way, she'd have a plan before they arrived.

"I wouldn't want to be in your shoes," Foloi said. He widened his eyes and looked away. She had a hard time resisting the cage fighter.

"How about in my bed?" she asked with a grin.

Foloi gave her a cheeky smile. "It's been a while. I thought you got bored of me. Look at my hands, though."

Foloi's hands wore white wrapping bandages covered in blood, bruised from the beating delivered to the other fighter the earlier night.

"What if I say you won't need your hands?"

"Maybe I'll drop by later, then."

"You *will* drop by, Foloi. Don't forget who's in charge," she said, leaning close enough to feel his breath, her eyes locked on his.

Foloi smiled and cursed something in his northern dialect that Gimlore didn't understand.

The wretched children came barging down the stairs and interrupted the conversation. Their talent for being able to appear like fairies one second and fiendish creatures in the next always amazed her.

Tinko tried to squeeze Thata's neck, while Thata fought back with punches and kicks. They fought day and night, but they were still inseparable.

The children then realised adults were present as Gimlore went to them.

"My little Bluebird and Sunshine. Do you know what happens if you don't behave?"

The children shook their heads.

"The Blood Collector will be upon you," she smiled as their eyes widened, filled with horror. "That's right. He will come for you. You will know once you hear him howl in the night. When you see his smoke and his blood-tainted sword. You better believe it. Now, will you test my patience or will you behave?"

Their mouths opened into beautiful, naïve smiles, complemented by the most innocent eyes she had ever seen. The old legends of the Blood Collector always worked. They had worked on her too when she was their age.

"Good kids," she said, turning back to face Foloi. "Look after them, alright? I need to take care of business."

"What, me? I can't handle these two."

"Just kick the shit out of them if they do anything stupid. You have my permission." Gimlore chuckled, knowing Foloi would never do it.

"You heard your mother?" Foloi asked the children as Gimlore left the Maiden's Hall.

Heleronde was quiet in the early hours of the morning, and the streets were still almost empty. Shopkeepers and business owners were preparing for their stands to open. The town folks had lived through too many battlefields and there were no taxes due, so no one was in a hurry.

After ten years in Heleronde, she no longer winced at seeing folks without arms or legs. She had built the town for them: the survivors.

A few merchants gave her side eyes while others bowed to her. She knew every single one of them by name, and every new town resident, too.

No one had put her in charge, but she still got away with things others couldn't.

"Good morning, Fanan," Gimlore said to the grumpiest merchant on the high street. His shop was narrow but in a prime location, next to the most desired shops in town, despite the grimy state of the shack. She had been trying to buy it from him for ages, but the stubborn man never budged. He never showed respect, either. Fanan scowled as he returned to work.

"Viper," he muttered, unaware she was still in hearing range.

Viper. Her reputation was catching up to her. She'd love to watch over the town, all handshakes and free booze, but she needed to show her venomous fangs every once in a while to get things done.

"What's up with you, old man? Perhaps show gratitude to the one who built this hole you call home. Or do you not remember how I welcomed you, fed you, and kept you cool for days until you felt more like yourself? So what if sometimes I need to get my hands dirty? I do it for the sake of the town."

"Keep telling yourself that..." he said with a scowl.

Gimlore felt the ire emerge but let it fade. "Have a nice day, yes?"

Fanan grumbled something, shook his head, and got back to business.

"Don't mind him, darling," an old, raspy voice interrupted. Gimlore turned and saw a familiar face. "He's just mad that his missus made him sleep outside last night."

"Good morning, Eshof. How are you?" Gimlore asked with a smile. The old woman was small and frail. Her skin was sun-kissed and wrinkled, and a lack of teeth often made her words unclear. Her hands were calloused from a lifetime of farm work.

"I'm alright, dear. What about you? And the children? It's been so long since I've seen them! Now that they're grown, they don't need auntie Eshof to take care of them when you're busy, and they don't visit anymore."

"They're getting on my nerves. I'll take them over to meet you one of these days."

Eshof laughed. "If you ever need someone to watch over them, I'm always available. Just like I was when they were tiny. We have to care for each other. Don't we?"

Gimlore nodded. "I couldn't agree more."

"And how's everything else going?"

Gimlore hesitated. She couldn't tell Eshof about the previous evening's events, and she had to come up with a plan to keep everything the way it was. "It's been better. But I'll manage. Don't worry about me."

Eshof nodded but saw through the lie. "Always show them what you're made of, my dear."

Gimlore contained a chuckle. The woman had more fibre than all the youngsters put together. "Always. See you later, Eshof."

Eshof winked at her. "See you," she said.

She studied her surroundings. Heleronde was a small, shabby town by mainland standards. The houses were sturdy, and the grand buildings such as the Maiden's Hall were three stories high, but most properties were nothing more than wooden shacks where the farmers slept.

It wasn't much, but it was only a ten-year-old settlement. It was still growing and Gimlore had grand plans for it. If it was up to her, Heleronde would become the capital city of Alarkan, a new free land with no inter-fering from any mainland kingdoms. For that, Alarkan needed to become a nation, but nations need wealth and armies to protect it. Maybe it was about time she started investing in that.

Pinesy's shack was on the outskirts of town. The small pinehead sat on the fence overlooking the space he had used to feed his vile bloodsleuths. His small stature, soft skin, and nimble body concealed his advanced age, as was common in his race. Even the eldest pineheads like Pinesy were never taller than four feet and always looked like children. His stiff hazelnut hair was short and grew densely, twisting around itself, as though he wore a large pinecone as a helmet.

The sound of Pinesy's beasts cracking the bones of their feast echoed loudly enough that Gimlore heard it from two blocks away. Blood was their favourite. They would eat anything with its scent.

Pinesy noticed Gimlore, but stayed quiet, as usual. Pineheads didn't like the company of humans but had made themselves useful by acting as long-distance messengers and filling any societal roles humans didn't care to fill.

"I brought your gold," Gimlore said, tossing a small but heavy purse filled with continental gold coins at him. Pinesy grabbed it with no effort, opened the sack, and counted its contents, to be certain it was all there. It didn't matter how many times she had proven she was trustworthy and reliable. Pineheads trusted no one beyond their own.

"It's all there," she assured him. "As always."

Pinesy was the only one in town who she could trust to dispose of a body and stay quiet. This time, she had sent him plenty of bodies to dismember.

"Your bloodsleuths have been eating since last night, huh?"

It was pointless to try small talk with Pinesy, or any other pinehead. Though much to her surprise, he spoke.

"They've been making fun of me," he said. His accent was odd, but she could understand him. His old voice did not match the childish body. "Those drunks come out of your tavern. Pass through here. Insult me. That is unacceptable. Make them stop."

Gimlore raised her brow. She never saw these things happen, but it didn't surprise her. She eyed Pinesy and realised he seemed like an easy target with his strange bright eyes. Pineheads were harmless to most people because they never fought, not even when provoked. But Gimlore took care of her folks, and Pinesy had proved to be a reliable asset.

"I will make sure it doesn't happen again. I promise, Pinesy."

He looked at her with gratitude and nodded. She watched as the bloodsleuths devoured the bodies. It soon revealed to be too much, even for her, so she waved goodbye.

"Wait."

"What is it?" she asked, turning back to him.

Pinesy pointed at the corpses of the Sirestine entourage being devoured by the beasts. "He's been looking for them."

Gimlore's chest thumped faster. "Who's *he*?"

"The handsome one," Pinesy said.

Gimlore realised he might not know anyone's names. She thought about who it could be. Handsome could mean a few people, but if Pinesy was warning her about him, it must be someone she disliked.

"The new one," Pinesy said, and she realised who he meant. A nosy one, that newcomer. Gimlore hated when they—whoever they were—started interfering with her business.

"Is it Keryon? The smokesmith?"

Pinesy gave her half a nod.

Bastard. The man was nothing but trouble. A dangerous mess. Now she had a smokesmith and former lawman sniffing around and asking about the missing Sirestine entourage. Great.

Just thinking of the smell of smoke made her shiver. She would recognise the smell of the smokesmith's herbs burning in a heartbeat. But it wasn't the smoke itself or its scent that made her shiver. It was the memories of death and destruction that always came with it. These were times of peace, but how could it be different?

"Thanks for staying quiet, Pinesy."

She turned back to the main street, her mind spinning in a thousand different ways. On shaky ground, she was sowing enemies both close and far away. She needed to outsmart them all. If the Herald was telling the truth, the Sirestine army could appear without notice.

Deception, Madam Mazi's voice said in her mind. But how? If she failed...

When she returned to the Maiden's Hall, the tavern was livelier than she'd seen it in the last few days. The drunks had come early to catch up on their drinking.

"All taken care of?" she asked Edmir.

"Yes, boss." His face looked stern, somewhat apprehensive. "But the newcomer has been asking questions."

"Pinesy said as much."

The tavern's main door opened and she glanced up to see the smoke-smith enter. He *was* handsome. His jawline was as sharp as she'd ever seen. He was dressed like a lawman from the mainland in clothes far too clean and expensive. Perhaps his vanity was something she could exploit. He was tall and elegant but his posture also reminded Gimlore of soldiers she had met on the battlefield during the Crimson Wars. They always refused to break rules even under the threat of death. She hid a glance at his belt and spotted two herb pouches. Reminders for everybody of the powers he held.

How insufferable could someone be?

Gimlore sighed. "Imagine my luck. I'll sort this out."

Edmir glared at the smokesmith. "Let me handle him, boss. Please."

"I'll handle it myself."

The newcomer scanned the Maiden's Hall before choosing a place to sit, his back straight.

Gimlore gritted her teeth as she watched him. Would he fall for her deceptions?

Mustering courage, she picked up a bottle of cerro wine and two small mugs and walked over to his table. She set the bottle and the mugs down. "Mind if I sit?" she asked while pulling up a chair.

Keryon didn't seem surprised by her boldness. Gimlore kept her poise. She couldn't lose her cool against a man who was so well-put together and had charmed so many in town with his pathetic chivalry. A man who could turn her to ashes at the snap of a finger.

"Sure," he said. "Can't say no to the owner's company, can I?"

"You can, but you would miss out."

A smirk curled his lips. "Yes, yes. Seems missing people are on order today."

Bastard. He knew where to poke to get her tilting. Gimlore did her best to keep cool. She poured cerro wine into the two cups and gave him one. "Are you referring to anyone specific, Keryon?"

Keryon grabbed the mug and chugged its contents. "I've been trying to find the Sirestine entourage you welcomed last night." He paused, then pointed to the pouches on his belt. "My shop requires suppliers from the mainland. I was hoping to get a deal with the Sirestine, but no one knows where they are. They vanished. So, I came to look for them. I am good at that, usually. Finding people. It used to be my job."

And then you choked them with smoke.

"Well, thank you very much for your visit. I never turn down a customer, but in this case, I am going to disappoint you. The Sirestine left first thing. If you ride fast enough, you might still find them on the road to the old continent."

"Interesting. I've been speaking to everybody, and no one saw them leave."

Gimlore swallowed.

Shit. He knows.

"Of course nobody saw them. They snuck out first thing in the morning, saying they had other dealings to attend. No one was asleep by then. You can't rely on anyone here to wake up before the rising sun. Why would anyone?"

Keryon's eyes narrowed as if he was scouting her for signs of lies. "Perhaps you're right, Madam Gimlore. I wonder then, who can I rely on in this town? You will not suggest I rely on yourself, will you?"

Gimlore frowned. "What is that supposed to mean? If not me, then whom? I'm an established business owner *and* legitimate landowner. I built this place. People know who I am. I just want this town to be better."

"Better by *your* standards, of course," Keryon said as he poured himself another shot. "Am I wrong?"

That struck a nerve. Gimlore leaned in and met his gaze.

"Every wooden board, bolt, tile, and square foot of gravel on the mud in this town came from me. When kids get sick, who do you think their mothers take them to? When the gamblers lose all their earnings, who sends them home with their bellies full? Everyone in this town owes me something. If you think otherwise, please ask around. That's exactly who I am, and I won't tolerate insinuations from you or anyone."

Keryon took another shot, crossed his arms, and spoke, "Now *this* is the truth, Madam Gimlore. Meekness doesn't suit you. Viper. Isn't that what they used to call you?"

No. Don't.

She gritted her teeth, clasped her hands in her lap, but looked away in shame. *I'm not like that anymore.* How dare he bring up her past? No one in this world had clean hands.

Keryon started singing, never taking his eyes off her.

She is the Viper, loose into this world.
For days and nights, ruthless she came.
All lies. No truth.
Deceit is her game.

Don't send spiders to prey upon the snake.
She will divide them, their land she will take.
From a distance, she will strike.
Your head will end up on a pike.

Those lyrics hurt more than she would ever care to admit. Every word felt like someone was thrusting a knife into her stomach. That might have been the old Gimlore. Not who she was now.

"How did I do?" the bastard asked. Then he leaned forward. "I know the truth. What you did to the Herald and his people. Even if I don't spread rumours, the people will wonder. And I have no reason to stay quiet."

Gimlore swallowed, cursing herself for deciding to kill the Sirestine entourage. Killing always came easier to her, but it was often the only thing to be done, even if she was now dealing with the fallout. "What do you want, then?"

"Ah, first you take them out. Now you're trying to bribe me."

"The alternative might be you finding out if your shop survives when your rent goes up and you can't find land for sale," Gimlore hissed.

Keryon chuckled. "You are used to having it your way, aren't you? I've met so many people like you. Do you know what they had in common?"

"Enlighten me."

"They have all been beheaded." He paused, looking up at her. "By me. I used to be a man of the law. I thought I was coming to Heleronde to start fresh, to chase peace and wealth. Turns out people here aren't that different from those I left behind."

"The difference is, here you are not a lawman."

"I'm a man of the people," he said.

"The people? No. In here, you are *nobody*," she said, getting as close to him as the table allowed. "Nobody gets to decide what is justice here. And nobody sends smokesmiths after their own people on a whim. There is no *law* for you to uphold."

Keryon sighed, took another shot, and stood.

"Maybe. But the tide is turning, madam. Who knows how long you can keep doing this? You helped nurse this town in its infancy, but are you the best person to take it to new heights?"

Gimlore fumed as Keryon left.

"Utter disrespect, boss," Edmir whispered. "Want me to take care of him?"

She shook her head. "I wouldn't mind, but we need to lay low on that front."

The bastard had just arrived and was already trying to take her place and undermine her authority. Gimlore doubted the townsfolk would be swayed by the man, especially one that used to punish people like them in the old days. *But he's young, handsome, and powerful. Could he do it?*

Keryon was a problem, but she had to track him rather than have him killed. She couldn't risk him trying to seize any kind of power, unless she could control that too...

Gimlore had another sip of her wine. It was still early for this much drinking, but her problems mounted. She only wished she could find the solutions at the end of the bottle.

Eight

Unwanted Neighbours

Gimlore

*T**he Old One awakened again. The deep came rising and crawling.*

— From *Mother's Memories*

Gimlore had Nosema and Nork counting the profits for that day as she stood behind the counter next to Edmir. The patrons were loud as usual and the smell of spilled beer mixed with the stuffy moisture in the air.

The last few days had been as stressful as when she first set foot on the continent. Difficult, but the other claimants realized she wasn't a woman to be crossed. Now she worried about a Sirestine army on their way to set up colonies and, if the Herald was to be believed, ruin everything she had accomplished. She thought about what Keryon had said, too. Just thinking about him made her snarl.

"Edmir," she said, calling him closer. This was embarrassing. Perhaps with another shot of cerro wine, things would get easier. "Have I gone soft?"

Edmir put the glass he was wiping back onto the counter, a frown deepening the lines on his forehead. "What do you mean, boss?"

"You heard me."

Edmir hesitated. He knew her well. "You haven't."

"That bastard got to me," she said.

"Please, let me handle him, boss. I'll get him real good."

Gimlore shook her head. She couldn't let that happen. Not again. Painful memories returned now that the wine had dulled her thoughts. A scene from her time in the Crimson Wars. The blue uniforms walking into the ambush as she and her men watched from afar. But then a faint column of smoke emerging on the horizon, next to her hidden brigands and all their bodies lay motionless later. Dead.

She shook her head, forced the memories to fade, and did her best to keep her eyes dry. Edmir, at least, she would keep safe.

"No. I can't let you. He's a smokesmith."

"So? Sorry, boss, but I've ended plenty of those."

"But we were bushwhacking back then. They were stepping into our steppe. This one is a fucking veteran and it would be too obvious if we threatened him in any way. No, there has to be another way to neutralise him. Keep him close to us. With whom does he associate?"

"A fellow named Pie," Edmir said. "It's his business partner at the herb shop."

She frowned her brow. "Pie? What kind of name is that?"

Edmir shrugged.

"Get your best fellows to tail him. Follow him, see what he does, who he meets. I can't have him plotting something right under my nose. We need to make sure he doesn't spread rumours. Understood?"

"Yes, boss," he said and left to organise the plans.

Gimlore stayed leaning on the counter, drowning herself in cerro wine. The drink muddled her thoughts. Sometimes she just wanted to inflict destruction on people. Instead, she just stayed put and let the alcohol destroy her instead.

"You seem like you need me to cheer you up," Foloi whispered from behind her. She jumped, then spun around to face him. "Next time you creep up on me like that, this bottle gets acquainted with your skull."

Foloi raised his hands, grinning at her, as if promising not to do it again. She calmed and handed him a glass. "Here, drink with me."

Foloi leaned on the counter next to Gimlore and his arm touched hers. His muscles were both hard and smooth, like a well-polished rock. She had a lot on her mind, but she also needed... comfort.

"What do you want?" she asked, raising her eyebrows.

"My hands are healed now," he said, stretching out his enormous hands and fingers. Instead of eyeing her, he glanced at the patrons.

"Is that so?" she asked, taking another sip of the wretched drink.

"Yup. I think I'm going to go settle in my room."

"You have my blessing, if it's permission you are asking for," she said, knowing well it would annoy him.

He cursed something in his native tongue and then took off.

She was about to follow him when she heard footsteps outside. Her lust would have to wait to be satiated.

Nosema and Nork came running and panting hard, their hands resting on their knees. "Boss! You've got to come now. It's terrible!"

"What in the underworld happened?" Gimlore asked, recognising the pain in their eyes. She picked up two of her knives and jogged outside to meet them.

"The mossbacks... they're dead."

·········

The speed of the ride made the humidity more bearable, but the sun was still soldiering above them and the sweat piled up inside her clothes. When they reached the western lots at the border of her lands, Gimlore pulled the reins.

"Where is it?" Gimlore asked.

"It's further ahead, boss."

The red vegetation was dense and crowded and they still had to avoid the deceitful water puddles that were far deeper than they looked. Most of them were circling the little creeks that crossed the swamps from north to south. Perhaps using a raft to cross the creeks would have been a better idea, but she still hadn't had the courage to see what creatures hid in that dirty river water.

A few hundred sweaty farmers tainted by mud and wrinkled by the sun scattered around the swamp. And then the stench of rot entered her nostrils before she even saw the carnage. Dozens of mossbacks lay dead in the red clearing, their crimson blood blending with the red grass. Someone had cut the skin in their bellies, that much was clear. And their guts were hanging out.

Shit.

Gimlore stopped, unable to continue. The farmers waited and eyed her, eager for her reaction. She couldn't afford to stand there and cry while her operation crumbled before her eyes. This was just one lot, but what if they targeted her other lots?

She kneeled by a carcass. "Anyone saw anything?"

"No," Nork said, his voice shaking as he scratched the head with his hook.

"How is that possible? They haven't been dead long." She reached with her hand inside the creature's guts, but the liver was still there. "It seems like whoever did this knew the elixir comes from the mossbacks, but they didn't know it came from their liver. So, none of our farmers talked. I wonder if the smokesmith is involved..."

An icy shiver ran through her as she considered someone targeting her farmers to extract the secrets of the elixir.

"Boss, allow me to disagree," Nosema said, while giving her a short, courteous bow. "I don't think it was the smokesmith."

"Why do you say that?"

Nork swallowed. "There's more you need to see."

·············

They rode and Gimlore let them take the lead towards the very edge of her claimed lands. Nork and Nosema stopped their hearthspears at the edge of the swamps. These portions of the land were harder to take care of, given their slight inclination.

Nosema pointed to the horizon, and Gimlore squinted, trying to focus on something in the distance. Then she saw little dots moving around like ants, carrying things. Those were not her people; those were settlers from a foreign nation.

Gimlore froze. Her breath hitched.

The Herald wasn't bluffing after all.

Sirestine settlers. Hundreds of them. They had come for her elixir. But killing her mossbacks like that? She had forgotten how entitled and vicious the mainland kingdoms were. They had assumed she would sell the land and were already building the camp without having confirmation. The old continent's monarchs weren't used to having their wishes denied. Especially not by people like her.

The bastards didn't wait for the Herald to return.

"Do you know how many they are?"

"Our pineheads counted a few hundred."

"Settlers or soldiers?"

"We believe they have soldiers with them as well."

A shiver ran down her spine as she imagined the soldiers marching towards Heleronde, swords in hand. Gimlore brought her hands to her face, stress and anxiety building. How could she say she was in charge if she couldn't protect her people? Her world wavered and trembled as it seemed about to crumble. All the hardships and the struggles for what? Just to let a foreign monarch grab it all.

"The Herald was right. They are already here. They poached our moss-backs, so we can exclude any good intentions from them."

Nork nodded. "Friendly neighbours wouldn't attack the mossbacks, boss. There is nobody else here. They're not even trying to hide it."

"We can't let the fuckers do whatever they want, but we also can't send them to the underworld without a thought. I need to think about this. Have scouts watch them. I want to know everything—what they are building, how many soldiers they have, and if they are slaves or loyal patriots. And we need to move the rest of the mossback herd closer to our settlement."

Nork nodded. "Yes, boss."

···········

As Gimlore rode back to Heleronde with Nork and Nosema, she glanced at her farmland. Everything she had was now under threat, in danger of collapsing. She had enemies everywhere she looked—on the mainland, in Alarkan, and in the town that she built with her own two hands.

Her hands trembled as she gripped the reigns of the hearthspear. Keeping her cool was turning into a monumental task these days. She envisioned what would happen if the Sirestine or other opportunists tried to seize her lands or destroyed the town while seeking the elixir. The thought of it made her sick.

When they arrived back in Heleronde, Gimlore felt more eyes on her than normal as they rode along the high street. She had helped so many build their homes and their businesses, helped vendors connect with suppliers and offered a place for them to cool off and have fun. She had offered jobs to hundreds of lost souls, nothing but washed-out criminals who ran from being hanged or beheaded in their native lands. Even now, everything she did was to expand Heleronde, create more jobs, and build more homes.

How in the underworld would she protect everything she'd built?

Gimlore and the men dismounted from the hearthspears and she handed the reins to Nork before they entered the Maiden's Hall. The tavern was bustling, although the noise quieted as she entered. Were they... afraid of her? She stood behind the counter as Edmir poured drinks and entertained their most inebriated patrons. She rolled up her sleeves and got to work. Behind her, in the second chamber, she heard the lively banter of those who watched the cage fighting.

"Edmir," she called. "What's with them tonight?"

"Rumours of the Sirestine emissaries having their fate cut short. They're worried about a fallout. Could have been the newcomer talking his mouth off, I'm not sure. My scouts didn't find any evidence of it, though."

Just great.

"I, too, am bloody worried about a fallout," she whispered. "The Sirestine have already shown they're not here to play. I need to find a way to stop them."

"You will, boss."

Gimlore sighed before she turned to the patrons. "I'm feeling generous tonight. One round on the house to everyone in here."

The drunken patrons forgot their fears and cheered.

"I've decided what to do about the smokesmith," she said to Edmir, as they both served the patrons. "I'm going to need you to come with me to pay him a visit tonight."

Edmir looked at her, surprised. "I will sharpen my knives."

"No," Gimlore said. "Not that kind of conversation."

If she mishandled anything it could all come tumbling down. Maybe she could bring the smokesmith to her side.

....

When the patrons had moved into the second room to watch the cage fighting, Gimlore took Edmir and left Nork and Nosema in charge of the Maiden's Hall for a while. It was already past midnight, and the chilly evening was a blessing after another scorching day. It made the air feel easier to breathe, although the humidity was strong, like they were breathing water.

The merchants were closing their shops, and she noticed how many young children there were. Some held onto their mothers' skirts and others ran around in chasing games. That's what Heleronde had granted them: a peaceful life outside the clutches of the kings eager to grow their smoke-smith ranks. There would be no orphans there, as she had been. They would all know what it was like to grow up with a family, as broken and trauma ridden as it may be. Seeing it gave her strength. *I'm doing the right thing, here. I'm on the right path.*

Finally, she saw the small herb shop, a tiny shack even by Heleronde standards. Gimlore smiled as she saw how far removed the shop was from the high street. If it was up to her, they would stay in that crappy shack forever, or even better, they'd go back to the mainland.

A modest lamp feeding on belleaf oil lit the shop. A hint of sulphur reminded her of the smokesmiths she had seen in combat years ago, dousing their herbs with it just before they set it on fire.

They were all alone. She knocked on the door three times. "May I disturb you?"

"Depends. Are you buying?" a man asked from inside the shop.

Keryon was there as well. His companion was almost as tall as him, but his hair was longer and more dishevelled and his beard thick and unkempt. He was bulkier than Keryon, with stronger arms and a wider chest and belly. The man looked like a blacksmith or a cook, not a merchant.

Gimlore found a few gold coins in the pocket of her sweaty trousers and flicked them at the man. "Sure. Whatever that buys. May I speak with Mister Keryon?"

Keryon looked at her and took his time. "What brings you here, Madam Gimlore?" he asked with a hint of annoyance, before going back to his affairs.

"We have matters to discuss," she said.

"I didn't think you'd come for me so soon after our conversation. And you brought your goon with you. At least now I know you respect me."

Gimlore had to contain Edmir, as his gaze rested upon Keryon. His eyes were fiery, ready to kill. No. She needed him to be a quiet menace instead.

"You flatter yourself, Mister Keryon. If I wanted you to be gone, I wouldn't bother paying you a visit."

"You are very confident."

She took a seat on top of one of the wooden boxes that cluttered the inside of the shop, but Edmir stood, without taking his eyes off Keryon. Crates and boxes stacked, still full of herbs. When sellers were sitting on large stocks, it meant they were struggling to find buyers. That was especially problematic while selling herbs because only the dried ones lasted a long time. These two were in deep shit.

"So, if you don't want me gone, what *do* you want, madam?"

"I will make you a proposition. One that pains me more to make than you could imagine, but once I explain my reasons, you will understand."

"My, my. A proposition. Hear this, Piesym? This is going to be good."

She didn't let his mockery stop her. She swallowed and continued. "I want you to take on the same role you used to have. To be the warden of Heleronde."

NINE
THE HOLY KING

ORBERESIS

*M*y *horror is here. I can always recall the moment they rose.*

— From *Mother's Memories*

Orberesis stood as three servants around him got him dressed. He could barely stand on his own, so big was the pain. After all this time, he'd started being able to distinguish between the different kinds of headaches. Sometimes, it was a swathe of pain across his forehead, while sometimes it was an excruciating pressure in his temples. These were bearable. Migraines, however, were the worst. They felt as though there was a specific spot inside his head—sometimes on the side, sometimes the forehead, sometimes the back—that thumped and pulsed relentlessly, tiring him, defeating him, making him collapse and tighten his jaw muscles. Keeping this persona was hard enough without trying to ignore such stifling pain.

The servants were silent and worked to exhaustion, taking his measurements, and making sure the robe had the best fit for his slender body frame. He could hardly stay still. Orberesis wasn't sure whether they noticed it, or whether they were believers, but they were aware of who he was. In their meekness they showed their gratitude. *Va Binit*, they said. Their saviour, it meant, which made him wonder just how poorly Doemus and Thura had treated them. "How long have you been in the Palace of Brilliance?"

That startled them, poor servants. They exchanged glances, none daring to open their mouths while also fearing not answering a question.

"You can speak freely. Think of it as a confession. Whatever you tell me within these walls is a secret I shall take to the grave. And I'll look out for you and maybe your children. Understood? If you go hungry, let me know and I'll feed you. If someone beats you, let me know and I'll see what I can do."

They still didn't dare look at him but their wide eyes hinted at their minds racing with anticipation. Hopefully they'd see in him an advocate. And they needed one badly, as much as he needed spies and allies within those treacherous halls.

"Well?" he insisted. "Speak freely with me. Always."

"All life, Highest One," a young, long-nosed boy spoke. "Born here."

Orberesis did his best to shake away the migraine and focus on the conversation. "A good life?"

The question was a test. He could never *fully* trust them. They could already be spies from Taishay or from somebody else, sent to watch his every move. But he could test their allegiances first and assess how likely they would be to listen in on things for him.

Long Nose spoke again. "Only one." *The only one they had.* That was promising for him.

It would take time, as much of a rush as he was in.

"Well, let's work on making it better, then. Here." Orberesis reached for the small, purple purse on the table, produced three small silver coins from within and placed a coin in each of their hands. "I'm not like other lords and ladies. I see everyone being worth the same—rich or poor. I treat everyone the same and I *help* when I can. You'll *never* catch a beating from me or any of my people. Understood? Just keep doing your job and... *talk* to me. I like company."

The shocked servants couldn't stop looking at the silver coins, which Orberesis reckoned were probably more than a whole month's worth of pay, if they got paid at all.

"T-Thank Highest Lord!" a curly-haired woman said.

"No need to thank me... I might be God Himself now, but just ten years ago and I was a city-dweller. Now, tell me all about your life here in the palace. Do the King and Queen treat you well?"

....

After a long wait and a long conversation, the now happy servants told him all about the inner workings of the palace while measuring him and getting him dressed. They commented on how the head servant responded directly to Queen Thura and chased them around day and night with a small whip that he kept hidden in his sleeve. For what seemed like hours, they talked their lungs out. Of course, not much of what they said was relevant to him, but any context was good. They seemed agreeable to him at the very least and, even better, his migraine subsided.

The servants provided him with a mirror. The white robe fit him to perfection. He wore leather sandals crafted by the best artisans in the world and his long, dark hair rested over his shoulders. They had brushed it to perfection, too.

"Thank you for your work and for the company. You may go, now," he said, summoning the gentlest manners he could.

All the servants left smiling after bowing perhaps a tad too long. When they closed the door to his chambers, he fell in one of the enormous, padded chairs present in his chamber. He pressed his hands to his temples, clinched his teeth, and screamed. Sometimes he wished he could use a hammer and a chisel to forcibly remove whatever was causing the pain. Or at least lie in bed all day, vegetative, until the pain was gone. He might be in a palace, but he still hadn't earned that luxury.

The migraine didn't leave him, but he had to believe it one day would.

Someone knocked on the door.

Orberesis sighed, his peace broken. "Yes?"

Solvi opened the door and entered the room, staying by the doorway. "Highest Lord, it's time," she said.

Orberesis jumped to his feet. "Ah, yes, yes. Won't you come here for just a moment, Solvi?"

"Yes, Highest Lord," The woman said and knelt in front of him.

"No, no, you don't need to kneel, Solvi." He held her gentle hand, colder than he would have imagined. "How do you like it here in the palace?"

"Your will is my will, Highest Lord. Your wishes serve a higher purpose that I must enforce. And I'm glad the King appreciates your counsel."

His eyes fixated on her cheeks and the perfect freckles that speckled them. She blushed as she noticed his unbroken gaze, and her eyes shied away from him to focus on the clasped hands over her lap. The migraine was a constant reminder. A constant parasite, feeding off him, but Solvi almost made him forget.

"I'm glad you feel that way. I'm only as strong as my followers. Thankfully, I have you as my strongest follower." He cupped her cheek. Resisting was hard. "You fought for me. Bled for me. And I'll never be able to thank you enough. Are you fully recovered?"

Her face reddened. "Yes, Highest One."

She would follow him to the bowels of the earth, he knew that, but he wanted her by his side in a different way. Perhaps one day, with his maladies healed...

"You were the first devout follower I ever had. Words are scarce for the appreciation I have for you."

"When I heard about your miracle, I knew I had to find you. To show you my devotion," she said with a smile.

"If only they were all like you... My doubts come from my followers," he said. Solvi's eyes perked up. "There are people in court who do not share your thoughts on this matter. They doubt my intentions. They make me question my own will. Councillor Taishay was against me when we first arrived. It wouldn't surprise me if he and his cronies were plotting something. But there are many others, surely. In and out of the palace. All over the Two Nations."

Solvi's eyes turned from surprise to a fiery rage Orberesis knew so well. "Highest One, that is unacceptable. Whoever these people are, they are wrong. I will look into it if that pleases you."

Orberesis nodded and placed his right hand on her leg. "That would please me very much. What would I do without you?"

Solvi blushed once again. "I'm not worthy, Highest One."

"Yes, you are. You are," he said. "You've come a long way since I've met you."

"Only because of the Highest One."

"No, no," Orberesis said, shaking his head. "Your faith has a strength of its own. I can see it. Remember how it was when I met you?"

Solvi swallowed, stiffening. "I do, but I meant what I said, Highest One. It was thanks to your miracle that I get to be who I am, that I no longer have to fight."

"And the warlords can no longer use you as their personal war machine," he said, grabbing her hand. "It's alright. You are free now and look how far you've come, always brightening my day. You're perhaps the most important person in the Order of the Red Orb."

Solvi's eyes welled, and she nodded. "Thank you, Highest One. For you, I will always fight."

Pleased to see her loyalty was still unwavering, he got up from the padded chair where they sat. "You said it was time already?"

"Yes. Everyone is waiting. Please follow me."

The two guards who stood outside bowed as he passed before closing the doors to his chambers. They walked through one of the palace's main hallways where the history of the Two Nations of Sirestir and Yab was told in oil portraits, tapestries, and glasswork, telling tales of dynasties both old and recent, of kings fallen and conquerors being born. Beautiful ancient queens in intricate gowns stood with hundreds of men kneeling at their feet. An old tapestry caught his eye as it showed a strange depiction of hundreds of children arriving from the skies and being received in Ushar. He didn't recall ever hearing that legend.

"Perhaps the King will let me have my portrait hung in here as well one day," Orberesis said as the two of them and a small group of guards walked through the wide hall. When he thought the headaches were gone, they returned, and he struggled to keep it hidden. As always.

Solvi looked back and smiled. "I shall arrange it, Highest Lord. Perhaps your portrait should replace these."

He chuckled at that, but Solvi had been serious.

When they reached the end of the hallway, the doors opened, and Orberesis entered the ceremonial room. Servants had decorated it with red banners. He knew the worship leaders of the Order and Solvi were behind those efforts. He would be a governing councillor now after all. An enormous crowd of noblemen and their courtesans knelt. No one wanted to be seen trying to stand taller than God Himself. Clerics and priests from other religions stayed out.

That must have been Doemus' doing. They wouldn't kneel voluntarily.

Orberesis mustered any hint of regal spirit he possessed amid another splitting headache, walked towards King Doemus, and kneeled before the throne that was guarded by five armed soldiers in full armour. Ten years ago, those same men would not have hesitated to take his head for coming near the palace and now, they would swear to protect him.

"Miraculous One," Doemus said, picking up a ceremonial sword adorned with precious gems. "It's a pleasure to raise my sword and appoint you, God Himself, a governing councillor of the Two Nations of Sirestir and Yab. Despite the attempts of traitors to block you from this council, I welcome you to the palace with arms wide open. I vow to always seek your counsel and to bestow upon you my trust."

The Queen helped the King's sword touch both of Orberesis' shoulders and the crowd applauded in a much more subdued fashion. Funny how wildly they cheered when they didn't know he wanted to be one of them. Now here he was, and they'd much rather throw stones.

He sought their faces. How could he trust anyone? Taishay and other councillors could stab him in the back. Other nobles. Even soldiers could be hiding covert allegiances. He had obtained the power he sought, but that didn't mean he'd be able to keep it with ease. That, in itself, was enough to fill his head with aches. All of this, he reminded himself, was to end the pain. There was no room for failure.

"Thank you, Your Majesty. You saw reason and truth before most. You were selfless and welcomed me with no doubt and no fear. I vow to provide you with counsel, wisdom, and friendship. I have no interests other than those of the realm."

Everyone except Solvi and the King seemed to know that was not true.

Orberesis looked at the other people in the room. He could still see doubt, prejudice, fear, hatred. And those were supposed to be the peaceful ones. The ones agreeable to the King's decision to bring him into the governing council. That much was clear in Taishay alone. The old councillor didn't bother to hide his distaste, so Orberesis would have to trust that Solvi would keep an eye on him.

Perhaps I could start asking more direct questions to the servants too.

Kene and the direct conspirators had been arrested or killed, but they would surely have plenty of friends in the palace. Orberesis couldn't parade himself too much without knowing exactly who they were.

"Thank you, Highest One." The King turned to face the crowd. The nobles, merchants, and councillors had their eyes on him. "With God Himself as part of the governing council, we have a great opportunity to sail waters never sailed, pave roads never travelled. We'll have wisdom, bravery, and boldness to spare. But despite the Highest One's miraculous achievements, I count on *all* of you as well. You are the heart and soul of these Two Nations. You take care of my land and of my ships and you keep my people safe. You also stood loyal when the traitors tried to dethrone me. For that, I am thankful."

Orberesis searched for Tavanar in the crowd and found him at the back of the room, leaning against the stone wall with arms crossed, smiling deviously. Orberesis was the one who should be thankful. Thanks to the orb around his neck, he'd been able to fool millions—one of them a king.

I've done it. I've fucking done it.

Ten

Goals and Ambitions

Orberesis

I cannot go back. I cannot stop. I cannot resist.

— From *Mother's Memories*

Orberesis was tired. He drank the most expensive cerro wine in the world from his crystal glass and it blurred his senses, giving him the buzz he had been craving for months. The alcohol, at least, would dilute his migraines and dull his senses a bit.

His red orb lay on the large study table by the stained-glass window and he sat on a comfortable, cushioned chair, with his head leaning against the backrest. He opened his mouth and the northern servant fed him a cerro berry. Another held his wineglass for him.

Orberesis had chosen those northern servants for this evening because they didn't understand his language. He didn't want anybody spying on his conversations with Tavanar. His friend sat on the chair in front of him, also surrounded by three servants.

"I could get used to this," Orberesis said. The worst was behind him. It had taken them ten years to get to this point. He wasn't healed yet, but he couldn't complain.

"You *will* get used to this, once you're cured," Tavanar said as a servant fed him another cerro berry. "I've summoned the best healers, medics, and shamans of the Two Nations. I didn't give a reason for it. We will cure you soon, my friend."

"And I'll become an insufferable little runt with high standards, like the rest of them," Orberesis said

"You're already pretty close to that."

Orberesis chuckled. In here, they were alone and he could relax, lower his guard. "I wish we could just drown ourselves in wine."

"Don't dream too big, you bastard."

"I know. I have to keep my eyes open. I'm doing my own little investigations with the help of a few servants, and I also asked Solvi to investigate those vocal against me."

Tavanar nodded. "Why don't you call her over here?"

"I can't do that. I still have to keep the farce. To her, I am God Himself, her saviour."

"That's a shame. What about these servants?" Tavanar asked as he fondled the breast of one of the northern servants.

"What about them?"

"Shouldn't you be with someone closer to your station?" Tavanar asked. "What will your people say if God Himself, the Miraculous One, only lays with the lowest of servants? Will they say you have poor taste? There's nothing wrong with these fine young men and women, but—"

"Yes, yes, I get it," Orberesis said. "I keep thinking of my dad. Maybe one day I'll have the power to free the people from all the tyranny and avenge what the crown did to him."

"Cheeky little bastard. Be careful," Tavanar said. "Well, as long as I can keep living like this, you have my full blessing to do whatever the fuck you want."

"I haven't forgotten how Doemus' mother ordered my father to be burned alive, along with my entire village. All because of a fucking necklace." He sighed and raised his glass. "But for now, we celebrate."

Tavanar mimicked him. "Cheers, my friend. To being fed and spoiled!"

"Cheers."

Orberesis chugged whatever was left in the glass. At the bottom, he found only the guilt of not having told Tavanar he had no control over the orb's powers. They were friends, but it was a matter of survival. "Listen, Tav. You are all I've got left. I know we're not good men. We haven't been for a while, but after all the shit we've been through together, you deserve this life of a lord, too. We were always together."

"Always."

"Do you think we can make the world better?"

Tavanar was silent for a moment, then they both burst into laughter, spilling the liquor.

Tavanar pointed at the round window behind him. It was at least ten feet tall, and its glasswork was iconic. It was visible from anywhere in the city, its depiction of old religious figures. "Remember when we used to sleep on the rooftops and point at this very window? I always said it would be our biggest heist. We would rob the King while he slept."

"Not a real theft, but we did, all because of this orb," Orberesis said.

"The bloody orb indeed."

Orberesis reached for the orb around his neck. "You mentioned something about pilgrims earlier. What did you mean?"

"There are hundreds of them outside the palace. Thousands, even. They're from all over the world. A lot of them come from beyond the Seven Peaks of the Benaven mountains just to see your ugly arse. To adore you, pray to you, or whatever it is they do."

Orberesis nodded. Word of his miracle had continued to spread over the past ten years and, with a little help from his worship leaders and Solvi, many had made it their mission to preach about the Order. But to travel the world just to see him was nerve-wracking.

Soon they would start asking for more miracles and they would realise he had done his miracle by chance and no merit of his own, that the orb had acted alone. Maybe King Doemus would realise Orberesis couldn't perform miracles and throw him in the catacombs where horrible men would torture him until they decided he should die. Those thoughts plagued him and brought back a gruelling migraine. A sharp pain occupied his mind and erased everything else. He lifted his hands to his temples, but it got worse, and his legs became shaky, forcing him to drop to his knees. Tavanar noticed and grabbed his arm.

"Migraine?"

"They're getting worse."

Tav nodded. "What are the nightmares like, anyway?"

Orberesis shrugged. "The last one was about the time when we found the orb. The ruins where we found it, and how disappointed we were. Us, doing our best to find someone to sell it to. And then it all goes dark, and I wake up sweating."

"I'll line the healers up in front of you first thing in the morning."

"I must at least try the elixir as well, Tav."

Tavanar gave him a light pat on the shoulder. His face was serious. "You will. We'll get it."

One too many drinks after that, Tavanar was already slurring his speech and unable to open his eyes. Orberesis ushered all the slaves out of the room and started whistling before he caught Tavanar frowning at him.

"What was that?"

"What?"

"You were whistling. Since when can you whistle?"

Orberesis stopped himself. He *had* been whistling. That was an odd one. "I didn't realise it."

Tav shook his head. "People don't just learn how to whistle out of nowhere. You've always had it in you."

Orberesis nodded and his eyebrows shot up in realization. "I guess I did."

Shrugging, he drank more cerro wine. Perhaps this phenomenon had been related to the alcohol he was drinking, since it also seemed to make him crave foods he never remembered enjoying either.

As he brought the glass to the table, a sharp spasm took over his arm, making him cringe. "Ah!"

"What is it?" Tavanar asked.

The spasm expanded, as though his muscles were no longer in his control, folding and contracting through his back, towards his other arm and his legs. Then the pain climbed up to his neck just as he was about to answer.

He could no longer answer.

And there was only pain. He couldn't move his body and dropped flat on the floor, hitting his head on the table, breaking the glass top.

"Doi!" Tavanar rushed to his rescue. "What is happening?"

The pain spread from his neck to his face and Orberesis couldn't explain the paralysis. Where did it come from? With all his muscles tensed and pain coursing through them, he felt tears running from the corner of his eyes, down from his crooked mouth while his jaw muscles locked outward. A wet warmth built around his groin.

Fuck.

Tavanar tried to massage his muscles, soothe the pain. It was no use. The was no way to massage tense muscles without causing Orberesis a greater pain. This was his to bear. Alone. He hated that Tavanar had to see him like that, crying and drooling and pissing himself. How very godly of him.

"Shit. You hit your head too. You're bleeding."

As though that wasn't enough, his vision blurred. Too much pain. He could see the fear in Tavanar's wide eyes. His friend looked like he might just piss himself too.

"I need to call the medics."

Orberesis tensed even more as he heard that, but he could express no reaction. There would be rumours, true ones at that. Who would believe him to be God Himself if people saw him like that, lying flat on the floor like a rug? It hurt him badly, but he managed to grasp Tavanar's shirt, hoping his friend would understand.

No medics! He tried to say, to no avail, though Tavanar understood the look in his eyes, nodded, and sat next to him, covering the cut in his head with a cloth.

The paralysis was just that. It was extremely painful and degrading, and came without warning. But he wouldn't die unless he bit his tongue with the spasms or hit his head too badly. It would just be a long night.

Bathing in sweat, tears, and piss, Orberesis' shame only grew larger. With a paralysed body, he only had his thoughts, his angers, his fears, and his pain. He wished for *some* change. Maybe revenge for his father's fate. A painless future.

He wished to have patience.

All in due time.

Eleven
Defiance

Orberesis

Their screams are mine, and I hear their horrendous replies.

— From *Mother's Memories*

"What do you mean, no elixir?" Tavanar asked the healers, his voice echoing throughout the chamber. "You are the King's healers. How is that possible? How can you not have it?"

Orberesis sighed as he glanced at them, all dressed in ridiculous clothes to strengthen their eccentric reputation.

"A wizard, a shaman, a spatial herbalist, whatever that means, yet none of you have a sample of the famed elixir," he said.

"We've heard much about it, it's true, but we've had none in our possession, I'm afraid," the shaman said. "Ships are being sent to buy it. What's the hurry? Is it so urgent that you need the elixir now?"

"Indeed!" the spatial herbalist said. "You can ask King Doemus. Where is he?"

Orberesis found himself with gritted teeth and frowning. Thankfully, nobody else was in the room, save for Tavanar, his guards, and three servants who always followed him now.

Tavanar took a step forward and got up close to the healer. "*King Doemus* is a busy man and has no time for this. The Highest One is a member of the governing council now. He must be treated with respect."

"Apologies, apologies," the healer said, his face red as he took a bow.

Tavanar sighed and walked over to Orberesis. "They're useless. I'm sorry, Doi. I thought they'd have it."

"It's not your fault, Tav."

"Maybe you can finish them with the orb."

Orberesis gave his friend a faint smile, and his chest tightened. Tavanar was his best friend, yet he didn't trust him enough to confide that he couldn't control the orb at all.

"Not worth it. If they don't have the elixir, I have no use for them. Get them out of here. We have the council meeting now," Orberesis said.

Tavanar pulled Orberesis aside just as he was taking off.

"Look, Doi, I know you're trying to be reasonable," he whispered. "But you've already tried every medicine and cure in the Known World except for the damn elixir. You can't let it go like that. It's their job as healers to, well... heal people."

Orberesis nodded, patting his friend's shoulder. "I know, I know. But if I threaten them or hurt them, I'll only be making everyone wonder why I need a cure so badly. We need to seek the elixir in silence. Patiently."

"It doesn't matter what anyone thinks. You can lie. Tell them it's for one of your miracles. Or say it's for me. I don't care."

"Lies always have short legs, Tav. You know that. You can't keep them running forever. And I say that as an expert liar too. Let us go and see what the governing council has to discuss. We'll find the elixir elsewhere."

Tavanar sighed but he understood.

They left the healers behind and walked the halls of the Palace of Brilliance. Orberesis did so at a slow pace to avoid follow-up cramps from the paralysis of the previous evening. Unlike the name suggested, the palace wasn't so bright. In fact, it was rather dark, he realised, with the wide windows not enough to lighten up the halls and chambers. And it was rather cold without the sunlight. Dozens of sconces hung on the walls, supporting torches throughout.

On their way to the Council room, they passed through the hallways that branched out into the King's quarters, then the Queen's quarters, then the Ceremonial Room.

"Highest One," his servant said. Pircela was her name. "Look."

Orberesis narrowed his eyes as he noticed two figures close to one another. They quickly disappeared into a hallway, but Orberesis thought he still saw a glimpse of them for a split second. One had been a soldier or a guard. Someone wearing a military uniform of the palace. The other was a woman of dark hair and dark skin.

"That looked very much like..." Tavanar said, but Orberesis shushed him.

The Queen...

That was very useful information for him to hold, but he couldn't make a big deal of it yet. Could have just been a friendly conversation. But why so secretive, then? And why were they talking so close to one another? It wasn't uncommon for rulers to have affairs, but he couldn't be quick to make assumptions. That was something to investigate.

"Thank you, Pircela," Orberesis said as he held the servant's hand and discretely placed another silver coin in it. "That was *very* good."

....

Those gathered around the council table were silent. "What is it?" the King enquired.

Taishay swallowed and spoke. "We must discuss protection. For you and the Highest One, Your Majesty. I fear you might find enemies lurking within the Two Nations, yes, but not only within the realm. Seirgrave, our greatest ally, have got word of our internal struggles. My spies say the Seirgravians perceive it to be a display of an exploitable weakness. There are rumours bubbling that they are considering an invasion."

And perhaps you're in bed with them.

"I'm sure when General Taishay mentioned our internal struggles he meant how stoically you handled the traitors, stopped the uprising, and prevented a coup from taking place," Orberesis said. Taishay bit his lip and frowned at the jab. "We'll show the Seirgravians our strength if we must. Let's keep our eyes open, especially at the border."

The King nodded. "The Highest One is right, as expected. We shall do just that. Now, is there anything else that requires my attention, Taishay?"

"There is, Your Majesty," Taishay said.

The man snapped his fingers, and a polite aide walked to the table, handing him a rolled piece of paper. Taishay took it, unrolled it, and spread it across the table. It was a map of the Known World with many careful annotations. He placed a pebble in each corner and pointed at a specific point Orberesis struggled to see.

"What is it?"

"A few months ago, we sent one of your heralds to enquire about buying a very interesting plot of land on the new continent, Your Majesty. Alarkan, the one the Highest One created during his miracle. There has been nothing but silence ever since."

Oh?

"Is it related to the elixir?" Orberesis asked. *The healers did say something about ships being sent.*

Doemus nodded. "They say the elixir doubles a man's strength and has healing properties. No one said where it came from, but I asked Taishay and other councillors to investigate. They tracked it to a ratty settlement. But the ships won't be back here for at least another month. Most likely more than that."

I can't wait that long... "I understand."

The King swallowed. "It's a worrying find, Highest One."

"Worrying?"

Taishay answered instead, "If one of our rival kingdoms was to get hold of this elixir, they could give it to their armies and—"

"And we wouldn't stand a chance," the King said. "Do not interrupt me, Taishay."

"Apologies, Your Majesty." The man was fuming.

"That is why I tried to get ahead of the enemies and seize the elixir. I had hoped to set up a colony on Alarkan."

"I'd love to be of assistance, Your Majesty." Orberesis needed something. Any opportunity to be involved in this. The earlier he could try the damn elixir the better. "In any way I can."

Doemus scratched his chin. "Yes, that sounds like a good idea. It is the continent you created, after all. Perhaps you could find out what happened to the Herald."

"If I may, Your Majesty. I was in charge of the expedition..." one of Taishay's cronies said.

"And what news have you had? What happened to the Herald you sent?"

The lordling stayed quiet. There had been no update yet.

"That's what I thought. You know nothing." Doemus spat, then turned to Orberesis. "Very well, Highest One. If that's what you wish, I'll leave you in charge of that effort. We can send more settlers if we must. Please keep me updated on any fresh developments. Tell me when you have a sample."

Not until I bloody try it myself. "Of course, Your Majesty."

Doemus nodded and everyone at the table remained quiet until another one of Taishay's cronies with a funny moustache cleared his throat. Orberesis refused to believe they were always this quiet. This fearful. They were all throwing knives at him with their eyes.

"There is another topic, Your Majesty."

"Go ahead," Doemus said.

The tinted glass window shattered, and shards flew across the room, covering the table and everyone present, putting an end to the conversation. Orberesis closed his eyes and raised his arms to protect himself from the falling glass. With shards covering his head, arms, and shoulders, he finally looked up to see what had caused the window to break. When he did, a shadowy figure stood between him and the sunlight that poured from the now broken window. By the time Orberesis saw it was a man sliding down a rope and leaping towards him, it was already too late. The man landed with his boots on Orberesis' chest, shoving him onto the floor.

It all happened so fast.

In a chaos of broken glass and cuts all over his skin, the man's gauntlet had a powerful grip on Orberesis throat. Through the corner of his eye, he saw the dagger in the assassin's right hand.

Orberesis couldn't breathe with the man's gauntlet digging into his throat. His heart raced and his face must have been purple as he fought against the man's grip, grabbing his wrist. The worst of all was the dagger. Soon, he would find it stuck in his brain, or his heart. He tried screaming for help, but he couldn't utter a word. In that moment, before Solvi, Doemus, or anybody else in the room could get the assassin off him, impending doom weighed on him. This was how his dream would end. His meaningless existence, finished at the edge of a blade.

The red orb glistened under Orberesis' robe and the assassin's grip loosened. His dagger hand froze and with impossible force, the man's back hit the stone wall with a surge of power. Then he fell to the palace floor, gasping for air. Orberesis gasped too, promptly caressing his neck in newfound relief. What had that been? The orb still glistened. His other hand touched it and he appreciated it with his eyes wide. It had saved him; he was sure of it. The orb saved him from the assassin. It had manifested in his favour, and this time, he remembered it.

Another miracle.

"Kill the assassin!" Solvi hissed.

"No, wait!" Orberesis said. "We need to know the culprit and who ordered it!"

The soldier who had been standing guard at the door snapped out of his daze, advanced towards the assassin with a small, compact crossbow pointed at the man and kicked his arm. Orberesis thought he'd seen the guard somewhere before, but he couldn't remember where. The assassin didn't move at being kicked, so the dark-haired soldier removed the assassin's mask to show his identity. As soon as he did, the mouth foamed, and his eyes went blank. There was nothing special about the assassin's face. Could have been any man in the Two Nations.

"Poison, Your Majesty," the soldier said, putting his crossbow away. "He poisoned himself. Probably to avoid questioning."

"This is an outrage!" Doemus screamed. "From now on we need reinforcements and tighter security around me and the Highest One. The traitors still walk among us, it seems. We must root them out once and for all."

Orberesis was too stunned to speak. He'd been expecting traitors and noble merchants trying their damned hardest to get rid of the problem—him—but he couldn't take his eyes off the orb. It had protected him. Maybe now they'd believe him, the bastards.

He smiled as he held the orb. *Thank you.*

"I need to know who he was. His name and his master," Doemus said as Orberesis composed himself. "Everything about him. Trying to kill God Himself should deserve the worst of fates."

"I will find the culprits, Your Majesty," the crossbow soldier said, before storming off with his guards carrying the assassin's body.

Orberesis still couldn't say a word. Everyone must have seen the second miracle and how he'd handled an assassin with impossible power. Good. The story would spread.

Orberesis picked off pieces of shattered glass in silence. "Now I understand what you meant, gentlemen. It seems you were right. I hope whoever is behind this understands I'm God Himself, not any man. It will take more than daggers to get rid of me."

....

Just a few hours after the assassination attempt, and they hadn't come to a conclusion yet. The King liked to tout his power, but it was all a front. The man was insecure, maybe more troubled than Orberesis.

Solvi stood and leaned across the table, eyes locked with Taishay. "They are jealous. And like the underworld creatures that they are, they hide in the shadows and spread lies just to tarnish the purest reputation of the Highest One. And now they try to assassinate him."

"What are you insinuating?" Taishay spat, surprised and irritated.

As much as Orberesis appreciated seeing the old man uncomfortable, it was better to deescalate the confrontation. Solvi would discover if he had been involved in the assassination attempt.

"How should we bring the culprits to justice, Taishay?" Orberesis asked the room, pretending like this failed murder had been nothing. With the shock gone, however, there were ripples of anxiety and a million questions popping up. What if the orb hadn't stopped it? He would have died, surely. Could he count on the orb again? Had this been a fluke?

"Well, I—. His Majesty should invite the merchants to the palace again, spend time with them, explain to them your religion and give them time to soak it in. To understand faith in the Highest One. A consensus can still be found. Diplomacy," Taishay said.

Tavanar leaned forward, crossed his arms and furrowed his brow. "Are you suggesting His Majesty and God Himself kiss the arses of those traitors to prevent them from trying to stage a coup?"

Taishay stopped for a moment. He still believed in peace. In a solution where the old ways would work with the new. But all chance of that had been crushed when Kene took up arms. It had been one thing to try and focus on Orberesis but challenging the King on that would prove fatal.

"I will pretend you didn't say that, Taishay. And I'll keep giving you the benefit of the doubt until my patience runs out," the King said, frowning. "But I'll *never* sit with traitors, no matter who they are. As king, I should be prepared for false and careless words about me. Insults, even. But plots to take the throne? And to have God Himself murdered? I will not have it."

The King's words had left everyone in the room silent. No one dared interrupt. It was nice to have someone with power by his side, he reckoned. Perhaps there was a way to make sure the King wouldn't let this go. Both their lives depended on it, after all.

"Your Majesty," Orberesis said, doing his best to sound wise, even if his condition almost always made him wonder if it really came across that way. "May I ask what is the punishment for those who have been proven to slander the King or the governing council in the Two Nations?"

"The gallows," the King said. "Do you have any suggestion, Highest One? I feel as though I should make it up to you somehow. This is not how our realm should be. We should be better than this. What a horrible first impression it must be."

Orberesis shook his head and spoke to the whole council. "Well, there has already been an attempted murder and an attempted coup. How do we make sure people know the price of injuring the King's name or plotting against His Majesty? I say we chase them down and *show it* to them. We do have smokesmiths at our disposal."

"You're not suggesting chasing down citizens of the Two Nations just to make a point, are you?" Taishay asked, and the indignation was spread across the rest of the advisors. "Cracking down on the citizens? That would create chaos. Revolt. It would be an outrage. His Majesty would lose the support from all the lords and merchants. From our allies. It would be madness, Your Majesty?"

Queen Thura, who usually minded her business stepped forward, placing her hands on Doemus' arms. "Darling, surely you can't be serious? Listen to Taishay. He's always been a good councillor."

All eyes focused on the King, who scratched his chin. Perhaps he needed another push.

"Your Majesty, the rule of law is important to keep the peace. After the coup, the disruptors tried to challenge your rule. They questioned your authority. Keeping the peace and establishing justice sometimes must go hand in hand. Great people must make great decisions to avoid great consequences. I'm afraid it is such a time.

"The traitors of the realm have proved they're still willing to challenge your rule. They won't stop at anything to get what they want, especially if we let them go with a slap on the wrist. Actions demand consequences. This is about protecting the realm and strengthening your position as the king. Kings are always tested in their lives. This is your time to be tested. Your enemies think you weak, so it's time to prove just how wrong they are. If you fail to do so, the consequences could be dire, Your Majesty."

Taishay was shaking his head so vehemently it was as though his skin was about to slide off his skull. "Insanity! Utter insanity! We haven't had a public execution in decades. We're a forward-looking nation. Peaceful and prosperous. We only need to keep our eyes peeled for Seirgrave and other kingdoms. Let the merchants do their work."

The King seemed divided. "What do you say about this, Highest One?"

Orberesis swallowed and wondered if the King was ready for honesty. "I say general Taishay hasn't toured the Two Nations like I have. He hasn't communed with the subjects as I have. And it shows. He seems to have no knowledge of their living. I don't remember seeing much peace or prosperity. The streets are riddled with brigands and bandits doing as they see fit. And I'm sure there is prosperity somewhere, but most of the city-dwellers are starved, sick, and depressed. By striking against the traitors, Your Majesty, you have an opportunity to present yourself as the man of faith that you are. A man of justice and strength. A man of the people. Loyal subjects would never betray their king. Unhappy ones, on the other hand..."

Doemus mulled this over in silence and rose his hand every time Taishay or the other buffoons in the governing council tried to speak. Just as they babbled incoherent words, trying to talk over one another, Orberesis was stifled by a puncturing headache on both his temples. It was as though nails were slowly being inserted into his brain on both sides at the same time, such was the pain.

The King cleared his throat. "How would you go about finding these traitors and bringing them to justice?"

Orberesis noticed Tavanar's frown fixated on him. His friend must be confused about why Orberesis was so insistent on this punishment. In truth, he was afraid the orb wouldn't work anymore. He was afraid there would be more assassination attempts. He was afraid he wouldn't get the elixir in time and would have the most miserable life until he became truly insane because of it. He'd seen people like that, driven mad from illnesses uncured and did not want to become one of those. If a few hundred treacherous bastards were hung, so what? Tavanar didn't know it. What it felt like to be in that much pain so often. After a while, the well-being of others becomes much less of a priority.

"I have a few ideas, Your Majesty."

············

The weather had cooled. Sirestir was never as cold as the northern nations. Despite the chill northern breeze, Orberesis could still wear his white robe without feeling cold. A few weeks after the failed assassination, he no longer needed the slaves fanning him with large tree leaves, but six of them still carried him in his chair.

"A lovely day, isn't it?" he asked Solvi. Except it was not a lovely day. There were bulls rampaging inside his brain, stone masons chiselling his skull while a musician played the drums directing into his mind. It was a bloody *miracle* he could still sit there and talk without screaming into the skies or trying to rip his hair out. He'd also had a horrible nightmare the previous night, with the giant man chasing him across the crop fields. At least there had been no paralysis.

"Indeed, Highest One," she said.

The day would be much lovelier if he found a cure for the migraines, the nightmares, and the paralysis, elixir or not. He'd seen ten healers, five shamans, and three doctors. Not counting the dozens he'd met over the years. They had prescribed different lifestyles, herbs, and pastes. Even praying rituals. Orberesis had tried all the recipes and they had all failed. They'd looked at him with risen eyebrows and said it was 'not natural' or 'not from this world'. Well, he was very much *in* this world, so that was a problem.

Ten years of perfecting his acting skills and building up a reputation, all with gaining access to the world's best doctors and healers in mind. And none of them had known what illness he possessed. He almost slipped and let out a tear of desperation but ended up bottling it. His choice was between infinite pain or death, and neither option was appealing.

Solvi walked with him to the courtyard of the Palace of Brilliance. His personal guards surrounded him. Orberesis looked towards the city. The view was as wonderful as he had always dreamt it would be. The tiled rooftops of all sizes and heights leaned against each other, sprawling from the Palace of Brilliance to the walls in the distance. The city's largest avenues were wide, marked by trees taller than buildings alongside the roads where both pedestrians and riders transited. Ushar was an architectural marvel. Much of that ancient knowledge was now lost, of course. He didn't comprehend how a kingdom that prided itself on having no wars and traded so much could still have so much misery.

But he understood misery.

He had bathed in it for most of his life, scrambled to prevent it from drowning him. Perhaps he should feel sorry for the people they were about to target, but he did not. Nobody had helped him when he was an orphan, an urchin roaming the streets of Ushar. He had to look out for himself. Now wasn't any different. Tavanar was shifty, scratching himself as though he was deeply uncomfortable. Tav had always been soft. He'd shake his enemy's hand if it was extended to him during a battle.

"How many people left the city walls?" he asked.

Solvi shrugged. "Few, Highest One."

"Is everything in place? Are the smokesmiths ready?" King Doemus asked the rest of his advisors.

Taishay and the other councillors hesitated. With regret painted all over his face, Taishay took a step forward and bowed, his jewellery clinking. "Yes, Your Majesty. It should start any minute now."

Orberesis hadn't understood it when his father had said 'good people need to do bad things, sometimes'. Now, he did. He needed to find the elixir and stay alive until then. This world wasn't for the weak minded and even less so for the weak hearted. He wished his father was still around so he could stand next to him and watch as the same ruling class who'd burned him to death faced the same fate.

They stood in the Palace of Brilliance's courtyard, looking upon the city. Moments later, Solvi pointed to a column of smoke on the left side of the city. "So, it begins."

Orberesis squinted and saw threads of smoke coming from buildings and roads. A few at first, but more and more appeared, creating a cloud of smoke above Ushar. He could smell it. First the sulphur; then, burning wood; and finally, traces of a scent that turned his stomach – burning meat.

The smokesmiths were already at work. They had instructions regarding who they had to send to the underworld: merchants, traders and industrious business folks who the spies had discovered as traitors. No urchins. No beggars. Only conspirators and known opposition to Doemus' rule and Orberesis' appointment to the governing council. This was no different than what the King had ordered done after Kene's open rebellion, only on a larger scale. Like a show, to dissuade any others and promote the King as a friend of the poor.

Orberesis froze in a cold sweat as the pillars of smoke spread.

Why should the lady sleep in silk when the lumbermen sleep in mud? He found comfort in his father's words.

"Let us sit, gentlemen," Orberesis suggested.

Taishay and the other councillors looked petrified. They didn't dare move a single inch, as those they were expecting to be next. They all sat in the palace courtyard. The King stared at the table in silence, his slouch more pronounced. He couldn't see the smoke across the city but the way he moved in his chair showed doubt.

Orberesis counted almost a hundred threads of smoke around the city.

Solvi had deployed smokesmith inquisitors, soldiers, and spies to find out who the opposition was within the city. Their names made no difference now—they were burning.

Orberesis heard screaming from outside the Palatial walls but no one moved a finger. Orberesis grabbed a glass of wine and drank from it, earning a frown from Tavanar as squeals and screams echoed all around.

"No, please!" someone screamed. A woman. "Please, we'll do anything."

"No!" that scream was her last and her voice was extinguished by a cloud of smoke.

Wooden soles clanked against the cobbled floor as surely more merchants and nobles got what was coming for them.

"Would you like some wine, Your Majesty?" Orberesis asked and the King snapped out of it.

"No. No, thank you, Highest One. Not right now."

Suit yourself. Orberesis had another sip.

Screams turned into gasps as the smokesmiths caught up to the fugitives, he reckoned. And then it ended. Those must have been the last ones to find their way to the outer walls of the palace, hoping for a solace that wouldn't come.

Tavanar's heavy gaze fell on his. He said nothing, but his friend's feelings were obvious.

·············

Orberesis spent the rest of the day locked inside his quarters, surrounded by slaves. He had shown Ushar's upper class he had the King's *full* support and should not be messed with. All these displays of strength were useless, though, unless he could cure his bloody maladies.

Every gulp of wine he had should make him forget about what he had done and forgive himself for doing it. He had condemned people to smoke and flames, and still he hadn't fulfilled his goal. That's what the sickness did to him. It turned him into those he used to hate. Into a selfish monster, unable to think beyond the tiny borders of his own needs, and he hated himself for it. The worst was, he knew he still wouldn't have done it differently, so he cursed himself he had to do it in the first place.

Good people sometimes must do dreadful things.

But if he had done what he had to do, and sometimes good people had to do bad things, then why did it sting so much?

His servants didn't mind. They never looked him in the eye but kept smiling, pouring him drinks, and dropping cerro berries into his mouth. They were great spies, informing him about everything the King, Queen, and other councillors wanted to keep private. Their company was empty, however.

A heavy knock on the door interrupted his thoughts and scared two of the blonde servants. "Yes?" he asked, slurring a bit.

Tavanar emerged from the two heavy doors and glanced inside the room. He wore his typical black garments with a heavy belt, where he carried a sheath with a small dagger and the scabbard where his sword rested. Orberesis had never considered Tavanar an attractive man. Too skinny and too tall. He could not wield the sword well and lacked the intellectual prowess of a king or a scholar. His oily dark hair flowed backward, showing his wide forehead. But he was a good friend.

"What do you want?" Orberesis asked. Tavanar had spent his days fucking and gorging on the best food he could find. He'd had no difficult decisions to make. No pain to deal with. Somehow, that irritated Orberesis.

Tavanar hesitated but approached. "Leave," he said to the servants, pointing at the door so that they could understand what he meant. Orberesis sighed but nodded and the servants left.

Tavanar started pacing and when Orberesis thought his friend was going to say something, he continued as if he had something stuck in his throat.

"There are many places to go for a stroll that aren't my chambers."

Tavanar stopped and eyed him. "You've gone insane, haven't you? Slaughtering hundreds of people at a time, burning them alive. How could you?"

"I did no such thing. The King ordered it."

"You planted the fucking idea in his mind!"

"Did you forget they tried to kill me? They were plotting against me. Against *us*. You saw the assassin. Since when do you care about rich merchants?"

"They're... still people, Doi."

Tavanar was voicing what Orberesis had already considered himself. But there had been no way around it, or at least that's what he told himself. He paused, poured himself more wine, and squinted, facing Tavanar. "I'm the one who has to make the hard decisions for you and me. And the burden rests on my shoulders, Tav. I'm aware of that. If you want to talk about it, at least sit down and have a glass of wine. Isn't that why you're doing this? So you can have a better life?"

Tavanar was silent, but he sat and leaned against a padded chair, his eyes blank. "I don't know anymore."

"You don't know what?"

"*Why* we do this," he said. "It's obvious you have no problem with getting people killed as long as there's a chance to get the elixir, but I'm not as cold-hearted as you."

Orberesis scowled. "Please! I do this because I *have to*. I'm desperate to feel something other than pain and regret. It gets so bad I often wonder if I should just stop existing. Maybe that'll give me peace. You have no idea what it's like. Cold-hearted? How dare you? Didn't you see me raise the orb and make the ground shake to swallow the swarms of beasts?"

"I did," Tavanar said, as if he still couldn't believe what he had seen.

"Would I save millions of lives if I was cold-hearted?"

"How the fuck do I know? I know nothing anymore. Maybe my eyes were playing tricks on me back then."

"But I did it. I opened the ground and lifted a continent from the ocean. I sent the assassin flying from me, too, remember?"

"You really think you are a god now," Tavanar said, his voice cracking. "You really think you are God Himself. I thought this was just another con, but I barely recognise you these days. Sometimes I look at you and I don't see the Doi I knew, I see someone else. You're different. You've changed."

"Different how?"

"The way you talk. The little things. I don't know."

"Look, I don't care about any of that," Orberesis said as he shrugged, though he agreed he had changed. He just wasn't sure how much and whether that was a good thing. And when had he changed? He couldn't tell. "All I care about is finding a cure for this illness. Don't I deserve peace? Don't *we* deserve peace? For years, the world stomped on us, abused us, and we worked until our bodies could no longer continue. We did things we are not proud of, and they all led nowhere. This is the final scam. We can't go back now. We deserve this."

"Do we?" Tavanar asked, and Orberesis remained silent. "What about them? The ones you just killed. Did they deserve it?"

"They never gave two shits about people like us. You may think I'm a wicked man, a bad person, but I am doing what I need to do."

"No remorse, huh? I told you. Cold-hearted."

"It's survival, Tav. If I sit, get fat, and forget about things, I will end up with a knife in my heart. We made it here, but I need to find a cure. The King's enemies are our enemies. People want me dead. You think the neighbouring kingdoms wouldn't want a shot at me too, if given the chance?"

Tavanar nodded and then shook his head as he headed towards the door.

"Hate me all you like," Orberesis said. "For every traitor, I've got a thousand worshippers who would die for me if I ordered it."

Tavanar stopped as he reached the doors and looked back. A hint of sadness and pity hid in his eyes and he did not raise his voice. "You shouldn't be careless, my friend. And I don't mean about the enemies, I mean about yourself. I see the darkness in you now. You think you have the world in the palm of your hand, but I know who you are, remember? Others could find out as well. Every day you live, you are at risk."

Tavanar left his room and closed the door behind him.

Twelve

A Necessary Hero

Gimlore

*H*e *will return and carry with him the soul which he has won. The soul which will bring me into my peaceful demise.*

— From *Mother's Memories*

The breeze was a relief. The air was still humid, but it was bearable, and the sun no longer burned. She studied Keryon. A dangerous man like him left to his own devices, unsupervised, would be trouble.

"That's an interesting turn of events," Keryon said. He frowned as if he did not believe her. He smirked first, before he puffed up his chest and lifted his chin, cockiness galore.

The bastard. It's like having justice isn't as important as him delivering it.

"Why do you want me to be the warden?"

She leaned against a large wooden table where they kept the herbs and crossed her arms. Edmir looked just as confused. "Although I *did nothing*, contrary to what you may think, Mister Keryon, I felt bad that the Sirestine left so fast. I realised the town may no longer be safe unless we take care of it ourselves. We need to keep our people secure and safe from outside influence. As one of the original settlers and landowners of Heleronde, it's my duty to make sure people are safe. Plus, it's bad for business if someone attacks us and people die."

His eyebrows rose and he twitched in excitement. "But why me? You hate me."

"You're right, Mister Keryon. I don't like you. That's why you'd be the perfect warden."

The men furrowed their brows.

"If you dislike me as much as I dislike you, and you are the warden, then no one will point fingers at me and say I'm trying to grab power. You can uphold justice as well as you wish. It's what you did before you came here, isn't it?"

"Smokesmiths answer only to lords, madam. There is no lord here. What would you propose?"

"You would answer to the *people*, wouldn't you? Be a little open-minded. Didn't you call yourself a man of the people? It's a role of significant power and notoriety."

Keryon remained silent and crossed his arms as well. His eyes assessed her, her intentions, her motives. His business partner, Pie, looked doubtful. He shook his head and packed the herb satchels in the small wooden boxes where they would stay during the night, leaving the matter to Keryon, but still with both his ears pricked.

"That is a most interesting proposal, Madam Gimlore, but I will have to refuse. I still don't understand how, but you are playing me."

He is playing hard to get, hoping I would sweeten the deal.

"You are right. You understand nothing, Mister Keryon," Gimlore said with a feigned scowl.

She glanced at Edmir. The way his eyes shifted between her and Keryon suggested he had realised she had a plan, but he hadn't figured out its nature.

"We need someone to look after the town and I don't think there's anyone more qualified. You're the perfect person for the job."

Keryon scowled. "It's been a long time since I've used my abilities, Madam Gimlore. And it's not something I'm eager to show. Have you seen a smokesmith at work?"

Gimlore nodded and felt a shiver down her spine.

"If you have, then you'll know it's not a pleasant experience. It's not pleasant for me, but even less so for my enemies."

"If everyone knows you are a smokesmith, no one will dare challenge your authority. You could start a force to protect the town. Recruit a few local boys and girls. People are looking for jobs. We can find local benefactors."

Keryon looked at Pie for an opinion, and Pie shook his head. He was considering it. Perhaps Pie was the one in charge? She would have to convince him, too.

"Would I still be able to keep the shop?"

"Of course. What you do in your free time is none of my business."

She waited for a reply. Her case was strong and a proud man like Keryon had to accept.

"If I were to accept the job, I would *not* be under your thumb like the others, Madam Gimlore. You realise that, right? If that is the warden you're looking for, you must know I won't be one of your goons."

Gimlore smirked. That was exactly what he would be. He just didn't know it yet.

"If I wanted more goons, I would talk to somebody else, Mister Keryon."

"You have no business with Keryon. I do," Pie said. "He's my business partner. He is no longer a lawman. We are here to work hard and get rich. Isn't that why everybody is here?"

Gimlore hated the intrusion. The bearded man was hideous. Greedy and yet he couldn't resist sticking his nose in other people's conversations. After forcing herself not to respond, she took a sharp breath and walked a step towards him.

"Listen to me, fool. I don't know who the fuck you are, but when you talk to me, you talk with respect, you understand? You think you're an entrepreneur, do you? Look around. You live in a shithole, in the worst part of town, and you sell these useless herbs and spices that nobody buys or needs. That tells me you either don't understand business or you don't plan to be here long. I wouldn't have to ruin you, because you're ruining yourself."

Pie flushed, and Keryon adopted a confrontational stance that she hadn't seen. "Madam, you won't talk to Piesym that way."

For a moment, Gimlore wondered if she had exaggerated, but now that was too late, so she ignored Keryon.

"*You* are nobody," she said, looking at Pie. "But Mister Keryon still has the chance to do something meaningful if he takes the job. I can see how much he misses it, for better or worse. I won't be the one paying the salary. All the gold will come from a fund supported by the richest landowners in town."

They didn't need to know that was her three times over.

"You won't be in business long if you don't look after the people in town. Keep them safe, Mister Keryon. It's for your business, too. There's no point in keeping your business open if your customers are at the mercy of invaders."

"I have no such obligation," Keryon spat, but she could see uncertainty in his eyes.

"Oh, you do. You do. You are a lawman. The only one we've got. For fuck's sake, here I am, offering you a good job, an excellent opportunity, and yet you're acting like I'm trying to manipulate you. If that doesn't weigh on your conscience, Mister Keryon, maybe I came to the wrong person. Maybe I should appoint one of my men as the warden. Or perhaps I should start a private army. I can pay for weapons, uniforms, wages, and rations. Let's see how many townsfolk would oppose that, shall we?"

"Wait, madam," Keryon said.

Gimlore turned around and walked away.

"Let's go, Edmir. These fools are thicker than my arse on a bad day."

"Wait, Madam Gimlore!" Keryon said. "I will consider it, alright? I won't decide yet, but I will think about it."

Gimlore almost let out a smile, but she hid it well just before she turned to face him.

"Don't take too long, Mister Keryon. You do not know how many candidates for the job I already have, and my patience with you and your friend is wearing thin. You have until tomorrow morning."

Keryon swallowed and nodded. She had put him in a tough spot. She could sense the disbelief and doubt plaguing his mind. Pie looked stunned.

She waved goodbye as she took leave with Edmir on her tail. She wiped sweat beads off her forehead. As they walked on the muddy ground, she tied her hair into a bun.

Edmir watched her but didn't ask questions. The bald man looked confused as they walked to the Maiden's Hall.

"What?" she asked with a sigh.

"Hmm? Nothing, boss," Edmir said. "I almost believed everything you said about making him the warden, I guess."

"Well, that part wasn't a lie, Edmir. I intend to make him the warden."

"I guess I don't understand why you want that son of a bitch to be the warden. Isn't that bad for us?"

Gimlore took a deep breath. "Before I ended up in the steppes ambushing soldiers, before I found you, I was a fucking delinquent, like my kids are now. I didn't have parents, though. I only had this woman named Madam Mazi who would give me food. The only condition was that I needed to steal things for her. Madam Mazi could be a fucking bitch, Edmir, but she was the smartest person I've ever known. She taught me everything. Her key lesson was to keep my friends close and my enemies closer. I had no fucking friends, so I didn't know what in the underworld she was talking about, but now I do."

Edmir seemed confused. He nodded, but Gimlore was sure he didn't get it.

"Keryon knows we wiped out the Herald and his entourage, he just doesn't have evidence. Everybody else in town knows it too, but they keep quiet, which is why he hasn't accused us directly, because he's a foreigner and he's new. But he's a lawman, which doesn't make the fucker very corruptible. I'm appealing to his sense of justice instead of his greed. If Keryon is the warden, he will have certain duties and roles he must fulfil. People will expect things from him. If he's busy keeping us safe, he is unlikely to sniff into our affairs. Do you understand now?"

"Brilliant, boss." Edmir nodded. "You'd never told me about your child-hood."

"It's not something I talk about," she admitted. "And speaking of wars, I have a strong suspicion we might as well prepare for another one. Too many people sticking their noses where they don't belong. I don't like it, Edmir. And we can't let the Sirestine bastards take over Heleronde."

"If there's war, there's war, boss. We'll take care of it. Do you think he will accept the job?"

Gimlore shrugged. "I think so. He reminds me of the rich folk I used to rob as a child. His clothes. His hair. Everything is fancy. All the smoke-smiths I've met were like that. They always went about trying to prove how important they were. How much they'd endured. Keryon is no different."

Gimlore wished she could be as certain as she sounded. She was used to being in control and calling the shots, now it was slipping away. She had worked too hard for everything she had. Keryon would still be a thorn in her skin, but she could work him, massage his ego, his pride, pull his heartstrings. Let him be the town hero. Having a smokesmith on her side would be like controlling a small army, but not enough if there were hundreds of enemy soldiers.

"What are the Sirestine settlers up to?"

"They're still setting up camp, boss."

Gimlore sighed, confused. Her instincts told her to prepare for battle. To gear up for a harsh skirmish, prepare the citizens for an invasion or other attacks on the mossbacks. The old Gimlore would strike first. She would march straight into the enemy camp and burn it to the ground just to show she wasn't to be crossed. But that was too reckless. Too many things could go wrong.

She shook her head and took a deep breath. "Maybe I'll do the right thing, eh?"

"What's that, boss?"

"Maybe there's no ill-intent. Maybe there's a misunderstanding and they didn't kill the mossbacks. I'll give them the benefit of the doubt for now. I'll be the bigger person. Give and take—that's what doing business is all about, isn't it?"

Edmir shrugged. "Whatever you decide, I'll do, boss. But the settlers might be missing the Herald already."

"I know."

They reached the high street. Nearly all the shops were closed. The Maiden's Hall was the only establishment that was still open and full of patrons. Edmir opened the door and she entered with enough confidence to shut up half the loudmouths.

"Good evening, madam," ragged old man Veir said, licking his lips. His long, grey hair almost touched the ale inside his glass. "Always a sight to behold."

"Drink more and I'll look better," Gimlore said.

Nork and Nosema were still behind the counter. She set them to other tasks and left Edmir in charge of the drinks. Resting her forearms on the countertop, she scanned the room where her kids were on the verge of fighting once again. There were only two empty seats, and the patrons resumed their loud chatter.

"I think old man Veir needs a reminder that he is already past his bedtime," Gimlore said.

Edmir nodded and whistled, calling two of his men.

Gimlore wiped the glasses clean, her mind elsewhere. It was a dangerous game she was playing. How long until Keryon and the town folks realised there was an enemy nearby?

Edmir had sent the men to escort old man Veir out of his chair and Gimlore smiled as they dumped him outside the tavern face first. She was sure he would still come back the following day. That was the appeal of the Maiden's Hall.

"Edmir," she called.

"Yes, boss?"

"Why did you come here?"

"Because you told me to, boss."

"No, Edmir." She sighed. "I mean, *here*, in Heleronde, on the Alarkan continent. Why did you follow me here?"

Edmir frowned. "Because you asked me to, boss," he said.

Sometimes it was difficult to handle someone who took everything literally.

"But what was the reason? Did you come to chase your freedom? To get rich?" she asked.

Edmir shrugged and shook his head. "It was a blur when you found me in the steppes. I was ready to let myself go. Perhaps I'd be buried somewhere nice. I thought I was going to die, but you pulled me out of the hole, boss. You showed me there's more to life. You saved me in more ways than you know. It's as I told you before, it will take a lifetime to repay you. I'll still try, though."

She choked up a little.

"If I may ask, boss, why are you asking this now? Are you planning something?"

Gimlore shook her head. "No, no. That's not it. I was thinking about how easy it's been. How peaceful, until now. This has been the only quiet period of my life."

"That's a good thing, no?"

"No. It's the worst. It makes me nervous. Everyone is soft and happy, and they forgot how to fight. They would rather surrender to the first invader than fight for the land they own, as long as they stay alive."

"You are right, boss."

Gimlore picked up one of the secret bottles of cerro wine she had stashed under the counter and poured two mugs before sliding one to Edmir.

"Drink up, Edmir," she said, lifting the mug. "May the Gods or whoever is in control of this shit force that bastard to take the job. And may the rest of the Sirestine bastards die flooded by a giant wave or attacked by swamp creatures on their way here."

Edmir smiled and clashed his mug against hers and they both downed the strong cerro wine, which burned all the way down. Edmir's face reddened.

She nudged him with her elbow. "No puking, Edmir. This is my best stuff."

"Yes, boss," he said, struggling to keep the wine in his stomach.

Gimlore laughed.

THIRTEEN

PARAGON OF JUSTICE

GIMLORE

He shall tread through the ages until the treasures of kings turn to dust, until the flesh of men rots.

— From *Mother's Memories*

Gimlore tidied her clothes and hair with more care and took off with Edmir, leaving Nork and Nosema behind to take care of the Maiden's Hall and the kids, although the youngsters would most likely take care of themselves.

The townsfolk headed to the old building she had donated to the new warden patrol, and they followed the crowd there. The building was nothing but a two-storey shack with rotten wood and no furniture.

She saw the other three donors to the warden patrol fund that she had created. They were there to lend their name to the cause while she was the real benefactor and contributor. Without them, she stood to face criticism and accusations of having too much power. They were there as she had instructed and said nothing.

"Any news from Keryon?" Gimlore asked. Pinesy was setting up the podium for the ceremony, hammering the nails that joined the boards together, so he just shook his head. She wouldn't trust anyone but her own people with performing important tasks, but if there was an exception, Pinesy was it.

The crowd continued to gather. She guessed at least three hundred people were outside the building. About half of them were resident drunks to whom she had offered free drinks in exchange for attendance.

"Edmir, do you know where he is?"

"I think that's him right there," Edmir said, pointing to the edge of the high street, where a tall, slender man walked towards them.

He wore shiny boots and a large, ridiculous, flat hat. Gimlore frowned and suppressed a chuckle. Keryon had probably thought it a good idea to wear his best clothes for the ceremony, but in Alarkan, the terrain was unforgiving. Mud covered his boots and a layer of sweat tainted his dark linen vest, inappropriate for such a muggy climate. The townsfolk looked unimpressed. Nobody enjoyed dealing with a fancy fool rubbing his wealth on their faces, after all.

As he arrived, Keryon removed the flat hat and wiped the sweat off his forehead with his sleeve. He must have been terribly uncomfortable inside all those clothes. His face poured sweat like a fountain. "Am I late, Madam Gimlore?"

"You're right on time, Mister Keryon. Nice choice of apparel, although I hope you don't intend to go around chasing criminals in those."

"I thought I'd try something special today. I'm surprised by your mockery. Women often fall for my sense of style."

Gimlore scoffed. She hadn't got him wrong after all.

"Should we get started, then? I have plans."

"Sure, sure," she said, glancing at the crowd to make sure it was large enough.

Gimlore made sure the improvised little podium was ready and when she got the nod from Pinesy, she climbed on top.

"Good morning, citizens of Heleronde," she started. The crowd didn't even flinch. "Today is an important day for our town. Today we appoint our warden."

A man raised his hand and Gimlore looked at him, startled by the interruption. She hadn't seen him around much. "Yes?"

"Why do we need a warden?"

"Yes!" another man said right away. "Why can't we keep the justice ourselves! Many of us ran from smokesmiths our entire lives. I think it's time we leave behind the old ways."

"Yes! We want to keep the peace with our own hands!"

Chatter spread among the crowd, and Gimlore forced herself to take a deep breath.

"With all due respect, dear *citizen*, this is less about justice and more about protection. Don't all our citizens need protection? There won't be any smokesmiths chasing orphan children, or anyone innocent, for that matter. I can promise you that much. Mister Keryon is new, but we must give him a chance despite his choice of apparel, don't you think?"

The crowd laughed. She took no further time after the two men stopped talking. "As I was saying, today is an important day for *everyone* in Heleronde. For those not yet familiar with this man, I'd like to introduce you to Mister Keryon."

Keryon stepped onto the small podium next to her and waved his hand as if he was a king waving to his subjects. Except no one waved back. Instead, a few people spat.

"How lucky are we to have him?" Gimlore asked, doing her best to sell him as a warden. "This man has served citizens as a lawman for decades. He is a trained smokesmith, too. A veteran!"

"Excuse me, Madam Gimlore?" another man from the crowd asked. "If he works for you, why do you bother introducing him to us? You can keep your own smokesmith..."

"What? He doesn't work for me! He works for *everyone*!" Gimlore said. "For the citizens of Heleronde."

"But you pay him."

Shit. This wasn't going well.

"Well, I am one benefactor of the fund that supports the warden patrol, but not the only one. Mister Keryon holds no obligation or responsibility towards me. Isn't that right?"

Keryon nodded. "I am no longer chained by loyalty to anyone. I'm a free man. My purpose is to protect this town and its people."

A few in the crowd shrugged, other nodded. Still a hard sell, but it wasn't like she needed their approval.

She pointed at Keryon. "This man is the paragon of justice!" she said.

Edmir walked onto the stage and handed her a small tin badge. Gimlore lifted it for everybody to see.

"When he receives this badge, Mister Keryon will become the warden of Heleronde. He will serve the people and justice, and will scrutinise anything he deems suspicious," Gimlore said.

Then she turned to Keryon. "Do you swear before these people, to do them justice, to keep them safe and protect them?"

"I do," Keryon said, swelling with pride.

"Do you accept the job of town warden, with all its benefits and burdens, rights and responsibilities?"

"I do."

"Here is your badge," Gimlore said with a smile. "The job is yours. Congratulations."

Keryon grabbed the badge and pinned it to his vest. In small towns, there was no need for the stupid badge because everyone knew the warden. Judging by his expression, though, he looked as if he had won a pot full of gold. Gimlore let him celebrate as the crowd greeted him with reluctant applause. She didn't expect a town of criminals to be excited about a man who was supposed to be the epitome of justice, but they couldn't argue against it in public.

"Mister Keryon, do you care to speak to the people?"

Keryon started, but composed himself and nodded, turning his attention to the small crowd.

"Brothers and sisters, I'll be brief. I think myself a man of honour and I promise to keep my vows and the oaths I swore, and to protect the town of Heleronde with my life. I will chase those who don't care for justice, those who seek injustice, and unruly. This town is in good hands."

Gimlore pointed at the lawman and the man displayed a broad smile filled with pearly white teeth.

Incredible how the bastard becomes so amicable now that I've given him a position of power.

It was as if she had just introduced a predator to a cave full of prey.

"Are you going to protect us against the Sirestine bastards?" a loud voice boomed from the back of the crowd.

Gimlore's heart skipped a beat. Who was that? She looked around and saw old man Fanan.

"I don't follow..." Keryon said, scratching his chin.

Fanan raised his voice and addressed her. "Madam Gimlore, is it true that the Sirestine has soldiers just north of Heleronde? That they are settling there?"

Shit.

She hated being caught in a lie or a deceit, but there was nowhere to run. Nothing more to hide, now. No point in lying anymore.

"It is true, but I—"

"This is an outrage!" Fanan said as he faced the crowd. "Isn't it suspicious that Madam Gimlore welcomes emissaries from Sirestir in her establishment and right after, Sirestine settlers and soldiers arrive on our continent, close to our town? I wish I could have heard what businesses you discussed inside your filthy tavern that night. It must have been serious, since they left so early in the morning! Is our dear Madam Gimlore selling her lands to the Sirestine bastards behind closed doors? Is she exchanging them for a prominent official post in the Sirestine capital? Or did she piss them off so much they came for us? Which is it, madam? We *must* have answers!"

Tension filled the air and she felt the weight of the citizens' gazes resting on her.

When they expose the truth, make it your own truth, Madam Mazi's voice echoed in her mind.

"I assure you all I'm not going anywhere. I sold nothing and I didn't take money from the Sirestine fellows. Nor did they promise me anything. Their visit was... unsuccessful. And that's why they left early and unseen. But I admit I knew the Sirestine had arrived in greater numbers... than they led me to believe. That is why I am certain we need a warden. For our own protection."

The crowd erupted into shouts.

"It was your fault the negotiations failed, madam!" someone shouted.

"And now she acts like she knows nothing! Deceitful as always," another man said.

"We should have never trusted the Viper!"

"You only wanted a warden because you're worried they will take away your land. But you don't give a shit about us, you never did!" Fanan said, leading the insurgence. It was baffling how easily he could sway these people. "Do you know what their intentions are?"

Gimlore forced her hands to steady. "I expect anything between indifference and hostility. I'd like to be naïve and believe in peace, but I don't want to lie. They are looking for the elixir."

"She means she won't lie to us *anymore*. Isn't that right, madam?" Fanan asked as he scoffed.

She nodded.

Keryon turned to the crowd. He didn't puff his chest, but the bastard might as well have. This was a man used to getting what he wanted.

"You can leave, now. I'll get to the bottom of this," he said and what little opposition was left in the villagers drifted away.

The crowd hesitated at first, but then they hurried out of there. And then Keryon focused on her. His handsome face was menacing. Serious. All the pride and vanity gone.

"Not an impressive start, is it? I wonder... If I were to ask you what your intentions were with this, would it matter? Would you be truthful with me?"

Gimlore paused and gathered herself. "I meant to talk to the foreign bastards myself. This has nothing to do with you. I admit I never intended anyone to know besides my men, but that's because the town folk didn't need to know. Why would they need to worry if I will deal with the foreigners?"

Keryon studied her. "What will you do?"

She was cornered. The pressure mounted, and she didn't have the answers.

"A chat for starters," she said. "Beyond that... It will depend on their reaction."

············

Later, the last drunkard had left the Maiden's Hall and Gimlore gathered her crew before the clean-up duty.

Edmir sat while Foloi slumped on the chair, his legs stretched. Nork and Nosema were sitting with Edmir, still in their white kitchen uniforms covered in grease stains. The tension was palpable. It reminded her of the time spent in the steppe. Death hid behind every bush.

Control. Be in control.

"We have serious matters to discuss. I suggest you drink."

Gimlore took hold of her mug and chugged its contents. As usual, Edmir struggled to keep the alcohol in, and his face reddened.

"Our new neighbours. They are after the elixir, but don't want to pay a fair price for it. The Herald admitted as much. They see us as slaves, as vassals to a king, and believe we must do as we are told. There is no confirmation, but I believe they killed our mossbacks too, searching for the elixir. Who knows what they'll do next? I can't risk them invading Heleronde and taking people hostage until someone decides to tell them how to extract the elixir. We need to do something about it fast, or they will."

"What are you going to do?" Foloi asked.

"I want to pay them a visit before jumping to conclusions," she said. "Nork. How many people are in their camp?"

"My scouts say over two hundred people and they suspect other ships are on the way with more building materials, supplies, and soldiers."

"That's almost as many people as we have working the the mossbacks."

Nork and Nosema nodded.

"They're going to start missing the Herald. If they haven't already," Gimlore muttered.

"So, what are you thinking?" Edmir asked.

She took a moment to think. This could turn into a dangerous game.

"You know, after I found you three..." Gimlore looked at Edmir, Nork, and Nosema. "What did we do? We laid low, we learned to bushwhack the enemies, to sabotage them, to deliver smaller but consistent blows to their objectives until we could flee. What did I always preach?"

"Low risk, high reward," Edmir said.

"That's right."

"So, what do we do this time?" Foloi asked as he leaned forward. It was the first time Gimlore had seen him hungry to take part in planning.

"We need to set up surveillance at night, next to the mossbacks. But our risk is already too high in this scenario, so we need to play it safe. We must prepare traps. That's for our own security."

Her crew was silent. The last time they had ambushed someone had been in the early days of Alarkan, when the land had just emerged from the ocean. They wanted to get on with their lives, and so did she.

"I am going to march into their camp and ask to parlay with their leaders to see if we can reach a non-aggression agreement. But because they've shown they can be aggressive. I'm going to need Edmir and Foloi to come with me."

"What about us, boss?" Nork asked.

"You, Nosema, and Pinesy will stay outside of camp, hidden in the marshes and watching us, in case it goes to shit. You'll be armed and carrying some greasy bombs. Just for insurance. But they mustn't see you.

Nork and Nosema exchanged looks and nodded.

"Why does this feel like ten years ago, when we were preparing for war?" Edmir asked.

Gimlore swallowed and shrugged, without an answer. She had been thinking the exact same, but she had to do something now. If she waited before more Sirestine soldiers arrived, they could wipe out Heleronde in an evening even if she fought back. This was about preventing a war, and yet, it felt like the other side wasn't interested in preventing anything.

Fourteen

Gasho

Rednow

The brave are weakened and horrified.

— From *Mother's Memories*

Rednow's riding party had disbanded as soon as they stepped on Gashoine soil. It was nice to come down from the Benaven Mountains and to be out of the battlefield. There was no bone-chilling wind, but the winter continued to chase them and they found themselves in a thundersnow or two along the way.

Now he was indoors, warm, and well-fed, but sat alone.

He looked at the long table where wine filled expensive glasses and unfinished roasts covered the silver platters. He observed the commotion around him inside what they called the dance room of the palace, larger than many temples he had visited. These guests weren't praying, though. They followed the music of the drums and string instruments played by the servants. Men and women wore long silk robes and gowns of all colours.

Many of the guests of Gasho's royal palace had a dozen palm-length metallic spikes piercing their faces, almost disfiguring them. It was a tradition in the nation which made them look as if they had meat skewers pierced to their faces. More piercings in their faces meant they were higher in society, which left King Caligo with almost no visible features left. Rednow tried not to stare as the monarch, old as he was, sat on his throne overlooking his party and guests. His facial skin sagged after decades under the weight of the long piercings, making it impossible for Rednow to guess how the King had once looked. Next to him sat a much younger man, his son Eterstan, who had less than half of his father's piercings.

Rednow took a sip of his wine and relished the buzz. He was just there to collect his gold, and wished they would get on with it, but the King had insisted he stayed for the party to celebrate his victory, so he had to wait.

You've always chosen gold over glory, that is a fact, Rebma's voice said.

He shook her voice away and scanned the large room ornate with antique paintings, flowery details, and abstract statues for the members of his entourage. Among all the colours the guests wore, it was easy to spot Rednow's comrades, the only ones wearing fabrics of poor quality and in darker shades. He almost let out a sigh of relief when he realised they weren't doing something as stupid as dancing among the Gashoine nobility.

Tellwoon and Merey sat against a wall, holding each other's hands, all smiles, and Zatak and the pineheads had been told to stay outside until they found manners. Rednow imagined Rebma being there, her red hair flowing as she walked over towards him, carrying a glass of wine to celebrate his win and tell him not to do it again. And he would shrug and tell her that was all he could do—hide in the bowels of civilisation and sell his services to people he hated for a few bags of gold.

But Rebma was long gone.

Lighten up. At least put on a smile. This party is for you.

He had won, yes, but he could also still feel the heartbeat of the blacksmith's son he had failed to save. The look on the man's face upon realising his son had died would forever be engraved in his mind.

You're allowed to enjoy yourself from time to time, Rebma's ghost insisted, and he bit his tongue, cursing. Why didn't it just leave him alone?

Rednow scowled and turned to the Gashoine guests and their dancing. A servant in a long robe appeared by their side.

"Excuse me, sir?" the servant asked while he bowed. His Gashoine accent was noticeable. He was slim and well-dressed. "Would you care to come with me? His Majesty would like you to sit with him."

It was about time he got his audience with the King. And collect his gold.

"Nothing would make me happier," Rednow said as he got up from the chair and followed the servant.

The closer he got to Caligo and Eterstan, the easier it was to see their faces. More starkly, Rednow noticed their vivid eyes. The metal piercings stretched their skin and forced their eyes open wider.

The servants had set up a table before Caligo's throne and a modest but expensive chair, ornate with precious metals. The young man who had fetched Rednow pulled the chair and nodded for him to sit. Rednow acknowledged Caligo and Eterstan and bowed as deeply as his back allowed before taking a seat.

"Well met, Blood Collector," Caligo said in a raspy voice. "The face of all the legends."

"Well met, Your Majesty," Rednow said, swallowing again. It was a good thing he only drank a small amount of wine. "As old as those legends too, these days."

"My son Eterstan was just commenting that you have barely touched the cerro wine. Are you not satisfied with it?"

"There's nothing wrong with the wine. I just can't handle much of it."

"Ah, a religious man, perhaps?"

Rednow shook his head.

"No? A non-religious moderate drinker. It's the first time I've met one. Aren't you afraid of what the gods might do to the unfaithful? Don't you fear?" Caligo asked as he drank from a crystal glass. His robe's sleeve slid down, exposing the entire forearm. The whole robe itself must be more expensive than all those of his guests.

"No. If the gods are so powerful, they can come for me. I'm always ready."

We both know this isn't true, brother.

"Most of my guests would not enjoy those statements, Blood Collector," the King said. "Perhaps it's a good thing you decided not to mingle with them this evening. You strike me as a wise man, but a rather bold one."

"That's not for me to say, Your Majesty."

Eterstan leaned forward in his chair. "See, Father?" he asked, his accent less formal. They had shaved his head, just like his father, but his clothes were less traditional, with a tighter fit, more proper for younger people. "This is a man of fearlessness! Of courage and boldness!"

Caligo scowled. "And what of it?"

Eterstan took a deep breath and was about to respond to his father, but ultimately turned to Rednow. "Blood Collector, perhaps I should get your opinion on something. My father and his advisors think we should let the Nohani be after your victory, negotiate a peace treaty. I say we push forward, cut through the border, to make this victory count. Conquer them! What do you think?"

Rednow was caught off guard. He wasn't paid to give strategic counsel to any of these despots. "Why would you risk doing that?"

Eterstan's eyes widened, and a smile appeared on his lips. "If we take Noha, then I'll marry the princess and we'll grow into something bigger. An empire. Wouldn't that be glorious?"

A glorious blunder, Rednow thought. *The kid is thinking with his cock.*

King Caligo laughed, to his son's dismay. "My son's dreams of grandeur are as amusing as they are nonsensical. The world is always changing, yes.

Now we're hearing about better trade routes, faster ships, clothes being weaved in half the time they used to when I was a child. It's no time to invest in old wars. My warlords speak of nothing but explosives and cannons and even have small long-range weapons more deadly than crossbows and carry them in their scabbards, like a dagger. There are other things more worth fighting for."

"We can fight the old wars in new ways, Father!"

Caligo scoffed and shook his head. "Ah, the youth! All bravery, bluster, and presumption. I'm more curious about the potion the Blood Collector said the Nohani were using. May they rot in the underworld, as far from me as possible. But the potion intrigues me."

Rednow nodded. He didn't want to intrude between the King and his son and was even less eager to pick a side. He didn't give a rat's arse about gods, technology, or any of the forced intellectual blabber. But the King was the one paying him.

"The youth are always rushing," he said. "They always want things done faster, better, and stronger. But you can't dwell on the past. My Prince, you must understand what I am talking about, do you not? I thought you'd understand me, Blood Collector, as someone who knows true strength. I'm not worried about my father's legacy, but I worry about mine. I don't want to just do what I'm told by the advisors. I want to build something. I want to know greatness. Be loved by the people and admired even by my enemies."

"You'll have plenty of time to craft your legacy. And, believe me, I care little about strength or legacy, as long as my warriors are well and fed. I'm an old man with no honour, no family, no land, no kingdom, and no gods. All I've got left is the trust of my warriors and a bunch of promises I made to people who no longer walk among us. You must listen to your father. He knows a king's duty is to protect his people. Dreams of conquest belong only in our sleep, my Prince. You don't want to get as old as I am and be full of regrets, torn by ghosts of the past. Our purpose as leaders is to lift those who put their faith in us."

"That might be true of someone as lowly as you, but that's not my purpose as heir to the throne. I am destined for greatness, no matter how many times the Nohani bastards reject a betrothal between the princess and me."

"Eterstan!" the King shouted. "The Blood Collector is my guest. Mind your manners."

As though the taste in his mouth had turned sour, Rednow felt a powerful urge to teach that smug brat a lesson and rip every metal rod from his face. Instead, he contorted in his chair and gripped the armrest. *I should leave before I say something stupid.* But there was Merey, Tellwoon, Zatak, and all the others left in camp, who were still training and needed full stomachs. "Lowly or not, my Prince, your father still relied on me to do what your soldiers couldn't. How would you even expect to conquer Noha?"

Silence hung in the air between them until Eterstan broke it.

"My father should have let me do it. I wouldn't have taken as long as you did."

"Eterstan..." the King snarled.

Rednow chuckled. *This little brat.* He could feel his temper worsening.

"Are you laughing at me, Blood Collector?" Eterstan asked.

Rednow resisted a quip, wondering if the brat had ever left the colossal palace. He was used to the best wines, the best food and wore the best clothes. He spent his days with servants and guards, sheltering him. Rednow hadn't been born a warrior, he had made himself one after his parents were burned alive in wars they knew nothing about. He had crawled, lived among beasts, and eaten from the soil. But he'd survived. So yes, he dared laugh at the little shit. But perhaps a more peaceful approach was needed...

"Come on, my Prince, we're not so different. I may not be a scholar or a man of faith, or have any noble blood, but the world belongs to people, and I *do* understand people. No matter who we are, we all like gold, wine, and lusting for one another."

Caligo and Eterstan stared at him.

"Peasants always think it's easy to rule a nation." Eterstan scowled. First, he looked at his father, then turned to Rednow. "You think there's no responsibility, that all I do is drink wine and fuck?"

Pretty much, yes.

"Eterstan, mind your words," Caligo commanded, then he turned to Rednow. "You are my guest, Blood Collector, and I'm grateful for your service, but this is my *son*! The future king of Gasho. I won't allow you to challenge him like that."

"Your Majesty, I didn't say—"

"Enough!" Caligo shook his head, and his eyes rested on the stone floor in front of him. He took a deep breath. "If this was anybody else, I would have their head, Blood Collector. Instead, I'll have you escorted out of here. I don't want to see your face any longer. Take him!"

The King snapped his fingers, and six guards took hold of Rednow. He could have fought back and escape, but that was far too dangerous. *What did I even say?* He made no sense, and yet he was being escorted like a criminal from what was supposed to be a party to celebrate his achievements.

He would never understand royalty.

FIFTEEN

DUEL

REDNOW

Today I lie defeated, as if I knew the truth.

— From *Mother's Memories*

Rednow couldn't remember the last time he had stayed indoors for so long. Living outside in tents had prepared him for the toughest of lives, not for sleeping in padded mattresses. He had spent the entire night sleeping on the fur rug on the floor, instead. The King had sent him and his entourage to the lowest floor of the palace, considered the least luxurious one. They were not supposed to have access to servants of any kind. None of it was a punishment, Rednow reckoned. If Caligo had intended to inflict humiliation upon him, he had failed.

He was the first to wake. The others took their time to recover from the boozy evening. With time to think about how he hadn't been paid for his service yet and had now fallen into the King's bad graces, Rednow couldn't shake off the doubts about his imminent retirement and the impossible question of who would replace him.

Does it really matter? Rebma's voice teased him.

"Of course it does…" he whispered.

He sat on the rug and assessed the space. The walls were decorated with fine southern tapestry. There was a cedar desk by the window with folders and papers scattered around and letters inked in a flawless calligraphy left behind by past guests. Rednow grabbed Rebma's messenger bag, opened the flap, and peered inside, where similar parchments were kept. Probably the songs and poems she had written. He still couldn't make himself open the folders and read. It was still too soon, made worse by her ghostly voice which always hung around him.

"I'll read this when I find my peace. I promise. When I retire," he muttered.

With another glance at the window, he realised he was so used to the cold he no longer remembered what the scorching sun felt like on his skin. He hadn't been back to Shari, where he was born, and probably never would. There was nothing left for him there. He would retire elsewhere.

It doesn't matter where we're from, but who we are, brother.

And who was he? A killer for coin. At least Rebma had died an inspiration for everyone at camp after saving countless orphans from the clutches of smokesmiths. She had been so much more than him, Not tainted.

That isn't true, brother. I remember everything. How the smokesmiths treated us, how they burned Ma and Pa. How you held on to me so hard I had bruises on my wrist for weeks. You saved me.

Rednow covered his ears and shook his head, wishing the ghost would leave him alone. He would retire soon—as soon as he chose a replacement. And he would go somewhere warm, as Rebma had wanted.

Perhaps that would appease the ghost.

To forget all of it, Rednow closed Rebma's bag, put it aside and grabbed his sword instead. He slowly pulled it out of the scabbard and started oiling the blade, admiring the shades of red that inexplicably tinted it, resembling bloodstains. That sword alone had scared enemies enough to make him the Blood Collector.

Tellwoon and Merey snuck out of the nearby room, like two lovebirds waking up in the early hours of the morning. They nodded, exchanged pleasantries, and sat next to him. "I've always wondered how you ended up with such a sword." Merey said, scratching her hair. "It's... old. And there are better ones out there. Not out of reach with all the gold you've earned."

Rednow gave Merey a glance.

"An old sword for an old man," he joked. "But it has sentimental value and a certain allure to it, since these red stains should be impossible. I bought it in Abirad. That day is still engraved in my mind as if it was yesterday. Rebma must have been seven winters old. We were strolling through a market with our hoods up, trying not to get anyone's attention. Especially not the city's smokesmiths'. Rebma saw the sword for sale at a merchant's stand. The poor man must have been trying to get rid of it for ages, because he was trying to sell it to everyone that passed by, lowering the price at every turn. Rebma must have seen this, grabbed my hand hard, and begged me to buy it."

"Why?" Tellwoon asked.

Rednow shrugged. "I never understood. And now it's too late to ask. I told her the sword was old. That there were better ones, but she shook her head, stomped her feet, and said 'Brother, I'm not going anywhere until you take that sword with you'. I had never seen her so serious before and needed her to be quiet, so I ended up buying it for a bargain. Once I did... I just ended up using it. I've always liked its weight. The way it slices. It might be old and strange, but it's a part of me now."

"You must never get rid of it, then. Not even after you retire," Merey said, her gaze dropping to the floor. "I know how much you miss her. We all do."

Rednow turned grim and nodded, a strange silence filling the room. "I still hear her voice, sometimes. It's random. But it's like she's still... a ghost, following me around."

Merey and Tellwoon exchanged looks but said nothing, silence filling the room.

Though they were on the ground floor, the palace was at the top of a hill, granting them an unrestricted view of the sprawling city of Mewon. Flocks of dark birds huddled close together for warmth, like ink stains on the snow-covered rooftops, in a perfect winter portrait.

"Rednow," Tellwoon started after clearing her throat once again. "I'm still wondering what you told the king for him to kick us out of the party."

"It wasn't that bad."

"What do you mean?" Merey asked.

"It doesn't matter. It was all fluff. We were wasting our time there. It's better this way. Now we just have to collect the gold and leave."

"Speak for yourself. *I* was having fun. But he seemed furious at you. His son even more so," Tellwoon said.

Rednow shrugged and decided to change topics.

"Something the King said stuck with me. The world is changing. Warfare is changing. Everything I taught you is becoming old-fashioned. The Leeth have been effective this entire time because we adapt. It is time to conform to the new age. When I do retire, you should investigate the potion the Nohani berserkers were taking. It could be useful to the Leeth," he said, producing the vial with the silver fluid from his pocket.

"We will," Merey said with a nod as she looked outside the window. "Are you not going to try it?"

"No. Could be dangerous. And I might need proof of it later," he said.

Merey nodded and let out a sigh. "Right."

It made him jittery to think any average soldiers with that potion could rival the Leeth. A potion like that would be highly coveted by all monarchs in the Known World. Maybe they would not even need his services anymore. If the Leeth could get a hold of the potion, however... they could become even more powerful than before. Choosing the right replacement was crucial. As much he believed in these two as individuals, none of them stood out enough yet. Which one deserved his full trust?

His attention drifted to the peaceful winter scenery outside, tinted by the birds claiming the rooftops as their own. He needed to get the gold quick. If the snow was already in Gasho, then the soldiers in Mount Melchor would be freezing and endangering themselves while hunting just to get food. They needed gold to feed all those mouths, and they needed it fast. Every day of delay put the survival of his camp at risk.

Rednow left Tellwoon and Merey flirting by the window and walked across the main room, determined to ask for a swift audition with the King to collect the coin, but once he tried to open the door, he couldn't.

"It's locked," Rednow muttered, trying to force it open several times. He then knocked on the gate and called for a guard.

"What's the matter?" Tellwoon asked as she and Merey walked over towards him.

"Someone locked the door," Rednow said again. The King had ordered the guards to lock them inside.

"What did you tell him for him to make us prisoners?"

"We're not prisoners. They must explain this."

Merey and Tellwoon looked at him as they crossed their arms.

"Fine, alright. We're prisoners," he admitted. "We have to think about what to do."

Rednow imagined what Rebma would say if she was there, cursing at him for screwing it up.

Nice retirement plan, but not quite what I had in mind, the voice said, as though it had heard his thoughts.

He shook it off.

"We need to consider the possibility of escape," Merey said.

"Wouldn't an escape put the city on alert? I don't think we would want to attract attention," Tellwoon said. She would always be cautious.

"We could do it, though. This is the first floor. It's not that tall and we have Zatak and the pineheads outside the palace. They could help us," Merey said.

"You don't know that. For now, we can't assume anything," Rednow said. "They locked us here without warning. We don't know what their intentions are or what else they've done."

An ominous silence reigned.

"If we knock the door down, the palace will come crashing on us," Merey said. "Now, I have no problem chopping off heads, but I say escaping through the window unscathed is a better way. There would be fewer casualties that way."

"You're acting as if they have locked us up for days. Look at where we are. This is where they accommodate their *guests*. It's not like we're in a dungeon chained to a wall. Just wait," Tellwoon said.

Rednow shook his head. "No. You're being too naïve. This is a game for him. I don't have the time for kings who don't know what they want. I mean, is he trying *not* to pay us? I'm not leaving without the gold."

Tellwoon sighed. "You and he are competing to annoy each other. They will come and get us soon. It's only morning, anyway."

Rednow sighed and sat on the floor again. Tellwoon was sharp in her comments, but she had the gift of always leaving him wondering if he was doing the right thing. It was the only way for him to learn something. Most of the times she was right.

Rednow fiddled with the buttons of his vest. Part of him just wanted to blast the door and confront the King, hold him by the throat, and snap his neck. Old men were supposed to be wise, so Rednow should at least be that if he was going to be so damn stubborn.

"Let's wait," he said, just loud enough for them to hear.

"Why can't we just exit through the window?" Merey asked.

Tellwoon shook her head. "We can, but if we do, we are abandoning this job and the gold. How are we going to get through the winter? We can't afford that."

"It's still not guaranteed *this* king has any intention of ever paying us either," Merey said, frowning.

"We wait for a few more hours and then we'll see what he is planning. He knows who we are. I don't think he would try anything stupid," Rednow said, feeling the sword in his scabbard. "They didn't even take our weapons."

Tellwoon nodded, touching her sword, and then sitting beside him.

Merey still paced. She wouldn't rest until she had convinced them to leave. "Don't you think something strange is going on?" she asked. "Who locks guests in their palace?"

"Well, the skewer-face does."

"It's about power," Rednow said. "Caligo is old, like me. He feels his power slipping. His son is old enough to challenge his rule, so he needs to show his superiority. He is bullying us, trying to force us to decide between breaking out of here and risking disrespecting the host, who is a fucking king, or staying here and letting *him* decide when we can get out. He can do whatever he wants now. Even if we leave, we've wasted time and resources in doing all of this. He wasted nothing."

"Then, let's leave and take a few souvenirs for our trouble on our way out," Merey said as she smirked.

"Chances are that's something he planned for as well. We get out and have the entire city guard on our heels."

"You must have pissed the bastard off," Tellwoon said. But Rednow shot her a firm glance, and she lifted her hands and smiled.

Merey gave up and sat with them on the rug, sharpening her sword with a whetstone.

"I don't understand what this will accomplish."

"It's a punishment, Merey."

"For what you said to the King's son."

Rednow swallowed and sighed. "Yes."

Merey sharpened her blade and the big black birds cawed outside the window. For what seemed like hours, he sat there, either oiling the blade or simply watching the birds, until the door's lock clinked, and it opened.

"They unlocked the door!" he said.

"I bloody told you!" Tellwoon said with a smile as she hit him in the chest.

As the door opened, the young man who had seen serving him the previous night entered the room dressed in formal attire. Two guards accompanied him, armed to the teeth.

He's not taking any chances, Rednow thought.

"Why were we being kept here?" Rednow asked, without giving the servant or the guards any chance to escape the topic. The guards tensed up as they heard him but didn't shift their straight posture. The young man turned his head and bowed to him.

"Good morning, Blood Collector. They did not inform me of those matters, but I shall conduct the most thorough investigation and get back to you with my findings," he said.

Rednow scoffed. "Sure."

"We are here upon command from His Majesty, King Caligo."

"What does the King want?"

"You'll have to ask him. I'm here to escort you to a duel with His Highness, Prince Eterstan himself."

Rednow's mouth gaped, as though the servant had the power to stun people with his words. It took him a moment to even understand their meaning. The bratty prince couldn't want something so utterly stupid and old-fashioned as a duel, especially not one with Rednow. It was comedic that he thought he could. And the King approved of it? It didn't make sense. He still didn't understand exactly what he'd said that had offended the lad so much.

"Look, tell His Majesty to rethink this. I can stay here a little longer, until he cools his head, but I won't duel anyone."

"I'm sorry, Blood Collector. That is not a choice. My instructions were to escort you to the duel with the Prince. No matter what."

As the young man made his intentions clear, Rednow saw the guards hardening their stance, preparing to be met with resistance.

"Just let me go, then. I want no part of this. I'm tired of these games. You can tell that to the King. I'm sorry if I offended him, but I will not fight the Prince in a duel."

The servant didn't move, determined to fulfil his task. The guards looked ready for a sudden charge. Rednow's patience was at its limit, and he was about to shout at them.

It's not a good plan to reject or desert upon an offer for a duel, Rebma's ghost whispered.

It was also not a good idea to *kill* a royal heir. If he accepted the duel, he was supposed to kill the young man with honour, but everybody knew it would be an outrage if he did that. They'd hang him for it. The Prince was trying to trap Rednow. No matter what happened with the duel, there was no positive outcome for him.

There has to be one. You'll have to find it, the ghost of Rebma said.

He looked at Tellwoon and Merey for advice, but they had deep frowns, as confused as he was. He then turned to the servant. "Maybe I can talk some sense into them."

Rednow never worried about dying, but this was the first time in his life he worried about having to kill. Before he followed the servant out of the room, he stole a glance at the snowy rooftops outside the palace.

This wasn't a good day to kill a prince.

Sixteen

The Smokesmith

Gimlore

I can sense a shadow beneath me. Underneath me. In me.

— From *Mother's Memories*

The sun had already set and Gimlore made sure she strolled past the decrepit building that was now the warden patrol just to confirm Keryon was still there. She had a good look at it and it was lit up, so she continued towards the Maiden's Hall.

When she entered the building, followed by Pinesy, there were no customers there any longer. The room was filled with equipment. Blades, ropes, and black powder. Nork and Nosema were sharpening all the knives they hid in their belt and under their clothes. Next to them were all the materials they would need to make greasy bombs: small throwing knives, thin leather, black powder, and belleaf oil. The twins scooped about a handful of black powder with a spoon, placed it on top of the knife, and wrapped the tip of the blade and the powder inside the thin leather before finishing with a knot over it. Then they dipped the whole ball-shaped leather that now covered the edge of the throwing knife inside a container of belleaf oil to soak it.

"Greasy bombs? We're only supposed to go there for a conversation," she said.

Nosema nodded. "Better safe than sorry, boss. You might be going in to talk to them, but we're going there to make sure you get back out."

She sighed. That made sense. She couldn't shake off a dread that had settled in the pit of her stomach. She wasn't afraid of fighting—she had done it all her life—but they didn't stand a chance it if came to that. She wanted everyone to be safe. Her children, her men. Heleronde was supposed to be a safe haven, not a battleground.

Outside the Maiden's Hall, she told Pinesy to prepare the mounts. Travelling in the swamps required one that saw well at night. The weather was humid, but temperatures dropped in the swamplands, so they wore dark, hooded cloaks for warmth and to conceal themselves as well. Once everyone was ready, Gimlore left the Maiden's Hall, followed by Edmir, Nork, and Nosema. She had to kick Tinko and Thata for them to stay. She couldn't trust those two yet for stealth.

Pinesy stood with five hearthspears in his reins. The creatures roared, eager to gallop. Their reptilian scales were as light as desert sand and dozens of large, spiked bones shot out of their lower backs, upper thighs, and tails, resembling the pointy edges of spears.

Gimlore threw Pinesy a smaller dark cloak. The pinehead grabbed it and put it on as he climbed up with extreme agility onto the saddle. Gimlore took longer to get on hers as the animal kept neighing, begging her to go faster. She ushered the creature through the muddy high street of Heleronde until the outer edge of town, followed by her crew.

The mount was on a race against itself. While its weight and build didn't allow for sustained high speed, it was the perfect beast to ride in rugged terrain in small bursts, especially if there were ponds and water holes where humans often got trapped.

She continued riding, and as darkness enclosed, she lit a torch. They approached the farmlands under Gimlore's ownership. The small bushes and trees that surrounded the uneven ponds of dirty water had been almost all chopped off for lumber and to allow the farmers to tend to the precious mossbacks more easily.

In the main trails, she saw mossbacks with their red heads peeking out of the water, then diving back in as soon as they heard the heavy steps of the hearthspears on the surrounding ground.

"Edmir," she called, and he rode to catch up with her.

"Yes, boss?"

"No one is following, right?"

"No, boss."

"Well done."

They reached the edge of her farmlands. She halted the hearthspear and took cover behind the enormous trunk of a dead tree overlooking the enemy encampment, already riddled with basic timber buildings. She glanced at the rest of the camp, which already had a few small wharfs for small boats and canoes. There was a large fire pit at the centre of camp. She also saw guards. They posted the soldiers on the brink of the encampment, staring off in all directions. They wore the tight, dark-red uniforms of the Two Nations and carried a thin rapier sword, a dagger, and a wooden apparatus that resembled a spear, except it was hollow and seemed to have a lever of sorts in the handle.

"What the fuck are those soldiers carrying?" Edmir asked.

It was Gimlore's first time seeing the long-ranged weapons, but she had heard about how they could blast through plate armour.

"Well, I'll be damned," Gimlore said as her mind raced. "Those are muskets."

"Muskets," Edmir repeated.

Gimlore swallowed. "Time to go in."

She walked slowly with Edmir and Foloi towards the Sirestine settlement with arms raised, keeping a distance of about six feet between all three of them. They were still far from the camp, but they couldn't take any chances with those muskets, which could shoot long-range. As they walked, Gimlore's heart raced. Ideas and thoughts clouding her mind, her judgement. On one hand, she loved Heleronde and everything she had built. All it represented. She would do almost anything to keep it safe. To keep everyone safe. On the other hand, she had spent her whole life avoiding the oppressive thumb of the mainland rulers, their smokesmiths and their obsession with power and control. Even during the Crimson Wars, she fought for survival, not for any monarch. She would never kneel for them, and she sure as the underworld wouldn't allow them to step on her neck.

Gimlore stopped when they reached a considerable distance to their camp.

"We're here in peace. I'm from Heleronde. I just want to talk to whoever is in charge," she said, raising her voice.

Five muskets pointed at her. "Say that again."

She swallowed. "I just want to talk to whoever is in charge. I came in peace."

The Sirestine guards exchanged confused looks, but one of them muttered something and another went on running inside the camp.

"Wait right there. Don't move," the first soldier said.

Gimlore feigned a smile. "What if I have to scratch my nose?"

The soldier didn't laugh. She wasn't going to give him the satisfaction of complying. She had come voluntarily, but she wouldn't *obey* them. She only hoped Nork, Nosema, and Pinesy were watching, prepared for action if it came to that.

It didn't take long for the soldier who had left to come back with someone else, a bald, middle-aged man with brown skin and a dark beard peppered with white. The soldier pointed at Gimlore and the bald man walked forward, with two guards covering his rear.

"State your name and business."

Here we go.

"I'm Gimlore. I'm here representing Heleronde but also my own interest as a business owner in town. I came here to hold a peaceful conversation with whoever is in charge of your camp. Is that you?"

The bald man scanned her from top to bottom, not revealing much. "Gimlore? Are you the Viper?"

She swallowed. "I don't go by that nickname."

"But it is you, then. How interesting. I'm Sergeant Dase of the Two Nations of Sirestir and Yab. Come into our camp, then, and we'll talk."

She was almost tempted to accept, but if she stepped a foot in that camp, she would be offering herself as a hostage. "I would prefer to speak out here, in the open. On neutral ground, if you don't mind."

Dase frowned and pinched the bridge of his nose. "Fine. In that case, there is something I'd like to talk to you about as well. Mind if I start?"

Gimlore dropped her hands. "By all means."

Dase gazed at her first, then his eyes switched to Foloi and Edmir, then back to her. "I've heard a lot about you back in the day. There are many tales about those who fell victim to the Viper during the Crimson Wars. Are all the rumours true?"

Flashbacks of explosions and bodies lying on the ground flashed in her mind, "Me and my squad did what we had to do to survive. It was war."

Dase nodded. "War indeed. See, before King Doemus sent us here, he sent a Herald to assess the land and establish a trade relationship with your town. The thing is, he hasn't been seen since. It has been a mystery for me and my superiors."

"I saw him, I can confirm that. I took him, his interpreter, and his bodyguards in my abode, fed them, treated them to a bath and lodging and we held trade discussions. Unfortunately, we couldn't reach an agreement that suited both parties, so the Herald left in the early hours of the morning. And I didn't see him after that."

"Is that so?" Dase asked, but it was rhetorical. "And how long ago was this?"

"A few days ago."

"And where would the Herald go? He had instructions to come here and yet he never showed. We're growing a little restless as you can imagine."

Gimlore swallowed. "I can imagine. Unfortunately, he didn't say where he was going."

Dase produced a yellow smile, but let the silence hang in the air, so he took the liberty to speak. "I have a few things I wanted to ask myself."

"Please do."

"Yesterday we found a worrying number of our esteemed mossbacks slaughtered, with their guts hanging out in a vicious attack. The problem is, the mossbacks have no predator in Alarkan, so I'm struggling to understand who could have done such a thing. None of your soldiers happened to see anything, did they? The mossback pastures being just around the corner from your camp and all."

"That is very regrettable. I'm afraid nobody saw anything, or they would have told me. We have a very strict chain of command."

Fucker. He knows damn well they did it. "I see. Then I'd like to ask: what are your plans for this settlement? I don't mean to intrude, but it is awfully close to our settlement. Alarkan is a new continent, full of unexplored land, so I find your choice of location interesting."

Dase smirked. "I admire the honesty of your question, but I'm afraid we're all just following orders. The orders were for us to build the settlement in these exact coordinates. We're all just playing our roles."

He's just playing dumb now. "Would you, then be willing to sign a peace agreement with Heleronde? I'm willing to establish favourable terms for your camp, as long as the safety of our town and our farmlands is guaranteed. I'm also open to trade talks, just as I'd discussed with the Herald."

Dase sighed. His eyes turned sharp, locked on her. "As I said, I'm just a sergeant following orders. I can't do business on behalf of the King. That was the Herald's job. I would need to wait for a new Herald or someone to supervise the camp."

Well, I tried.

"That is regrettable. I think that concludes everything I came here to talk about, then. I'll take my leave."

She raised her arms again and slowly turned around. Edmir and Foloi mimicked her and the three of them started walking back to the woodland area just outside the Sirestine camp.

"Regrettable indeed," Dase said. "If you hadn't killed the Herald, he might be kind enough to negotiate some kind of treaty with you swamp rats."

Gimlore froze, anger building in her. She clasped her hands and bit her lip to prevent herself from exploding. She slowly turned back to face Dase and found the muskets were once again pointed at them.

"Do you have any evidence for those accusations?" she asked. "The Herald issued threats about the safety of our town unless I sold my farmlands under their value. He's the one who didn't try to negotiate."

Dase laughed. "Evidence? Cut the crap. Out here, we don't need any of that. I know you killed the Herald. It's a shame he died. He was a smart man, the Herald. But our orders are to get the elixir, so we will do as we were asked to do."

Bastard. "Then do it. Get the elixir. Just leave us alone."

Dase shrugged. "I'm afraid I can't do that. Our King doesn't like waiting. We can't wait for us to figure out how to extract the damn thing on our own. We have to deliver results and deliver them quick, if you catch me. And here we are. You came to us, so I'm thinking we keep you for a while and persuade you to tell us all about that elixir of yours."

Gimlore's mouth went dry. They wanted to capture her. Torture her until she handed the elixir on a silver platter. Why did she ever think talking to these bastards was a good idea?

She turned to Edmir, and Foloi. "Let's get the fuck out of here. The muskets are still out of range."

"I wouldn't do that if I were you," Dase said. He whistled and Sirestine soldiers rose in a circumference all around her, Edmir and Foloi. Probably about fifty of them, maybe more. "My troops are well-trained."

Panic settled as her mind raced at full speed. If they obeyed and stayed there, allowing themselves to be captured, they were as good as dead and the enemy would get the elixir. Maybe the Sirestine could still spare the lives of everyone in town, though that was unlikely. If Gimlore and her men were to fight back, they were at a serious disadvantage, just the three of them against fifty enemies. *Shit.* Running away was the only option, and even that was risky.

"Run!" she shouted. The three of them started running back and away from the Sirestine camp. Loud bangs of muskets being fired echoed in the air and Gimlore gritted her teeth, praying to gods she didn't believe in that no shrapnel from the muskets would reach her or her friends.

Survive!

Maybe they could still defend the town somehow. Maybe the enemy soldiers would fall back, since they weren't enough in numbers yet to stage a siege or conquer a whole town. She brought her right hand to her mouth and whistled as loud as she could. They needed help to escape.

Three objects flew towards the Sirestine guards that were now surrounding them. Greasy bombs! Gimlore protected her ears and waited. The greasy bombs landed about a hundred feet in front of her. As they hit the ground, they exploded in bright surging balls of fire in loud bangs that deafened her ears, forcing her to close her eyes and shield her face from the debris. Dirt, wood, and body parts from the soldiers hit were still falling to the ground in clouds of smoke and dust, but they now had a clear path.

For the gods, thank you.

Gimlore kept running, Edmir and Foloi still covering her rear. She could now see Pinesy, Nork, and Nosema throwing greasy bombs at the Sirestine soldiers, who were still marching forward with muskets in hand. Flurries of black powder shot from those weapons were loud and frequent as the Sirestine soldiers pushed forward, protecting their camp, avenging the comrades who had now fallen.

Then, the soldiers in her right flank started firing muskets too. Gimlore threw herself into the ground. "Get down!" she shouted. Foloi and Edmir wasted no time in doing the same, but their progress had been impeded. They were heavily outnumbered, and soldiers armed with muskets were coming from her rear and the flank. Those were weapons that had in power and deadliness what they lacked in accuracy.

"Nork!" she screamed across the mount and amid the sound of the muskets firing. "How many greasy bombs do you still have?"

"About half a dozen," he shouted back.

Shit. They were doomed.

"I'll distract them and you move forward, boss," Edmir said. "You need to survive."

"No, Edmir. That's not—" she said, but Edmir was already on the run, making his way towards the enemies in the flank, putting himself in arm's way, finding shelter in tree trunks as he got the enemies' attention.

"You stupid man," she whispered as her heart sank, cursing herself. Why would he do such a thing?

"We need to move. Now." Foloi grabbed her arm and pulled her upward. Forward.

Nork, Nosema, and Pinesy threw three more greasy bombs at the enemy, keeping them at bay for a time. They'd be left with only three, but Gimlore kept looking to her right, at Edmir. Her breath intensified, a mix of nerves and running as she crouched, not to be hit by the metal pellets shot by the muskets.

She should have never come here. She did what she could, but she should have known they were not reasonable. They'd never negotiate after the Herald disappeared. At least she knew that now. Survival needed to be the new focus.

The scenery between the farmlands and the Sirestine camp looked like an inferno of burning trees, flying debris, and burning soldiers, running out and screaming, trying to put out the fire that burned them.

She stole another glance at Edmir as she closed in on Nork, Nosema, and Pinesy. She couldn't see well in all that smoke, but all she could think about was getting him back to safety. She remembered the first time she saw him, lost in the steppes, shivering in cold and hallucinating after having deserted his unit. A man broken by war. Ten years later and here he was again on a battlefield, putting himself in harm's way for her. How could she accept that?

The musket sounds stopped.

"What happened?" Foloi asked.

"They must have run out of ammunition. They're charging with melee weapons now," Nork said.

"We must go back for Edmir, then," she said. "I can't leave him behind. You cover my rear with the remaining greasy bombs."

"Wait, boss. It's too dangerous!"

Gimlore ran towards Edmir, anyway. She knew it was dangerous, panic demanding all the air in her lungs. She could reach him before any enemy soldiers would.

When she caught up to him, behind a tree trunk, her eyes widened. Blood soaked Edmir's shirt. He gave her an apologetic smile and a half-assed shrug. His breathing was slow, and his eyes struggled to focus on her.

Please, no. Not this.

"I'm sorry, boss," he whispered. "I got shot."

"Shh," she said, trying to rip open his shirt to use it as a tourniquet to stop the bleeding. It was in his stomach, with multiple entry wounds, as bad as she had seen during the Crimson Wars. Some of the shrapnel was still lodged in the skin and his rib bones. It was a fucking miracle Edmir was still alive and breathing.

"I'll do my best to get you out of here."

Edmir lifted his head, trying to get up. "Boss! No! You must go. They're coming. I'll take care of myself."

"Don't be an idiot," she hissed.

How did I let this happen?

"Boss!"

A sharp blow to her head caused her to collapse. Her vision blurred, and she struggled to get back to her feet. An enemy soldier, dressed in red and dark, had used the back of his musket to hit her. She dodged a close second blow by rolling in the grass but found blood on the side of her head.

She was bleeding for the first time in ten years.

The enemy used the blade in the muzzle of the musket and tried his luck at stabbing her. Gimlore struggled to dodge the vicious motion amidst all the panic. Looking for something she could use to defend herself; there were only throwing knives in her cloak.

The soldier screamed in fury as he pursued her, holding the musket in both hands. Another soldier appeared and his comrade bellowed something at her.

Gimlore kept glancing at Edmir. She feared for him, hurt like that. He had put himself in front of the enemy to save her. Now it was her time to save him.

Gimlore could finally reach inside the cloak and find a few knives. She slid them between her fingers and threw them at the soldiers. The first one landed on a soldier's throat, but the others missed the targets.

She picked up more knives and faced the second soldier.

"Boss! Run!"

"Not a chance!"

Gimlore stopped, struggling to evade the strikes from a third soldier. But she wasn't thinking about the enemy or the plans any longer.

"Gimlore, leave!" Edmir screamed, his voice cracking in a mix of despair and concern for her. "Save yourself!"

Edmir's pleading eyes branded themselves in her mind like an iron. How could she let them slaughter him like that?

She produced another knife. This time, she stabbed the soldier, but another group was already on her tail. A salvo of fiery arrows lit up the sky, and then started descending. All the grass and the surrounding bushes burned, the fire spreading fast. Soon, the flames would reach Edmir. He was only fifty feet away.

She winced. He didn't deserve to die like that. Abandoned. Burned to crisp or in a blast.

"Let's try to get you up! Can you walk?" she asked with gritted teeth, looking both ways for more incoming soldiers. She pulled him up and held him by the armpit. For the gods, he was heavy.

Soot and sweat covered his face. His breath was hoarse, and he moaned in pain, eyes shooting to the back of his head. "Thank you," he blabbered.

She gritted her teeth, struggling to carry his weight as she scoured the field for new enemies. Nork and Nosema waved at her to join them. Could she close that distance without being attacked again?

The weight became too heavy and Edmir slipped onto the grass, falling.

"What is it?" Gimlore asked, feeling a sudden dread looming over her, as if she knew what it was. Edmir looked from his feet and to her and remained silent at first until a tear flowed from his eyes. "What is it, Edmir?! Come on, get up!"

"I can't," he uttered, his face unfolding into defeat.

Her eyes welled. For once, she said nothing.

"You need to go," Edmir said.

Gimlore let her tears flow and his face softened.

Fuck. Fuck. Fuck.

Then she ran away, as though her legs moved on their own, though the more she moved, more regret took hold of her, the more she wanted to go back to her old friend. She glanced back at him slumping, barely moving any longer.

Then he looked at her and raised his hand to wave.

It cut deep into her. And it hurt.

Gimlore yelped like a child, dumbfounded by Edmir's firm resolve even as he took to the underworld. Her right-hand man, best friend, and confidant. He didn't deserve to die. And it was all her fault. She had led him astray into this poor attempt at negotiating a peace treaty. She had put herself in danger, prompting him to protect her.

She cried and clasped her hands, angry. At the world. At her useless self. She panted and gasped, her eyes turning into a blur of smoke and tears. Edmir was gone. It wasn't fair. The world wasn't. It was as though the good part of herself had been forcibly removed and all she had now was the rotten part.

The sky lit up again as part of the Sirestine camp burned from Nork's greasy bombs. Several of the rudimentary buildings burned in flames as tall as two men. Boxes of black powder exploded and sent shattered pieces of wood flying at incredible, dangerous speeds. Settlers shouted and scrambled around in fear as the soldiers did their best to figure out where to go when their entire camp burned.

She didn't know—didn't care—if she was running or walking. She had no idea how close she was to reaching the rest of her crew. Her chest was tight, and it was hard to breathe. Her body tensed and locked, her mind became foggy. It all felt like she could go to sleep and by the time she woke, none of this would be happening. It was as though she was captured in a daze.

It can't be true. He can't really be dead. The infuriated soldiers kept shooting arrows. Their companions kept coming for her, dozens of them, armed with muskets and spears.

It was as though the strength in her legs had vanished and a hole opened in her chest. Was she still walking? Her heart tightened. She felt dizzy and her stomach hurt. She was getting sick. She dropped to her knees and looked at the grass as enemies surrounded her.

She couldn't continue any longer. That was it for her. If the arrows didn't catch her, the spears would. But then, even more light came into her field of vision, expanding like the sun. Amid the chaos, she recognised a trace of sulphuric smell, different from the rest of the smoke.

Hands grabbed her.

"It's time to get out of here," Keryon said.

A white cloud of smoke surrounded the man, clinging to him as he dragged her away.

She ran alongside him through the outskirts of the burning camp just as settlers tried to get out. Gimlore could still walk, her body beaten and bruised, though she could not think straight.

"Nork... Nosema..." she struggled to say. After jogging for a few moments, she spotted them, back-to-back and trying to fend off a dozen Sirestine soldiers, with muskets pointed at them.

Another shot of fear consumed her.

Nork and Nosema struggled against the better trained soldiers. They were out of musket ammunition, but the edge of their spears looked sharp awfully enough.

Keryon continued, urging her forward.

The warden blew air into the herbs in his hand, and his white smoke returned. He took a large whiff of it and started running faster than should be possible. As Keryon ran, the smoke brightened, and turned red. The smoke ignited and turned into a cloud of fire, engulfing Keryon and following him around without burning his body or his clothes.

He became fire.

He has a special ability, she realised.

Keryon reached the men and, effortlessly, spun and the fiery smoke around him twirled in a whirlpool before it stopped and exploded in all directions, burning, consuming the enemies.

He circled his enemies. The smoke followed and ignited, setting the grass alight. He made a circle of fire around the soldiers. The Sirestine soldiers cried for help that wouldn't come, and Keryon let the smoke subside as he urged Nork and Nosema to escape.

Then he jumped into the fire and took another whiff of the smoke, which expanded into an enormous cloud around him. Then he waved his arms, and the smoke turned to fire again, swallowing the soldiers and everything else in its way. They couldn't fight *that* with a sword or a musket. They could only run in the other direction and hope he didn't pursue.

Keryon emerged with charred clothes, hazy eyes and spitting blood, but he had been victorious.

SEVENTEEN

TRUE PAIN

REDNOW

*E**mpty promises take every breath I still have.*

— From *Mother's Memories*

Rednow saw more of the innards of the palace as he and his companions followed the servant through the vast hallways and down different staircases. Confident in his duty, he didn't even seem to fear the guards or the guests. There was not one bit of anxiety in him. Something was off about the young man, but Rednow wasn't sure what.

"What's your name, boy?"

The servant glanced sideways on his way up in the narrow stairwell. "Monder," he said. "Apologies for not introducing myself. Guests never ask."

"You seem clever, Monder. Why don't you tell your Prince this isn't a good idea?"

"Many thanks, Blood Collector, but the Prince cares not for my opinions," the young man said. He continued climbing the spiral stairs with the rest of the group on his tail.

"But he should, shouldn't he?" Rednow asked. He felt the guards glaring at him, but Monder didn't even flinch. His speech was eloquent. Perhaps he had grown up among royalty.

"You are very bold, Blood Collector. I suppose that's only natural for someone who has cultivated a reputation like yours and has nothing to prove."

The little bastard isn't stupid, Rednow thought as they kept walking through the hallways. "And what reputation is that?"

"Someone who knows where the next battles will be. You're always there, and you win more than you lose, at least according to the tales."

"That speaks only for the efficiency of my troops. I can't take credit for that," Rednow said.

The servant did not engage further, and they continued to cross hallways, passing through a few that had no natural light and were lit up by oil torches hanging on the walls.

They stumbled upon the men and women that made the palace run—all wearing ratty clothes. Bony-faced carpenters, builders, maids, and cooks stopped when they saw Rednow and his entourage pass. Those were people of multiple origins and pasts, with different skin tones and hair colours, but they all had one thing in common. Their faces showed a displeasure Rednow had grown up with.

As Rednow locked eyes with them, he saw their pleas for help. Ten, twenty, thirty years ago, Rednow would not have rested until he had taken them under his wing and made something of them. He would have made hunters, warriors, and killers out of them, never again forced to serve ungrateful, cruel lords. But now he was old, and the wisdom granted by a lifetime of war prevented him from saving everyone. Not everyone was to be saved.

He felt for them as their eyes drifted from his. Surely, they assumed he was just another lordling, another guest to whom they had to bow their heads. Rednow felt an incredible urge to go back and meet them, tell them otherwise, shake their hands and explain he was different. But words meant nothing unless he did something.

And he did nothing.

Merey pulled mutton wraps from her pouch and handed them over. The servants' faces brightened as they looked at her while she joined the group again.

Monder opened one last door and Rednow realised they were on the third floor, not too far away from the large ballroom, where they met Caligo for the welcoming feast the previous night.

Monder guided the group to the large ballroom. Once the guards opened the doors, Rednow recognised the room, but it was now empty except for enormous banners of the Gasho kingdom between every vertical, diamond-shaped window. King Caligo and his son, Eterstan, stood at the far end of the room with their faces skewered by countless metal piercings. Their honour guards stood behind the King and his heir. Eterstan wore a casual white shirt and black linen trousers, while Caligo maintained the formal, colourful blue robe representative of their kingdom.

"Your Majesty," Monder said as he bowed, kneeled, and stayed low. "I brought the Blood Collector, as instructed."

"Thank you, Monder. You can stay and watch, if you'd like," Caligo said, then turned to face Rednow.

Eterstan locked eyes with Rednow. "Are you ready, Blood Collector?"

Rednow shook his head. "This is a bad idea, my Prince. Your Majesty."

"*This* is more mercy than any commoner would receive after talking to me in such a way."

"How can you accept this, Your Majesty?"

The King stayed silent.

Eterstan waved for the nearby servants to approach and a short man who looked like an armourer brought him a sword. The weapon was still inside a scabbard embedded with all kinds of colourful, precious gems. As Rednow observed Eterstan unsheathe the sword, he could almost feel the burning glare of his travelling companions reaching the back of his head, blaming him for this predicament. The Prince's sword looked like a blade of quality, but Rednow could tell right away it had never tasted blood. It was a ceremonial weapon, never meant to be used, even in strange situations such as duels. Was it sharp?

"This is ridiculous, my Prince. You can't be serious."

"Oh, I am serious. Don't you see my weapon?"

"I've been fighting for survival my entire life. I have the instincts and the appetite of a caged bloodsleuth. This won't help anyone." *Especially not you...*

"Self-congratulatory blabber from a commoner who overstepped his position and badmouthed my name and my status. I am quite the swordsman if you must know."

With every word from Eterstan's mouth, Rednow's disgust towards the brat became harder to contain, all the anger and frustration bubbling to the surface.

"You wouldn't know a good swordsman if you saw one," Rednow spat. "You surround yourself with servants and lordlings, eager to please and to earn your favour. They tell you how good you are. They lie. It must have been a shock when you didn't get that false reverence from me. You never even realised it was possible for commoners not to kiss your arse."

"Blood Collector... That's enough!" the King spat.

"I helped you defeat your enemies, Your Majesty. I'm not here to hold your hand or to tell you how wonderful you are. Let's stop this nonsense. I just want my gold."

Eterstan's grip on the sword tightened, and he flexed his legs, readying himself to lunge.

"This man doesn't know civilised ways, Father. I'll teach him some manners."

The King leaned forward and whispered to his son. "He didn't mean to offend you, Eterstan. It's just how he speaks. Forgive him and we can end this. You don't have to go through with it."

The King still has some sense, Rednow thought.

"Please step aside, Father," Eterstan said, his eyes dead set upon Rednow. "I will honour our bloodline and your throne against this mercenary scum."

Rednow felt sick. He would ruin everything for everyone he cared about, but the urge to kill the prince was strong after failing to make him and the King see reason. Perhaps he could get away with it. Everything told him to back away, apologise but his pride wouldn't allow it. His pride made him want to teach the young prince what genuine respect meant. He wanted to teach him no man was better or worse than another, especially if they could fend for themselves.

"He would kill Prince Eterstan if necessary."

Eterstan smirked. "I will let my blade wipe that filthy mouth of yours."

Monder stepped forward and bowed. "If both parties are ready, I shall be the judge."

Rednow saw Merey and Tellwoon looking stern, with their sword hands resting on their hilts. He had to think about them. He couldn't let this escalate into something even worse.

"This will be a duel where our accused, the Blood Collector, will respond to accusations of insult and perjury put forth by His Highness, Prince Eterstan. It will be a trial by sword. It ends when one of the two men dies. No one else may intervene on behalf of the accuser or respondent. Understood?"

Rednow nodded, and Caligo did the same.

Eterstan started with a rash strike. As soon as Rednow saw it, he unsheathed his sword and the red stains in the blade made their full display, making the steel weapon look like something else in the eyes of those who didn't know about it—a weapon of lost ancient times. A blade that blood could not rust and, instead, seized it, drank it. The shock was visible in Eterstan's eyes as he saw the sword. The Prince had never thought the legends of the red-tinted blade were real.

Rednow parried and used his right foot to make the brat trip and fall onto the stone floor. He gave his opponent time to get up and prepare another attack.

"I'll have you know that I'm not the true Blood Collector."

Eterstan scoffed and flexed his legs, clutching his fancy blade, trying his best to leave no openings. "So, who is it?"

Rednow lifted his right hand that held the blade. "The sword. I really don't want to add yours to the collection, my Prince."

Eterstan's disgust was palpable as he struck at Rednow's head and then at his gut. Rednow blocked both strikes, studying how fast the Prince could move at his quickest. He wasn't the worst Rednow had seen—perhaps new warriors of the Leeth could still lose in a duel like this, but not him.

Rednow blocked two more blows and parried the third, finishing with a leg sweep that left the Prince without balance, falling on the ground and sitting on his arse. Looking down on the young man, Rednow smiled. "Most people think swordsmanship is about strength and speed, when it really starts with grappling."

That was how he liked his kings or princes—sweaty, humbled, and defeated.

The soldiers around the room shuffled in their stances, and so did King Caligo and Monder. Nobody was allowed to interfere.

"I'll show you swordsmanship," Eterstan said as he tried another desperate stab Rednow saw coming from a league away.

"You have shown me everything you can, my Prince. You have shown me you don't know pain, fear, or chaos. And I conquered those before I could even grow a beard. This duel was never fair to begin with. Let's stop this. I don't want to kill you."

Tellwoon and Merey had their arms crossed.

Eterstan was silent as he tried to slice through Rednow, studying him, trying to find an opening. Sweat beads built around his disfigured mug.

"That blade..." Eterstan said. "It must be sorcery. You must be cheating."

"When someone confronts you, you accuse the opponents of cheating. How *regal*, Your Highness."

Eterstan looked around the room but found no help. The penalties for intervening in a crown-sanctioned duel would be severe.

Rednow blocked another blow that made the Prince scramble to not fall on his arse again.

The Prince's honour guards shifted their stances and clasped their halberds. Rednow picked up the pace and, in a flurry of blows to the left, right, and an elbow to the chest, sent Eterstan to the floor on his knees, as though he was training a new recruit. Rednow extended his right hand and, with the tip of his blade, lifted the Prince's chin.

Eterstan remained motionless, but with hands shaking. His last grip on the fancy sword loosened, and the blade fell to the stone floor, its clinking echoing across the grand room before stopping still. The Prince's head bobbed left and right, and tears formed under his eyes. He was on his knees, humiliated by the failure of his own games, by his own machinations. He kneeled as he should before a stronger man.

Rednow smiled, as if years of amassed anger and frustration had reached a cathartic conclusion. "Can we put a stop to this? I don't need to kill you."

"You must. That's how it's supposed to be. I need to die in honour," Eterstan said, tears flowing down his face.

Rednow scoffed. "Fuck honour."

"Of course *you* would say that. You wouldn't understand."

Rednow sheathed his sword back into the scabbard. "I'm done with this. I won't kill you. This was supposed to be a duel, but it's over, as far as I'm concerned. I can't be forced to kill you."

Rednow took a few steps back, sheathed his sword and stood with arms crossed, waiting for someone to stop the duel. King Caligo sighed, shook his head, and walked towards his son. Rednow wondered if he was about to console or scold his son for the decision. Perhaps he'd call the duel over since Rednow had clearly won but no one had died. There must be no precedent for this.

"That was... embarrassing," the King said.

In a swift motion, Caligo produced a dagger from his robe, grabbed his son by the collar, and sliced his throat. Rednow froze, his eyes widening and mouth gaping as Caligo then stabbed Eterstan in the neck and in the chest.

Covered in blood, the King snapped his fingers and his honour guard attacked Eterstan's overwhelmed retainers with halberds, swords, and even bolts from covert crossbows. The poor soldiers didn't have orders to follow and were caught by surprise. They still tried to defend themselves, fending off some of the attackers, but ultimately fell to their demise. Other guards loyal to King Caligo locked all the exits of the room.

Rednow tensed, assessing what had just happened, unsheathing his sword. It had all happened so quickly he had barely had time to process it. Nearby, Tellwoon and Merey did the same, but it didn't take him long to realise he and his generals were not the targets. This had been something else.

Rednow was careful with his words. "What is the meaning of this, Your Majesty?"

King Caligo let his son's body lie on the floor and the blood pooled underneath. The King's blue robe now had countless blood stains and there was splatter on his face as well, which he couldn't wipe off due to his piercings.

"Ridiculous," Caligo said as he spat on Eterstan's dead body. "Pathetic child. He had to humiliate his family like that even as he died."

Rednow dared not to move as he watched, still waiting for answers.

This is a first.

Why would the King not only have his son killed, but kill him with his own hands? Eterstan was supposed to be the heir to the throne, groomed by the crown to take his dynasty to greater heights. So... why?

Rednow had taken the King for a sensible, reasonable man—as sensible and reasonable as autarchs could ever be—but now all he saw was a cold-blooded murderer with no remorse. Rednow's eyes switched between the King and his dead son. This was no spur of the moment, he realised. Caligo had been planning to kill his son and had tried to get Rednow to do the dirty work. Thinking back to the previous evening, the King's disproportionate reaction to Eterstan's offence made sense. The King had seen their little argument as a way to pit him against Rednow, perhaps even planted the ideas of a duel in Eterstan's mind, since he was always eager to prove himself. It probably hadn't even taken much. But he hadn't expected Rednow to have mercy on the young man, so he took it into his own hands. This made Rednow wonder just how safe *he* would be after witnessing this, but also why the King had committed such a gruesome act.

The King looked as if someone had lifted a heavy load from his shoulders, even with his son's blood all over him. His honour guard celebrated behind him as well.

They had left Monder alive. He walked towards Caligo.

"At last!" Monder said. "I wish you would have done it sooner, Father. That was hard to watch. How humiliating, even for me."

The King embraced Monder.

"This was for you, my son. No one will ever deny you again. You are the son of a king. My rightful heir." He grabbed Monder by the neck and gave him a fatherly embrace. "Now, there's no time to lose. We must hurry to squash Eterstan's loyalists. They have been quiet, but they are still hiding in the shadows."

"I'm already on it, Father. I gave word for my assassins to strike in the wee hours. I also ordered the Mewon city gates closed, so there will be no escapes. No time for our enemies to gather allies. It will be a few days, but we'll manage it. Some will survive, yes, but not with enough backing to stage a revolt of any kind. Eterstan was loved by the peasants, though. I'm more worried about *them* staging protests."

The King shook his head. "I'm still the king, and they'll grow to love you just as much. They'll accept whoever is my heir, eventually. There will be tension, and we must stay alert, though. It's probably best to stay inside the Palace."

"Yes, Father."

Caligo turned to his honour guard. "Tell the smokesmiths they'll be needed. If any crowd start rebelling or even raising their voices, unleash them. These people need to remember *I'm* still the king."

"Yes, Your Majesty," the guard said as he bowed and left the room immediately.

Rednow bit his lip. He couldn't believe what was happening, but the King hadn't seemed to notice he and his companions were still there.

"You! Get the scribe master to write a public announcement. We must get the word out that the Prince was murdered with his retainers. A full investigation is being conducted into this horrible act."

"Of course, Your Majesty." The soldier bowed and immediately took his leave.

Rednow cleared his throat. "Your Majesty. Everyone will think I murdered the Prince now."

King Caligo turned towards him and walked a few steps closer. "I'm sorry for all this, Blood Collector. For everything you have just seen. It was long overdue. I assure you no one will accuse you or your mercenaries of this."

Rednow swallowed, still baffled and unsure of what to say. Caligo walked closer to Rednow and patted him on the shoulder.

"Your gold is ready, but I still have one thing more I'd like you to do for me," he said. A radiant smile took over his face, despite all the metal sticking out of it. "Shall we go somewhere private and talk?"

Rednow shook off the surprise and nodded, following Caligo. He looked back at Eterstan's body lying there on the floor over a pool of blood. A stark reminder of how nothing in this world could be taken for granted. There was always something more, something new. Even family didn't always meant love.

A pressure built on his shoulders. He was following the King, but how could he now trust a man who didn't bat an eyelid upon killing his own child? And how could Rednow reject whatever someone like that wanted him to do?

I'm still useful, he though, releasing the breath he was holding. *And I'm still alive.*

EIGHTEEN

PROPOSITIONS

ORBERESIS

The one who would not die haunts them with his eyes.

— From *Mother's Memories*

Orberesis laid motionless in his large bed. He had spent the last few days in a daze after the migraines and all the wine he drank to dull them. Too soothed, however, and he'd become vulnerable, even with guards and servants all around. His theory that the Queen had a lover inside the palace wasn't confirmed yet and the servants didn't really offer much insight into Taishay and other noblemen. If they were in fact plotting against him, they were good at covering their tracks. The King had also taken to spending his days in his study, surrounded by his books about history and poems and old maps. Nobles were more boring than most people would ever believe, but perhaps he should spend more time with the King until the emissaries to Alarkan arrived with the elixir.

He had got used to fear when he was a thief and scavenger, but now he had enemies in and outside the borders and still hadn't found the damn potion. His only friend sometimes looked indistinguishable from the enemy.

He drank another glass and let the wine send him into dreams.

Sand kissed Doi's feet as he walked. The red orb had been a disappointing discovery in the tomb, the only thing hidden in a place that promised many riches, but perhaps this warlord was interested in buying it.

His eyes shifted between the orb and the strange horizon above the ocean, where clouds gathered in bizarre shapes, as if moulded by human hands.

It was a beautiful sight.

Doi realised he had been walking but going nowhere. He tried running. His body moved, but it was as if the world under his feet moved at his pace. Desperate, he tried changing direction. He tried running towards the ocean too, but something paralysed him, even though his body moved.

A powerful roar echoed in the distance and the branches of the trees that surrounded the beach turned to flames burning in light shades of orange. Dark creatures snarled and hounded him, their fur dark and thick. They didn't belong on a beach.

No!

Someone, help! But no words would come out.

The creatures charged, their maws revealing sharp fangs. Marcrunchers, bigger than five men. Bloodsleuths, following his scent from a mile away. They sprinted towards him, but he couldn't move. They got closer and closer until a giant human emerged on the horizon. A naked male body with no legs but blessed with piercing bright eyes.

This impossible figure clapped, and everything turned dark.

Orberesis woke gasping and covered in sweat, a weird, slimy feeling in his throat. His heart raced. His pants were wet stained in the groin.

Rushing, he stood, cleaned himself with soft towels and changed into his white robe, still shaking. Orberesis let his long hair fall over his shoulders and back and forced himself to control his breathing. *Breathe.* But it didn't work, and he fell on his knees and brought his hands to his face amidst tears and rage.

Why couldn't he just be normal?

He left his quarters, followed by his guards, not really knowing where he was going. He just couldn't be in the chamber anymore. He wished Solvi was there to comfort him, but she had him on a pedestal. She wouldn't take it kindly if she were to find out he was the most ill man in the Known World. Not really God Himself. He walked through the now deserted inner chambers of the Palace of Brilliance. The place was a marvel, but it was still eerie to walk the large corridors and hallways with only his personal guard or the Order's worship leaders after the King had ordered tight security measures for his safety.

When he reached the westernmost corner of the Palace, he found the hidden corner window overlooking Ushar. The city sprawled before his eyes, all the way until the ocean, where the large nine-mast vessels of the Floating City Fleet had docked in wharfs just as big. The smoke had dissipated and the sky was clear, yet his heart was racing.

His instincts told him he was all alone and would always be. He feared it was true. No one really *knew* him. He lived in a world populated by those who hated or feared him. Continuing the con was dangerous and foolish. And yet... he still did it. He *had* to do it until he found a cure.

Steps on the stone floor echoed throughout the room and pulled Orberesis from his thoughts. Solvi walked towards him, wearing the long dark gown. There was beauty in so much simplicity. She didn't try, he knew, but she had an unexplainable aura of effortless flawlessness. He noticed the little red gem she was wearing around her neck. He reached for the pendant and the orb, locking eyes with Solvi for a moment.

"Your pendant," Orberesis said. "The red orb is just like mine. Smaller, but just like it."

Solvi nodded. "It is, Highest One. I had them made. I've decided that members of the Order will wear these to honour God Himself."

"That pleases me," Orberesis said, turning his to the window. "The city, Solvi. It looks so peaceful now."

"Yes, Highest One. That is because we purged the heretics and the blasphemous from the underworld. I would say no one will miss them."

Orberesis turned to her and studied her expression. Solvi was even shy with him. She had respect and admiration, but perhaps something more. Or at least that's what he hoped.

She sat opposite to him and looked at him, expectant.

"Are you happy with your life now?" Orberesis asked.

Solvi raised her eyebrows at the question but nodded. "I am, Highest Lord. Life in the palace is good, despite the quietude of the halls and the attention we must pay to everything we do. There was only war and misery. The wretch used to plague our towns and cities every week, kill us and our children. And for years I thought my purpose was to kill horrific creatures and even worse men. It's all over now."

"You used to protect people too," Orberesis said. "You were a smoke-smith. You kept the peace. A woman of the law."

"The law of monarchs far more wicked than those we have here, Highest One. I'm glad that's not who I am anymore. Everything changed when God Himself saved humanity from the wretch that day with the Miracle. I changed as well. I suppose I'm just... still trying to find my role. What I'm supposed to do now," she said.

Orberesis thought he saw a tear in her eye. He turned his away from her. "Perhaps your place is at my side."

He let the words hung in the air and Solvi's face filled with realization.

"Highest One? Do you mean…"

He nodded. "You're the perfect woman. But it's not time yet. We must wait until the safety of the realm is guaranteed for now. And then we can go and spread the word of the Red Orb. Together."

Solvi's eyes were wide. "But I'm just a woman. You're God Himself. You saved millions with your Miracle."

"Many people died because of me too," he said, failing to stay in character. He'd try to hide it. Bottle it. But the screams of the dying merchants were still sharp as a knife in his mind. He remembered every single one of them. Blood on his hands.

"No, Highest One." Solvi leaned towards him and cupped his face. "They died so others might live. If I can help relieve God Himself from the weight He carries, I will do it. It would be my greatest honour to be by your side."

"You've been the greatest asset. I'm very thankful," Orberesis said. Solvi was leaning so close to him, he noticed her lips, her neck. Those damn freckles which made her a creature of the heavens. He almost didn't pull back.

"I only hope to please the Highest Lord," she said.

Orberesis resisted, smiled back, and nodded. He wondered what would happen if she found out he was a fraud. The thought sent a chill down his spine. "What brings you to my presence today?"

"The banquet," she said. "The King and Queen are expecting you."

Orberesis nodded. He had forgotten he promised to have supper with them. Just thinking about the meetings, discussing politics, and warfare was exhausting enough. Doing so with perpetual migraines that came and went like the tide was a million times worse. "Let's go, then."

············

The King had ordered the servants to prepare the ceremonial room and set up a long wooden table to host a feast for around thirty guests. Doemus sat at the top of the table, Queen Thura sat at his left side, and Orberesis to his right, to the visible discomfort of the other councillors.

Orberesis felt the velvety arms of the chair and leaned back. His chair had been painted in red, to match the colour of the orb he carried around his neck. It had several rubies embedded as well. The King was really trying to show the extent of his faith. Solvi and Tavanar had been given honours to sit by his side, while Taishay and some fools whose names Orberesis hadn't bothered to remember sat across the table. They were Taishay's cronies, with their thick, curved moustaches and golden jewellery. They wore ceremonial attire, proper for a royal banquet. Taishay and the Queen held a friendly conversation about one of Taishay's many estates where he spent the wet season. Orberesis noticed that the same guard with the crossbow who had rushed in and found the assassin dead was posted in the room, stagnant like a statue.

"First, a toast!" the King said, tipsy as he lifted his cup of cerro wine and spilled a bit. The servants and slaves around the table made sure everyone had their glasses full. "A toast of gratitude to the Highest One for his stellar advice."

The King downed the contents of the glass and Orberesis was about to do the same but noticed the Queen and the other councillors didn't follow through.

"Music! We need music," the King said, clapping his hands to summon the musicians, unaware of the mounting tension.

The troupe came and started playing their uds, gishgudis, chitaras, dizis, sodinas, and drums. Their melodies told tales of adventures and triumphs that transported Orberesis to his childhood, when he used to dream of fame, glory, and wealth. He recognised the songs, the lyrics, and the tunes.

It made him want to get up from his chair and dance without care, like the men and women from his village. He understood the King's yearning for something more, something to cheer for. Unfortunately, music only caused his migraines to worsen, these days, making it a bittersweet experience. Even the small, pleasant things the world had to offer had been taken away from him.

Orberesis looked around to the table and noticed the stern faces of all his guests. Sometimes they avoided eye contact with him, and when they didn't, they seemed to show no pleasure in being there. In truth, he wished he didn't have to be there either. He had waited for news of the elixir for weeks now. Not a single word. Ships had been sent. So, where was the news he sought? The samples he needed?

"What's the matter?" The King realised not everyone shared his festive mood.

Only the beautiful instruments playing in the background extinguished the silence he got in response.

"I asked a question."

One of Taishay's cronies shuffled in his seat, cleared his throat, and fiddled with his moustache. "Your Majesty," he started. "I can only speak for myself. I ask your forgiveness for my insolence, but this feels almost like a celebration, while... the Two Nations are still facing challenges."

"What do you mean?" Orberesis asked.

Taishay hesitated and fidgeted with his moustache. "There have been no more uprisings. The purge was very effective."

"Then what is the problem?" the King asked.

"But, Your Majesty, the people we purged were... prominent members of society. They were merchants, business owners, and landowners. With them gone, there's been hunger and disease in the kingdom. For example, in Yab, fishermen are turning to piracy. We're losing sea routes and getting plundered because of it."

"Prominent members of society? They were heretics, and they paid for their sins," Orberesis said. *They're trying to pin this on me.*

Taishay's eyes spewed anger. "I'm talking to His Majesty. Not you. And you would do well to stay silent. The purge was your idea, after all, *Highest One*. Now without the purged ones, those gaps in our society are being filled by criminals. Our industries are failing. No one wants to trade because of what we did. We can't sell our goods and we can't buy any of theirs! They're calling us a failed state."

"Well, it was the Highest One's suggestion. We shall replace the heretics with even better trade, commerce, and industry! We can do anything with the Highest One on our side, isn't that right, Thura?"

The Queen didn't share Doemus' enthusiasm and gave him only half a nod. For the first time in a while, Orberesis found himself wordless. They were cooking him. Throwing him into the fire and seasoning the boiling water. And there was little he could do to stop them.

Taishay's eyes were wide. The man looked like he had something important to say. "That is a splendid idea, Your Majesty, but there's a problem."

"Another one?" The King crossed his arms.

"Yes. Our financial situation. It's very regrettable, but our idea of the purge cost a lot of gold in the form of tax revenue. It did not leave us with much. We don't have enough to feed our paupers. I'm sure you've had the chance to hear about our citizens here in Ushar. Many of them are starving, many more have died from hunger and disease because we raised their taxes already. They were left with nothing."

Orberesis stiffened. "Can we tighten the belt further? Or perhaps increase our gold reserves?"

"Your so-called pilgrims have been an issue, Highest One." The general's words might as well have poison in them.

All the other councillors hummed and nodded.

"The pilgrims are protected by the Order of the Red Orb, Taishay. They have my blessing to be here," Doemus said. "Why have they been an issue?"

Orberesis swallowed. This was not how he wanted any of it to be going.

Taishay faced the King. "With all due respect, Your Majesty, the pilgrims are here. They are being fed by the Order with resources that could feed our people."

"The pilgrims *are* our people," Solvi spat.

Taishay turned to her. "Are they labouring? Do they pay taxes?"

Solvi clenched her hands and narrowed her eyebrows, but didn't respond, which meant the old buffoon was right. Orberesis felt the pressure mount.

"Like I was saying, Your Majesty," the old councillor said. "If we can't find a way for the kingdom to sustain itself, it might collapse altogether. We need more resources or more gold. But we have God Himself on our side, so perhaps he can perform a Miracle and help free us from this most burdensome situation."

Orberesis gripped the wineglass so tight he thought he'd break it. Everybody else at the table remained silent, expecting him to say something. They must be all thinking the same thing. Wasn't that why he was around? Why he'd been promoted to the governing council? After all, if he could do miracles, why would he choose to let his devout followers starve? He could not envision an answer that did not end with him drowning or losing his head. The thought left Orberesis almost shaking. He struggled to keep his composure in the chair.

"Miracles are hard to come by. They're complex. Difficult to perform. Just because I can perform them, it doesn't mean I'm able to do it all day, every day."

Doemus sighed, his joyous mood souring. Even doubt was starting to seep in. "I'll discuss this with the Highest One later. In private. Anything else, councillors, or we can we continue the banquet?"

Taishay cleared his throat. "There's also Alarkan, Highest One. I've yet to hear from the emissaries we sent. And the Highest One hasn't taken any action yet. Something must have happened."

Son of a bitch.

"The pineheads said the herald sent to the settlement disappeared, but I'm confident we are close to a full-fledged colony there. We will produce the elixir soon. I'm just waiting for word. What else do you suggest I do, Taishay? Allocate more resources there without knowing what the situation is? That would be unwise, don't you think? No. With soldiers enhanced by the elixir, we will save gold on warring efforts or we can just sell it and improve our financial situation. But we must be *patient.*"

"I'm inclined to agree with the Highest One, I suppose. The gold from the elixir or the elixir itself would be a welcome addition, indeed, but we already sent ships with settlers and soldiers."

Taishay could have snarled at him. The other councillors furrowed their brows and some clenched their hands. But if Orberesis had to wait for a sample, they also had to wait for the riches the elixir could provide. *Mind your own fucking business.*

Doemus turned to Orberesis again. "Do you think the herald deserted?"

Orberesis had no idea what had happened to the Herald, but to simply shrug and admit as much was inexcusable. He just didn't have the spies to obtain that kind of information yet. When he was about to make something up, Taishay spoke in his stead.

"They suspect he died along with his entourage. But there's more, Your Majesty. The rumours say someone attacked and destroyed our settlement. They even had a smokesmith."

Doemus couldn't help but widen his eyes. "Who... Who is behind this?"

Orberesis swallowed again, his lack of focus coming back to bite him. How did Taishay know all of this? That's what councillors did, he supposed. They governed and knew things.

Shit.

Taishay shrugged. "Savages. The ones running the export business for the elixir. They say they own the land, but they are just that — savages."

Orberesis ground his teeth and scratched his chin. If that roll of bad news was true, he was *far* from getting the elixir, and there was no guarantee it would help, anyway. What was he even doing here, playing thrones with these fools? He had to find a way to salvage this, somehow, while he still had the King's trust and faith. Perhaps this was the perfect opportunity to fix everything. Alarkan was the key. It had the elixir he needed and the resources the Two Nations needed. All they had to do was seize it from the savages. He could keep waiting for news or for the ships to come back with the samples, but he couldn't endure the suffering for much longer and the other councillors were doing a damn good job at destroying his reputation with the King. Must he chase the elixir himself?

"Your Majesty, it seems we all agree the Alarkani elixir would help our finances. It could be the solution to many of our issues, isn't that right, Taishay?"

Taishay sighed and nodded in acceptance. "Perhaps... But I maintain that if the Highest One could do a miracle on our behalf..."

"How dare you!" Solvi erupted, her chair falling to the ground. "How dare you ask the Miraculous One to use his divine powers!"

"Let's calm ourselves," Orberesis said. As much as he enjoyed watching Solvi restraining herself not to behead the old fool, he needed civility, not chaos. "This isn't the time to be pitted against each other. Your Majesty. Let me pursue this avenue of the elixir. I know Alarkan. I created the place, after all. Just say the words."

Doemus sighed and scratched his chin. "It seems like what was supposed to be a joyful banquet has turned into another governing council meeting. I'd like to discuss this with the Highest One. Thura will stay, but the rest of you will leave us."

They bowed as they left the ceremonial room.

"I accept your proposal, Highest One. In truth, I just wanted some peace. I don't like how divided the council seems to be. It reminds me of my mother's governments." Doemus waved a servant to bring him a large folder stacked with bursting papers. "I was hoping I could share with you my interest in scholarly matters."

Orberesis could see the disdain in the Queen's eyes as she tried to hide it with a sip from the wine glass. Her eyes rolled inside the eyelids.

Orberesis picked up a glass of wine too. Anything to get the King in his good graces again. "I can't count myself as a scholar of any kind, but I'm your councillor, Your Majesty. I'm here for whatever you need. If what you need is a friendly ear, I'm here. Spiritual counsel is my specialty."

Doemus scratched his head. He kept the papers in the folder. "These are my studies. It shouldn't be a secret to you at this point how much pleasure I find in the company of books. Mother thought nothing of it. Nothing of anything I was interested in, in fact."

"And what is your field of study?" Orberesis asked.

His head pounded.

His future as a councillor was in jeopardy, with people trying to kill him.

The elixir was probably still in another corner of the world and his best friend had started resenting him.

He didn't give a shit. *The things I put myself through.*

"I grew up in the Palace of Brilliance. I have lived nowhere else. This city feels like my home. It always has. But since I was a child, the history of the city has always interested me. We know so little about it and its relation to the Ancient Ones, who built the city, as you well know."

"I see. What do you find interesting about it?"

"Let me answer that question with a question of my own, Highest One, if I may?"

Orberesis nodded.

"Have you found Ushar different from other cities?"

"I suppose I have."

"Many things about this city make no sense, though. The Ancient Ones dug up the ground and built canals, but for what? No water runs in them. Certain roads are too large, with avenues of massive trees that still stand to this day. No other part of the world has those things. I find it interesting that *nobody* knows why they built Ushar this way. There must be a reason! The scholars always look for clues left behind by the Ancient Ones. Several schools of thought exist.... My apologies, Highest One. I'm boring you."

Yes, indeed. "Not at all. Please continue."

Doemus nodded and cleared his throat.

"The key clue was the art," he said as he pointed at a painting on the wall, depicting two warriors—a man and a woman—about to face each other in combat. "That painting tells a very common story found in paintings, pottery, tapestries, and even poems by famous poets such as Eimorcreba, Nosrednas, and Nitram. It's the myth of Mother Nature and Father Time."

Orberesis' eyes widened. He had heard of those, but he let Doemus continue, the passion flaring in his eyes; the confidence building up in his speech.

"Mother Nature and Father Time are battling and all the stories told show them in a constant, almost eternal struggle. Different schools of thought propose different ways to interpret this. The Balancist Theory interprets their constant battling as a metaphor for a balance where one can never overpower the other. When Time passes, it takes away. But Nature grows things back. I believe it's a beautiful balance, and it tells me that the Ancient Ones wouldn't have built Ushar in this manner at random."

"That is an interesting thought, Your Majesty," Orberesis said. He had never cared much for studies and schooling. He found it all an *enormous* waste of time, the whims of spoiled rich, bearded fools. "But you mentioned other theories?"

Doemus nodded. "War Theory scholars corrupt the myth of Father Time and Mother Nature into something I find untrue. They claim the tale to be an inspiration for war, that the legend shows humankind can only continue to progress if they compete and wage war against one another. They think the Ancient Ones built Ushar like this because they could, because they wanted to surpass themselves and their rivals."

Orberesis had to contain a scowl. If these people were good at something, it was at using art and books to justify atrocities. He turned his attention to Thura. "And what about you, Your Majesty? What do you believe?"

Thura scoffed, as if she was putting on a show. "I think they are both wrong."

Even Doemus seemed surprised at that answer. "How so?"

"Mother Nature and Father Time fell in love after millions of years of infinite wars. They stopped their wars so that we could now have peace. Time is smooth in its course and Nature lives long and slowly decays. Humanity can only live and thrive when people let themselves follow love. With love, people can do anything."

Thura picked up a glass and stood there, proud, facing them. Even their bodyguard nodded a short and vehement nod of approval.

"Perhaps your theory could be the Love Theory. You could start the Lovist school," Orberesis said, trying not to cringe at his own words.

"I think I'll leave the studies to my husband," she said. She wrapped her arms around Doemus while he stood as if she had caught him by surprise. Orberesis noticed a tension there, between the two.

"Drink with us, Highest One," Doemus said, getting rid of Thura's arm. "To new ventures in Alarkan."

Orberesis lifted his glass and chugged its content, hiding a migraine flare. Pound. Pound. Pound. At every heartbeat,

"May I trouble you, Your Majesty?" Orberesis said, summoning a regal tone again.

"Of course! What is it?"

"I realise I'm still not in the favour of some of the governing councillors and I wonder if there's anything I can do to appeal to the people's faith more. If my people are not with me, then I lose my purpose. Is there anything I can do?"

"Miraculous One," Thura started. "If I may?"

Oh?

Orberesis nodded.

"Why not go into the city?" she asked. "Show yourself to the people and show the governing council just how much they love you. Let the citizens see you in the flesh, among them. Thousands of pilgrims are here for you, anyway. Let them see the divine red orb."

That did not sound like a bad idea, but the fact that it came from Thura left him slightly worried. He'd never pegged her as a believer at all.

"Do you agree with the Queen, Your Majesty?"

"I find it a great idea, as long as you're well protected, Highest One. You would need many guards and perhaps worship leaders from the Order as well."

It wouldn't accomplish anything, but this was his life now. Parading himself like a fool for other fools to see. The headaches would continue and so would his utter need to keep them tame. Why was it that when you tried solving a problem, others unfolded and demanded you solve them first? He needed a cure for his illness, but for that, the elixir was the only solution. He might not get to try it at all, though, unless he stayed cosy with the King, but that might not be possible unless he mitigated the threat that Taishay and other councillors posed. He couldn't have Solvi kill them, though. No, too much. What then? A fucking parade. If Thura had tried to humiliate him, this had been a genius move.

"That sounds like something I could do," he said, cursing himself at every word that left his mouth.

Nineteen
A Whistle in the Air

Orberesis

*E*mpty *promises take every breath I still have.*

— From *Mother's Memories*

The winter winds appeared in the morning, but Orberesis refused to wear anything other than his white silk robe. It made him look more... Godly. And he needed all the divinity he could muster when his head pounded with the might of a blacksmith's hammer on the anvil that was his skull. *Is it me or are they getting worse?* He held on close to the pendant around his neck and wished the orb to do something. He didn't need another miracle, but if the orb did something to help him keep the city-dwellers entertained, everything would be easier.

Orberesis went out to the city inside the circle of soldiers and worship leaders who controlled the crowds. It didn't take long for word about his descent to the city to spread.

He waved at the women peering outside their windows to see him. The merchants kneeled, and he waved again. When a fishmonger offered him his best fish, Orberesis contained a chuckle and waved as well.

"All hail the Orb Bearer!" someone chanted. The words reverberated through Ushar as he walked the streets. Behind him, a small procession followed. They wanted to see him, to be as close to him as possible. Crying mothers held babies for him to bless.

How can these people have so much faith?

It was still daunting, so many willing to accept him as their god, their saviour, when he was still fighting to save himself. He was a survivor first, and he would let people believe what they wanted to believe if that meant he lasted another day.

Reality set in fast and he knew what the councillors meant. The rotten teeth, the bony faces and limbs. There were large groups of mud-marked children with soil caked on their dishevelled hair. A strong stench of shit and piss emanated from the alleyways leading up to the road he was in as well. It asked for no permission to invade the nostrils. So many people, living in absolute filth.

Ushar was a beautiful city with so much history and ancient architecture. Now it was becoming... degraded, so depleted.

He almost blamed himself, but no, he had been in their shoes, too. He used to be the one running away from the smokesmiths so they wouldn't turn him into one of them. He used to fight hounds for the leftovers and steal garbage just to feed himself. People like those around him now had given him nothing but beatings. They set him up to die before he could grow a beard.

Orberesis continued down the slope, blinking as the migraine blurred his vision. He tried to forget the instinct to feel remorse and guilt for lying to them.

Soon, he reached one of Ushar's main squares, where the ancient bronze statue of an ancient king riding a shadesgrowl stood at least thirty feet tall, dwarfing everything else in sight. The square was large enough to hold about one third of Ushar's population. Perhaps he would put that to the test now with his procession.

An immense crowd of thousands gathered in the square. On his left, Tavanar furrowed his brow. He barked orders at the soldiers to strengthen the security circle. They wouldn't risk letting diseased peasants cross and reach him to ask for a blessing or something of the sort. But even with all those soldiers around Orberesis, it intimidated him. If devotion was this overwhelming, he had no intention of being reminded of hatred.

Despite the noise, Orberesis heard a whistle cut the air. Suddenly, the whispering intensified and ended just as an arrow skidded over the stone floor, right in front of him, not two feet away.

Orberesis froze, and the world around him turned into a blur. Solvi embraced him and covered him with guards to serve as shields. Her voice strained in panic and utter devotion. Her shouts were primal enough to scare anyone who was still around there.

"Archers! Protect God Himself!"

Again.

There it was again.

Where did that arrow come from? He looked for the culprits. And the orb hadn't reacted either. He grabbed it as if for reassurance, but once again, felt nothing.

Why didn't it protect me?

His hand clasped the orb. In the chaos, he could never trust no one would steal it, even with the metal pendant supporting it. Even with guards around him. Tavanar, however, hesitated, fearing for his own life.

Some friend...

Petrified, Orberesis let Solvi and the three soldiers shielding him act as guides on where to go, where to take cover. Fear flooded his mind and took over as a million questions arose.

He had *almost* died again. And he could still die unless they found the assassins.

The crowd vanished in a trampling sea of chaos. The impetuous rushing stampede of the people looking for safety was followed by screams and yelps. If someone was trying to kill God Himself, how could *they* be safe?

"Search the rooftops! Find the assassins!"

Solvi picked up the arrow. It looked greasy, with a green and purple hue. She brought it close to her nose. "It's poisonous..."

Orberesis shrugged with a mix of shock and panic. He could think of a million people who would dare try to kill him yet again.

His body shook. It was the most ungodly he had ever looked. If the peasants had seen him like that, they would lose faith.

But whoever the assassins were, they would curse themselves for missing.

TWENTY
THE ONLY SOLUTION

ORBERESIS

I hear voices. Conversations I've never had. They guide me through pain.

— From *Mother's Memories*

Orberesis moved from side to side in the silky bed sheets, but they provided no comfort, and neither did the gentle servant hands that caressed his arm and back. He ignored it, just as he had for the past few hours. His head burned and pulsed, as if it was going to explode. But also like a tapping knife, slowly serrating his skull from within. Two assassination attempts already and he was no closer to finding a cure.

He froze. The councillors would raise questions. The King. How could a god be so human? So killable?

Perhaps the assassin had been pondering those questions, too.

He wished Solvi was lying next to him, to comfort him. Caress him. Tell him she'd protect him and kill his enemies. All he could think about was the arrow that nearly got stuck in him and the orb which hadn't worked when he needed it most. Everything was in jeopardy again, and he had no way of knowing what else the failed assassin could be planning.

He had already purged the city, so what was he supposed to do now?

He reached inside his nightgown, pulled out the perfect red orb and inspected it. Why wouldn't it work when he needed it? For a moment, he even considered throwing it away, covering himself in a cloak and escaping, but he knew what life was like for exiles and refugees. And what of his maladies? He would rather get killed by a flying arrow than go back to the miserable life he'd lived. Orberesis needed to figure out who it was that the purge had missed. If they were brave enough to try and kill him in plain sight, perhaps they wouldn't shy away from trying something much worse.

He removed his nightgown, put on his white silk robe, and combed his hair, then opened the doors of his quarters and left.

"Distance," he said to the four armoured soldiers posted outside the room. "You shall not approach me unless you're protecting me from imminent danger."

"Yes, Highest One."

Orberesis couldn't help but feel threatened. Even the walls looked like they could hide invisible men ready to strike him. Even his mind seemed to be trying to overthrow him from the inside out.

He shook himself and hurried, always making sure the guards stayed at a distance. He strolled through the hallways and was relieved to find that the soldiers had cleared them as he commanded.

He was the first to arrive at the council room. It was still early and he hadn't been able to sleep. He took a seat in his large, ornamented chair, and the guards stood on both sides. And he pushed away the bottle of wine, despite the headaches.

The governing councillors arrived all together in animated chatter and sat in their normal seats. He wondered if they were making a mockery of him in their local dialects. Solvi came in after them, eyes puffed in sleeplessness and dark rings around them. Tavanar on her tail.

"Good morning, Highest One," one of the councillors said.

Orberesis still didn't know his name and simply gave him a nod. Instead, he looked down at the table in front of him. The King came in last, the Queen holding his arm and guiding him through the halls. Guards all over them. Once everyone sat, he shifted his eyes to see them.

"Do we have news about the assassin?" the King asked.

Solvi cleared her throat. "I've been all night with the best trackers in Sirestir, Your Majesty. Trying to find the archer. They are still searching with their bloodsleuths. We will find whoever was responsible for this horrific attempt on the Highest One."

"Yes, you will. Gather the best archers in the Two Nations and investigate anyone skilled enough with the bow to try that shot."

The King looked pale. Did he blame himself for what had happened? Orberesis doubted the man was capable of anything other than navel-gazing and talking about histories no one cared about. The more he thought about the archer and the assassination attempt, the more he realised it didn't matter. Someone had ordered it, but perhaps finding the archer was key in discovering who had been behind it. Killing someone wasn't cheap and killing God Himself would certainly cost even more than the average person. It had to be someone with access to archers or enough money to convince one to shoot the arrow.

"Highest One, if I may?" the grey-haired councillor asked after adjusting himself in the chair.

Orberesis nodded.

"Many people have yet to experience your grandeur. There were hundreds of witnesses to your miracle. You also showed your might when you took care of the assassin. Your worship leaders have written their accounts multiple times. It is clear we are looking at God Himself, but even if many of the commoners believe it, they have yet to see it."

Orberesis grimaced. They were trying to deflect the attention from the *real* culprits. "Are you suggesting it was a poor ragged man who did this?"

The moustache man shrugged. "I'm suggesting no such thing. It's just that... There's a lot of poverty, hunger, and disease in Ushar. And we... purged the not-so-poor folk."

So that means it must have been someone in the palace, you fool.

"Clearly, we didn't purge it enough," Solvi said.

The councillor adjusted himself in his chair, his hands twitching once again, but said nothing.

Orberesis sighed.

The King was quiet and looked down at the papers in front of him. "I am sorry that I didn't prevent this from happening. Assassinations aren't common and they are even hard to predict. I hope we can find the culprit and bring him to swift justice."

He wished to break the earth once more, but the fucking red orb just wouldn't work at his will. It wouldn't surprise him if he and the rest of Taishay's cronies had ordered the assassination, but he couldn't halt everything just to find the assassin and those who filled the pockets. He needed to plan his next move.

He needed the elixir.

....

In the comfort of his quarters, Orberesis took a deep breath. "I'm going to end up dying here, sooner or later. I'm sitting in the palace and that isn't deterring them from trying to kill me. I want to go to Alarkan myself."

Tavanar swallowed as he rested his boots on top of the large table. "Do you have a plan?"

He assessed his old friend. Was Tavanar still a friend? Their relationship had turned sour of late. They no longer drank together. Laughed together. Tavanar looked colder to him, now. But if he wasn't trusting his oldest friend, then who would he trust?

"The Two Nations are scarce in resources right now. At least that's what Taishay says. All of his cronies are saying we need to get gold or resources. The kingdom needs the elixir as much as I do, just for different reasons. It just so happens that stupid island is where it comes from. I'm going to ask the King for more ships and more soldiers so that we can take the place. We already have a settlement there with soldiers. It's probably not hard to conquer. There is no one there but savages."

"Are you sure?"

"From what Taishay said, they are farmers, refugees, and exiles."

"That sounds crazy to me," Tavanar said, scratching his head. "Crazy to think no one has tried to conquer it."

"But it makes sense. Everyone thought it was worthless land, filled with nothing but insects and mud. That's what I assumed, too. It was the shithole where those with nothing left to lose ran off to die. Who would want to seize a place like that? Now the elixir changes everything. I suspect not many people know about it yet, which is why we should be first."

Tavanar nodded. "That's true. But I have inspected the Sirestine army and I can tell you it leaves much to be desired. It was as if they didn't have enough practice. The useful ones were those posted at the borders. That makes sense, given how everyone knows the Two Nations for its trading routes."

Perhaps Tavanar was right. But he needed the elixir, something that he could show his people. And most importantly, it was an excuse to get out of there and find the cure for himself on the king's coin. "I think we could storm the island. Take their land. Take their elixir. If it goes well, I'll be cured and the Two Nations will start producing the elixir. Become healthy again and rich while we're at it. We've got the ships and the manpower. We can do it."

"You make it sound so simple."

"Perhaps the savages are even devout, who knows?"

"I don't imagine I can say anything to convince you of how delusional you sound," Tavanar said, grinning.

"Delusional? It's a realistic plan. Plus, I have to get out of here now, while the King still holds any kind of faith in me and is agreeable enough to give me resources. I thought we could stay here and live like lords while we wait for the elixir to come, but it has been a hurricane of trouble and we're drifting. And you saw the pilgrims yourself. They all love me for reasons that I still don't understand, but they do. It's got to mean something, right?"

Tavanar chuckled. "Aren't you forgetting something?"

"What?"

"Your assassin, you dimwit! How about you solve that one first? Perhaps the one who shot the arrow came in, hiding among your beloved pilgrims."

An icy fear slithered through him as he realised that was a possibility.

"No," he shook his head. "I have my suspicions about who is responsible. If I'm right, it won't take long until I get this settled."

"I assume you will not tell me."

"Not yet. There's something I need to find out first."

"Well, don't take too long, if you really want to go to Alarkan, that is. The other councillors will try to block the King from giving you the ships and the soldiers, as they do with everything you do. If you want to send troops to the other side of the fucking world, we need to prepare for such a journey. And we need to explain the decision pretty damn well."

Tavanar was right, of course, but Orberesis' plan made sense. He would find the assassin and convince the King after that.

TWENTY-ONE
STORMBANE

ORBERESIS

*T*he hilt of my sword is one with my hand. The blade has the blood of the cardinal red. Of the old dead Sun.

— From *Mother's Memories*

Orberesis sat on his chair. The mighty piece of wood was ancient, glittering with gems and other metalwork crafted in intricate ways no longer known to humanity. He would soon say goodbye to it, which left a bittersweet taste in his mouth. He hadn't achieved anything, just left a trail of dead bodies and failed attempts at finding a cure for his illness. Now he was leaving, like a coward.

Silence filled the Ceremonial Room, something eerie about it. It was the only proper room to handle important business. He wasn't the king, but his right-hand councillor. He wasn't *powerless*.

Instead of calling the court and the city's merchant class as the King would have, Orberesis summoned a smaller group, including King Doemus and Queen Thura and the rest of the governing council. He had soldiers and servants—his true friends—in all corners of the room, watching the doors and windows. Doemus and Thura wore tight, beautiful, gowns, and she held his right arm. The two councillors that always backed Taishay looked uncomfortable. Tavanar wore his practical black garb, the same shade as Solvi's robe.

"Solvi?" he asked with a tender smile. "Would you be so kind?"

Solvi bowed, smiled, and rose to her feet. "Certainly, Highest One," she said.

She took off at a quick pace, marching across the room towards the doors. The long red carpet muffled her boots. The guards opened the doors for her, and Orberesis waited for her return without uttering another word.

"You haven't told us yet what this is about, Highest One," the King said.

"Soon, Your Majesty. Very soon. I beg your patience."

Solvi returned with two guards, dragging a man by the arms. He was strong and well-built. A strange brown sack covered his head and the strong iron cuffs tied to his hands and feet rattled, shattering the silence into pieces.

The guards tossed him to the floor, and he landed on his chest and shoulders, uttering a guttural cry of pain.

Solvi nodded and walked a few steps until she was close to the man. She grabbed him by his shirt, pulled him up to his knees, and removed the sack from his head. Before looking at the man's face, Orberesis glanced at the King, the Queen, and the councillors, fishing for an unintended reaction. Then he allowed himself to see the prisoner.

It was the guard. The same man with the crossbow who had rushed to the first assassin. A man who had been near him countless times for months on end. A man he thought he trusted. He was brown-skinned like most in Sirestir, with neck-long dark hair and a stubble of a few days. More obvious were the bruises on his face. There would be more after Solvi's interrogation.

"This is the man who fired the arrow at you, Highest One."

Muffled gasps took over the room. Guards and the guests—they all knew him.

"Is he? And how did you find him?" Orberesis asked.

"It was hard, but our trackers are superb. We used the arrow to let the bloodsleuths follow the scent."

"Is there any doubt he is the right man?"

Solvi shook her head. "It's him, Highest One."

"Interesting," Orberesis said. Nothing showed on the man's face. He knew what his fate would be. But he was also hiding something.

"He is an archer. He used to be a captain at the western border, before being posted at the Palace. Isn't that right, Taishay?"

Taishay swallowed. "That's right."

Orberesis' brow rose. "A traitor, then."

The archer shot him a deadly stare and spat on the ground in front of him. "I am no traitor, you greasy coward!"

"Verbal offence to a governing councillor. Punishable," Orberesis said.

The guard smacked him in the head with the heavy steel gauntlet, but he continued as if he could feel no pain. "You were lucky, you spineless lizard. A gust of wind saved you. It was the first arrow I missed in years, from that distance."

"Oh, he confesses!" Orberesis said, hiding the chill those words had caused him, knowing how close he had been to the end. "And he seems like a talented archer too. What's his name?"

"Rarder," Solvi said.

"Rarder," Orberesis repeated. A *proper* Sirestine name. Judging by the way he carried himself and spoke, he must be from a prominent family, too. Even better. "Who paid you to kill me?"

"He wouldn't say, Highest One, even though we asked in different ways."

"Nobody paid me. I would never take money to kill a bastard like you who has put the realm in jeopardy and weakened the King's resolve. I did it with pleasure. For the Two Nations," he said, spitting once again at Orberesis' feet and getting another swift smack in the head.

"That is very brave of you, Rarder, but why do you hate me so much? What have I done to you?"

"You are darkness. You sow discord and reap destruction."

"I'm touched," Orberesis said, coming out of his chair and taking the four steps into the place where the man was. "Very interesting, indeed. You think you know me, Rarder. It takes great wisdom or great stupidity to be that confident. Of course, I did my research on him as well, Your Majesty."

The man tensed but remained silent.

"Well, what did you find?" the King asked.

Orberesis turned to Rarder again. "It seems like your job as an army captain ended and you came to Ushar to serve as the archery instructor for new recruits. How am I doing so far?"

Rarder remained silent, so Orberesis continued. He'd deployed all his servants to gather this information. It didn't even take that long.

"After years of fighting border disputes, you were ready to pass your experience and knowledge to the youth. You were very good at it, Rarder! You were so popular they would sometimes even allow you inside the Palace of Brilliance. What an honour it must have been. You mingled well with royalty, because your wonderful parents raised you right, didn't they?"

"Don't you use your filthy mouth to talk about my parents."

"But you were too ambitious, wouldn't you say? It's tough to navigate the court. Everybody is richer than you. And your commendable military achievements hold little significance in a country that treats merchants as if they are kings, isn't that right? But there was someone who saw through all of that. Someone who cared for you. Someone who saw you for yourself."

Orberesis gave Solvi a nod, and she produced a dagger from underneath her tunic and grabbed Rarder by the scalp, exposing his neck, where the sharp edge of the blade rested.

"But notice how everyone is quiet now that you face consequences. Now that you stand here, accused. Why does nobody save you?"

"I don't know what the fuck you're talking about."

Orberesis smiled at the lie. Honourable men always made terrible liars, and they were always the first to die because of it.

"Oh, you *know* who I'm talking about," Orberesis said, turning to another guard. "Bring her to me."

One guard loyal to Orberesis—a devout follower—marched forward and hesitated in front of Thura, before grabbing her by the arm.

"Highest One, what—what is this? Doemus?" she asked, her face turning pale.

"Highest One. What is the meaning of this? That's the Queen!" Doemus turned to the guard who held Thura's arm. "Do not touch the Queen or I'll have your head."

"She did a lot more than you realise, Your Majesty. I'll explain everything" Orberesis said with unmasked contempt, then turned to Rarder. "Would you die for the Queen, Rarder?"

"Of course I would. She was the queen before you showed up and ruined everything. And she still is. I would die for her."

"Would you kill for her?"

The man was silent.

The guard stopped but Thura and Rarder exchanged looks. Orberesis saw the love and all the pain in those eyes.

"I have to admit, Rarder. Before I showed up, your plan was brilliant. You seduced the Queen and had plotted something to get rid of the King, didn't you? Long before I arrived."

"Nonsense!" shouted the Queen. "Doemus?"

The King remained silent. Curious. Orberesis continued.

"You are from an excellent family. You are a well-respected war veteran, so you could gain the favour and the respect of the army generals. The navy and the army would side with you and start martial law if necessary. No one would find it strange if Thura picked you as the King-regent after Doemus was dead. There are no heirs, so you could still give her one. Everything was perfect for you."

"Liar!" Rarder screamed, but his eyes said otherwise. Orberesis had discovered the affair a while ago, after his servants pointed out the figures hiding in the hallways, but it was only when he asked them for more information that Rarder's background started making more sense.

"I thought you said you were an honourable man. Where was your honour then? You're just a traitor to your king. To the Two Nations," Orberesis asked.

He then turned to Thura, who wept still under the guard's strong grip.

"Lies! All lies..." Thura whimpered.

"You were ready to let His Majesty die for a stronger, younger man. Perhaps His Majesty's blindness isn't natural. I wonder if we'll find evidence of any poisons or herb extracts in your quarters. Anyway, your plan was going rather well, but then I showed up and *everything* changed, didn't it? When His Majesty brought me into the governing council, you didn't expect it. And you were ashamed. His faith is stronger than any pull you might have on him. You felt shunned. Perhaps if I was dead, everything would go back to normal. And you knew His Majesty is a truly devout man, so I needed to go. So, you had to turn to the best man you knew to finish me. The only man you could trust. Your one and only gallant bodyguard. Your conspirator."

"He lies!" Thura shouted, a mess of tears and snot.

"Truth. He hired the assassin and was right there to take the body away so no one could tie it back to him. When that didn't work, you even convinced me it was a good idea to take a stroll into the city so that I would expose myself. The perfect shot for Rarder to be your hero, but he missed. You fooled everyone; I'll admit as much."

Digging all this out had required a lot of cautious investigating from servants that were now loyal to him. Planted in the Queen's quarters and all around the palace. Servants talked. The gossip spread and Thura had a reputation for governing the palace with an iron fist. No one hesitated too much when telling the truth about her. Granted, not everything he'd said was a guaranteed fact. But a few leaps in logic here and there. A few assumptions... and they'd think he'd seen through all the deceit.

"You ruined everything," Thura said. "You repulse me, you monster. Vile excuse of a human being."

There it was. The confession. No more evidence needed.

"Thura?" The King was dumbfounded, immobile like a statue. "You plotted the assassination attempts? And you've been poisoning me? Making me blind?"

Orberesis addressed Thura. "Do you want to know what your mistake was?"

She eyed him with watery eyes.

"You let your ambitions cloud your judgement. You were so convinced no one knew about your torrid affair with the bodyguard that you never thought there was any danger in convincing him to take a shot at me for your sake, for his, and for the country's. But the Palace of Brilliance is rather large. The walls can hear things. They host hundreds of invisible people who never really liked you. See, I like to surround myself with servants. I like their company. I like their presence. They're good people and they know more about what is happening than you would think. If it wasn't for them, I would have never known you and Rarder were meeting like young lovebirds behind everyone's backs. Now what happens to you two is His Majesty's decision."

Orberesis felt a weight being lifted from his shoulders, but emotions were still running high, and he couldn't let himself rest. Thura's wallowing continued and Rarder's resigned face froze as he faced the floor. Doemus was still shaking, and his face muscles twitching hard.

"Adultery I can tolerate. But murderous plots, vengeance, and treachery I cannot. It pains me to admit the evidence for all this is very sadly compelling." The King stuttered, as though he was still processing all of this.

The other councillors stood like marble statues, not daring to say a word or move a muscle. Orberesis wondered if they had other schemes and plots going on the side. They certainly didn't seem innocent, though he'd found no evidence against them.

The King hesitated, his lips wavering, and walked over to a guard. "Your sword. Give it to me."

The guard unsheathed the blade and placed it in the King's hand. "Bring me to this treacherous bastard."

The guard walked the King to where Rarder knelt. A snarled formed on the monarch's face. "Any last words?" he spat.

"You are a fucking momma's boy, still clinging on to her skirts even though she is long gone. You've brought nothing but ruin to the realm, bathed it in filth with your incompetence. You are blind now, but you have long been *blind*, you absolute—"

"No!" Thura let out a bone-chilling squeal.

Doemus' blade pierced Rarder's chest and Rarder gurgled in pain. The King pulled the blade away from Rarder's chest and, in a terrible rage, cut the man with a harsh downward strike, as though he held an axe and was chopping wood, blood splattering all over him and the guards.

Once he was done, he threw the sword onto the floor and knelt, panting. Blood now stained his formal apparel, and he wheezed in a gruesome blend of pain, exhaustion, anxiety, and trauma. "Arrest her," he whispered, his face becoming a pool of tears and snot. His eyes blanked as he cried.

Thura's knees dropped to the cold floor, and she sobbed.

"Doemus, no! Please. I'm sorry. I'll be better. I'll retire to my father's estates. Please."

The King didn't honour her with a response and two guards escorted her from the room at a hurried pace.

Orberesis took a deep breath, too. Again, the weight vanished from his shoulders. Now he could focus on his most important task yet—getting the elixir.

"I'm sorry I kept this from you, Your Majesty. I had to be absolutely sure of it."

The King didn't reply, which made Orberesis swallow. Doemus got up, wiped his eyes, his nose and his mouth and cleared his throat. "I know I don't always understand faith and what it means to believe in something. In someone. I do have faith in you, Highest One, but it is tested every day. Challenged every day. And I have the Two Nations to govern."

Shit. Orberesis fiddled with the orb, anticipating what the King would say. "Of course, Your Majesty. I don't envy you."

Doemus was still a nervous wreck, not knowing what to do with his hands. "I need to focus on what my government needs, which is why I decided it's best if you take on another role for the realm. I'm rescinding your position on the governing council, but as a token of my faith and appreciation for all you've done here, I've decided to take you upon your offer. I'm deploying you to Alarkan to seize the elixir from the savages who hold it."

"But, Your Majesty—" Taishay said.

The King snarled, wiping a smudge of blood off his face. "No. Not now."

Excitement washed over Orberesis. The King was acting as though this was a punishment for all the trouble he'd caused. Yes, Orberesis would like to have a wealthy life at some point, but he was tired of the farce, of not being able to be himself. Of the bloody migraines. The past ten years had been a never-ending cycle of thinking he was close to a cure and never finding one. The elixir was the last one left. Now he could finally go and get it himself.

"I understand, Your Majesty. I will not disappoint you." Orberesis could not promise that, just as he could not promise miracles. "I will seize the elixir and we will sell it to support our nation. Use it to strengthen our armies and destroy our enemies. I will issue a warning to all the countries with settlements there that they must leave by the time we arrive, or our forces will crush them. The elixir shall be ours and ours only."

....

Orberesis arrived at Ushar's monumental harbour and enjoyed the breeze caressing his face. The smell of the sea blended with the scents of rotten fish, piss, and shit from sailors and other drifters. There was rare excitement in his heart. After several weeks of preparations, it was ready. Fifteen enormous monsters of wood and steel floated in the waves as if they owned them.

The Floating City Fleet.

Or part of it, since the other vessels had been too far away to be a part of this campaign. He was going to do this. He would sail to the unknown land he had created and seize the elixir, take over the resources, and give the Two Nations the wealth and prowess it should have always had. If luck was on his side, the elixir would heal his headaches.

The opportunity to sail in one of those gargantuan nine-mast vessels didn't hurt either. He had longed for it since he was a child.

"The ships are prepared, Highest One," Solvi said. Her smile never failed to lift his mood. Or perhaps he was just happier than usual. She had a purpose now. Something to look forward to—being at his side. And how he longed for that. Tavanar stood right next to her, less thrilled about the trip, although he recognised the opportunity outweighed the risk.

Orberesis nodded.

"Right this way," Solvi said.

She guided him to a small rowboat that would lead to the large fleet. As he jumped on the small wooden vessel, he felt it shaking with the added weight. Tavanar and Solvi joined him as two slaves rowed towards the largest ship of all.

"Am I the last one to board?" Orberesis asked without lifting his eyes off the massive ship.

"Yes, Highest One. We didn't want to keep you waiting. All the crews are ready, and they prepared the fleet to sail."

Orberesis smiled. The winter wind blew, lifting his hair about his shoulders. No bloody migraine in sight. That was almost a miracle in itself. The ships appeared even larger as the rowboat edged closer to them. They could hold hundreds of crew members and tons of cargo on journeys that could last years.

"What a beauty," Orberesis said without taking his eyes off the leading vessel.

"*Stormbane*, that's her name," Tavanar said.

Stormbane, he thought. *How fitting.*

There was no doubt a ship as large and strong as *Stormbane* could resist the worst storms with ease.

Once they arrived at the ship, someone threw a rope ladder and Tavanar and Solvi held it tight as Orberesis climbed. Once he reached the top, a crowd welcomed him with bows. Many of the sailors even kneeled and others refused to look at him out of respect. A short, stocky man with coarse arms and hands reached out to him. Orberesis identified him by the round hat he wore and his drooping moustache—a tradition among ship captains.

"All hail God Himself," the captain said. "On behalf of the *Stormbane*'s crew, we hope you have a pleasant journey. We would like to have your blessing, Highest One. For the trip."

Sailors had always been superstitious.

"Get up, my good captain," Orberesis said, picking up his rough hands. "What is your name?"

"Captain Chamas, Highest One. At your disposal, as is the crew."

"Well met, Captain Chamas," he said, as Tavanar and Solvi joined him.

"Would it be too much if you could say a few words before we raise anchor?"

"Absolutely not," Orberesis said, clearing his throat and raising his voice. "My dear crew, I bless you and your loved ones. As God Himself, I will ensure we reach our destination safely."

"Thank you, Highest One," the Captain said, as if he still expected something.

"I can promise this trip will be without trouble." The words slipped out of him and a slight pent-up tension turned into an aching flair at his temples.

He could promise no such thing. No one controlled the weather and sailors were fools for believing *he* could.

TWENTY-TWO
PROMISES

GIMLORE

*P*lease, *if clarity is no longer a choice, then mercy.*

— From *Mother's Memories*

Gimlore stood behind the counter holding a bottle of wine. Her clothes stuck to her skin with sweat. Blood, dirt, and ashes caked her hair. A thousand minor cuts and scratches made her want to peel the entire skin off and get on with it, but those were easy to clean. The hole in her chest, however...

She poured another shot of the liquor and downed it in an instant, but it didn't numb the pain. How does one numb a phantom pain? She passed a shaking hand over the tough wooden counter while the other one held the bottle.

At least she still had the Maiden's Hall, her most prized possession. It was everything she had dreamt of since she was a child. A place that felt like a home. That *was* her home. Now that Edmir was gone, what was the point of having a cosy place to sleep at night? What good was that if she lost those she cared about?

Wherever she looked, she saw him. Behind the counter, pouring drinks, wiping the tables, carrying food around, or even trying in vain to teach Tinko and Thata some manners. The stupid man was the heart and soul of her operation. The steady force behind everything she did.

She glanced across the counter. Nork and Nosema looked a little worse than her. Instead of their uneasiness and twitchy demeanour, they were even more quiet than usual. They looked as if they had the floor swept from under them.

She had failed them, too.

Foloi sat at the edge of his chair, eager to speak. Gimlore was ready to smash the bottle on his head if he dared open his mouth. She might have survived the Sirestine settlers for now, but if she was going to keep this operation, she would need to change something. But what?

She jumped over the counter to sit at the table, and someone knocked on the door. Nork stood and everyone reached for their weapons.

"Who is it?" Nork asked.

"It's me," Keryon's familiar voice sounded from the other side. Everyone put their knives away and Nork opened the door. The new warden walked in, still covered in soot and dirt. He still looked like a majestic thunderbuck in his prime. Men didn't deserve to look like that.

"May I?"

"You're already here." Gimlore said, rougher than she should be. If only he had got to Edmir earlier... "Sorry. Yes, come in."

He nodded, pulled up a chair, and sat near the counter, facing her. Behind him, his business partner Pie emerged, looking meek. He entered the Maiden's Hall and removed his round hat as he did so. "I'm sorry for your loss."

"Thanks," she said, observing Pie sit next to Foloi. The two men were the largest in town, although Foloi had bigger muscles, Pie's girth was in his gut.

"Can we talk in private?" Keryon said, forcing her to look him in the eyes.

"Sure," she said and snapped her fingers. Nork, Nosema, and Foloi went into the other room, and Pie followed them.

She should thank him for everything he did, or at least hear him out.

"Look," Keryon said after they left. "Before you say anything, I want to say that I am here in peace. No tricks. No snark. Nothing. You run everything here in town. You gave me the job to keep me out of your way, but I care about it, believe it or not. I think these people deserve a chance to be left alone, to build something new here. They've been through a lot. And so have you, I can tell."

No. He couldn't say things like that. "You seem to know a lot of things."

He leaned in with his piercing eyes. "I know you care. You cared about Edmir and you care about these people. They are your people, like them or not."

"What's your point?" she asked. She just wanted him to leave her alone with the bottle.

"I'm saying you can depend on me. That you can trust me."

"Sure."

"For the love of the gods, Madam Gimlore, you can *trust me*. You are not alone. You can rely on people."

Gimlore took a sharp breath and drank another shot of cerro wine. Keryon didn't take his sharp eyes off her. What the fuck was he staring at? "Are you implying I have trust issues?"

"That's right."

The fucker's nerve. "Are you suggesting the negotiations didn't work *because* of my trust issues? Because that is really fucking stupid. I trust people all the time. All of my employees."

"What about friends?" Keryon asked as the corner of his mouth rose into a little smirk.

"Friends? What are we, ten years old? I don't need friends. If I needed friends, I would get a hound to keep me company. I need my people to do their jobs and strangers to leave me alone. That's it."

Keryon stayed silent, tapping his fingers on the counter. His smirk remained intact.

She sighed. "Alright, fine. But it is hard out here. You've just arrived, so you do not know. I can't ever trust anyone. Not anymore," the words slipped out of her.

She no longer relied on Edmir. Now, this bastard walks into her establishment, points out her faults and fears and expects her to just acknowledge them? She liked her flaws and fears. It was what kept her grounded. Although she tended to order people. She *did* like being in control.

"Thanks for coming here and telling me I got my only friend killed," she said.

Keryon poured cerro wine from her bottle into her cup and drank from it. "You're a tough nut to crack, I'll give you that. But you know damn well that was not what I meant, madam."

"What did you mean, Warden?"

Keryon had another shot and paused for a second, perhaps picking the right words. "I guess I am offering help."

"Are you saying you want to work for me?"

"Not *for* you. *With* you. As equals. Of course, you have this place and your land, and I have my shop. I will not ask for a cut in your business. But I want to know what *really* goes on in this town and get involved in it. I actually want to be the warden. In exchange, you can have my help and my opinions. As you saw tonight, I'm still in my prime as a smokesmith. I could seize this place by myself if I wanted. I could burn it down. But I'm a peaceful man. An honourable one. Admit it—I can be very useful. You'll have to tell me things, though. Ask me for my opinions. That isn't so hard, is it? You're a businesswoman, so you recognise it's a good trade-off."

This had to be a trick of sorts. No. She had to stay lucid. He was taking advantage of this moment of fragility and grief. She would never relinquish control of *her* town to a foreigner, as charming and handsome as he might be.

She tapped her finger on the counter. "You must be out of your mind. What makes you think I would agree to that?"

"Because I saved your friends' lives," Keryon said. "And I saved yours, too. If I wanted you dead, I could have achieved that a long time ago."

Gimlore didn't find any words to rebate that.

"You know I'm right," he insisted. "And this was probably the last time you got away with being a little careless. Enemies will return sooner rather than later. Once they realise the hounds of Alarkan don't just bark... that they bite too, they will bring entire armies and cannons."

"You're right," she admitted, drinking another shot.

She was still so focused on Edmir that she hadn't stopped to think about what to do next. She was thankful that he had shown up and saved them. If only he had got there early enough to save Edmir too... As much as she hated to admit it, she would need help.

He smiled, pleased. "I know I'm right. So, what are you going to do now?"

"I have not accepted your offer, so it's none of your business."

"No, madam. This *is* my business. If they come, I cannot stop them all by myself and neither can you. And they *will* come. It's just a matter of who comes first. Are the Sirestine going to wage revenge on us? Or are other kingdoms already on their way? This is the only sensible thing to do—put our differences aside. Let me help you and let's build defences. Let's protect people."

For the gods, she hated when men were right.

There wasn't much more that she could say. She didn't have to like it, but perhaps they *could* work together. Perhaps she should give up full control. "You win, Mister Keryon," she said.

Each word was like chewing on a rotten fruit for a minute and then swallowing it. The grin on Keryon's face widened. Even his pearly teeth were all straight and shiny.

"Good, good. So, the first thing to do is start hoarding all the mossback elixir, no? We're going to need as much as possible. Everybody knows you're making a fortune with those farms, which is why people have turned sour towards you." Keryon could not keep his smile to himself. "But if we're going to protect this town, we need the elixir."

And he *still* wanted to help her? There had to be something she was missing.

"The elixir makes people go mad for a while," she said, composing herself from the surprise. "It's not good for anyone to use it often. It can be addictive, too. All that power... people get drunk on it."

"With all due respect, it's not very different from the smoke I breathe for my transformation. We need it."

Gimlore took a breather. She wasn't about to let him tell her what to do. "And where the fuck am I going to get the gold?"

"That is not the most important thing right now. We *need* military power. We need the elixir."

"But even with it, who do you think these people are? Warriors? They're drunks. So damaged and broken they can't think straight. They sit around and wait to die. They will not fight any war, not even if you give them an elixir. You're just making addicts out of them."

Keryon nodded. "You may be right. But it's better than nothing, which is what we have right now. Nothing."

Gimlore sighed but saw no alternative.

Thudding from somewhere outside shook the Maiden's Hall, and Gimlore realised they were still in the tavern. Someone could have been listening outside. She grabbed a knife and ran outside to chase the spy. Keryon followed. Instead of a spy, she found Pinesy standing outside, with three bloodsleuths wearing muzzles and with harnesses tying them to a small wagon.

"Pinesy! What the fuck happened to you?" she asked, feeling tempted to hug the little man until she saw his spooky bright eyes and backed away. "I thought you were dead. Nork and Nosema couldn't find you anywhere."

Pinesy shifted his eyes from her to the top of the cart. There was a large, dark wooden trunk covered in burn marks.

"I was hiding. You know I don't fight."

"Right," Gimlore said. She couldn't blame him. The little bastards lived long lives for a reason. "So, what do you have in the trunk?"

"I was hiding. I went back in their camp. And I got these," he said in his old man's voice.

Pinesy jumped into the top of the wagon and shoved the trunk out onto the floor with a strength someone that size shouldn't have. He then opened it.

Gimlore and Keryon approached the wagon, expecting the worst. She wondered if he had the remains of Edmir's body or something even worse and her stomach turned, somewhat reluctant to see what was inside.

"Pinesy!" she said. "I love you, you sneaky little bastard."

Inside the trunk was about two dozen state-of-the-art, brand-new muskets like those the Sirestine soldiers had been using.

"I wanted to bring these to you," Pinesy said as he prepared to leave. "All right, bye."

"Wait, Pinesy!" Gimlore called. "I can't pay you for these."

Pinesy shook his head. "No pay. You keep them. To protect our home. And my boys," he said, glancing at the dreadful bloodsleuths.

She smiled and her eyes watered. "Thank you."

"Now, this we can use," Keryon said, hypnotised by the weapons. "These are like miniature cannons. I've seen no other army use these things, or even looked at them up close."

"Did you see them in action? They are more powerful than an arrow, but they only work if you have time to recharge," she said, picking up one and scrutinising it. They made it from wood, but because the metal barrel was hollow metal, it felt light in her hand. Lighter than a spear would, at least.

"Remarkable," Keryon said, his eyes locked on the weapon. "It's like harnessing the power of an explosion to shoot metal pellets."

If she could figure out a way to replicate the craftsmanship of these weapons... They had blacksmiths and woodworkers. All they needed was a model, and now they had many. It would take time to perfect it, but any musket was better than none.

"We need to study the elixir, too. I don't want people to turn on each other if they have a quarrel. We should conduct experiments," she said, putting the musket back in the trunk.

Keryon helped her carry the trunk. "I can help with that. I am good at seeing what people's limits are when enhancing themselves," he said.

"That sounds very good, but we need someone to oversee this experiment. I, for one, know fuck-all about science," she said, grimacing as they hauled the heavy trunk.

"That makes two of us, but I have a friend who might help," Keryon's smile came back.

"Let me guess," Gimlore said, dropping the trunk on the floor and wiping the sweat off her forehead. "He knows a lot about herbs and has the name of a certain pastry."

Keryon smiled. He didn't break a sweat while carrying the trunk. "The man knows things, but Pie is just short for Piesym."

Gimlore shrugged. "As long as he can help us figure out the elixir, his name could be Meatloaf and I still wouldn't care."

·····‹·······

The heat and humidity seeped through Gimlore's clothes. It covered her in multiple layers of sweat mixed with dirt from the grave she was digging, but she could only stop once the hole was deep enough.

Edmir deserved it.

He had to have a proper burial, even if his body was left behind. With no corpse, she would bury his things instead. Digging the grave was the least she could do. The world had turned into chaos. She had made an unlikely alliance with Keryon, but she missed her old friend.

She dropped the shovel and let herself fall back on her buttocks. Insects hovered around her, some biting. At least down there, in the swamps, the ground was soft and muddy, easy to dig. She was alone with her thoughts and with all the pestilent rodents plaguing the bushes and trying their best not to turn into supper for a mossback or two.

Once she recovered, she stood, shook off the mud, and walked to the hearthspear, petting the creature's scaled maw. She opened the large saddle mounted on the hearthspear's right side and pulled out some of Edmir's belongings. Going through them left her strange. With all the scuffles they had been in, the bald man hadn't had any time to collect things. He refused to keep a spare bottle of wine by his side, the weak drinker that he was.

Gimlore let Edmir's clothes and baubles fall into the grave. She had been hoping to find out where he was from but he left her no clues. The past was the past, as they always told each other. Shit, she didn't even know if he had relatives in another dirty corner of the world.

Before it was time to fill up the grave with the dirt and mud she had removed, she took out her own cerro wine, looked at the hole, and gave it a nod.

"Take care of yourself in the underworld," she whispered before she lifted the bottle to her lips.

Every time she loaded the shovel with dirt, it felt like she was burying part of herself. It was as if the dirt was pressing on her, mounting on her shoulders. Tears fell from her eyes as she poured more dirt into the grave. She would never see him again.

After breaking into more sweat and perhaps a few tears, she finished and Edmir could rest in peace. Or maybe not.

Not too long after she finished, Gimlore heard the loud galloping of another hearthspear coming from the east. The sound intensified and she saw Nosema riding one of the large animals, his red bandana flowing in the air. He looked as thin as a spear on the large, muscular creature.

Nosema dismounted and noticed the grave. His hands were as twitchy as ever, even when he attempted to hide it by stuffing them in his pockets. "May he rest in peace."

"Indeed," Gimlore responded. "What is it?"

Nosema glanced back at her. "Trouble, boss. It's more trouble."

"Of course it is. It's always more trouble. What is it this time?"

Nosema shook his head. His hands shook. "No, boss. This time, it's real trouble."

"What the fuck do you mean?"

"Pinesy's cousin from the mainland said the King of Sirestir is travelling here himself. He wants to conquer us, too. Says the whole continent is his to take."

Shit. "How many soldiers?" she asked.

"It's difficult to tell. But he's coming in those large ships. There are over ten of them, if the information is correct."

An entire army at his back.

That was everything she didn't need.

She stole one last glance at Edmir's grave and jumped up on her saddle. "Goodbye, old friend. Wish me luck."

....

The Maiden's Hall was full—but not with patrons. Gimlore sat on top of the counter as Nork and Nosema sat in a nearby chair to her right with their arms crossed. Every evening Gimlore had to close the tavern to hold meetings, she made less money but she would find other ways to make it work.

"If we're all here, let's get started," she said, eyeing Keryon, who gave her a vigorous nod. To her left, Tinko and Thata pretended to be playing around, but they perked up their ears.

"Thanks to Pinesy, we know we will be under invasion soon," Gimlore said. "We don't have stone walls around the town. We don't even have an army. That being said, one would think we are fucked."

"I'm tempted to agree," Foloi said with a smile.

"We have a trunkful of muskets and the mossback elixir, which will help, but we still need soldiers," Keryon said, combing his hair with his hand.

"And where are we going to get those soldiers, boss?" Nork asked, his voice shaking. He hadn't been the same since Edmir passed.

Gimlore sighed. "This is not a straightforward decision. That's why I wanted to talk to you first. The only realistic solution is to hire the Leeth."

"The Leeth," Foloi said, his eyes widening. "I thought they were a legend."

"No, they're very real. I don't think we stand a chance against the armies of Sirestir without them." She tried her best to stay calm and collected though there was nothing calm about her. She wanted to flip around all the tables and chairs in the tavern and shout into the air until her voice collapsed.

Or stick a knife into somebody.

"If we want Heleronde to continue independent, and Alarkan free of lords, it's time to stand firm. Only the Leeth can help us with that. They will fight anyone... for the right price."

"But they are difficult to find, are they not?" Nork asked.

Gimlore nodded. "Yes, but our friend Pinesy can pass a message to them through his cousins."

"Can they get here before the enemy? I don't see how that's possible."

Gimlore leaned in. "Not everybody knows this, but the Leeth operates as an idle army. I once met one of their soldiers who slipped that out when he was drunk. They have core units, of course, but the bulk of their power comes from soldiers around the world, doing normal work until they get the call to battle. No matter where it is, chances are, they will have soldiers nearby. That's what makes them scary. They are unpredictable and extremely efficient. I'd wager they have enough soldiers to take it to the most powerful kingdoms. But that army would be impossible to hide in plain sight as they do now." Gimlore said.

"We'll call them, but I have a question first," Keryon said, turning to face her.

"What is it?"

"How will we pay them?"

That question was one she wished she didn't have to answer. She had her ways, but people didn't always condone them. In the end, she opted for a half-truth.

"We can raise taxes. I can pay some, but we will need to collect taxes too. Since we're taking care of their security and all," she said.

Pie sighed. "The merchants won't like it. They will see it as an attempt at becoming lord-like. Might as well proclaim yourself queen," he said, raising his eyebrows.

She swallowed. Half the truth didn't cut it. She needed to be honest with them. "What about paying with land? With freedom?"

TWENTY-THREE

BEFORE THE STORM

GIMLORE

A nother child birthed from the confusion, birthed from the chaos.

— From *Mother's Memories*

The swamplands sprawled to the horizon as Gimlore rode the hearths-pear through the muddy ponds and bushy patches of land that made up Alarkan. The ponds were deceivingly deep, and what looked like a puddle would sometimes turn into an underground water cave. Gimlore and her people had allowed bushes to grow around those to show which ones were too deep for the hearthspears to stomp. Without the fear of getting stuck in a water hole too deep, the creature rode like a ferocious predator hunting for prey.

Through trails, pathways, and sometimes stepping on deep puddles, the hearthspear moved like there was nothing in its way, splashing muddy water with each step. It was light and fast, almost too fast for Gimlore to hold onto its back. She was deep into her land, and it was clear how much there was left to explore. How many more mossbacks were there to discover still or hearthspears for her to capture, breed, and tame? She would take in more people, and give the poor bastards work and a purpose.

But those were all childish dreams now.

Foloi and Pinesy had sent a quick message to the Leeth requesting help through the strange yet useful networks of pinehead families that extended around the world. They had mentioned how urgent it was, but whether the Leeth would arrive on time, that was another matter.

She continued to ride towards the farmlands until she was far from Heleronde, where her land extended for leagues and leagues on end. The air was rough to breathe, and the humidity rested on her skin like it wanted to belong, but the relentless hearthspear continued, thriving in the muggy forests. But Gimlore didn't let it continue forever. She pulled the reins, and the beast whimpered as if stopping there was an injustice.

"Sorry, fellow," she said, touching the cold scales on his long, muscular neck. "I'll come back soon, I promise."

She jumped from the saddle. It was time to collect taxes. No one had volunteered to do it and, since she was the one taking possession of the gold, she might as well be the one asking for it. The farmers would not be thrilled, but this time she had a good reason to pester them.

Her smile faded when she considered that even with the Leeth, fending off the enemy for good wasn't a guarantee. And even if they won, other lunatics could come for her. She would have a much tougher time paying for help a *second* time.

Shit.

She needed walls, warriors, weapons, and maybe even warships. And a lot more gold to fund all of that shit. Or more elixir.

She had been on the losing side before, though this time she wasn't fighting other people's wars for them. She was fighting her own.

Gimlore continued to walk through the mud and the thick bushes until she reached a large clearing where about thirty shirtless peasants took care of logging, fed the mossbacks, or grabbed those that would have their livers removed.

Farmers stopped what they were doing and removed their straw hats in respect.

"Madam!" a wimpy woman named Clafa said, kneeling.

"Stand up, Clafa. No need for those formalities."

The skimpy folks all stared at her. She saw fear and pain in their eyes. They were used to bad news. If the landlady took the trouble of travelling to the farmlands, she wasn't there to spread good news.

"Gather around, folks," she said.

Their anxiety became clearer. Clafa's hands clasped the straw hat against her chest. "What brings you here, madam?"

Gimlore sighed. She needed to sell this.

"I come here to tell you about something I wished I never had to say," she started as she scanned their worried faces. She heard mossbacks chewing rodents and cubs playing. The humidity was oppressive, especially so close to the water.

"What is it?"

"It's about this," she said, extending her arms. "The ponds, the moss-backs. Someone wants to take it all away."

"What are you going to do, madam?" Clafa asked.

Gimlore sighed again. "We don't have soldiers. We don't have an army, but we also can't let them take our land."

The farmers nodded. Their bony, sweaty torsos reflected the bright sunlight.

Gimlore summoned her bar maiden charisma. "I will recruit the Leeth mercenaries to come to our aid. With them, we can fight this dreadful enemy and keep our land and our independence."

Hope showed on otherwise numb faces. Clafa nodded and scratched her chin. Gimlore figured they had selected her to be the one representing them, which meant she must be the brightest among them. "That's very good, madam."

"There's something else, Clafa," Gimlore said. "I alone cannot afford the high costs of these mercenaries. They are the best, which means they are also the most expensive. I must collect a tax to pay them. It's hard on you and it will be hard on everyone. But it's necessary if we are going to keep what's ours. Protection comes at a cost."

The farmers exchanged looks. Clafa was pulling on the straw hat so much she could have torn it apart. Even with no taxes, salaries were low, but the job wasn't the hardest. It was a safe environment unless they were drunk. There was no killing or dying involved. But of course, any talk of taxes would leave them thinking she was just trying to become like old-fashioned feudal lords and kings.

"It's a tax for protection?" Clafa asked.

"Yes."

"A temporary one?"

Gimlore nodded.

Clafa scratched her chin again and exchanged looks with the other farmers. "How much will this tax be?"

"Ten *palleans* of gold per head," Gimlore said, knowing how much they would hate it. "It's a lot, but it's a one-off contribution."

"Madam, with the utmost respect," Clafa said, "that's more than half of our monthly wage. How are we supposed to feed ourselves? We have young children. Others have elderly folks to care for."

"By going to the tavern once a week instead of once a day," she said, doing her best to appear firm. "I will channel most of my funds to pay them, too. And I will lose gold from all of those who like to wet their lips but cannot afford it anymore. Am I being unfair here?"

Clafa looked desperate, on the verge of quitting. "Madam, if that is the case, then we are going to join the other farmers. That way things will be fair! You might be the landowner, but we are the ones risking everything.

We remember how they attacked the mossbacks. What if we had been there? We will only pay the tax if we are free to cooperate with each other."

They didn't realise they *were* free to create whatever they wanted.

This wasn't like the mainland. This union of farmers would not help her, but she still had ways of getting what she wanted.

"Absolutely, Clafa. In fact, I *encourage* you to work together," she said, making it seem like they had a say in it, like they were a part of the discussion. "Do we have a deal?"

Clafa took a deep breath. "Yes, Madam. But once we shake hands, it will be agreed in front of all these people that the tax is ten palleans on a temporary basis. Until the invasion is over."

Gimlore smiled and extended her hand. Clafa's rugged hand grabbed hers and they shook it on the agreement. Not bad. She let out the breath she was holding.

"Thank you for understanding," Gimlore said.

"And you, madam. May the gods bless you for your bravery and for trying to do the right thing." Clafa put her straw hat back and walked back into the field with the rest of the farmers.

"I don't need any fucking blessings," Gimlore whispered to herself.

She walked back towards the hearthspear and the creature neighed, eager to ride again, as always. Once it saw her, it went mad, bobbing its head back and forth as if it was already riding indeed. She had convinced the farmers, who were an important group in Heleronde, but it still wasn't enough.

············

Gimlore spent the entire afternoon going from shop to shop, speaking with all the merchants about the taxes. By the time she spoke to the third vendor in town, everybody already knew about it.

Bad news spreads quicker than disease, she thought as she exited the small mouldy shop where a strange toothless man sold ratty clothes at a price too high for most. That wouldn't last too long.

Stepping into another shop brought Gimlore memories of when she first settled in Heleronde and started building the Maiden's Hall with Edmir and the rest of the brigands. She had known nothing of carpentry or managing a tavern, but those refugees and exiles needed something like that if they were going to settle. Back then, she used to smile at every new shop that opened and at every new wagon of refugees arriving. She had helped build most of those shacks. She even offered the wood and the nails sometimes.

This was *her* town in more ways than people realised.

She continued through the high street, her boots splashing in the mud at every step. With the sun covered by the clouds, the humidity created a layer of sweat across her body. This time, though, she had brought company.

"What I told you earlier. Repeat it."

"Behave well. No talking and no fighting," Tinko and Thata repeated. They dragged their words with exaggerated marked disappointment.

Gimlore smiled. "Good kids."

"Where are we going, Mama?" Tinko asked.

"We are going to visit the person who gave you your nicknames. She asked to see you and I need to talk to her, so you are coming along."

They sighed. "The old woman?"

Gimlore smacked them in the heads. "Old woman? She's an old *lady*! She took care of you more than you ever deserved, ungrateful little runts. I'm telling you. If you don't act like heavenly creatures, you will regret it."

"Fine, Mama!" the kids said.

Gimlore smiled again. She was their mother, after all. For ten-year-old kids, it meant she had no weaknesses. She would always win.

Gimlore and the kids arrived at an old shack, one of the oldest in Heleronde. The logs and wooden boards looked older than the shops.

Ten years of humidity had damaged it and the scorching sun had blasted through it. Nobody had repaired it, of course. Gimlore knocked on the door three times, even though it was open.

"Yes?" a slow, raspy voice asked from the second room. An old woman followed the question. Her face was weathered by the sun, age, and war. Not even the wrinkles could hide the scars covering her cheeks and forehead.

"Eshof. It's good to see you again," Gimlore said. The woman's surprised expression turned into one of joy when she saw Gimlore, Tinko, and Thata and came out into the main shop.

"Dear! And my little Bluebird and Sunshine!" Eshof said, dragging her words. Her movements were slower than Gimlore remembered. "They are so big now! Look at those faces. They are their mother's children."

"They are getting worse by the day, Eshof," Gimlore said, then turned to the children. "What do you say to Eshof?"

Tinko and Thata put on their best fake-pleasant faces. "Nice to see you again, Madam Eshof," they said, dragging their words.

"What do you mean by getting worse? They seem lovely to me, as always!"

"You don't want to know," Gimlore said. "Alright, you two can go. I want to speak with Eshof."

Tinko and Thata left the mouldy shack and Gimlore sat against a wooden beam. "I'm sure you've already heard why I'm here."

Eshof shrugged. "I've heard a thing or two, my dear."

"I promise this will be a temporary tax, Eshof."

She shouldn't be making such promises, especially if they were going to be difficult to keep.

Eshof shook her head and walked towards Gimlore, finding a seat on a small broken stool. "I'll pay for as long as it's necessary. I know how hard you've been working all these years, dear. I remember what this place looked like when we got here."

Gimlore smiled. "I remember that too."

"About the tax... I have a story for you," Eshof said. Gimlore wasn't very fond stories or pointless conversation, but she could at least indulge the poor woman. "How much do you know about me? Before I arrived, I mean."

"Not much," Gimlore admitted. That was the case for everybody. Whoever arrived left their past behind them and nobody would pry. Everyone deserved privacy.

"I was born in the deep north in a place so remote, it's not even a kingdom. It's run by chieftains. Fajar. Have you heard of it?"

Gimlore shook her head.

"There's not much there, either. I was a child when warring began. They killed our chieftain, along with most of the warriors, but I escaped with my parents. They took me south for a better life. I remember feeling the warm and pleasant wind that I never felt until I crossed the Seven Peaks. Rivers where I could swim in without freezing. I could take naps on the grass. I thought life was going to be different, but I was wrong."

Gimlore swallowed, not daring to interrupt.

"There was war there too. Kingdoms and lords fighting for land that I didn't know anyone could own. I had always thought land belonged... well, to itself. That was always our belief. I had never met people capable of destroying nature. But the farmstead where my parents found a job burnt down in a border dispute between Gasho and Noha. My folks were inside the stables when it happened. It was my introduction to life."

"I'm sorry to hear that."

Eshof shushed her. "I travelled south alone. The weather was better. The landscape was prettier. But the people, my dear, were filth. I became a farmer like my parents and lived for a few good years. Even found myself a man, but then the war took him too."

"I never knew that, Eshof. I'm sorry."

Eshof shook her head as if to say she still had more to say. "I was taken prisoner, even though I didn't take part in any war. The Nohani sold me like cattle from lord to lord until they said I was too old to do what they needed. I was in another war when I heard about Alarkan. A new land. A land untouched by the greasy hands of humanity. Warm or even hot. Do you know what made me travel here? There were no lords here. No fighting. No wars. I found peace."

Gimlore grimaced. "Not for long," she muttered.

The pain Eshof must have felt was far greater than her own. How could she take money from these people? *What the fuck am I doing?*

"No dear, you don't understand," Eshof said. "I paid taxes all my life, even as a slave. And for what? I still lost everything and everyone I cared for. I could have died so many times. This time it's different. This time, I *want* to pay taxes, because I know you work hard on my behalf, because I know no one is taking advantage of me. People think I have nothing else to lose, but they are wrong. We're all in this together, working for a common goal of freedom and prosperity. I've seen first-hand what selfishness does. This time, I found peace and freedom. If I have to pay taxes to keep things the way they are, I will do so without even blinking."

Gimlore's eyes watered.

"Thank you, Eshof," she said, unsure if it was because she felt sorry for the old woman or because she felt bad about how much of an arse she was trying to be. How could she even think of trying to steal from people like Eshof?

Gimlore wiped her eyes and stood. "I will do whatever I can to keep the peace," she said.

Eshof smiled. "I know you will, dear. You are a fighter. Much more so than I ever was. But you fight for the right reasons. You don't let them step all over you."

Gimlore had to leave. Eshof had been through so much and she still deposited so much trust in her. A trust so fickle... so easy to betray. She could never put Eshof or anybody else at risk, ever again.

"Thank you. See you around," she said.

She left the shack, turned towards an alleyway, and vomited. Only then did she calm down. Her arms still shook as she used the sleeves to wipe her mouth.

I'm sorry, madam, she thought, struggling to find composure. She had to abandon Madam Mazi's teachings. They'd served her well, but she needed to give up control now. She could no longer deceive them.

They needed her.

TWENTY-FOUR
THE PRICE OF BLOOD

REDNOW

I may be broken, but so is he. We have won. May the prison take as much as I gave away.

— From *Mother's Memories*

Rednow, Merey, and Tellwoon followed the guards through the hallways of the grand palace, swords ready for any... incident. Traditional blue Gashoine tapestries covered the grey walls, but there were no paintings of former monarchs. Rednow had received the gold, but the King hadn't wanted him to leave yet, due to the bedlam that Mewon had descended into after he'd announced Eterstan had been assassinated.

The King had launched his smokesmiths after the population as an excuse for finding whoever murdered his son and bodies had been piling up on the streets. Mostly nobles and apparently other Eterstan loyalists, who saw through it and accused the King of attempting to dirty the crown's dynasty and dilute the purity of the bloodline.

Staying in that cold palace left Rednow shivering. The lights were dim, and it made no sense that the place was still so cold and damp. Occasionally, they had to fend off rebels, assassins, and other guards who had changed their allegiance or had been favouring Eterstan all along. Troubled days in Mewon, those were, with blood running on the streets. All of it because a king didn't think his heir was worthy enough and wanted a new one. For that, everyone was now required to suffer.

I'm still not convinced the King will spare you, Rebma's ghost said, almost reading his mind.

But there wasn't much he could do. Even if he could leave, carrying the gold out when the king was trying to prevent his nation from turning into the epicentre of a civil war wasn't the best idea. So, he would hear the King out.

As they walked and passed through a side room, a group of servants stuffed tree branches in a fireplace, several dead bodies lying next to it. Traitors who had been ratted out.

The guards steered them to a smaller, more private part of the palace, where hallways were narrower and there was no natural light at all. It was as though the Palace of Mewon had been designed as a maze to confuse invaders and assassins while providing several escape routes for those who knew it well. Instead, a larger number of guards stood alongside the hallways with their backs to the stone walls. The King must be paranoid, now, even if he still held a firm grip on the kingdom.

Not many tyrants can have peace, the voice said. Rednow shook it off again, unable to ever get used to it.

After a right turn to the main hallway, the guard knocked three times on a large, dark door with his heavy gauntlet and muttered something in Gashoine. Another guard opened the door and ushered them inside quickly, as though he expected action at any moment.

Rednow and his two generals entered the small room where there was an ancient Gashoine desk crafted with at least three types of wood and layered with an expensive resin that allowed it to survive for centuries. With the desk as the centrepiece, the King only needed a few trinkets and baubles for the room to be complete. A large parchment map of the world hung on the wall and a more detailed one stretched across the old desk where Caligo rested his arms as he sat on a large chair with a tall backrest.

"Come on in, come on in," the King said, sounding harsher than usual. He looked sleepless, with dark rings around his eyes. "Sorry about all this. It's been a mess. I guess I underestimated how many bastards were waiting for me to die and for Eterstan to take over the realm."

"How goes the effort?"

Caligo let out a weary sigh and punched the desk lightly. "Finding them is proving harder than we anticipated, and keeping the gates locked means we're not getting all the supplies we usually need, which isn't helping us cool tempers one bit. But this is a matter with which Monder and I must deal. Please, sit."

The Leeth leaders found chairs and sat as commanded.

"May I ask, Your Majesty, why you did it? Why kill your son?" Rednow asked.

Tread carefully, Rednow. Do not poke the beast.

"My son was a peacock made of vanity and pride, unfit to rule this kingdom. But times are changing. Monder is everything I ever wanted in a son. He's a bastard, however, which a lot of people have problems with," Eterstan said.

"I see," Rednow said, doing his best to cut it short. He had to keep reminding himself of why he was there at all. He was far from his troops, in the monsters' den. He needed to leave. "I'm sure you will come out on top."

Rednow wasn't sure of anything. In fact, he had never been so unsure in his life. A sense of powerlessness washed over him. World's most feared mercenary his ass. The palace guards were armed to the teeth. Warriors, soldiers, and smokesmiths at every corner. Even with his sword and his herbs to burn, it would be a nightmare to leave without the King's blessing. And once he was outside the walls, there would be even more chaos.

Perhaps he'd even be accused of murdering the Prince. All he could do in that moment was swallow whatever the King had to say, even if the man had tried to take advantage of him to kill Eterstan. Better not even mention that, for the sake of the Leeth.

"I have *grand* plans for this kingdom," the King said, looking at the map and pointing his finger at it.

"I'm listening," Rednow said, leaning forward.

"That potion you retrieved, that the Nohani were using. We'd long been hearing rumours of it. Super strength and rapid healing, they said. I even had offers of a supply sample, but we didn't pursue it. I thought it was a shaman-type looking to swindle me, but after your reports, it seems like it was true. I didn't buy it and the Nohani did. That's a problem and my mistake. With the potion, or elixir, as they called it, I could protect the realm's borders better against my enemies. And I could squash any internal dissent too."

Interesting. "So why don't you reach out to the seller and buy the elixir?"

"I'm afraid the time for bargains is over. They are no longer in the market. I suspect they sold all their available volumes to the Nohani. Perhaps they are sitting on a few more crates of it, but it's not up for sale yet. And I can't wait too long, you see. I still have Nohani prisoners I can exchange. I might buy me some time in avoiding another invasion from the bastards, but if I have to wait months or years for another batch, I might already not be here when it does."

"You want me to go and find the elixir."

"Precisely," Caligo said,

Not all was lost. If the King was being honest and this was a legitimate job, perhaps he had no interest in him and the Leeth getting decimated. "And do you have any idea where we can find it? Such a secretive product must be hard to trace."

Caligo scoffed. "Our smokesmith inquisitors can be quite persuasive. We traced it back to Alarkan. The new continent. Have you heard if it?"

Interesting. "I have."

Rednow had no interest in doing this for the King. As soon as he was out of Gasho, he'd pick a replacement and retire. Especially after the King had tried to get him to kill a fucking prince. As soon as he was safe, he would never look back. But maybe Merey and Tellwoon would be interested.

"I'm thinking of sending a little group of soldiers with you. I don't think you will have a problem in securing the elixir, but what good will it be if we kill those who know how to produce it? No. I'd like to produce it too, for the use of my own army. It wouldn't hurt to have soldiers who don't hesitate to strike and heal fast."

"Well, we're not murderers, Your Majesty. We can take the elixir and leave the people alive if you wish. No need for any of your soldiers to join. We can take care of it."

"I trust your resolve, Blood Collector, I do. The problem is the elixir is being produced in Alarkan and the Alarkani are a bunch of dirty savages who have already claimed much of the explorable land. It will take military persuasion to make them see reason, but also some diplomacy. In fact, I hope I'm not too late for that."

The King's eyes sogged and he sighed.

"What makes you say that?" Rednow asked.

"My spies say the Two Nations have sent diplomats there, with a proper entourage, and none of them returned. Nobody knows what happened to them. They claim the Herald never left the settlement."

Rednow wondered how true the rumours were. Perhaps he could try it himself. Perhaps the elixir would even restore his youth, heal his lungs. "Maybe we could help with that," he said.

"Excellent," Caligo said.

"I understand," Rednow said, and those two words almost made his stomach turn. Here he was, again, the lap hound of people he hated. Doing what he had to do. But for how long? When would he be able to break this cycle of shame and misery? Rebma had been right. It was time to retire once and for all, with or without the elixir. He stole a quick glance at Tellwoon and Merey, the future of the Leeth. But there wouldn't be much future if they couldn't feed themselves.

Grow up, he told himself. *Everybody does things they don't want to do.*

"How many soldiers do you need for the raid to Alarkan?"

"I was thinking of five thousand heads."

"That is going to cost you."

"What is your price?"

It wouldn't hurt to try his luck. "I will still need to meet with my generals before I accept, but I need five thousand *malleans* of gold for that many heads."

Caligo's eyes widened before they dropped and set on the desk. "You weren't kidding. I'll need to think about it as well, then. Tonight is Monder's Piercing Ceremony. It's something small and private, given the state of things. I will sleep on the issue and let you know tomorrow. And if I decide your price is worth paying, we can discuss my plans."

Rednow nodded. One more night in that dreadful place. One more night still alive. He forced himself to be positive. That much gold would not only keep everyone fed, but it would also be almost enough to feed the entire army for half a year. If he decided not to do it, he could still run away with the gold from the previous campaign at the border. Not bad.

"I never had children myself, but you must be proud of Monder. To risk everything for him, I mean."

The King nodded. "Everyone rejected him because his mother was a foreigner. Can you believe it? Spent his whole life in the shadows, rejected by his own... Not by me, though. I've always kept him close. One of the brightest minds I know. He was the one who suggested I hire your mercenaries."

"I guess I should thank him," Rednow said, smiling.

"You can join us at the celebration. Well, Monder will heal from the piercings with anaesthetic herbs, but he will celebrate like he deserves."

Rednow sighed and glanced at Merey and Tellwoon. These fucking people celebrated too much. Even when the realm was close to a civil war, they still took time to get drunk. He wanted no part of it, but the faces of his comrades told him he should accept the offer. He couldn't reject another act of courtesy lest he anger Caligo.

"We would love to go, Your Majesty. It would be an honour," Tellwoon said before Rednow could say anything against it. "We'll be there."

....

"I can't stay here for another night," Rednow said, shaking his head as light snowflakes landed on his cloak.

Snow covered the courtyard and far were the glorious days of summer, with parades, courting dates, and other foolish things lordings did. The snow absorbed his steps and turned into a grey slush at his passage. It was still a mild snow, though. And there was no wind. It didn't compare to the Seven Peaks in their wintry blanket.

"Maybe you can sleep outdoors with Zatak and his hounds," Tellwoon said, tapping him on the shoulder.

Rednow turned to her and widened his eyes. "You think I would mind that?"

"We know you wouldn't, Rednow. Don't be so cranky. You did well in the negotiation. He won't even know he's overpaying," Merey said.

Rednow grumbled and carried on walking through the snowy courtyard, hurrying to get out of there. The dark birds cawed above them in a large flock. They dove into the ground to grab a few unsuspecting rodents. They, too, were merciless killers by nature.

While the courtyard was still too regal and formal, its openness almost made Rednow breathe lighter. He wasn't made to be inside, not even in a palace. Still, they remained under the watchful eyes of several guards, though the lack of commotion outside the walls and smoke in the air hinted at a peaceful evening. Rednow looked at them looking at him. Did they think he had killed Eterstan?

Let them, he thought, shaking those suspicions off his mind.

When they reached the courtyard walls, Zatak turned around. The man was like a hound himself. Even in the courtyard, he must have felt like he was in a cage. Next to him, two vicious bloodsleuths lay on the wet ground. Awake or asleep, Rednow didn't know, but he wouldn't go near the beasts.

"Where is the pinehead?" Merey asked as she sat.

"He just got back with news and went to meet his cousin."

Rednow sat by the fire, enveloped by the pleasant heat it produced. That would always be one of the best feelings in the world. "What did the pinehead say?"

The hound master grimaced, stopped sharpening the sword, and sat closer to the rest of the group.

"The pinehead says there's another offer for us. Someone else is interested in our services," he said.

"Well, who is requesting our swords?" Tellwoon asked, warming hands over the fire.

"No names yet, but it's from Alarkan."

Rednow exchanged looks with Merey and Tellwoon. "It's the second time we have heard about that name now."

"Second?"

"Yes. The King wants to send troops there, too. I'll tell you later. But what's the proposal from these people in Alarkan, then?"

"The pinehead only said it seemed pretty urgent, which means they must be desperate." Zatak revealed his crooked smile.

Rednow nodded. "What else?"

"He said they could pay with land ownership. No taxes. A chance to start again. A chance at a new life. That crap."

"Crap?" Rednow frowned. "They're exiles and refugees. Broken people dealing with an enemy far stronger than them. Not too different from us."

There was silence among the group. If the Alarkani people were a bunch of refugees and half-dead bandits, they wouldn't be able to pay, but they could offer land, freedom, independence, and a complete lack of monarchs.

You must go and help them, brother. You simply must, Rebma's ghost told him.

"What do you all think? I'm not keen on working for this king again."

Zatak grunted and shook his head. "This one is better money. No one cares about having a piece of land in a place in the back of beyond. What's that good for? I can always take my hounds back to the Seven Peaks, live there and I don't need to say it is mine. That would be silly and so is this."

"We need the gold," Tellwoon said. "I'm sorry. I know you have a soft spot for refugees and those that are... well, like us."

Rednow turned to them. "And you don't?"

Zatak shrugged. "We already have common folk to worry about. And that's why we're here. To get paid so we can feed them. You can't save everyone. You know that."

Rednow swallowed. "But this is different. If we take the King's money, we might get the elixir, but we'd be fighting against people like us, not minions of a monarch. Are you all prepared to do that?"

Merey shrugged. "We don't even know exactly what the Alarkani need us for. We can't decide yet."

Rednow remained silent, switching his focus to the fire once again.

It would be the perfect place for you, Rednow. A fresh start. Redeem yourself from all this killing.

Rednow shook his head, but the ghost was making sense. So much sense. It was a warm place where he could retire. Where he could build something. Rednow pictured himself living in a humid, swampy land. He had been born in the south and retirement was imminent. What else was he supposed to do, die in combat?

"Let's hear more about their offer and then I can make a decision."

TWENTY-FIVE

TARNISHED

REDNOW

My blade given away. My soul... shattered. And yet they play, forever ignorant.

— From *Mother's Memories*

The heat from the fireplace warmed the room. Rednow extended his arms forward and let his palms soak in the languid warmth of the simmering tree branches. Sitting on a small stool meant for servants, he took a sip of a very light winter wine the palace staff had given him. Tellwoon had already downed several mugs of the spirit, but she still appeared to be alright, though the alcohol left her face red and eyes vacant, locked to the flames as they waited for Merey.

"If we're lucky, we'll be out of here by tomorrow morning," Rednow said, compelled to distract the general from her own thoughts.

Tellwoon turned to Rednow before producing a quick, shy smile. She pulled her knees towards her chest and hugged them, then looked back at the fireplace. She had combed her hair and cleaned her clothes as much as possible, considering the distance they had travelled.

"I hate this King and the way he crushes his subjects," she said.

"I'd be worried if you didn't," he said.

Rednow nodded, knowing all too well Tellwoon was talking about the way the King had deployed his guard and his smokesmiths to squash the faction that was in favour of Eterstan taking the throne.

He hadn't been outside to see it yet, but he overheard servants and guards speak of the atrocities. The bodies littering the streets. The screaming in the middle of the night. The King's enemy faction had apparently put up a bit of a fight, but they were now being chased outside of the capital city. Something like this, though, could never be rooted out completely. Dissent would be expected and common even among the nobles, who were surely not happy about Caligo's idea to host a Piercing Ceremony for his bastard son who was now being raised as the heir to the throne.

Rednow needed to get away from there. The bloodbath wasn't over yet.

This was what monarchs did. They stomped on those who weren't at their height. This was why his job as the Leeth's leader was so important over the decades—rescuing children who had suffered from the acts of kings like Caligo.

"How can these people stand it? Being told what to do, every day? Why don't they rise up?"

Rednow shrugged. "Tradition, to begin with. But the power is skewed. Those in power have no interest in sharing or letting it go and those not in power have no way of reaching out and grabbing it without being destroyed. So, they compromise and place their faith in the next best thing. A kind ruler is better than a vicious one."

"We have an entire army. Why don't *we* do something about it? How come we've never tried?"

Rednow sighed. "We're killers for hire, but we barely know politics. We could rally the people if I was a charismatic man, sure, but other kingdoms would test our grip on the realm. We wouldn't be able to hold it for long without proper trade partners, and we would end up losing more than we ever gained. Plus, I have no aspirations to be a bloody king. That's why we do the next best thing and compromise as well. We take the monarchs' coin and do our best to help those affected by their actions. It's little, but it's something."

Tellwoon nodded. "You're pragmatic. That's part of what makes you a good leader. We can always count on you to cut our losses. I'm not sure if I'd be ready to replace you."

Rednow had wondered the same thing himself. "What makes you say that?"

"I find myself... distracted." The general rubbed her hands together. "I should be grateful, shouldn't I? That you're considering me? Thinking about ways to improve upon your methods and your legacy. And I do that, to an extent, but I spend most of my days thinking of something else."

"You mean *somebody* else."

"Yes," Tellwoon admitted, almost as if she was confessing a crime. "I think about her all the damn time."

"I suppose that's normal."

"I'm in love. I know it. And she is too."

Rednow produced a grunt. What was he supposed to say to that?

"And that's not all, Rednow. I think about life with her and what that means. I think about things I've never considered. Children, somehow. Me! Raising children! Am I being foolish or soft? It makes me less eager to fight."

He adjusted himself on the little wooden stool and produced another grunt, followed by a vehement nod. He couldn't picture Merey carrying children around. She was a warrior, always eager to fight. She wasn't a mother. Tellwoon was softer and more level-headed, but she had always been better with the blades too.

"How come you never had children?" Tellwoon asked.

"The way I see it," he said, taking a sip of wine, "all of you are my children. I took care of you since you were scrappy brats with your faces covered in soot and grime."

"But how come you never found someone? A companion?"

"I don't know. I was never interested in those things," he said. It was hard to explain things he didn't understand himself. "It seems like I never felt the things other people did. I never spent days and days thinking about *anyone* the way you do about Merey, for example."

"Never?"

"Never."

Tellwoon widened her eyes and looked away. "Well, that is alright too."

Rednow gave her a nod of appreciation.

"Yes. If you want to know, I'm glad I avoided a lot of the pain that comes with loving someone like that. But that wouldn't make you a poor leader. You have to think of the soldiers as if they were all your children. As if you and Merey handled all their lives."

"That seems like an awful load to bear."

"It's heavier than many people realise, but it's worth carrying. You'll come to understand that. If I pick you to be the leader, that is."

"Cheers, Rednow," Tellwoon said, raising her mug.

"Cheers," he said, raising his own mug and bringing it towards his lips. "It seems like we ended up having our own celebration. Where is Merey, anyway?"

"She was taking care of the shadesgrowls. Said she needed fresh air. Maybe I nagged her too much."

Rednow chuckled and nodded. Perhaps he had underestimated Tellwoon. Worrying was a good thing in this line of work.

The two of them stayed by the fire, ruminating on old tales of the past and thinking about what the future would bring. Perhaps sunny days, surrounded by farm creatures and the sword put to rest, his promise to

Rebma finally kept. Then, Rednow set his eyes on a large rectangular oil painting adorning the wall.

"What do you think of that?"

It depicted a battle scene, with soldiers fighting each other, while another set of soldiers emerged from the skies to join the battle.

"I don't know. I've heard stories about the Ancient Ones... Do you think they could really fly?"

Rednow shrugged. "I very much doubt they could, especially without wings, like in the painting."

"You're probably right."

"Rebma used to write songs about them. I never understood the lyrics or how she knew all that. I was always moved by her singing voice."

Tellwoon swallowed. "Do you still hear her? You said you—"

Rednow nodded. "Every day. I wish I could make it stop. It almost feels like she's right behind me, but not quite. I've wondered if I'm cursed, or perhaps going mad."

The sound of footsteps echoed through the hallway, interrupting their discussion about the art. Merey appeared, dressed in comfortable pants, shirt, and a tight dark coat, but her hair was tight around her scalp in a spiral braid.

"What do you think?" Merey asked. "I clean up pretty nicely, don't I?"

"Of course!" Tellwoon almost shouted. "Beautiful!"

Merey smiled and walked over to her. That look in her eyes showed Tellwoon was right after all. They loved each other.

"Should we go?" Tellwoon asked. "The celebration must have started already."

Rednow nodded.

The three of them took leave and walked around the halls of the palace. At night, it was like a different place. Even the torches hanging on the walls were barely enough to lead the way forward. An experienced assassin could put those lights out and move without being caught.

They passed through a group of stationary guards. One of them pointed to another hallway on the left side, near the King's office. Two more escorted them to wherever the celebration was taking place. Led by the guards, Rednow's entourage walked towards the big event. While doing his best to memorise the innards of the palace in case he would need it later, Rednow found himself wondering how much he knew about the Piercing Ceremony.

"The young fellow's face will swell," Rednow muttered. "Be prepared for that. It won't be pretty."

Merey and Tellwoon nodded.

After three turns to the right and another to the left, they reached a heavy door reinforced with metal strips. One guard opened it and a wave of sound and colour flooded Rednow as they ushered him inside, along with his friends.

Rednow's eyes widened, and yet he didn't look away. The room was full of large, exotic trees inside ceramic vases, and there were padded chairs so comfortable one could sleep on them next to small tables with Gashoine cerro wine and bowls with cerro berries scattered around the room.

"What the—" Rednow couldn't help but say as the guards left and closed the door behind him.

Even stranger than the decoration were the people. About two dozen nude figures paraded themselves with intricate plume hats and intricate headbands, nibbling on berries, drinking and, to Rednow's horror, fucking. Their moans blended in with the fast-paced melody of a band playing at the back of the room.

Rednow gritted his teeth, a quiet fury bubbling inside. There were corpses on the street and they were... dancing? Celebrating? Fucking? If he wasn't inside the palace, Rednow wished the other faction would have stormed the place and slaughtered all these bastards. Perhaps Eterstan had been right all along, and the King lacked focus on what really mattered.

He turned to Merey and Tellwoon. "This was a mistake. We should leave. Let's go."

"Blood Collector! You're here!" Caligo said between breaths. He grabbed the hips of a naked young woman as he thrust his pelvis against her from behind.

This is the celebration? Disgusting, Rednow thought. It went against everything he knew. Something so detached from the realities of the kingdom could only come from the twisted mind of a lunatic murderer. Rednow noticed another man lying on his back next to the king as a woman rode him. He was the only one besides Caligo who had piercings, but they looked recent and his face was bloated. There were remains of dried blood around the holes punctured by the metallic spikes. That had to be Monder. This was how these fools had celebrated.

"Blood Collector!" Caligo called again. "Come on. Have a drink. Or join us if you'd like. The same goes for your crew."

It was uncomfortable to see so many people fucking like that, but to see a king promoting it was something new. And inviting him in was even worse. Rednow's anger was too hard to contain.

"You've caught us by surprise," he said, loud enough that the King heard him from across the room amid all the music and the moaning. "We came prepared for a banquet."

"Well," Caligo said, keeping up his pace. "This. Is. Also. A banquet. Of sorts."

Fucking gross.

"Let's go," Tellwoon said, pulling on his arm.

"We came here to chat," Rednow said out loud. He wanted nothing more than to rub that bastard's skewered face on the floor until every piercing hole was bleeding again, but he had to stay calm.

Caligo finished in a loud and disgusting howl. "Fine," the King said, looking at Monder. The new heir seemed to still be drowsy from the pain of having his face pierced, the swelling continuing. Caligo wiped his face and his body with a silky cloth and put on a light robe over his body.

"Monder is still a bit out of it. Can't blame him. But he took it well," Caligo said, grabbing a new crystal glass of wine. The rest of the people in the room continued as if their new king hadn't stopped. "Let's go to the next room, then."

Caligo walked over to a door that led to the room inside that one, forcing Rednow and his crew to cross the entire room, passing awfully close to both male and female genitalia.

The longer Rednow stayed, the angrier he became. That place contrasted harshly with the solemn postures of the palace guards outside who had lost their brethren in the skirmishes. It was even more of a stark comparison with the devastation he imagined to be outside the walls. These people didn't care. Power was a game they could win or lose. They would still fuck around, drink the best wine, and eat the best food. There would always be someone to praise them and others for them to step on. Only their reputations mattered.

The room next door wasn't much better than the other one and decorations were just as wild, with draping curtains depicting wild exotic trees and the walls painted with abstract motifs over the grey stones. The centre of the room had a large sofa with about ten small, padded stools. Rednow wasn't sure what the room was for, but it looked like something either ancient or straight from the future.

"My artists exceeded themselves with this room, don't you think? I'm a big enthusiast."

Rednow grunted as he and the crew sat on the padded stools while Eterstan took the large sofa. The resolve it took not to lash out was grandiose. The old king seemed tipsy, but he had regained his breath already. Four soldiers from his honour guard stood at each corner of the room.

"Perhaps I should have told you what celebration we would have tonight. You'll excuse me for that. I was so... happy for my son to have his piercing done and then we have this fresh new batch of slaves that I wanted to... try for myself. Did you see them? A new batch from the northlands. I've never seen skin that fair."

Silence fell upon the room.

Rednow's fury flared. He had been born a slave. So had his ma and pa, born and sold like cattle. He still remembered the sound the whip made before lashing them on the back. There was no room for this in the world, but he alone couldn't change that. Slavery was forbidden for the Leeth. Almost every soldier he had trained had been a slave or born of slaves and other refugees.

Rednow closed his hands into fists. What would happen if he struck the King right there and then? He was sick of tyrants forcing others to do their bidding. He was almost ready to lay it all to waste for the sweet satisfaction of caving the fucker's skull in. "Are you their master?"

"Indeed," Caligo said, smiling. "Wretched beasts run rampant in the northlands and they come down here looking for help. This is the only help I will give them. They're quite an exotic lay. Very different from the Gashoine whores. I'm a man of refined taste!" the King said.

Rednow bit his tongue. Quiet. He needed to stay quiet.

He imagined himself lunging towards the King across the desk, stabbing him repeatedly. Perhaps transforming into his monster form and crushing the King's skull with one hand and a primal roar. He imagined the King's mouth bubbling blood, his eyes wide, pupils dilated in his last moments before the underworld. The King was just a man like any other. No more. No less. How glorious would that be?

He sighed. Unfortunately, Rednow couldn't do that. The King's honour guards stood paying close attention to him, and the entire palace was filled with even more. He was alone with Merey and Tellwoon. As prolific warriors as they were, there was still a massive numbers disadvantage. Any mercenary knew when to pick battles and when to shut the fuck up.

You've never been a coward, Rednow. You have nothing to prove, his sister's ghost said.

He couldn't express himself against the King as he wished, but he also didn't have to continue being his lap hound. This wasn't *his* king. Rednow was free.

"It is with sadness that I inform you the Leeth will not be able to help you in this campaign to Alarkan."

Caligo remained silent, assessing him, as though wondering if Rednow was joking, or perhaps tasting the sour flavour of rejection. Either way, Rednow refused to cut the silence.

"That's unexpected. I was going to try and barter with you on the price. Are you sure?"

Rednow nodded. "I am, Your Majesty."

"But why not?"

Rednow swallowed. How to tell a despot his abuse of slaves made him uncomfortable? How to tell him he had another offer on the table, from people he actually respected? Or tell him the ghost of his dead sister spoke to him, begging him to take the other job instead? Perhaps he could tell the old man he didn't appreciate how the bastard had tried to get him to kill his son for him.

"I'm old, Your Majesty. I promised my sister I would retire and now I intend to honour it," he said, keeping the details of the promise vague enough that it could sound like a good excuse. "I'm sure you'll understand, the honourable man you are."

King Caligo scratched his chin and sighed. "I do understand. I thought I'd be able to purchase your services for longer, is all. Without you and the Leeth, my chances of successfully venturing into Alarkan are slim. Delayed at the very least, given all the trouble I've got at home. It will take time until I root out all the rats that dare stand against me."

Maybe you should have thought about that before you caused it all.

"Of course. It's regrettable."

The King nodded, then knocked on his desk and his face lit up as he looked at Rednow again and got up from the chair. "Well, no time to waste then. Let us get back to the celebration."

Rednow cleared his throat. "We're thankful for the invitation and wish Monder all the best in his recovery, but we'll be taking our leave. We've got a long way back to our camp and the winter is near. The earlier we can head north, the better."

The King nodded and extended his hand for Rednow to shake. "Then it's been a pleasure, Blood Collector. If you change your mind about my offer, you know where to find me."

"Thank you, Your Majesty."

Rednow had never seen a king do such a thing. Usually when they did, it was with the expectation of it being kissed, not shook. He couldn't help but feel something was amiss.

Twenty-Six
Kingdom of Chaos

Rednow

I *am, so that you can see the sun setting. To hold you and protect you.*

— From *Mother's Memories*

Rednow breathed under his hood as he jogged through the snowy streets of Mewon. He thought the Gashoine capital would be quieter now, but it was still in a bloody turmoil of rioting peasants, burning buildings and smokesmiths chasing them though narrow alleyways. Nearly every street Rednow passed had bloodstained cobblestones and a sense of distrust was palpable, with everyone glancing at strangers as though they could be enemies. Upon seeing all of that, he could only wonder how much Caligo had overestimated his own popularity or his ability to keep the crowds under control. It had been many days now, and if this was what peace looked like, he was glad he had missed the bloodbath.

They grabbed the gold coffers and immediately mounted the shades-growls.

No one seemed to sleep in the frozen evening. Militias marched the streets, armed with batons, sticks, pitchforks, and hammers. Every now and then, there would be cheering, then shouting. Everyone looked excited, angry. Everyone had an opinion.

In the middle of all that, Rednow, his generals, Zatak, and the pineheads stood out like a sore thumb, even with hoods up.

"I heard it was an assassin," someone said. "Sent from the south."

"There is no heir! A bastard is a bastard," another one said.

Rednow and his crew had escaped the palace, and they had to get out of Mewon as soon as possible.

"Did you kill our prince?" a drunk asked Rednow, standing in front of his shadesgrowl.

Rednow steered the mount around the man, but the drunk moved again in front of the beast. "Move or the creature will trample you," Rednow warned.

"I asked a simple question." The man slurred his speech, but his eyes fixated on him. "Did you?"

The altercation attracted some attention. Several city dwellers gathered, arms crossed and spitting at the floor in front of them.

"They're from the Leeth! I heard the Blood Collector killed the Prince in a duel."

"Duels are legitimate, you thick fool."

Laughs.

"I don't care who it was or under what circumstance. No one has the right to kill our heir to the throne!"

The crowd erupted in cheers and Rednow felt something hit the back of his head. A pebble?

"We have to leave," Tellwoon whispered.

Rednow urged his shadesgrowl onward, but the beast hesitated, given the mob that had surrounded them. There must be about fifty of them,

They started throwing things at him and his crew. The drunkard that had stepped in front of him smiled.

"Move or you won't live to regret it," Zatak said, inciting his blood-sleuths against the crowd. The beasts snarled, but that didn't deter them.

Another pebble hit Rednow.

"No need to get so flustered, old man..." the drunkard said. "Just give us the gold and we'll let you go."

Reality hit Rednow like a brick. *The gold.* They were here for the gold. His mind raced and he glanced at the pineheads who carried the gold in their bodies, spread out to avoid attention. There was nothing about any of them that hinted that they had any sort of gold. Their clothes were ragged and the cloaks even more so. The packs on the side of their shadesgrowls were rather empty and none of them looked like well-off travellers or noblemen making a run for safety. Rednow reckoned they looked like what they were—mercenaries, trying to get by.

So, how did this crowd—and the drunkard in particular—know that they held a fair bit of coin? "We haven't got any," Rednow said, though he didn't expect much of it.

The drunkard laughed. "I'm not going to repeat myself."

He knows.

It had to have been the King. He had set him up to kill Eterstan in the duel, and when that failed, took it upon himself to do it, but that created the chaos they were all in. It wasn't in anyone's interest to prolong the civil war, so after Rednow rejected his last offer of employment, the King must have realised he could still shove the blame of Eterstan's death onto Rednow and, if he was lucky, get the gold he'd paid back, or let the crowd have it to appease their bloodlust. By using him as a scapegoat, he'd end the civil war.

Clever bastard.

If Rednow was correct about this, then this man wasn't a drunkard, and most of those people in the crowd weren't peasants, but instigators and assassins sent by the King.

"This is how the King reacts after all I've done for him?" Rednow spat.

"What are you…?" Tellwoon asked, then she gaped her mouth, realization hitting her.

Rednow cursed himself. More people gathered in the crowd, most of them armed. Even with him being a smokesmith, they were a small group against a massive crowd. All it would take was a sharp enough blade in the middle of the chaos and he could lose his life. But giving up the coin he and all his troops had worked so damned hard for? He gritted his teeth and grasped the reins hard, powerless. *Fuck.*

"Do you give us your word we can leave in peace?" Those words were as difficult to utter as anything he'd ever said.

The drunk-who-may-not-be-drunk smiled. "Of course."

"No, Rednow! We can't!" Merey shouted. "The Leeth will go hungry."

That was true, although most warriors of the Leeth were well-trained and capable of working for coin when they weren't fighting, so they wouldn't all go hungry. The children, however, were another matter entirely. He was being taunted by a king, pushed to his limits, and shoved around like a piece of the game board or a resource to be exploited. And for the first time in his life, he wasn't in a position to fight back.

"Give them the gold." Each of those four words bit him harder than a hound could.

"Rednow!" This was Tellwoon's turn.

She and Merey looked at him with frustration, but that was just the denial before the acceptance. They were all free to choose their own destiny, but when they'd decided to intertwine themselves with the powers that ruled the world, this was a reality that was bound to happen. They were free to try to escape or even fight back against the oppressors, but the chances of living to tell the tale were low, too low for his comfort. Perhaps if it was only him, he would still try it, out of pride. But Tellwoon and Merey needed him. And the rest of the Leeth needed a new, competent leader.

The pineheads hesitated, looking at him for confirmation.

"Give them the gold," Rednow insisted.

The pineheads reached inside their cloaks and undid the belts that supported all the pouches that carried the gold. They gathered it, in a total of fifteen pouches, almost enough to feed an army for a while, and threw it to the muddy floor. The crowd rushed to get their hands on the gold, scrambling to untie the cords. Then they started fighting each other for it.

"Let's go. Now!" Rednow ordered and shook the reins to get the mount moving fast. With a glance back, as they gained distance from the crowd, Rednow saw the chaos mist into a skirmish, different small groups emerging to take the gold.

You did the right thing, he heard Rebma's voice say.

He tried shaking it off, but the voice was still there, always there. It sounded like her. The same cadence, the same tone. It drove him mad, and he didn't think he could withstand it much longer.

It's not your fault, Rebma said.

That was too close to what she would say, to how she would forgive his wrongs. He shook his head to release himself from those cursed thoughts, but they held onto him. Her voice haunted him, as if she was watching.

It sure felt like it had been his own fault. First, for relying too much on gold handed out by kings, then for not being able to hold his tongue against the Prince. And then for angering the King by rejecting his last offer. He had always been thinking of what his people needed, but he had somehow also ended up jeopardizing all of everything. A pressure built in his chest, as though it was getting crushed by the impossible weight of loss all over again.

The rest of the city turned grim fast, but nobody else stood in their way. Many wanted upheaval and rebellion. Hungry peasants stole from their neighbours, acts of violence were gratuitous and unpunished, and the light of man-made fires in the distance lit the night sky.

The city guard was in peril, their numbers weakened by the riots. The soldiers that weren't being ostracised and attacked by the pitchforked peasants for selling their souls to the King were left clueless, outnumbered and without orders.

It was only a matter of time until the rest of the kingdom followed the example of the sprawling capital city. With a contested heir, there would be more scuffles, skirmishes and the richest lords would start power plays. The kingdom's conspirators were rubbing their hands, making plans and alliances to make a run for the palace. A weakened king was always an attractive premise to those of ambitious nature. This was a great opportunity for someone to take now. More death.

Rednow cursed himself, wondering what lies the King was spreading about the Leeth. How would the Leeth find future patrons if their reputation of integrity and trustworthiness was tarnished? Word of the crime would spread across the world, and it could very well peg him as the sole responsible soul.

And his word didn't matter. The truth didn't matter.

The group rode the grey beasts as fast as possible into the dark until they crossed the now unprotected city gates. With a glance back at the city, Rednow could almost see the bedlam. The shadesgrowls rode faster even on the snowy grounds as if temperature didn't bother them, but Rednow was cold, colder than he had ever felt. Like he had left something behind. There was nothing to do now. It was his fault. His pain to bear. He was good at that, at least—bearing pain. He would have to tell his warriors he'd let brigands take the gold. So much for the world's most feared mercenary. Looking forward was the only thing to do. Like a goddamned farm animal, he had to work through it.

Well outside the city walls, the group stopped in a clearing, and Zatak left to go find his hounds. One pinehead took the reins of the shadesgrowls.

The other did his best to start a fire despite the freezing cold. Rednow sat on the ground, covered by the thick marcruncher fur over his back, shoulders, and neck. Merey and Tellwoon sat by his side in silence.

It didn't take long for Zatak to return with the bloodsleuths. Their maws gnarled and dripped blood, revealing an early supper they had eaten in the woods. Zatak eyed Rednow and the other two and sat as well, with his dreaded tamed creatures lying nearby. The pinehead got the fire going after a few drops of oil added into it; the flames grew into a sizeable bonfire, good enough to warm the few of them in a freezing night.

"So, what do we do now, Rednow?" Zatak asked.

Merey shot him a deadly stare. Rednow shrugged.

"Well, what do you want to do? Just pretend we didn't hand our livelihood away?" the hound master asked as he chewed raw meat from his pocket. "It is a fact that we lost a pile of gold. And now, people might never trust the Leeth as an impartial mercenary force."

"We would have died!" Tellwoon said.

"I know. It's hard, but everybody dies. We fight for a living. We face those odds and go ahead anyway, so I don't understand what was different this time."

"We had to do it. That's the end of it." Rednow even struggled to believe his own words.

Tellwoon sighed and Zatak sat back, resigned. "What now? We could return to the Seven Peaks. I guess we could try to make it work there. Organise hunting parties to survive through the winter."

All eyes focused on Rednow.

"No. I have no intention of ever going there."

Merey and Tellwoon exchanged glances. "Then what do you suggest?"

"There's still one job we haven't considered yet, isn't there?" Rednow asked Zatak.

"Are you seriously considering heading down to those filthy swamps? It makes no sense to travel that far for one job. Even if it pays well, which it doesn't."

"I will stay there. I won't be returning to the mainland," Rednow said as if he had already decided. There was doubt in the eyes of his generals.

"Are you sure?" Merey asked. "Are you retiring there?"

Rednow nodded. "It's what Rebma wanted—a warm place. It's what she would have wanted me to do. One last job, then handing the reins to one of you and retiring in Alarkan."

"Won't you miss the mountains?" the hound master insisted. "It's where you grew up, where you raised us all."

You need a fresh start, Rebma's voice said again. It was vivid, crystal clear.

The Benaven Mountains were where he had lived and suffered. Where he buried his dreams and built himself into shape. Every bit of land tainted with his blood, sweat, or tears. He needed no reminders of that place.

"I want to live in a prosperous land as a free man. It's what my parents sought. Maybe I'll give up the sword and pick up a hoe. Become a farmer. I don't know yet, but maybe that's a good thing."

Merey and Tellwoon exchanged looks once again. "What about us?"

"You'll be more than fine. You're both capable. Whoever I pick to lead will be great at it."

Zatak cleared his throat. "Fine? Who's going to agree to pay us now that we are being accused of killing a king?"

Rednow shrugged. "We have one more mission to think about that."

They nodded.

"So, you've decided," Zatak said, his face dropping.

He would get used to it.

"You should tell the pineheads to take the offer from the Alarkani settlers. We also need to send more pineheads to rally all the idle troops we have closest to Alarkan."

Zatak took a sharp breath but nodded in agreement and went over to the pineheads, who gave him a quick nod and left to spread the message, as if their own lives depended on it. The message would get across fast, and they would arrive there on time.

....

The journey was long and arduous. After the third week riding the shadesgrowl, Rednow was giving. His lower back hurt and his inner thighs were still too sore from holding tight to the thick shadesgrowl's torso for so long. As if pain wasn't enough, Rebma continued to haunt his mind with thoughtful and nurturing comments. He should use his time on the journey to design a battle plan, to learn more about the enemy, but this time, it was hard to focus on those important things.

He was used to death, thrived in it, and was a master at delivering it. Then why did it hurt so much this time?

The group continued to ride and Rednow stopped listening to Merey's and Tellwoon's status reports about the terrain and the enemy they were about to face. For days, they had decided not to shy away from the main trails and roads since the group was small and attracted little attention. They crossed farmlands—wide fields full of luscious, red cerro berries that were strong even as the winter fell upon them. Farmers would stop and stare at the riders, and Rednow wondered how much they knew or cared about a dead prince and his murderous father.

In the south, the weather was an enormous improvement. Rednow had stored away his heavy marcruncher fur in the pack on the side of the shadesgrowl's saddle and, to his surprise, there was no snow covering the ground any longer. The air was still humid, but there was a warmth to it that seemed to enhance his sense of smell. Birds chirped and the little apes jumped from trees to trees above him, chasing each other in a game of catch.

I was such a fool. So stubborn for refusing to come to the south earlier.

Weather aside, the good thing about travelling across half of the continent was seeing old faces long forgotten. Little boys and girls he had trained years ago were now ready to be called for battle and fight alongside him. They earned money in other ways—farming, smithing, building—when there were no battles to be fought. And they always came up to him.

"I never thought I'd see you again," a woman said. She and another small group of cloaked Leeth soldiers in disguise had joined Rednow's little entourage on their way to Alarkan. Rednow had trained so many of them he did not recall who she was, but he smiled on the occasion.

They are thankful for everything you've done for them, Rebma's voice said, startling him.

How could he make it stop? "Stop it," he muttered.

"What was that?" the woman asked.

"Nothing, nothing."

Even before he saw the end of the forest, the unmistakable smell of the sea washed over him. He didn't see it then, but the swelling giant was there, so close he heard it crashing against the shore. The white sea birds became louder as they flew and dove towards the spray to find their prey.

When the forest ended, the beach took over the horizon in its loose white sand. Rednow stopped the shadesgrowl, dismounted into the sand, and stretched himself as he took a deep breath. It was as if the salty sea water could heal. The rest of his now large group stopped right behind him and dismounted as well.

"You never realise how much you've missed the sea until you find it again," Rednow muttered. He hoped Rebma would hear it, somehow. He watched the sea birds fighting for the caught fish as the winner flew away with the prize, chased by a dozen hungry followers. Rebma would have loved it there.

Tellwoon rested her hand on Rednow's shoulder. "After so many years in the mountains, this is a sight to behold."

Rednow squinted and, thanks to the clear blue sky, he saw another landmass on the horizon, far on the other side of the sea. "That's where we are going," he said, pointing.

Tellwoon squinted as well and then she could see it. "That land over there?"

Rednow nodded as he walked to the beach, leaving the shadesgrowl behind. He kneeled and dug a handful of sand, before letting it drop back onto the ground. He knew it hadn't been in that exact location, but slight episodes of his first years of youth flashed through his mind as he walked towards the ocean water. Him, running through the shores, chasing birds, digging up holes in the dunes. Running towards the sea for a swim, his tiny feet caught in algae. He wasn't sure if the memories were his or if he was wondering what it could have been if there was no war. No death.

As the bursting low tide reached his boots, he looked both ways and to his right, far in the distance, he saw a ramshackle harbour with half a dozen rowboats attached to it, floating in the waves. He whistled and pointed there. Zatak and the pineheads headed there as the group was still dismounting after emerging from the woods. Tellwoon and Merey caught up to him and the trio started walking towards the harbour, along the beach.

"This is going to be my last battle," he said, almost choking. It was too much.

Merey smiled. "Once you see the enemy, their banners flying, when you hear their war drums playing, your emotions will bury themselves. And they will meet the wrath of the Blood Collector."

"As much as I hate that name, it carries weight," he said, nodding. "Perhaps I can pass it on."

"Absolutely not!" Merey said. "What is yours is yours."

"Yeah. We'll get our own names," Tellwoon said. "I was already thinking about one. What do you think about the *Night Terror*?"

Rednow and Merey laughed, and Tellwoon had no choice but to laugh as well at her own poor attempt.

"The point is for *someone else* to give you a name like that, not for you to choose," Merey said, shaking her head as she laughed. Rednow saw her blush a little as well.

"It's for your enemy to be so afraid of you they'll name you after a monster out of their worst nightmares. And you embrace the monster. You become the monster. And you make them even more afraid," Rednow said.

They stayed silent.

When the trio reached the harbour, there were already three row barges prepared to bring soldiers. A hollow-cheeked old man with dark and sun-wrinkled skin was in charge of the light vessels. He spoke little, but his gesture of an open palm and a finger pointing at it was clear, and the pinehead placed a bag of gold coins in his hand.

"One day journey," the pinehead said.

When Rednow jumped into the wooden boat, it seemed anything but safe, but the old man insisted it could take at least fifty people. Merey, Tellwoon, and two other soldiers jumped in and started rowing, while the pineheads and Zatak stayed back to embark later on another vessel. They would need many trips to transport everyone.

As he rowed, Rednow felt the weather changing. Alarkan was further away than it looked at first. The air was thicker, warmer, and more humid. A constant layer of sweat insisted on forming on his skin, no matter how much he wiped it with his sleeves. The closer they got to Alarkan, the hotter it got, which made Rednow feel uneasy, as if they were entering a dreadful place in the underworld.

"How can it be so muggy?" Merey asked as she took off her coat. "The Seven Peaks are cold and dry. This is hot and wet. Do you think it will be a problem for our troops?"

"They'll adjust."

As it got hotter, Rednow understood why this place had remained undiscovered and unknown for so long. Explorers probably turned back as they realised the scorching climates they were about to enter.

The unknown land of Alarkan was getting closer and closer. Rednow squinted, but there were no buildings in sight yet, except for a makeshift port where they should dock. Another old man, like the one on the mainland, sat and took care of a good dozen of peaceful shadesgrowls that were busy munching on weeds.

Rednow had seen nothing like it. The trees and bushes seemed to grow on top of each other, in a deadly row for survival. Several holes in the ground preserved water, but it was the densest forest they had ever encountered. So thick Rednow wasn't sure he could call it a forest.

"I'm wondering how the fuck we're going to fight a battle in a place like this."

It would be difficult, but if they had enough time to make plans, this could even help them and cut the battle short.

"We'll make room," Rednow said.

TWENTY-SEVEN
FOREIGNERS

GIMLORE

I will see you smile in your dreams. I will warm you.

— From *Mother's Memories*

Gimlore poured herself a mug of wine and noticed her hands trembling. She chugged the liquor in a single gulp and turned her attention to Nork, Nosema, and Foloi. They had everything they needed to make greasy bombs, but none of them were as fast at it as Edmir had been.

She poured another mug and drank in the memory of her old friend. If he was still with her, they would have five trunks full of greasy bombs already—enough to blow up an entire battalion if planted the right way in the right place. By her estimations, they already had about five hundred of them, which was fine, but they needed more. Many more.

The Maiden's Hall was closed to customers now. So many years getting rich and now the gold was rapidly vanishing from her coffers.

On the left side, by the stairs, Tinko and Thata sat cleaning the muskets as instructed.

"No distractions. Clean them well. I want them working as they should."

The kids nodded and scrubbed the barrels with a long brush. Gimlore finished a third mug and glanced over the second room. What had once been the fighting cage was now the storage unit for all the battle equipment. A few dozen workers stacked everything according to her instructions, while others took care of producing more greasy bombs themselves at an even slower pace than Foloi and the twins.

Where the fuck are those mercenaries?

The commanders of the Leeth received the message and accepted the mission. Just thinking of the legendary Blood Collector left her shivering, even if the man was nothing but a myth created to instigate fear upon the enemies and not an actual person. There was still no sign of them. Without the Leeth, she might as well say goodbye to Heleronde and everything she had built.

"Did Pinesy say when they would get here?" she asked, tapping her fingers on the counter.

Foloi shook his head. "I can't get that bastard to say over two words. You're the only one he talks to."

The greasy bombs looked like berries between his fingers. His massive hands were less than suitable for producing something that required such finesse.

Gimlore sighed, pulled out her map of Alarkan, and stretched it across the counter. She flipped it to the other side, where a detailed and more specific map of Heleronde displayed all the shacks, roads, the farmlands, and the puddles, the ponds, and the untouched swampland.

Ten fucking years mapping out this town. Let's put it to use.

Even if the Leeth didn't show up, she still had the terrain advantage. It wasn't by chance that she had survived in the Crimson Wars, bushwhacking enemies, before coming to Alarkan. She could do it again.

Two workers interrupted her thoughts as they walked into the Maiden's Hall carrying a large, heavy trunk that went to the second room. Their frail bodies looked like they were barely strong enough to take it all the way inside the tavern.

"Careful there, boys. Do you know how precious that is? One broken vial means days of work wasted."

"Yes, madam," one man said as he struggled to keep the trunk from crashing on the floor.

"Did the warden say anything?"

The man's face was redder than a cerro berry from the physical effort. "Yes, madam. He said you could go over there whenever you wanted. He has news for you."

Isn't that great?

She grumbled and let the men go ahead with their arduous task. Everybody was busy these days and as nervous as she was. Perhaps even more.

"I'm going to see what he wants."

Foloi mumbled something, but no one objected.

She took leave from the Maiden's Hall and walked along the muddy high street. She wasn't the only one preparing. The poor citizens, merchants, and shopkeepers were busy strengthening their shacks, boarding up the windows and doors with extra wood to fend off invaders. None of that would resist an explosion or a fire, but it warmed their conscience and gave them peace of mind. Who was she to take that away from them?

Entire families packed up their belongings on the carts pulled by shades-growls. She couldn't blame them, either. She would do the same if there wasn't so much at stake. When she reached Keryon and Pie's small herb shop, she found the door closed. She knocked on it, but there was nobody there, so she walked back to the busier side of town and stopped by the old building of the warden patrol. She walked in and it was bustling inside. Squinting, she wasn't sure what to expect. The building was old, and the wood was mouldy. The creaking floor betrayed her presence at every step.

"Ah, Madam Gimlore!" Keryon said as his head peeked from the next room. "We were expecting you."

As Gimlore walked towards the next room, which she expected to be an office, they had now turned into what she could only classify as the chamber of a wizard from a children's tale. Pie sat on a small wooden stool, wearing strange protective equipment covering his face and neck. Gloves protected his hands, and he held two vials of what looked like samples of the mossback elixir she had donated. Many other vials of different shapes and sizes containing liquids of different colours sprawled across the room, occupying most of the counter space.

"What the fuck is this? Is this man a... wizard?"

"Wizard, madam? What stories have you been reading? Piesym is a man of *science*. He dedicated his entire life to studying how we can use nature for our benefit."

Gimlore nodded. She didn't like the man, but she had agreed to work with him. For now. A temporary truce. "Fair enough," she admitted. "What have you found?"

Pie cleared his throat. "I've... taken the liberty of testing it on a few subjects."

"Well?"

"It's very similar to my powers as a smokesmith, but Pie is still trying to figure out the connection between our herbs and your elixir. This is revolutionary, madam. Imagine the possibilities. Imagine if everyone was a smokesmith."

Gimlore felt a chill down her spine. She did not want to live in such a world.

"But the damned mossbacks are not like herbs. They live long and take a long time to grow. Once we take their livers out, that's it. They're gone. We might not have enough. Perhaps to battle against the Floating City Fleet, but not forever."

Keryon and Pie exchanged looks and shared a smile.

"What if I could replicate the elixir?" Pie asked, a devious smile spreading across his round face. Gimlore's eyebrows rose yet again.

"What the fuck do you mean, replicate the elixir?"

"I think I've found a way to produce more mossback elixir here, in this room," Pie said. He was beaming, puffing his chest. "It's still in the early stages, and it's rudimentary, but I've done it."

Pie produced a small vial from his worktable and handed it to Gimlore. The silver substance flowed within the glass, barely any difference visible.

"This is... I'd never thought... How can this be possible?"

"Listen, madam, you've got a grand business opportunity here. If you allow me to do this and assign more labourers to help me, your reserves of the elixir could double!"

Gimlore frowned and focused on Keryon, looking for confirmation, and the warden nodded.

"Now that's quite the tale if I've ever heard one," Gimlore said, taking another glance at the precious vial. If she produced those herself, she could very well be sitting on a gold mine, or even better. If she rejected his offer to help, nothing was stopping him from selling the secret to whoever invaded. *Shit.*

"If that is true," Gimlore said, still eyeing the vial. "How many can you produce for every hundred vials brought to you? With the right help."

Pie sat back down in the chair. "It would take a few days to get started, but with the right equipment, the right number of workers and access to raw elixir, I could double it, produce another hundred."

"And how long would it take to produce that much?"

Pie scratched his head. "It's difficult to know, but less than you take to harvest a hundred vials."

"But if you were able to do this, wouldn't other... scientists be able to do it too?"

Pie nodded. "There's that. But they can't keep replicating it indefinite-ly—they need a steady supply of the undiluted original. Which only comes from you."

Gimlore swallowed. She had to be very careful, then, about who she sold it to.

That was a most interesting discovery, but like everything good in life, it wasn't free. In fact, it would come at a high price. "If this is all true, why haven't you run away with the formula?" she asked.

Keryon took over. "I took an oath, didn't I? I'm not an oath breaker. Our herb business isn't booming. We need another source of revenue."

"You want me to *pay you* to produce *my* elixir for me?" she asked, feigning offence.

"No, madam. We could ask you for a meagre wage," Keryon said, still smiling as if the sun was ever bright and there were no evils in the world. "But because of this mutual understanding of ours, we've learned how much vision you seem to have for new business opportunities. We will trust you will make excellent decisions with the help you get from us."

She was being cheated. They sounded as though they had practiced all of this.

"What do you want, then?" she asked.

"We want a cut of the business. Not your entire business, just the elixir."

Bastards.

"What makes you think this will be a business? It's like a weapon to be used for battles. That's why we need it now. We're expecting enemies," Gimlore said.

Keryon chuckled again. "And weapons can be bought and sold. You expect us to believe you won't keep a heavy stash and start selling these for outrageous sums of gold? You're going to use that gold to strengthen the town, to help build this place up, train military forces, perhaps invest in industry, in trade. This is just the beginning for you, madam," Keryon said.

"I admire how much thought you've put into this, Mister Keryon, but right now I'm focused on defeating our most immediate enemy. I will think about your proposal and we can discuss it further after we send the enemy home in a coffin. For now, you can keep doing it, producing more elixir. I'll send more workers to help you."

They looked relieved as they exchanged glances. Their idea wasn't bad, but she needed time to think about the battle plans and only then would she think about business. There would be no elixir if she didn't save the town and the people first.

....

Walking back towards the Maiden's Hall, she found Nork at the door. He signalled with his eyes at a few weird figures standing against the wooden wall of her establishment. Two women and two men. All of them were taller than her. They had pale skin, as if the sun had never kissed it and put in the effort to make it seem like the climate didn't affect them. One man was older than the rest, likely their leader. Whoever they were, they weren't from around there, which could only mean they were enemy spies or...

Gimlore gave Nork a nod and proceeded towards them, raising her voice. "Can I offer you cold beverages? This is the Maiden's Hall. My tavern."

The strange folks turned around, and Gimlore had a better look at them.

"Thank you," the older man said, in a broken accent she couldn't quite place. His voice was raspy, a perfect match for his rugged appearance.

"No problem. Come on in," she said.

Nork opened the door and they all entered the building. The two women stiffened upon seeing that the inside of the Maiden's Hall looked more like the barracks of a military camp than a tavern, and they exchanged looks before proceeding back to the table.

"Cold water and cerro wine!" Gimlore shouted. She then turned to her guests, sizing them up as she did her best to be amicable. "Please, sit."

Gimlore pulled up a chair and sat next to them. They all carried swords in their scabbards. Just when she was about to ask if the Leeth had sent them to help her, they broke the silence first.

"I was going to ask who is in charge in this town and where I could find them, but it seems like you found us first, madam...?" the older man said, pointing at the war gear as Nork arrived with a cup of cerro wine and a large pitcher of fresh water.

"Gimlore. You have a keen eye," she said after pouring herself a drink. "Did the Leeth send you?"

The man picked up the pitcher and brought it to his face. He drank so deep water flowed out of the corners of his mouth. The other three did the same. They had been on the road for a long time, yet they didn't look dirty or too weary, which meant they had stopped often. Gimlore could barely blame them for refreshing themselves in such heat.

She narrowed her eyes at the older man. There was something about him. His face was lean, yet not fragile, and he looked in top shape for someone his age. He was almost... primal. Behind the beard, there were small scars and his eyes were piercing, but the grey hair and beard made him look like any other elder folk. Goosebumps built up all around her skin. There was something dangerous about him.

"Ahh," he said, wiping his mouth with his sleeve. "Thank you for this. We are from the Leeth indeed."

"I guess we should all introduce ourselves after you welcomed us and gave us drinks," a woman said. She had a long, beautiful dark braid well tied to her scalp, and her eyes were menacing. Gimlore had seen eyes like those, eyes that didn't trust anyone. That were alert day and night. "I'm Merey."

"And I'm Tellwoon," the other woman said.

The second woman had a very forgettable face, but she sported the same haircut as the dark-haired man sitting across from her, with the trimmed sides of the hair shaved to the scalp while the top was longer. She didn't look like a push-over either.

"I'm going outside to check on my boys," the younger man said, displaying crooked teeth that resembled fangs.

"That's Zatak," Merey said. "Don't mind him."

Gimlore nodded and turned to the old man. "And you?"

"I'm Rednow, but you might have heard about my nickname."

Gimlore gasped. "The Blood Collector."

TWENTY-EIGHT
INVINCIBLE

ORBERESIS

They took my love and trashed it. I gave them peace, and they shrugged.
— From *Mother's Memories*

The *Stormbane* rocked against the waves, resilient and hard. The furniture inside it moved wildly from left to right despite the hooks that were designed to keep it steady. Chairs clashed against the wooden walls and even the bed Orberesis sat on moved despite its heavy weight. There was no point in trying to sleep while the world tried to send him to the depths of the ocean.

When was the last time I slept? Unable to remember. He gripped the sturdy back of the bed as the waves crashed against the vessel like hammers, seeking to destroy it. Through his room's glass windows, the lightning flashed seconds before the thunder roared in the distance. The constant murmuring of the dense rain hitting the wood had long become a background noise.

Another wave crashed into the hull and a loud thud echoed. A vessel of such size should be sturdy and last for generations, but it didn't grant those within it the power of immortality. If the ship capsized, the underworld would take them.

His food had dropped on the floor. He couldn't let anyone see him in a state of panic. Sailors hated storms, but they were used to them. Orberesis did not know facing a storm at sea was like being attacked by a swarm of creatures so large that people needed to shut themselves at home and lock all the doors and windows for days on end.

And the migraines. It was as though he had an ocean or two inside his skull, with the tides sending weighty waves against the inside of it. But at least they kept him awake, away from the nightmares that he felt would devour him.

He was unkempt, with dried tears and sweat. His long hair hadn't seen a brush in days and stains of food and wine covered his white robe. How long were storms even supposed to last? Couldn't possibly be longer than that migraine flare, could it?

His hands shook when he tried to reach for the crimson orb inside his dirty robe. The tips of his fingers were so cold, he shivered and had to wrap himself in blankets. He knew what cold was, but not like this. Being out in the ocean, with blasting waves, strong winds, and the threat of lightning. He was already as close to knocking on death's door as he had ever been, but the cold made it worse, as if nature wanted to spite him, too.

It was as though Orberesis was slowly turning into a monstrous creature. A viscous taste had built in his throat and his guts growled and gurgled as though he had been roosting an underworld spawn. There were moments when he felt almost refreshed and others of pure exhaustion. How was that possible? His mind wavered, between flashes of self-aggrandisement and periods where non-existence seemed like a grand idea. This strange bipolarity extended to his senses. Certain foods he'd always liked, he'd now be grossed by; others he had always hated, he'd found himself craving.

Madness. I'm going fucking mad.

He had no idea if they were any closer to their destination or how much the storm had set them back, and other worries ate at him, too. He had promised the crew that the journey would go well and now, well... it hadn't. The white lie had turned out to be more pernicious than he ever expected.

The constant stomping of the sailors and carpenters above reminded him they weren't sleeping either—they were making sure the *Stormbane* didn't sink. In the first few days, shouting had been normal as the chaos took over. The captain and the main deck officers shouted orders left and right about what needed to be done, but the storm was the new normal now.

It was too late now for Orberesis to make himself presentable, climb up to the deck and boost the crew's morale. What was he to do? Freeze to death in the piercing rain? Get swallowed by a wave? No, staying put was his best choice, but he wasn't sure if by now they saw his presence as a blessing or more of a curse. Sailors were always the most superstitious.

I'd be superstitious too if I exposed my arse to Mother Nature for a living, he thought as he picked up another blanket to cover himself.

They would see him as a beast of the underworld, destined to drag them there with him. Sailors on the other ships were probably thinking the same. Would the soldiers even fight for him now? Fucked. Fucked, is what he was.

"The bloody ship is called Stormbane. You would think it would fend off storms or get rid of them," a muffled voice said from a nearby room. Orberesis couldn't tell who it was, but the scratchiness and the accent hinted at it being a lowly sailor.

"You're telling me!" another sailor said. These two were hiding or on a quick break. "Not even God Himself's blessing was enough to rid of this fucking storm."

The first one chuckled. "I once saw a turd that looked more like a god than that fellow does."

Bastards.

"Shh. Someone might hear."

"And do what? Throw me overboard? I'm telling you, being on the deck isn't much better at this point."

"Oh shit, someone's coming. Let's go," the voice said, and they were gone, hiding from duty somewhere else.

In a normal situation, Orberesis would very much like to see their faces, tell them he had heard them. But this wasn't a normal day, a normal time, or a normal place to be. Any mistake made by the crew could send them all into their doom, and fast. Orberesis wasn't so sure the crew wasn't ready to do that to him anyway, even if they all lived to tell the story.

There was a knock on his door, but Orberesis didn't answer. He huddled in his blankets and clasped the red orb inside his palm even harder. The stupid thing was still useless.

"You awake? It's me." Tavanar's voice asked.

"Come in."

Tavanar looked unrecognisable. His greased hair had turned into what looked like a dark rag. His eyes were heavy, and his face pale and bony.

"I look like shit, but you... you look like a shit that took a shit," Tavanar said, covering his nose as he entered the room and noticed the mess it was. His clothes were wet and ragged and there were still recent bits of frost topping off his shoulders.

"This trip was a mistake," Orberesis said, voice trembling.

"Well, it's our chance to get your elixir, and it will all be worth it. You said so yourself."

"It better be." Another wave crashed against the vessel, producing an overwhelming thudding sound. "I haven't slept. I feel like if I do, the beasts of the underworld will swim out of the ocean and pull me in."

Tavanar rolled his eyes. "Yes, yes. Poor you. All alone here in your private room, with your personal food, a comfortable bed, and warm blankets. I'm sharing a hammock with two other bastards who smell worse than my socks."

Orberesis frowned, but he had no retort. "If I were to get sick and die here, they'd think they're sailing on forbidden waters. They'd throw themselves overboard before the ship could even capsize."

Tavanar chuckled. "They're the ones keeping us alive. You know that, right?"

Orberesis sighed.

Tavanar walked over closer to him and held on to the bed as the ship rocked to the left and then again to the right.

"They're very curious about you," Tavanar said. "If it wasn't for Solvi keeping them in line, they would have already stormed in here with questions about your promises of a safe journey."

"I guessed that much." Just as he suspected, the sailors were ready for a mutiny. "And the captain?"

Tavanar shrugged. "I've seen him happier. He won't allow any upheaval, but if the crew rebels, he won't have a choice but to stand with them. And I don't see what the tipping point is."

"Shit," Orberesis said, shivering inside the blankets. It was even worse than he thought.

Tavanar paused and looked at him in silence. A sense of dread built, separating them.

"What?" Orberesis asked. "You're creeping me out."

"This storm got me wondering the same thing. Why *didn't* you do something?"

"What do you mean?"

"Well, the weather," his friend said. "You've got that orb. You're supposed to be this all-powerful man now. It's been two miracles I've seen you do with my own eyes. Why didn't you stop the storm? You promised them the weather would be favourable and it has been nothing shy of vicious. Why don't you do something about it?"

The question weighed Orberesis down like an overbearing beam or the load of a wagon. He needed to con his way out of this, too. If even Tavanar was wondering this, the entire Two Nations would soon ask the same questions. Tavanar had seen him split the earth with fissures, swallow villages, and raise mountains. He had seen him impossibly fend off an assassin in mid-air.

Stopping a storm should be easier than that.

He reached out to the orb inside the robe and the blankets, but remained silent for a few seconds, measuring his answer. "The truth is... I can't perform another miracle."

Tavanar frowned and stayed motionless for a moment and his eyes widened. Then he furrowed his brow. "I'd wondered this a few times but didn't want to believe you were lying to me the whole time. Pretending you were in full control. You don't have control of that orb, of those powers, do you?"

Orberesis instinctively gripped the orb tighter in his palm. An immense pressure built up in his chest, making breathing tougher. It was as if his tongue had stuck to his mouth. What was this pressure? A sense of antic-ipation and danger grew. Tavanar's face changed from disappointment to ire.

"You conned *me*," Tavanar said. "Made me believe you *had* the power, but you did it by accident, didn't you? You can't control it. You don't know what the fuck you're doing. And here I was, acting like your fucking lackey while you're treated like a god."

"I did what I had to do. You wouldn't understand," Orberesis was able to utter.

Something was wrong with him. His guts contorted, his muscles spasmed and it was as though something had risen from his stomach. Not food. Something else. That viscous taste on his tongue intensified again.

He shrivelled but clasped his red orb tighter, still covered in the blankets, only his face out. His bones and his joints cracked and snapped at every tiny movement he made, and his head pounded so harshly his vision blurred. There was this painful agitation, his chest tightening. Danger.

Tavanar paced around the room, unaware something was happening to Orberesis inside the blankets. Orberesis tried but couldn't call out to his friend.

Friend?

No. Not a friend. Scum.

Where had that come from? Fear washed over him, as though there was someone else there, watching both of them. *Something* else. A feeling of impending doom had seeped into his being and taken over entirely. He shook and crumbled underneath the sheets. Something wasn't right. *He* wasn't right. Tavanar didn't notice.

"These fools treated you like God Himself, but you're a little toerag who cares about only himself. I've been with you all along. We've been friends since we were children. And you cannot be arsed to be honest with me."

Tavanar was swimming in anger, but Orberesis couldn't see him properly in the darkness of the ship, especially with his vision blurred as it was, no matter how much he blinked. It got hot all of a sudden. His ears burned and an urge to rip his skin off took over. All the blankets were too hot and unnecessary. He needed to be free of them.

Tavanar faced him, now much closer, and Orberesis' head rang. "I'm so tired of this. Why couldn't we just sit back and enjoy ourselves? Little pigdog always likes to make things complicated, always needs to fuck everything up."

Tavanar needed to be put in his place.

No one talked to Orberesis like that.

He was just another fucking peasant, standing in the way of Orberesis' greatness.

What? No. Tavanar was a friend. His only friend. What was going on with him? With his head? Dread washed over him, but the strange anger hadn't gone away.

"What are you going to do, Tavanar? Kill me?" Orberesis asked and laughed.

A laugh he didn't recognise.

Was that really him? Yes, it was. It had always been him. Mighty God Himself.

"Kill you?" Tavanar frowned. "What are you talking about? I know I'm not a good man by any means, but I would never kill you, Doi. But you, however... Something is off with you. It has been for a while and I'm even mad at myself for taking so long to realise. For sticking by your side while you slaughtered an entire nation with your smokesmiths."

"They deserved to die. They're roaches. Nothing more," he whispered.

Why did I say that? It was as though someone had spoken for him, as though the words had a life of their own.

Orberesis shuffled uncomfortably as the blankets fell from his shoulders. It was too hot, and he needed to make Tavanar understand him. See his reason. Tavanar was supposed to obey him. Listen to him. He was God Himself, world breaker! He didn't need to justify himself. He did what he damn well pleased.

"You will listen to me, Tavanar," he said, moving towards his friend. No, his vassal.

Tavanar's brows widened, eyes filled with fear. And he staggered back slowly. Yes, fear was good. A surge of power filled every bit of his being. There was a mix of danger, fear, and pain, but that sense of power was addictive and Orberesis drank it all. Swallowed it whole.

"Doi... There's a—"

What is happening to me?

Just as Orberesis glanced at his own body, his eyes still blurry, the orb glistened, producing a red light so bright it was almost blinding. Orberesis covered his eyes and when the light subsided, he was no longer inside the dreadful ship.

A vision?

He scrambled to find out what happened, to find Tavanar. But he was back in a familiar place—a beach with red, wet sand, and constant waves crashing into the bank. The place of his suffocating nightmares. No good things ever happened in that place.

He glanced at the ocean, where a towering giant pillar of light emerged far in the horizon, connecting the sea to the clouds. Shaping them. Was it a dream or an illusion? He hadn't been sleeping, but he was sure mountains couldn't rise from clouds, and yet, they did there. The sky darkened into a mix of purple and navy blue. The sparse clouds covered millions of tiny, glistening stars.

A giant man appeared from behind the clouds.

A man as big as the sky, as big as the ocean. With piercing red eyes and a dark grey skin, the towering man looked upwards and his arms widened in an open embrace, as though he was showing himself. Revealing his presence.

Orberesis could not move. The cursed paralysis. But the orb's red glistening matched the eyes of the giant man. Impending doom prevented him from moving. Whatever was happening to him would be his end. This is where he would die. He knew it. All his nightmares brought him to such a place. And then Orberesis noticed for the first time.

The giant man was him.

The facial features were unmistakeably his, but when he rose from the horizon, there was nothing below his naked torso, as if the lower half of his body was missing. The clouds shaped themselves around the large, towering figure, creating space for him.

And then the world broke. The ground shook. The earth roared and Orberesis turned back in agony to see what was happening as hundreds of human bodies and creature corpses covered the beach where he stood.

Beyond the beach, villages were being swallowed by the fissures splitting the earth. Houses, roads, and trees were no more. Everything thrown into the underworld. Volcanic mountains and hills emerged in their place.

Orberesis recognised that place. That was where he had cracked the earth and rid humanity of the hordes of creatures about ten years earlier, sending both beasts and humans to the underworld in equal measure, putting an end to the Crimson Wars and lifting Alarkan from the ocean.

He remembered.

This was his doing. His power. His divinity.

He looked back as the orb kept shining around his neck. The swarming hordes of beasts forgot to fight when the ground crumbled beneath them. The earth spared no one and swallowed beasts and men. Before the soil closed again, the world stopped shaking, and the landscape had changed from chaos and destruction to a quiet, chilling nothingness. Far on the horizon, the impossible man stared right at Orberesis.

This can't be real. None of this is real. Am I dreaming? Dead?

Before he could answer, he was inside *Stormbane* again and his eyes adjusted. The orb around his neck was still glowing in a deep, bright red, but now it hovered in front of his chest, meeting his movements.

His rage for Tavanar was back. Something like he'd never felt. Such a powerful feeling, that. A burning heat and desire to indulge. His vision cleared and he found Tavanar's neck, choking under his palms, his hands uselessly clutching Orberesis'. Orberesis felt the power of his grip reaping the life from Tavanar, his panicked eyes begging for mercy. Like a maggot.

"You will listen," Orberesis said, though his voice was harsher, deeper.

What am I doing?

Orberesis caught himself. *What have I done?* He released Tavanar.

"I'm sorry, Tav... I... I don't know what—"

Tavanar gasped, his feet back on the wooden floor. He dropped to his knees, clutching his neck and throat, coughing, searching for his breath back. There was still a panic in his eyes, as though he had just seen something he'd rather never see again. Then he skidded out of the room without looking back.

Orberesis had fucked up. Truly. When had his hands reached out to choke Tavanar? He didn't remember any of it. He remembered glimpses of it, of a lust he could hardly tame, though. There was something wrong with him. Whatever it was, now he needed the cure more than ever. It might have cost him his best friend.

TWENTY-NINE
WAR CRIMINAL

GIMLORE

*R*ays of light pierce through the haze. A fragile hope for better days.

— From *Mother's Memories*

Gimlore struggled to keep the hair off her face as the wind blew stronger than usual. Maybe there was a storm on the way, but right next to her was another of human flesh and bones, aged by the harshness of battlefields and death. And yet, he looked so human.

She had been quieter than usual. She knew the tales of the Blood Collector, how he had defeated an army on his own, and how he was a restless monster that wiped out everything in sight. Was this old, white-haired man the real deal?

Gimlore glanced at the man through the corner of her eye and almost forgot what they were doing there, between the beach and the farmlands, but the hearthspears kept her sharp. A simple distraction would be enough for her to fall. The old man and his generals didn't struggle at all to ride the hearthspears.

"This is a most magnificent animal," the Blood Collector said, caressing the scales on his hearthspear's thick neck. The beast reacted and showed his dozens of sharp teeth in what should be a smile. "I'd never seen one of these, but they are gorgeous. What are they?"

She took a while to respond, half-stunned that the Blood Collector addressed her with such ease.

"Oh, these? We call them hearthspears. They can't ride for long, but they are the fastest I've seen. We couldn't get anything done in the wetlands without them."

The Blood Collector nodded and continued petting the hearthspear as the beasts rode through the uneven ground, indifferent to the obstacles in their way. The mercenaries still wore darker clothes, inappropriate for Alarkani weather, and the sweat built up in their faces.

"What do you think about our swamplands?" Gimlore asked.

Rednow glanced at her and his blue, weary eyes glistened under the sun light. "As a place to explore or as a battlefield?"

"Both, I suppose," Gimlore said.

She couldn't figure out the Blood Collector. He was quiet and reserved and did not seem a monster at all. Not vile, nor conceited or rude. He hadn't even made a single threat or insult yet. It was not who she had expected.

Rednow took a moment to reply. "Let's stop here and I'll look."

He pulled the reins, forcing the hearthspear to stop. He jumped off with ease, as if he'd done it a million times. Gimlore struggled to jump out of the saddle, as usual. She landed with her boots on the mud and let the Blood Collector walk around the swamp, surveying the terrain.

Rednow explored the bushes and many of the puddles and water holes that were scattered. He unsheathed his sword, and Gimlore felt her skin shiver as she saw a crimson red tainted the blade. Rednow kneeled and inserted the sword into a waterhole thick enough for a grown man to fall into his doom.

"How deep?" he asked after taking his measurement, pulling his sword out and wiping the water off with his sleeve. The blood stains did not leave the blade.

"We think some of them are underground water tunnels, connecting to one another," she said, walking over to another puddle. "This one is deep, but it's just a hole. But that one curves at a certain depth."

"Is this the first time Alarkan will be under attack?"

"Yes. I think this place is a perfect battlefield, though. We can set up traps and ambushes they'll never see coming. Your soldiers can come out and finish the job."

"It seems like you've seen the battlefield yourself," Rednow said, his eyes glued to her.

"A few too many fucking times," she said. "I'm hoping this will be the last one, though I also said that when I pushed the first baby out of me and there was still another one in there."

Rednow and his generals laughed. The old man had a regal smile if she had ever seen one. He laughed with the poise and confidence of someone with nothing left to prove. In that moment, Gimlore envied him.

"These water holes are going to make or break the battle," Tellwoon said. The woman was around Gimlore's age, but in much better shape.

Tellwoon picked up her dagger and cut out a thick and large horsetail reed and pierced it inside with her needle stinger of a dagger.

"Watch this," Tellwoon said as she jumped into the hole, holding the cane in her hand.

At first, Gimlore almost panicked, thinking the bastard had jumped to her own doom, but then she noticed the top edge of the reed on the surface of the water.

"She's using the cane to breathe," Gimlore muttered.

Rednow and Merey nodded.

"It's the perfect place to hide and ambush enemies. As long as we know *when* to get out of the water," Merey said.

"Hmm." Gimlore nodded while a drenched Tellwoon emerged from the waterhole.

"This is an interesting way to see what terrain we will face," Rednow said. "And you'll excuse my bluntness, but we're going to need to get paid now, as more of our soldiers are on their way."

"Oh. Let's take care of that, then."

She had hoped to sway them with promises of land. After meeting Rednow, she was not so sure that was possible.

....

"This is all we have right now," Gimlore said.

She sat at a table inside the Maiden's Hall. The room was vacant except for Nork and Nosema, who were there more for moral support than as bodyguards. "Each citizen paid a tax for this. I put most of what I have into it, too."

Rednow nodded and looked at a pinehead that had travelled with him, while pointing at the pile of gold stacking up on the table. The little pinehead had a lighter complexion than Pinesy, which suggested a more northern heritage. He jumped on to the gold and counted it faster than Gimlore would ever be able to. He then retreated to Rednow and spoke in his ear.

Gimlore swallowed and wiped her sweaty temple.

"This isn't what we discussed," Rednow said. His face changed. The charming and poised old man now sported a deadly glance, causing her hands to shake a bit. In that moment, she had no doubts he was the Blood Collector. "Is this a trick?"

"No, no," Gimlore said, sweat still flowing from her forehead. "We would never do that to you, Blood Collector. It's unfortunate, but it's all we have, though we can always negotiate. We have land. I'm willing to give that up, as I've already said."

Rednow commanded the pinehead to collect all the gold, and then he cleared his throat. "A little piece of advice, Gimlore. I don't know what games you've been playing with these people, but sometimes..." he said, leaning forward and closer to her. "The best way to win is knowing when *not* to play."

Gimlore froze.

"If I even smell that you're trying to play me here, this won't end well," he said. "Do you understand?"

Gimlore swallowed. It has been years since someone had spoken to her like that. And never in her own place. But this was... different. How naïve she had been.

"Yes, understood," she said. "But if you think I won't do what's best for this town out of fear for you, or admiration, or whatever, then you're wrong. I know when not to pick a battle."

Rednow raised his eyebrows, but his mouth stretched into a timid smile. "It seems like we're going to understand each other after all. You take care of your people and I'll take care of mine."

"Do you accept my deal? With the land as payment?"

Rednow hesitated. "Why don't we go see it? The land that you would use as payment."

Gimlore hadn't even thought of that.

"Sure, sure. It's a splendid piece of land. I'll show you," she said, turning to her crew. "You can stay here and continue to take care of whatever needs to be prepared. Have the scouts seen any sign of the Floating City Fleet?"

Nork and Nosema shook their heads at the same time. "No Boss," Nork said. "There's a big storm in the Southern Ocean. It might have caught them."

"Isn't that good?"

"Well, the longer they take, the longer we have to prepare. But if they come hidden in the storm, we might not hear about their arrival until too late," Nork said.

Gimlore scratched her chin and glanced at Rednow, as if asking for his take.

Rednow shrugged. "He's not wrong. We only need another day."

"You heard the man. You two stay here and I'll show the Blood Collector the lands we will be offering. And keep those scouts looking at the sea."

Nork and Nosema nodded and went over to the next room, where most of the weaponry and ammunition were.

"I see you're as prepared as you can be over here," Rednow said, glancing at the trunks, the muskets, and all the swords they had.

"Can't leave anything to chance," Gimlore said.

....

Gimlore and Rednow rode through the swamplands. The hearth-spears raced through the mud and the small puddles covering the ground. This was her poorest lot in terms of mossbacks living there and one of the farthest from Heleronde. She couldn't give up the good ones.

Upon arrival, there were rough bushes and wild plants hiding the water holes and the mossbacks made no sounds. She pulled the reins of the hearthspear and Rednow did the same.

"This would be it," Gimlore said, hesitant. No workers had maintained the land at all. It was unexplored. "From here to the horizon over there. I think it's quite generous. If any of you want to settle down here, we could really use people who can fight."

Rednow looked distracted, glancing around at all the trees, bushes, and muddy ground. Gimlore could not assess what the man was thinking.

"This is virgin land, is it not?"

"Yes."

Rednow considered her words and took another moment to scan the land. "This is still very wild. It will take a while to start up a farming operation."

Another bead of sweat flowed from her forehead. "Yes," she admitted.

Rednow nodded, unsheathing the sword and using it to slice the invading bushes to clear a path. "I want to see those mossbacks. Can I?"

Gimlore swallowed. "Sure."

She led the way through a part of the land where she detected footsteps from the beasts. Pulling a small dead rodent from her pouch, she tapped the surface of a large waterhole with the corpse. She did it a couple more times until there was a movement in the water. After a moment, the head of a mossback emerged from the water and Gimlore teased it with the dead rodent. It was a big one, larger than Pinesy's bloodsleuths. It was still twitchy, but eager to get an easy meal. Two more followed the first out of the water.

"Are they dangerous?" Rednow asked with his brow frowned.

"No. They don't trust us much, but they will only bite when they feel threatened. In my farms, they don't bite anymore."

"Is that so?" Rednow's eyes stuck to the creatures.

Gimlore threw the rodent about a few paces ahead and the creatures fought for it, snarling at each other. The strongest one got the rodent and dipped back into a water cave, chased by the other two.

"Fascinating. You know, I wasn't planning on taking you up on your offer, but a lot of... unpleasant things have happened, and this offer became a lot more attractive."

There was no ill-intent in his voice. No threats. No lies. There was only truth. "Can I assume seeing all of this makes up for the lack of gold?"

Rednow chuckled. "You can," he said as he explored bits of the land. "You know what I like the most about it here? There are no lords, no talk of tradition, honour or any such bullshit."

Gimlore produced another smile. "That is why we are here. Freedom. Independence. I used to say peace, but that's no longer the case."

Rednow nodded. "Peace is always temporary. When someone finds peace, there will always be some trying to protect it and others to steal it. That's the paradox. You extinguish it by trying to preserve it. And I say this as someone who could not make a living if there was only peace in the world. My usual policy is to let the lordings fight each other, and I'll come collect their gold."

"I want to keep it different from the mainland," Gimlore said. "But we need to stop the invaders. My scouts say they have a new king. A cult leader. Do you know about him?"

"They say he created all of this," Rednow said, still cutting down bushes to make way for himself and Gimlore. "Whatever that means."

"I heard he has the Two Nations in his pocket. You can't do that without some kind of ancient sorcery or a brilliant strategic mind, I imagine."

"You'd be surprised. Monarchs are proud and foolish. A cult leader like Orberesis harnessed a legion of followers all around the world. It's no surprise even kings and queens would also fall under his mantle," Rednow said.

Gimlore grumbled. "I wouldn't mind sending all those fucking tyrants to the underworld if they don't stay where they belong."

Rednow stopped and looked back at her before producing another smile. "My sister would have liked you."

"Would have? What happened to her?"

Rednow continued onwards and gauged his reply. They reached a clearing with a small pond. He kneeled and placed his hand inside the water, then produced a soft smile. "She is dead now."

Gimlore felt a shiver down her spine and had more questions than answers, though she said nothing. Instead, she walked over to the edge of the water, unsure of what the Blood Collector was doing. The man stayed silent next to her. Maybe he was enjoying being around nature, seeking peace before the battle.

They returned to the small hill where they had left their hearthspears as they heard a loud whistle. Gimlore recognised that sound. There was only one man in Heleronde who did that.

"Madam Gimlore." Keryon appeared, his eyes locked in on Rednow. "And this must be the legendary Blood Collector."

Gimlore was about to introduce the two, but she noticed the tense way they gazed at each other. Rednow's calmness and poise turned into a challenging stance and a deadly stare.

"Who is this man?" Rednow asked without taking his eyes off him.

"Th—this is Keryon. He's the town warden."

Rednow scowled. "A lawman."

"And the world's biggest war criminal," Keryon said with his charming smile. "Nice to meet you."

Gimlore's confused gaze shifted between the two men.

"Wait... what is the matter with you?" Gimlore asked, placing herself between them. "What do you have against each other?"

"He's a smokesmith. I can tell," Rednow said, spitting near Keryon's feet.

"Hypocrite. So are you."

"Hey. What's wrong with being a smokesmith? I am not the biggest fan either, but we need all the help we can get. Keryon is on our side," she said, then turned to Keryon. "And so is Rednow."

She pushed both of them in separate ways and Rednow took a deep breath. "That's fair enough. I have nothing against this man. I don't trust smokesmiths one bit, is all."

"And I have thoughts on how this gentleman makes a living, but I guess those discussions can wait until later," Keryon said. The smile returned.

"There will be no discussions, Mister Keryon. Rednow, why don't you trust smokesmiths if you're... well, a smokesmith?"

"You don't know how a smokesmith is created, do you?"

Gimlore shook her head. There was pain in Rednow's eyes.

"Those tyrants..." Rednow said. "They captured us while we were children. Stripped us from our parents. Took us off the streets. And exposed us to the smoke. Hundreds of kids die every time they do it. The kingdoms' existing smokesmiths force those who survive the smoke to train and become smokesmiths for the crown or for a lording's private army. By the time they are adults, they've bought into it. They're too scared to let go. It's all they know. Isn't that right, *smokesmith*?"

Keryon's smile vanished. "I was never enough of a coward to escape. I served the law well and they let me leave."

"Whose law? The law of your *owner*? Of stripping kids from their parents and doing to them what others did to you? The law of burning your lungs for the sake of your masters?"

"Most of us never had the luxury of escaping. At least I did my job with honour and pride."

"You think I lived a luxurious life?" Rednow asked, spitting to the side.

Gimlore froze. She did not need a fight breaking out between them. Keryon was younger and powerful, but this was the Blood Collector.

Gimlore sighed. "No one here had any luxuries, but you know who did? The cult leader who is on his way here. I'm not picking sides between you two. We don't have time for this. Can you at least pretend to like each other? If we don't work together, they will leave nothing."

Neither answered.

"Shit. You two... I'm putting my life, the life of my children and the life of everyone in my town, in the hands of you both. I'm giving up whatever control I still have left in all this in ways that sometimes make my skin crawl.

I have no choice but to rely on you. Well, I'm telling you both now—suck it up. What part of that don't you understand?"

The two men eyed each other furiously for a moment before Rednow broke the silence. "No promises," he said.

"Likewise," the Warden confirmed.

Scratching her face deep, Gimlore remembered how much she hated men sometimes.

THIRTY

CHOICES

REDNOW - GIMLORE

I rode the trails of the past, hoping the future would be ours.

— From *Mother's Memories*

Rednow wiped the sweat off his forehead yet again and smacked a bug biting at his neck. At night, the temperatures dipped, but the insects came in full force. The encampment set up on the outskirts of Heleronde was big enough for everyone. There was no need for a campfire, but he and his generals still sat on four large wood logs facing each other. Some habits were hard to break. Next to him, Rebma's bag with her paper, ink, and everything she had been writing. Everything he had promised he would keep. He would read it one day. Now was not the time.

"Are we still waiting for troops?" Rednow asked the trio of generals sitting in front of him. They now sported the much lighter clothing provided by Gimlore.

"The other houndsmen are still crossing in the rowboats," Zatak said. "But other than that, we are ready, so I hope this will be quick. Another week here and the insects will drain all my blood."

Rednow nodded and scratched his head.

Be honest with them, Rebma's voice said in his head. He tried to shake it off, but to no avail. Insanity was his destiny. That would be fine if his sister wasn't the voice of his nightmares. The ghost was right, though. Rednow's life would change after this, and so would the life of everybody else he led.

"I went to visit the lands we will receive as payment for this job," he said.

The generals exchanged looks.

"Any chance we can convince you to change your mind?" Tellwoon asked. She had her arms crossed and her feet tapping on the ground.

"No. Since I've been... hearing Rebma, I know what this means. It's time to say goodbye."

Merey furrowed her brow. "What do you mean, *hearing* Rebma? Are you alright?"

"Yes, yes. It's nothing. But listen. Let me finish. Now it's time for one of you to take up the reins of the Leeth and command all our troops. I have not decided yet, do you understand? Show me everything. Put everything on the line."

Both Merey and Tellwoon nodded.

"Merey. You're brave and strong, but you can be too reckless and impulsive. You must know contention when you're responsible for so many lives."

"Agreed," she said, before focusing her eyes on the ground below her.

"Tellwoon," Rednow said. "You're compassionate, and bright, but you have to show me bravery, tenacity. You still hesitate too much in moments where you should act on instinct."

"Right," Tellwoon said, tapping her foot on the ground.

"My successor should have the best qualities of both of you, but we can't have everything in life, so one of you needs to step up and do better."

"I'm glad you didn't pick me," Zatak said as he took out a piece of raw meat from his pouch and chewed on it. "This way, I can keep minding my little four-legged babies."

"You'd rather lead hounds than soldiers?"

"Hey!" Zatak said. "My hounds *are* soldiers."

For them, it was just another battle, but the enemy would be strong and Rednow felt as if someone had ripped out one of his arms. He needed proper time to grieve, but that wasn't possible on the battlefield.

I'll guide you, Rebma's voice echoed in his mind.

Those were words of comfort, and yet they hurt.

As the surrounding banter started, Rednow smiled at the generals, got up from the log and surveyed the simple tents the soldiers had set up for themselves. Old and new warriors laughed together, reminisced about old battles, and prepared to fight. The swords were well-sharpened; the uniforms were clean and well-maintained. There was no dishevelled hair in sight. The boots were, well, difficult to keep clean, even for Rednow.

They would be fine without him.

He would be fine with letting them go, although it still hurt to see how much they didn't need him anymore. Who was he without the Leeth? Without those condemned souls seeking life and a purpose?

He circled around camp, greeting the soldiers. He couldn't tell them that before a battle. Morale would suffer. The more he walked around the encampment, getting bit by the annoying insects, the tighter his chest felt. He went back to Zatak, Tellwoon, and Merey, joined by a large group of about twenty soldiers. They were weary, but as soon as they saw him, they almost glistened with pride and admiration.

"Rednow! Here you are!" one soldier said. Rednow couldn't remember the fellow's name. "I was telling the generals that I would like to play a song for you now that we are waiting for the call to the battlefield. What do you think?"

Rednow had always enjoyed music, which he did not hear enough now that Rebma was gone. He looked at the generals and they reacted with a mix of nods and shrugs. "Yes, go on, then. Please."

The soldier produced a confident smile and sat on one of the big logs. One of his friends pulled out a small flute, and he picked up his little drum, placing it between his thighs. And then the music started to the rhythm of the drum, in light but strong taps on the leather. The flute topped it off with an impressive solo, almost a voice itself. Then he sang of fallen brothers and sisters, of family waiting back home. His voice grew as he yelped and cried for fallen comrades; it dropped into a well of sorrow loud enough for the dead to take notice. His anger picked up then, rallying the crowd as the steady drum picked up the pace. He finished in a steady low chant, beating on his chest. Those who knew the lyrics joined in.

The flute came to a halt, waking Rednow up from his daydream. He wiped his wet eyes with the sleeve. He was getting too soft, too damn emotional for this.

Stop it, that's not true, Rebma's ghost said, which made him want to cry even more.

"That was beautiful," he said, noticing a sizeable crowd had gathered. Hundreds of faces, familiar and new. "But we haven't got the time to sit around and sing. All of you, back to your stations."

The soldier gave him an understanding smile and took off as the rest of the crowd dispersed.

"Singing mercenaries," a voice said somewhere in the distance. "Now I've seen everything."

Rednow looked around, trying to find the owner of such a recognisable, raspy tone, and found the dark-haired woman waving as she walked towards him. "Don't tell me you sing too," Gimlore said.

Rednow smiled. He had grown a certain affinity for her, perhaps because she reminded him of Rebma, in a way. "How can I help you?"

"The scouts say the Floating City Fleet has appeared from the storm. They should be here by dusk. It's time," she said. There was stress and anxiousness in her.

"Excellent," he said as he got up to his feet. This was his time. His last shot at showing who he was. "I'm going to need full military control of this battle."

"I know this land better than I know my children. I understand the terrain better."

"I'll start the battle behind, and then I join at the right time. Perhaps you can stay back with me? Tellwoon, Merey, and Zatak will each command part of my troops."

Gimlore scratched her chin and tapped her foot in the mud. "Fine. I guess that's fair enough. I hired you to do this, so I suppose I should let you do it your way."

Rednow smiled. "I'm sure I'm not telling you anything you don't know yet, but this won't be as easy as we make it sound. They have the numbers. And they have the massive fleet."

"Madam Gimlore, they're almost here!" a peasant came running at full speed. "They're anchoring their ships!"

"Well, shit," Gimlore said, swallowing, her heartbeat rising. "That's earlier than the scouts said," Gimlore said. "Let's look."

Rednow gripped the hilt of his sword and jogged towards the beach with Gimlore and a few of her men. The mud made the ground too slippery and dangerous for battle. A slip-up could betray even the best of warriors.

They walked across the small town and towards a ravine overlooking the ocean. Squatting to avoid being seen, Gimlore and Rednow peered at the sea.

"Fuck," Gimlore muttered. "*That* is the Floating City Fleet?"

Enormous ships sailed towards Alarkan with their sails down. Each of them had at least nine large masts, Rednow counted. Authentic monsters at sea. They looked worn out by the storm, but intact. Hundreds of sailors and crewmen moved inside like insects, scrambling to get the ships ready to be anchored. Rednow could only imagine how many soldiers those vessels could host in their innards. He counted fifteen ships.

"That is a sample of the fleet, but perhaps more than we can handle."

His eye caught a single vessel, bigger and stronger than the rest. The masts were taller and the deck much larger and wider. They had painted the wood in edges of dark blue and red highlights. The main large flag on the tallest mast was a black cloth with a red sphere in the middle.

"See that one? That's where their leader will be."

Gimlore nodded. "I'll make sure all my people know. I have a special gift planned for him."

....

Gimlore shouted commands at her troops. Soldiers, peasants, and farmers geared up, gathered their weapons and scrambled to their assigned positions.

"Rednow," she said, excitement and perhaps a hint of fear showing in her eyes. "Remember to keep your troops out of sight at first. He will come to talk to me first and offer me surrender, but his generals will assess my troops and how well prepared we seem to be. Our plans will only work if he doesn't see you and the Leeth soldiers."

"They should be in position now."

He left her and headed towards the swamplands between the shore and the town. He found his soldiers hiding behind bushes in silence, their faces covered in mud and grease for better camouflage. Rednow looked for Tellwoon and Merey and spotted them further back, out of sight, riding hearthspears.

"You know what my plans are. Now, it's up to you. Gimlore also has tricks up her sleeve."

"The woman is not as stupid as I thought," Merey said.

"Most definitely not."

The sound of a ship's horn echoed in the distance.

"Everyone in hiding. Under the water holes, if you must!" Tellwoon said.

Merey raced to her side of the troops and shouted similar commands. The troops obeyed with no delay. Soldiers picked up their reed canes and dove into the water holes. Those who rode hearthspears pulled back and stayed out of sight, closer to town and to the encampment.

Rednow followed them to a hill where they could see the sea, the beach, and the swampland. From there, he spotted three small rowboats departing the large ships, and he was sure Orberesis would be in one.

He saw Gimlore and four of her men walking towards the beach, careful about where they stepped in the sand. Or maybe that was how it looked like from there. It was in her hands now.

....

Gimlore took each step with the utmost care. The sand was tricky, and a false step could ruin everything. Nork, Nosema, Keryon, and Foloi followed her. The northern man was big, but not clumsy, so she had nothing to fear.

When they reached the part of the sand that was kissed by the waves, they waited. Gimlore's hands trembled, and she struggled to keep her legs from shaking. When was the last time she had felt like this? Over ten years ago, for certain. Was she still the same as she used to be? Edmir would say so, but she had got Edmir killed. She could not let the same happen to the rest of them.

A few small rowboats closed the distance between the anchored behemoths and her crew, carried by the waves as skinny sailors rowed on each side. Even at that distance, as the boats made their way to shore, she saw a squinty man, shrivelled and ill, but he was still compelling. That had to be the cult leader. His dark, long hair waved in the wind, but his white robe was full of stains and glued to his body. The bastard didn't even look godly. He was just a man.

"The fucker looks like shit. How does anyone believe he is God Himself?"

"Must have been the storm," Keryon said. "I bet the entire sailing crew is exhausted."

He was right. She inspected those around Orberesis. The darker-skinned folks looked pale, their clothes worn out, dirty, and ragged. That was a lot of nerve for someone looking to invade and seize a large piece of land.

"That woman," Keryon said, looking at the only woman in the boats. She stood next to Orberesis, dressed in dark except for a red crystal ball hanging from her neck. "She carries herself well."

"What do you mean?"

"I don't know," Keryon said, squinting and placing his hand over his eyes to shield them from the Sun. "I think she might be a smokesmith."

"How can you tell?"

"I think I've seen her."

Gimlore swallowed. Smokesmiths were never a good sign. Especially if they were with the enemy. "Can you keep an eye on her?"

Keryon's serious face unfolded into a big smile.

"With pleasure."

THIRTY-ONE

ABSOLUTION

ORBERESIS - GIMLORE

I taught you all I know, but you ignored it. When his blinding light came, my eyes burned. Now I will not be here to burn for you.

— From *Mother's Memories*

Orberesis was nauseous throughout the journey in the rowboat, wishing nothing more than to step on solid ground. After weeks of misery during the storm and the violent madness that had driven him to try and kill Tavanar, he was depleted and tired, but there was a new exhilarating feeling. He was more than glad to be in Alarkan, even if his best friend had been hiding somewhere for the rest of the journey. It was fine. He could do it alone or with Solvi's help. He reached for the orb and the anger and confusion he felt about the vision he'd had and everything else before that dissipated at the sight of the swampy wasteland that was Alarkan. He could almost taste the elixir on his lips. Even the migraines had subsided, giving way to a sliver of hope.

With his eyes on land, a hot and damp breeze slapped him in the face. The farmers, with their pitchforks and scythes, didn't seem to care about the weather much. They wore loose shirts and pantaloons designed perhaps a century ago, and the sweat built up in their skin was almost like an added layer.

Poor bastards, they're in for a treat, he thought as the tired sailors did their best to row the boats forward with their shrivelled, depleted arms.

Solvi sat next to him. From that close, he couldn't believe how beautiful she looked. Even the greasy hair after all that time on the ship didn't make him want her any less. Orberesis shifted his focus to the raggedy fellows waiting for him at the waterfront and the small shacks well behind them in the distance, invisible from the ocean.

That was it? That was the so-called town? *These* people had somehow sabotaged the Sirestine settlers' camp?

"It seems tiny. It will be an easy siege once we're done here."

"Yes, Highest One. You created this land, after all."

"Here is fine."

The rowboats were still at a considerable distance from the beach, but already close enough to listen to the poor bastards' pleas for mercy. Four men and a woman stood by the beach, unarmed.

Orberesis glanced behind them and saw less than a hundred men and women holding on to small daggers, kitchen knives, scythes, and other ridiculous weaponry. The four who stood by the beach, however, didn't look like they were going to be kneeling. Perhaps they would need persuasion. One man was large and tall, with blonde hair like the slaves he kept back at the palace. Good-looking, for sure.

"Well met," Orberesis said, addressing the blonde man. "I assume you know who I am. Who we are? Do you know why I'm here?"

No answer.

"I am Orberesis, the creator of this land where you stand. I pulled it from the depths of the ocean with my power. I am God Himself, the

Miraculous One. You might have heard of me. I'm here on behalf of the Two Nations of Sirestir and Yab, of King Doemus. All lives will be spared if you surrender," he said.

Orberesis waited for an answer, but the woman burst out laughing. She was older than him. Her dark hair was tight in a bun, and she didn't look tall or strong, but her laughter was unhinged.

"Listen, fellow, I don't know how much you've been drinking to say things like that. In a different world, I would invite you into my tavern and even let you drink for free if you came in telling stories like those. But you can go right back, shove the surrender up your shitty backside, and fuck yourself while you're at it. How does that sound?"

What?

How dare she speak to him like that? She would be the first to die. "And who might you be?"

"I'm Gimlore. And since you asked, this isn't your land. It's *my* land. *You* can get back in your boat or you will face consequences."

Orberesis could almost feel the anger in Solvi turning her into a monster, but he kept holding her arm. "You sure have much to say. I'm not sure if the people in that town of yours will be grateful for your words when I'm done with it."

"Why don't you come here to the beach for a fistfight? If you win, you can take the town. If I win, you fuck off," she said, a devilish smile forming on her face. "No weapons. Just our hands. You aren't afraid of a little defenceless woman like me, are you?"

His lips contorted in displeasure and his hands clasped into fists. The woman was a mouthful, humiliating him, provoking him. Him!

"This is an outrage! You dare insult him like that?" Solvi asked, her face nothing but hatred. "He is God Himself. You don't even deserve to breathe the same air!"

"You better control this woman. She's creeping me out a little," Gimlore said.

"Insolent fool. Later on, remember... You chose this. You've chosen to inflict pain, death, and extinction upon your people."

Gimlore scowled. "We've all seen those. We were born into it, lived through it, and survived it. It's not a big deal anymore. We've all seen tyrants like you, but we escaped them. We'll fight if we must. But you... you are something else. What kind of man pretends to be a god?"

"We will send you to your maker in the underworld," Solvi hissed.

"Great, then I can stick him with this," she said, displaying a long dagger.

Orberesis imagined himself choking the woman. Breaking her neck between his hands. People like her didn't deserve to be left alive. She was like those that had stepped on his neck when he was a starving child roaming the streets of Ushar. Ruthless. Vicious.

"Let's go back," he said. The idle sailors started rowing, but Orberesis kept his eyes locked on the dark-haired woman as she headed back.

....

Back inside *Stormbane*, Orberesis let his anger fuel him. With Solvi on his tail, he marched towards the captain.

"I want her dead, Solvi. DEAD!" He roared without facing her.

"With pleasure, Highest One," Solvi said. "I will arrange for her to be brought to you after we clear the area. You can give her whatever punishment you see fit."

"Perfect."

His mere presence made everyone flinch. They were tired, but it was up to him to remind them why they were there.

"Highest One!" the skipper said, emerging out of his cabin. The man was still pulling his pants up while a shy young woman left right behind him, still putting on clothes of her own. "I was just looking for you. Did the savages surrender?"

"No," Orberesis admitted and noticed the puzzled face of the seaman.

"No? They must have a death wish."

"It seems like it," Orberesis said. "How can we use our existing settlement here to our advantage?"

"The savages burned it mostly to the ground. There weren't that many soldiers to begin with, truth be told, but they await instructions, Highest One."

"Warn them and the soldiers in all the vessels. We are about to start our conquest."

"You heard the Highest One!" the captain said at his first and second mates, who took off running to pass the message. "Where is General Tavanar?"

Orberesis swallowed, ashamed of what he'd done. Tavanar had chosen to stay away since... the incident. Letting him was the least he could do. Heleronde was a group of savages too, so even he could lead the reconquest. This was going to be an easy victory. He noticed the enormous crowd of sailors, crewmen, and soldiers that had gathered around them.

"Solvi and I will lead the charge from here."

"But Hi..." the captain started.

"People of the Two Nations!" Orberesis shouted. "We're about to face our enemy," he bellowed. "The enemy of the Two Nations and of God Himself. They are foolish, but don't let them fool you. They are just as depraved as the beasts of the underworld! So, I will give my strength, my power, and my blessing to everyone who fights for me!"

Cheers and hails emerged, forcing Orberesis to pause for a moment. The sailors could complain, but they revelled in blessings and anything that would help them live longer, on validation from a higher power.

"I shall greet everybody who dies fighting in my name in the afterlife!"

More cheers emerged, louder than last time.

"I will absolve anyone who dies fighting for me!"

The soldiers and sailors cheered in an uncontrolled euphoria, feeding off his energy.

He positioned himself almost in an inhumane posture, with eyes wide and gesturing like a madman. "For every enemy life you steal, you will receive a thousand blessings from me! So, I ask every single one of you—fight for me! Fight for the Two Nations!"

Fight for my elixir.

The crowd continued to shout into maddening chaos. Roars, cheers, and hails turned into coordinated war cries. They weren't strangers to life and death. This was the same to them as getting a much-needed drinking break after a long and tenuous journey.

Orberesis glanced at Solvi. When she realised he was looking at her, she blushed and smiled back. In the tension of the upcoming battle, he braved up.

"What is it?" he asked, grabbing her hand and leading her away from the crowd.

"Nothing, Highest One. I was just thinking about how wonderful you are. I know it, yet you keep reminding me."

The soldiers geared up and collected their weapons. They pulled muskets, swords, halberds, and hatchets out of the crates as the sailors produced dozens of rowboats and pushed them into the sea for the soldiers to jump on.

"Your devotion inspires me to be more, to be better."

He stole a kiss from her and then smiled. He had longed for that for years. The taste of her lips was even better than he'd fantasized.

"You're my ultimate inspiration, Highest One," she said, her voice trembling, her eyes filled with reciprocal lust, love. Whatever it was. There was no explanation for that level of devotion. There was no rule against God Himself being romantically involved. And she had believed him from the start. Protected him.

Orberesis pulled Solvi into his room and closed the door behind them. Outside, the battle no longer mattered. It would soon be all over and they would put Gimlore's head on a spear.

His arms and legs moved by themselves. His hands grasped Solvi's hips and pulled them towards him, and his lips caught hers. Caught by surprise, she didn't take long to let herself rest her arms on his chest as he kissed her, feeling every bit of her body over her dark tunic. She kissed him back as if it was ten years too late and they needed to make up for lost time. His hands traced all the curves in her figure until he was familiar with them, from the legs to the hips, to the waist, to the breasts, to the neck. He held her jaw with his left hand and the back of her head with the right as they kissed again and again.

It felt right and wrong in ways he couldn't even explain.

Her body trembled at his touch as her hands wrapped themselves around his neck and shoulders. Orberesis grabbed her by the buttocks, lifted her up, and walked towards the bed, laying her on it. As he lay on top of her, the orb hung around his neck, between his chest and hers.

Orberesis took her wrists and spread her arms open against the bed. Eager, Solvi let him unbutton her robe and as he pulled the garment out, she let out a slight moan as she undressed. Orberesis felt himself harden and undressed his dirty white robe as well. They laid skin to skin, and he kissed her again on the lips, on the neck, and down to her chest as his hands compressed her breasts. His lips continued down to her stomach and below the waist.

He opened her legs and used his tongue to make her moan louder. Her hands found his back and scratched it hard.

"Highest One! What about the invasion?"

"You mean the slaughter?" Orberesis asked. He climbed up on her, his chest touching hers again. The outside did not matter. They couldn't lose a simple invasion like that.

He found the right path inside and took Solvi's face as a guide. With eyes closed and open mouth, she moaned at each of his pelvic movements. He continued to pick up his pace, fondling her breasts. Her moans were louder and louder as she held on to his back.

She rolled him on his back and rose, sitting on his lap and grinding against him. Each of Solvi's hip movements was pure bliss. He used his hands to aid her back and forth and rose to kiss her breasts. Her hips moved faster and faster. Orberesis felt it coming, the tidal wave of bliss, the erupting pleasure.

He then lay in bed, panting. By his side, Solvi panted almost in equal measure. Both covered in sweat. Orberesis looked at her and smiled. She blushed, smiled back, and lay there, glancing at nothing with a big smile on her face.

The chaotic battlefield seeped back into his mind. Soldiers were still circling around the ship; others jumped into the rowboats. Orberesis rose from the bed and walked over to the broken window as he put on his robe. Solvi did the same without uttering another word. His rowboats were reaching shore and all the savages were only a handful of armed farmers still waiting for them by the town.

"Poor souls." Orberesis said as Solvi joined him by the window. "They do not know what's coming."

············

Orberesis and Solvi walked towards the ship as his troops evacuated the vessel and rowed towards the foul-smelling beach. Through the innards of the Stormbane and the chaos of the battle preparations, his retainers cleared a path for him to jog towards the main control pagoda of the ship.

It was also the tallest and had the best view over the little swampy land that would soon become the battlefield.

In a hurry, he climbed the stairs to the pagoda's top, with Solvi right behind him. His hands clasped the steep wood steps as he hiked them. When he reached the top, he cleaned a hint of sweat from his forehead. The dreadful place was unbearable even in the winter.

"Highest One," the ship captain said and bowed. "I've given the order to send part of our troops. The soldiers that were left from our settlement are mobilising. What is your next command?"

Orberesis looked at the battlefield first, then the captain. Next to him, three aides stood like statues opposite a chest full of fireworks. "Is that the signal?"

The captain nodded. "One firework means sending another battalion. Waving a yellow flag means no more troops. Multiple fireworks mean even more battalions. And of course, waving the black flag is the order to shoot the cannons, although the Stormbane is the only ship equipped with them. Don't worry about the fireworks, Highest One, they sure are loud, but produce no visible flames."

Orberesis took this information in, then glanced at the other units from the Floating City Fleet. Years ago, mopping decks would have made him content, and now he stood as the supreme leader of the tallest vessel. From the vantage point, he could see fires lit in basins in every pagoda. Every ship's captain was ready and waiting for instructions. He could also see the savages, scattered on a small mount beyond the beach and the marshes, just outside their settlement. Not the height advantage they thought it was.

"Highest One? The order?" the captain asked.

Orberesis looked at the fireworks, and the captain seemed to read his mind. "More battalions, Highest One? I believe those we've sent are enough to take care of these poor fools. Perhaps now is a good time to use the cannons. To make sure we destroy their settlement, and survivors have nowhere to turn. If we wait too long, with our soldiers in the midst, we might lose the chance to use the cannons."

"We'll leave the cannons for later. Send every unit we have. We need to choke them out and take prisoners. They'll need to tell us all about the elixir."

··············

"Take the fucking elixir!" Gimlore commanded. The soldiers pulled out the vials with mossback elixir from their pouches and drank the whole contents. "They're rowing their boats here. Archers!"

A few dozen archers dipped their arrows in belleaf oil, raised their bows and aimed, waiting for permission to let the arrows fly. The makeshift bows looked scrappy, and that's because they were. Few people could shoot one well, but it would have to do.

"Arrows fly!" Gimlore screamed and the archers shot. The belleaf oil ignited the fast-moving arrows as they flew, turning them fiery, whistling through the air. Many of them didn't even reach the water and landed on the beach. Others hit the water, and it put out the fire.

"Shit! Again! Arrows fly!"

The archers aimed and fired more burning arrows. This time, they struck a few rowboats, but they didn't slow the enemy.

"It's not enough! Arrows fly!" she screamed again. The archers abided by her words. They shot the arrows and a few soldiers fell into the waters with arrows stuck in them.

"More, we need more!" She screamed and a fourth round of arrows caught a few more soldiers, burning others around them on the rowboats. But they were too close to the beach already. That had not been enough. Only about a dozen enemies were dead, while hundreds more rowed their way to her land. They were stronger and had better weapons, but they did not have her wits.

"Archers! Keep letting the arrows fly!" she called out. The peasants continued to aim at the shore and the shallow waters where most of the rowboats were heading. "Slingshots! Now!"

Roughly fifty men positioned themselves and picked up slingstones smaller than fists from their wood buckets. They placed the stones on the leather and swung the cords that supported it. Round and round several times above their head, the stones picked up the required momentum. At the right moment, one by one, they flew forward and onto the beach with incredible speed and strength, overwhelming the incoming soldiers. The sheer power of those stones hitting the enemy helmets and bodies was enough to incapacitate a few, but it was still not enough to take them all. There were still too many of them, those about to reach the sand and the ones still on their way to shore.

"Again, again!"

The farmers were not soldiers and did not have the accuracy of marksmen, but any enemy they killed was already a victory. They continued to swing their slingstones at the beach, hoping to hit someone.

Rowboats arrived at the break, and soldiers dressed in black and red swarmed the sands, most of them dodging the arrows and slingstones.

"Prepare the muskets!"

Nork repeated her command and the archers and slingshots aimed at the beach, often making a few enemy soldiers collapse. The beach had turned into a sea of burning arrows and bleeding bodies being caressed by the waves and mauled by the stones. No casualties on her side, but that was only a matter of time.

"It's almost time!" This was the moment she had been waiting for. The moment they had kept to themselves all this time. "They're about to taste the Viper's venom, boys."

Nork and Nosema gave her a smile and a nod, then scrambled to complete their tasks.

The battlefield was intoxicating.

The smell of death and burning was nothing to strive for, but as the first enemy soldiers marched through the loose sand, a misstep was all it took. Soldiers triggered the tripwire she had hid in the sandy beach and it activated one of her buried greasy bombs. An enormous explosion of red death lit up the sky, sending bodies of enemy soldiers flying along with sand, straight to the underworld.

Stunned by the explosion, the incoming warriors continued to race across the loose sand and, little by little, they fell for her trap. More soldiers' feet caught in the wires and the greasy bombs Gimlore had set up underground exploded again and again.

For Edmir.

She remembered his joy as they first landed in Alarkan.

Do you have a name for this place, boss?

She had vowed to turn that backwater swamp into a place like Madam Mazi's orphanage. She would leave all the death behind. All the killing. She would help those in need. That was all she could offer.

The Maiden's Hall, she had said.

But more killing had tainted her dreams again. More death.

"How do you like my seeds of war, bastards?" Gimlore whispered.

A sequence of bangs echoed as the explosives planted in the sand bloomed into a carnival of fire and heat, catching the enemy soldiers as they made their way towards Heleronde. The soldiers who hadn't died with the blasts stopped, thrown to the ground with the shake, stunned. Their eardrums were sure to be ringing. The braver ones, more war-savvy, realised there would be more greasy bombs buried, and they had to be careful.

"First muskets fire!" Gimlore said, and the most accurate shooters fired the pellets in their muskets, forming small clouds of smoke among them, to extreme effect. The first line of charging enemy soldiers fell, but they were still coming, gathering themselves after more rowboats reached the beach. They lost the element of surprise, but now the enemy knew there were greasy bombs hidden in the sand, so they slowed to avoid them. But more loud bangs continued.

Edmir would be proud.

It was impossible to predict where the bombs were. Something Edmir had taught her – sometimes burying too many bombs near each other would make for nice double explosions.

"Second muskets! Fire!"

The second line of muskets took over as the first line loaded their barrels with ammunition. From the vantage point of that small hill, the enemy would continue to suffer heavy losses. Only the numbers were in their favour.

Where is the false god, and why is he only sending the fodder?

The second round of muskets weren't as effective as the first. The enemy soldiers had greasy bombs of their own and threw them up the hill.

Gimlore took cover. It was not enough to reach her, but it was enough to buy them time to run up into town.

Shit.

"First muskets! Fire!"

The first muskets scrambled to take their position and aimed at the enemies. Many in the enemy ranks fell, but even more of them made it. Dozens of soldiers had escaped the traps she had set at the beach. Perhaps she had overestimated what her own talent could achieve. It was true—she had been a master bushwhacker, but guerrilla warfare only worked in small groups, not when enemies were in the hundreds.

"Retreat! Retreat!"

There was nothing much she could do now. It was all in the hands of Rednow and the Leeth.

THIRTY-TWO
AMBUSH

REDNOW - MEREY

I didn't lock him up in vain, but he will be back again.

— From *Mother's Memories*

Rednow smiled as he watched the giant explosion of light and fire forming above the beach. He heard the explosion too, and the smell of burning that he hated so much. But it was inevitable.

Gripping the sword's pommel, he watched as Gimlore and her farmers and merchants inflicted pain on hundreds of soldiers. There were rudimentary tactics, sure, but he had not expected her to be that resourceful. A lesson the little cult bastard would not forget.

As well as she had done, the enemy would eventually get out of the beach and get to town, but first they would go through the swampland and the water holes.

They wouldn't find solace there, either.

With a glimpse, he realised there were still dozens of rowboats headed to the beach, full of soldiers eager to spill blood. He then scanned the swamplands and did not see most of the Leeth troops, all camouflaged in the bushes, behind enormous tree trunks, or immersed in the water holes. Merey and Tellwoon were there as well. The incoming Sirestine soldiers had no idea what they were walking into.

But before the soldiers, the farmers came running back into town, passing through Rednow and the mounted troops he had put together. Behind them, running and panting, was Gimlore. The woman had seen better days, but she had done a damn fine job.

"Well done! I'll take it from here."

And off she went, following farmers and barking orders at them. It was no easy feat, killing so many enemy soldiers like that while suffering no casualties. No wonder she survived for so long with almost no help. She was... like him. A true survivor, at least.

A few hundred paces behind her were the first soldiers of the Two Nations, dressed in black and red uniforms. They had survived arrows, slingshots, muskets, and greasy bombs. Not bad for a bunch of dead meat.

Good luck surviving the Leeth.

....

Merey hid behind a tree and watched the Red Orb bastards marching through the mud and puddles of the swamp. The water was everywhere, and the bushes made their task of crossing the swamp harder. Unlike the innkeeper and her farmers, the enemy soldiers had never been in a swamp before and didn't know the dangers one would find in it.

Her sword arm itched, ready to go. But she had to be patient. Those were Rednow's words. She must lead with her head—not with her heart. That meant she shouldn't rush into danger when it wasn't the right moment.

As she bid her time, she looked for Tellwoon. Would she be alright? She would. As much as she loved her, Merey had to do better than her. She *wanted* to be the leader of the Leeth. She *knew* she wanted it more than Tellwoon.

Focus, she told herself. *Focus now. Be patient. Wait.*

The swamps were so quiet, no one would believe an entire army was hiding in them.

As drops of sweat flowed down her head, she knew the enemy soldiers felt the heat too, with no warning that the swamp would overwhelm them.

The soldiers continued to make their way through the swamp, passing her hidden troops without noticing them.

Patient.

It was hard to stay silent, but she needed to wait until the first group of the enemies was almost out of the swamp or that would alert those in the back.

Patient.

They were so close to her already, cutting bushes with their swords and hatchets. She forced herself to stay silent until enough of them were already so close she could jump on them.

Patient.

A few more seconds and the first soldier came through, skin covered in sweat. Soon, it would be covered in blood.

"Now!" Merey said in a prolonged cry as she jumped out of hiding and stretched her sword arm enough to pierce through the soldier's stomach. Hungry for more, she looked for another soldier, and another. Most of her troops came out of their hiding places, overwhelming the enemy. The Leeth soldiers emerged from the water holes with their swords first and slashed feet and legs before finishing them with a puncture to the neck or stomach.

What was this eagerness, this relentlessness?

She jumped from enemy to enemy. They were surrounded and ambushed from all sides, outmatched.

Is this the elixir? She wondered as she sliced through an opponent. It was as if her movements were loose. She felt better than she ever had. That feeling of power was there, and it was real, as though she couldn't lose.

She almost glided through the battlefield, not minding the slippery mud, the uneven ground, or the patchy bushes. Her focus was on the enemy hordes.

Why are they still coming?

Her goal was to defeat them, or at least contain them for as long as possible before they reached the town.

"Protect the town! Keep at it!"

A burst of swords and hatchets headed her way. Some of her soldiers had died already, but a leader only grieves when the battle is over. And it wasn't over yet.

She moved on instinct as she should. An enemy appeared before her, and Merey dodged his strike, her sword arm moving to cut him down. The sword felt light in her hand and her arm fast at cutting enemies. Another bastard came at her from behind and slashed her thigh, but somehow the pain was subdued. She barely felt a thing.

She turned around and cut the man down, then kicked him in the chest and he fell into the mud. Others piled up to face her, axes and spears reaching her and cutting even as she moved away from them. She turned to them and smiled, striking one in the foot, and quickly jumping to cut another's throat. It was almost too easy, despite the wounds. A gash like the one she endured in her right leg should be enough to slow her down at the very least, but she was stronger or... enhanced. There was no fear, only bloodlust.

"Cover the right flank! Don't let the bastards cross. Hold your position!" she said as she pressed on to make quick work of the enemy fodder. They

were many and some could even fight, but they hadn't trained like the
Leeth had.

In between slices and stabbing motions, she came to the same realisation
she always did during battles. Merey didn't deny it—she enjoyed warring.
No one could be at peace with themselves until they fought.

With no distractions, she focused on slaughter. But even if her troops
were competent, there was a limit to how many enemies they could face.
After a while, they buckled. Merey looked to her right side as she took a
few steps back. Tellwoon faced a similar situation, with the enemy swarms
overwhelming her forces too.

No distractions. Tellwoon is *a distraction,* she told herself.

A sharp pain in her leg brought her back from those thoughts. A soldier
stabbed at her, brandishing his blade high and low. She fended him off but
her thigh flared and blood surfaced. She had lost quite a bit of it now. This
wound wasn't as deep as it could have been. It still hurt like a bitch every
time she stepped on that foot.

Focus!

Merey shook her head. How long had they been in that swamp, battling
those enemies? Her breathing was harder, and it was as if she could feel the
hot humid air more in her lungs. She was still holding off Sirestine soldiers,
but the gash in her leg flared in pain and she was slowing down.

Gimlore said the effect of the elixir lasts for half an hour.

A quick assessment of her troops showed more casualties than she had
expected. With the overwhelming back-up the horde was still receiving, her
line of defence would break soon, too.

Shit.

In a normal situation, she would go with instinct and pride, and keep
fighting, but Rednow would tell her otherwise. Rednow, who lived with
the pain of every soldier killed while fighting for him. That was a burden
that she needed to carry as well if she was to replace him.

But before she could show him how mature and thoughtful she could be, Rednow came onto the battlefield like a storm. A few hundred soldiers with him.

Rednow ran by himself like the monster that he was.

And the smoke followed.

············

The scent of *Ominous Kas* burnt into Rednow's nostrils, flaring up his entire respiratory system. As usual, the lungs were a shadow of their former selves after decades of slow and self-inflicted destruction. The foul smoke followed as he ran and kept up with the mounted Leeth soldiers that rode the hearthspears into combat.

With every step, Rednow became stronger and weaker.

After spitting blood, he continued running forward and willed his transformation, focusing first on the legs and feet. They tripled their size, ripping out his pants. Claws emerged on the front side of his feet. As the calves and thighs expanded and took their form, he could outrun the mounts. His torso mutated and grew as the blood rushed inside him, being pumped through his veins, feeding off the smoke he held in his lungs. The arms reached several times the size of a normal man.

He was no longer human.

His skin was now coloured in shades of pink and purple, but much tougher and harder to pierce. His sword looked almost like a dagger in his hand.

Rednow rushed through the battlefield as if it was the last time, and the smoke followed. Stunned, his enemies stopped and stared before losing their heads.

Rednow crushed.

Destroyed.

Obliterated.

This was his rage. The force of an unstoppable storm. An unavoidable quake.

He saw Merey. She had a few deep gashes in her leg. Aided by the mounted soldiers, they could fend off the enemy's progress.

After inflicting death upon death, Rednow was more monster than man. His sword stayed firm and uncrushed by his tight grip, but his left hand was just as deadly and capable of snapping necks or piercing human flesh with his claws.

He continued to collect the enemy's blood.

The fear spread in the enemies' eyes as he feasted upon their frail selves. After clearing his lungs of the smoke for a time, he sang the long-forgotten song during the carnage.

That brutal day.
That brutal mountain,
We climbed that mountain!
We climbed that mountain!

Those who knew the lyrics sang, brave enough to sing as they fought. A song that was as old as Rednow's years spent at the Seven Peaks, where the rocks, moss, and snow had shaped him into who he was. What he was.

You didn't want to go
But you trusted me and
We climbed that mountain!
We climbed that mountain!

Our hands trembled,
Our arms fell off, but
We climbed that mountain!

We climbed that mountain!

Hearing the song confused and troubled the enemy soldiers. They hesitated. And for hesitation, they paid with their lives. The Leeth soldiers fought united and sang in unison as they had trained since they were toddlers.

Rednow continued to wreak havoc on the enemy lines, leaving behind a trail of detached limbs and rolling heads. He drenched his claws in Sirestine blood, but this was far from over. His soldiers fed off his words and kept singing with him as the enemy shrivelled in fear. Rednow had seen those faces.

The panic. The agony. But it was his job to finish them, and he had little time left. Every minute spent in that form; he would have to pay back later.

I can't stay like this forever.

He needed a final push.

Just as he was rushing his troops forward to confront even more soldiers, he felt a sharp metal hit his forearm, piercing his hardened skin. He looked into the distance. Hundreds of soldiers stood with muskets pointing at them, at him. There was only one thing to do.

Rednow broke through the enemy lines and rushed towards the marksmen. At the sight of him, they aimed their muskets at him and shot.

A twisted shot of pain rushed through him, but the smoke bottled it up. Dozens of pellets attached themselves to his carapace skin and those wounds would hurt the next day if he survived to feel the pain.

But he had to stop the marksmen.

He pressed on as they scrambled to load their muskets again. With a wild swing of his left arm, he wiped out five of them. A swing of the right took out another six. He couldn't stay there for too long, lest he become a target. But with him as bait, the soldiers of the Leeth could advance and cover more ground.

They moved forward, led by Merey. Rednow recognised rage in her eyes, and she shouted commands as she limped from her bleeding right leg. She had wrapped a piece of cloth around it, but it wasn't enough for a wound like that.

Many of the enemy marksmen retreated or fled. "The Blood Collector!" they shouted.

Rednow took out five with each arm as he walked forward. With the surging enemy line broken, many of the Sirestine soldiers didn't know what to do. They didn't want to charge into death by themselves, so they retreated or joined smaller groups of their comrades.

Rednow took advantage of their confusion. But the swarms weren't over yet. Even more of the bastards were running up the dunes and flaunting their weapons, while others rowed their boats to shore.

How many did they bring?

He inhaled the smoke again, needing more. Dangerously, more.

The strength and power surged through him again. Blissful and terrible, it burned him, and he spat out more blood as he continued the slaughter. He noticed enemy swordsmen making their way to the edge of the swampland before the town and raced back to catch them.

"Back!" he ordered his soldiers, who looked more weary and tired than their enemies who had just arrived. The wetlands and waterholes were now covered in bodies, either camouflaged in dark green or wearing dark and red. It was impossible to see how many warriors he had lost.

Then he heard a loud whistle and he knew what that meant. One enemy soldier, at least, had breached the line of defence and was heading into town from Tellwoon's side. It was time to call for help.

"Zatak!"

A few moments later, a swarm of wretched bloodsleuths stormed the swamplands and the Leeth did what he had taught them to do whenever he called the beasts. They ducked and took cover. The blind bloodsleuths sniffed the blood and sweat of the enemy and jumped straight for their necks.

It had taken training to avoid friendly casualties, but Zatak had dedicated his life to it. When the creatures latched their three-way splat maws on to an enemy, they wouldn't let go until that enemy was dead.

Confusion betrayed the enemy again.

There was no running from the bloodsleuths. The beasts of the underworld were faster and more powerful. A relentless drive for prey as they chased the soldiers in the swamp. Trapped between vines and bushes, they had nowhere to hide.

Rednow was free to move.

Zatak's minions knew his smell and even feared him when he was in that form. But he was still worried about that whistle. Something had happened to Tellwoon's side of the defence.

In the middle of his slaughter, he saw Merey struggling to get to Tellwoon, to close the breach and help her. That meant Rednow and Zatak's hounds would have to secure the areas she covered.

Shit.

There were still too many enemies coming from the beach. So many rowboats and even more men and women coming out of them. Even with the smoke, he was almost on his last legs. He couldn't go much longer. But if he fell, who would protect the town?

....

The whistle.

The dreadful whistle she never wanted to hear. Merey recognised it immediately. It was Tellwoon.

Shit.

"Cover the flank!"

She limped as she walked. The gash in the leg was bad and bled through the cloth, flaring harder at each of her steps, but Merey forced herself to go chasing the invading enemies. Tellwoon would never let the enemy through like that.

She ran across the swamp as her soldiers made room for her to run. Not as fast with the uneven ground slowing her down, but her chest tightened.

She had failed.

She had got distracted and was no longer thinking of the enemy and the town.

Only Tellwoon filled her mind. Her dark hair and her calm, confident demeanour. Her kindness, brightness, and strength. They made each other better. They were perfect for each other.

She was perfect.

Merey raced, stumbling a few times, cursing. A soldier picked her up and she continued to walk. She picked up another vial of the mossback elixir and drank it. Perhaps it would help with the pain.

She noticed the way Tellwoon's soldiers looked at her, their eyes defeated as they called her. Merey made her way to them, and her heart jumped when she saw a pair of legs lying in the mud behind a tree. She walked over and forgot all about the killing and dying around her.

Failing at her duty.

Failing to keep up with Rednow's orders.

And failing her love.

Tellwoon lay with her back against a tree trunk, with a sword stuck in her stomach, with the hand of the perpetrator still holding on to the hilt. A small line of blood dropped from the corner of her mouth and down to her chin. Her eyes were only half-open.

Merey choked up and kneeled by her side.

"She can't talk," one soldier said, and Merey did not take her eyes from Tellwoon. Instead, she shoved a vial of the mossback liver extract down

Tellwoon's throat, hoping it would at least give her a fighting chance. She ignored all her pain and wiped the blood from the corner of Tellwoon's mouth.

"You three! Press the wound and make sure the sword stays there. Find someone to help you carry her back to town. There should be an infirmary in there. If not, at least get the smokesmith... Perhaps she could survive the smoke."

The three soldiers nodded. They did as she had instructed and took off with Tellwoon losing consciousness, her eyes opening and closing. Delirious. "Together, we will live forever," Tellwoon whispered.

Merey's eyes welled, and tears dropped before she could wipe them away. She regretted not being someone of faith. If she was, she could ask the gods, or deities, or spirits to look after her love, her heart.

"Live, my love," Merey whispered, her hands clasped, and her eyes closed.

She took off in a rage. Anger, worry, and fear battled inside her as she fought her own enemies. Merey had failed in all her duties of leading the army. She had failed her promises to Rednow. Her dreams of taking over from him. But none of that mattered with Tellwoon on the verge of seeing the underworld.

She let her mind fill with ill thoughts. Revenge! She had to seek it. Inflict it upon those who had tried to take away half of her life.

Her gash no longer hurt so much, and she could run well on both legs.

Together, we will live forever, she thought, embracing those words as nothing else mattered.

Tellwoon had intended to live with her forever and that's what she was going to do. Tellwoon would survive and Merey would embrace her after all this killing. Still drenched in tears, mud, blood, and sweat, she kept running. Tellwoon would fight for her own life and Merey would fight for everybody else's.

Fuelled by the elixir, she pressed on, bottling up the tears and everything else. "Let's go! Let's catch up!"

She gripped her sword and started chasing enemies one by one, making them pay. The enemy soldiers were still in an overwhelming majority, but she pressed on through them, disrupting their line.

And then she saw Rednow, four feet taller than the tallest men. A swing of his spiky arms was enough to destroy five men at once. How long had he been in that form? His body was no longer the same and he would wear himself out too much if he continued like that.

"Tellwoon is injured. It's bad," she said, before spitting into an enemy as she pierced his stomach.

"How?" he asked in a monstrous voice.

"Sword to the chest."

Rednow raged and his blows to the enemy became harsher, less calculated. "Where is she?"

Merey swallowed. *Together, we will live forever*, she remembered.

"I sent her to the smokesmith."

THIRTY-THREE
LEVERAGE

GIMLORE - KERYON

O *h, how the acts of selfish minds can tear the world apart. Like fathers,*
like sons. Nothing but bones in their skulls.
— From *Mother's Memories*

Gimlore's hands shook as she watched the carnage from afar. The Leeth
soldiers had done their best at containing the charge of the Red Orb. The
way their troops had closed the enemies inside the swamp without being
able to get to Heleronde was unbelievable, but the surprising tactic didn't
last long.

The tension among her people was palpable. She had sent those who
could not fight into the middle of the farmlands. But that didn't mean
those who stayed were warriors.

She inspected them.

They could hardly hold a broom to save their lives, except for a few capable ones she had tasked with muskets, bows, and slingshots. The others
shook their legs with fear, worse than after a day of drinking.

Gimlore turned to Nork and Nosema. "Are the traps working?"

"Yes, boss," Nork said. "I prepared them myself."

"Good."

She tapped her feet on the floor. The muddy pathway between the swamp and Heleronde looked unassuming, but the Sirestine bastards would have another surprise. It pained her to see her own land being carved up like this, being the centre stage of a bloody battle, but surrendering had never been a choice.

"Why are you still here?" She asked, surprised to see Tinko and Thata, as if nothing had happened. As if they weren't children in the heart of a battlefield. "I told you to go with Eshof to the farmlands!"

"But Mama," Thata said with the most angelic pleading face. "We want to see the boom boom."

Fuck me.

"The only *boom boom* you'll see is my hand in your face if you don't find Eshof right now. Go!"

They knew she was serious. With sad faces, they went, but kept looking back, to make her feel bad about yelling at them.

"Little bastards..." she muttered, now even more nervous that something would happen.

She turned her attention to the swampland and the savagery in it. She could hear roars, shouting, and the clinking of swords and hatchets, but she couldn't see well inside as the vegetation blocked her view. Rednow was in there, scrambling to contain the enemy swarms.

No way he'll hold them forever, though.

She squinted and saw three of the bloodied Leeth soldiers carrying a fallen comrade. They waved at her as they emerged out of the marshland, asking for help. Gimlore ran towards them and recognised Tellwoon as the victim. She rushed to help them carry her.

"Is she still alive?"

The soldier grimaced. His accent was northern, not too different from Foloi's. "Barely. Sword in the stomach. She has been losing a lot of blood. Her only hope is the smoke."

"The smoke?"

The soldier seemed confused. "Yes. We need a smokesmith. You have one here, right? He'll have the herbs."

"You've got to explain that to me, friend."

The man's face pleaded, as if he was in pain, but he seemed to realise her confusion was genuine. "Sometimes when people are going to die... When they have terrible wounds... The smoke will keep them alive... Please, madam, we need the smokesmith now."

Gimlore nodded and hurried to take Tellwoon into the Maiden's Hall.

The smoke will keep them alive, she repeated the soldier's words to herself. It would either turn Tellwoon into a smokesmith or it would kill her.

She felt a shiver down her spine. How was that even possible?

....

Keryon looked to the door and stopped assorting the elixir vials for the soldiers, focusing only on Gimlore and the woman she had brought and laid on the bar counter. She was in rough shape.

"You must be confused, madam. I'm not a healer. I'm no doctor. My herbs are not the healing kind... And she looks like she suffered a serious wound. I don't..."

"Shut up!" she said. This time, Keryon detected no malice. "Blow your smoke! Do it. Slowly."

He hesitated and glanced at Piesym, looking for answers, but his friend shrugged.

Then the soldier that had carried the woman kneeled before him and extended his hands in a pleading motion. "Where we are from, the smoke from a smokesmith can sometimes help people survive mortal wounds."

What?

"That makes no sense," Keryon said. "If they survive, then they..."

"They can become smokesmiths, yes. It's true."

"I can't inflict that on somebody else, I..." he said.

"It's what she would have wanted. It's a custom in the Leeth. If the smoke doesn't kill her, then the wound will. Better to live as a smokesmith than to meet the underworld, isn't it?"

"Can I leave her in your care, Mister Keryon?" Gimlore asked with pleading eyes.

Keryon gave Piesym another look. His friend spoke. "We can try."

Keryon nodded and pulled out his herb pouch. "I'll do it, then."

"Thank you!" Gimlore said, running out of the Maiden's Hall.

As he doused the herbs with belleaf oil, he envied general Tellwoon. She was unconscious. She would either wake with healed wounds, somehow, and the knowledge she was a smokesmith, or she would continue on her path to the underworld.

Keryon still remembered the shackles around his wrists and ankles. Chained to a granite wall in a dark room, somewhere in the depths of the royal palace of Mosendel. Children crying for their dead mamas and papas. His tears mixed up with sweat.

And then the smoke had entered the room through the cracks in the door. One by one, the smoke consumed the lungs of each child, and they dropped dead one after the other. Orphans, useless and disposable.

Fodder.

Experiments.

And there he had remained, alive on his hands and knees. Coughing blood, but alive. Picked up and looked after, taught the rights and wrongs.

Treated like one of those who had put him through it. A miracle, they called him. The first new smokesmith in ages!

Funny how the thing that was killing him was also what had allowed him to live a normal life.

He steered his smoke to Tellwoon's face. Her breathing was faint, but it was still there, so he made sure she inhaled the fumes.

"How do I do this?" he asked the soldier. The man shrugged, so he turned to Pie. "A little help here, Piesym."

Piesym approached and started looking at the mercenary woman. He placed a hand on her stomach, where the cloth around the sword still inside contained the wound.

"She's still breathing. How long does it take for people to react to the smoke?"

"I don't know, I've never seen it done. Rednow made us swear we wouldn't tell anyone, but Tellwoon is like a daughter to him, so fuck that."

Was this possible?

"Piesym, keep measuring her breathing. I'm going to send more smoke towards her."

His friend nodded, and he blew on the smoke, commanding it to flow the way he wished as they taught him all those years ago. Using smoke to heal, huh? A first even for him.

Piesym perked, his eyes widened, and he smiled with the same face he made at the lab once he had discovered something. "I don't see how, but it's... working. Her breath is steadier now."

Keryon struggled not to show his amazement. He had no shame in his work as a smokesmith. Of course, he would take a lot of it back, but everything he did had a purpose—keep order and peace in the world. This time, though, his purpose was using his cursed ability to help.

Piesym approached him and whispered. "Do you know what this means? Half-dead people with the potential to turn into smokesmiths?

This could change the world, Ker. We must hold on to this information. If other kingdoms find out about this..."

Keryon tried to imagine a world full of smokesmiths and a cold sweat hit him.

He didn't like the sound of that.

·····‖······

Two soldiers dressed in the enemy uniform came out of the forests with their swords raised, as if it was a race to get to town and not a battle. Behind them, others came armed with muskets. They looked happy to be out of the swamp.

"Muskets! At will!" Gimlore bellowed. "Everybody else, take cover!"

Dying from musket pellets would still be a nasty way to go, she mulled while hiding behind a large wood table laid sideways. Her make-shift musketeers rose and fired back. She had a careful look, but only one of them had hit a target.

"Again!" The enemy soldiers stepped closer in the mud. She wasn't about to waste the entire array of greasy bombs on a few soldiers.

"Nork!" she called. "You and Nosema take care of the soldiers if they reach the entry point. I don't want to waste the seeds."

"Yes, boss," Nork said, pulling a handful of sharp throwing knives from inside his vest. His twin followed his motions almost identically.

"Get the ones with the muskets first. There are more Sirestine bastards coming from behind these. We'll get those."

Nork and Nosema threw their knives and four soldiers dropped dead in the mud, including two with muskets. Others were still pouring out of the swamps as if they had been to the underworld and lived to tell the story. This time, there were many of them.

Thankfully, she still had the seeds of war. Planted and tended to, they always bloomed into something magnificent.

"Get the muskets ready!" she said from behind the large table. About twenty enemy soldiers stepped into the mud.

Any second now.

Gimlore covered her ears and so did everyone who had taken cover.

The enemies continued to press on. A misstep. A Sirestine soldier tripped in the wire. When the wire stretched and the man fell to the mud, one of the buried greasy bombs exploded into a loud and bright bang. She never thought she would enjoy that sound after ten years, but she did.

The soldiers in the back stopped for a moment, uncertain about their surroundings.

Gimlore was going to make them pay.

"Muskets! Now!" Gimlore said and her handful of musketeers got up, aimed at the confused soldiers, and started firing. "Second muskets! Now!" she shouted. The second group rose from her right side and fired the pellets, hitting a large enemy group, now more cautious after realising this was no ordinary battlefield, no ordinary town.

An enormous monster emerged from the swamp. His hardened, spiky skin was a mix of pink and purple and his arms were so large they could crush several men at the same time. Gimlore felt chills down her spine when she noticed the monster was carrying a sword.

"The Blood Collector!" A soldier shouted. "Run!"

Rednow... that's Rednow.

With a roar, Rednow leaped long jumps as if it was nothing and caught up with the bastards who were not yet too close to trigger the rest of the greasy bombs. With his sword arm, he sliced through them, the sword a kitchen knife cutting through butter.

But Rednow's efforts were almost in vain. The Leeth army was tired and wounded. They had overwhelmed the Sirestine, but the invaders' sole goal was to wreak havoc in Heleronde and kill the citizens in the name of their false master.

They still had the numbers in their favour.

"Boss, look!" Nork pointed towards the beach. Dozens upon dozens of rowboats laid there, empty, floating in the waves as soldiers continued to venture into the swamp.

"What am I looking at here?"

"The sea! It's empty now. No more boats. They are not sending any more soldiers."

That was enough reason to celebrate. They had already killed so many, and even more fought inside the swamp.

"Gimlore!" Foloi called in the distance. "Gimlore!"

"What?"

"The scouts and the pineheads found an enemy official," Foloi said, panting from the run.

"What do you mean?"

"A man. They found a man. He's dressed in black and red, but not like these scrappy uniforms. Higher quality. Says he might have information we could use."

"A traitor, then. Convenient, that, no? Smells like a trap."

"Not unless they're willing to risk his life."

"We need to be careful. The false god might have tricks up his sleeve. Nork and Nosema—you two oversee things here. You know what to do. I'm going to *persuade* this man to speak his mind."

....

Gimlore took off, following Foloi from the town entrance and into the Maiden's Hall. Townsfolk scrambled all around, carrying ammunition, weapons, or more greasy bombs. She panted as she jogged over there, leaving the battlefield's sounds muffled in the background at the edge of town.

Inside the tavern, it looked like another battle had taken place. It was devoid of tables and chairs, which were now blocking the Red Orb army in the front lines, but there were leftovers of black powder all over the floor—a disaster waiting to happen. A tall and slim, brown-skinned man caught her attention. His clothes were fancy, of good quality. Almost tailor-made. Perhaps he could be an official, yes. But why was he here?

"Why the fuck is he unconscious?"

"Well, he couldn't keep his mouth shut. And we were waiting for you, madam."

"Just wake him."

Pie held the foreigner's head and placed an open vial under his nose. "This should do it."

"Shit," Gimlore said. She could smell the pungent liquid from where she stood. "That's nasty."

After a few moments, the man's right eye twitched.

"Come on, we don't have all day! This town will turn into a battlefield unless we can get information on the troops."

Pie frowned and took a deep breath. "Alright, alright."

He loosened the grip on the man's head and pulled up a second vial from his shirt pocket, placing both vials under his nostrils. It didn't take long for the dark-haired man to cough and come to his senses.

"Ah, there he is!" Gimlore said. The man still coughed and after a moment he realised he was surrounded, with knives pointed at him. "What is your name, fellow?"

The man looked up at Gimlore and his eyes focused on her as if he was trying to process her question. "Tavanar," he said. His Sirestine accent was strong. "Where am I?"

"Listen to me, Tavanar. I am fighting a fucking battle with that bastard who claims to be God Himself, so I need *you* to tell me everything I can use against him right now. Isn't that why you surrendered? Will you help me help you, or are you going to get acquainted with Foloi's fists over there, just to start?"

She was ready to continue with a threat or two, but the man spoke before she could say anything else.

"I'll talk," Tavanar said, still coughing.

That surprised her. "Well, talk, then!"

"He used to be my friend," Tavanar said, eyes locked on the floor, as though it pained him to utter those words. Gimlore raised her eyebrows. "For decades, we were like brothers. I even watched him unearth the orb. Break the world and pull this continent from the depths."

"Unearth the orb? What does that mean?"

"His real name is Doi. He's not a god. He's a peasant. A petty thief and a swindler. We were both running from our little scams. That time, we were in Ainis, far away from home, raiding an ancient tomb that seemed normal. We thought we would find old coins or jewellery. Things we could sell. Instead, there was only that red orb. We thought it was valuable, like a gem. When we tried to sell it to a rich warlord in Ainis, a big swarm of beasts attacked the city. It was bigger than we had ever seen. We were all going to die. I mean, how could we survive that? But then the red orb started glistening in Doi's hand and getting brighter and brighter. Next thing I knew, the ground broke in fissures, mountains rose out of the earth, and towns were destroyed. And the earth swallowed the entire swarm of the beasts, saving us all from imminent death."

Gimlore frowned and picked up a pair of pliers and waved them in the air.

"If I find out you are lying, you're going to apologise so much your dead ancestors will rise from their graves to help you."

"I wouldn't lie. The bastard almost killed me. Something changed recently. *He* changed... It's like he believes his own holiness, as if he is a god, indeed. I always thought it was a scam, we were always scammers. But I saw the Miracle, so I believed him chosen in some way. He fooled me like the rest. When I found out he didn't have full control of it, I confronted him and he... somehow... I don't know how, but... he lifted me, choking me. I thought he was going to throw me overboard, but he seemed to question himself and spared me. His eyes looked different, like he wasn't himself. Some days it's like I don't recognise him anymore. Ever since he picked up that orb. But it's worse lately. I'm scared of him. I wish he could go back to how he used to be. But I don't think that will ever happen, so he needs to be stopped."

"He's strong enough to lift you?" Foloi asked.

"He... used the orb, somehow."

"But you said he doesn't have control over the orb!" Gimlore blew up, picking up the pliers again. "Does he or does he not?"

Tavanar shook at the sight of the pliers. "I think he does, somehow. But I don't think it's absolute control. I guess it depends on the circumstances."

Gimlore sighed. "My *circumstances* are fifteen humongous fucking ships anchored in my shore and I don't know how many soldiers are fighting in my swamps right now. How can I defeat him once and for all?"

Tavanar stopped for a second. "The troops are decent, but they lack leadership. Without me and other generals, their only goal is to get here, kill everyone, and pillage, then question the survivors about the elixir. The Floating City Fleet is impressive, yes, but most of the people inside are sailors, carpenters, officers, and everybody else required to run ships that large. Not soldiers."

"Again... If you're lying..." Gimlore said, raising the pliers.

"I'm not. I swear." He swallowed.

"I'd trust an assumed swindler to tell the truth as much as I trust my kids to do so."

"He might be right. At least to an extent, madam," Keryon said. "Everybody knows the Floating City Fleet for global trading routes, not military prowess."

Tavanar nodded. "An assassin... You could send an assassin to kill him. Or you could send saboteurs to blow holes in the ships with these greasy bombs of yours."

"You've got no love left for your old friend, huh?"

Tavanar shrugged but faced the wood floor, silent. There was pain in that deep frown, as though he was containing tears.

Gimlore mulled over the man's words. *Sabotage*, huh? Could she trust what the man was saying? She could still give him a slow and torturous death if he was lying.

"Pie, stay here. Tie him up behind the counter. We'll talk when we get back."

....

A loud crashing sound echoed outside the Maiden's Hall.

It can't be.

Gimlore hurried to open the door and rushed outside. Something had hit a shack, and it was now turning into flames.

"What happened?" Keryon asked.

Gimlore looked over at the burning shack. She couldn't figure out what had caused the crash and the burning until she saw another burning projectile flying fast towards her.

"Take cover!" she screamed as she jumped to the side.

The projectile landed on another wooden shack close to the Maiden's Hall and after a loud crash, all she heard were beams snapping and wooden shards being sent into the air in a burst of sawdust and sharp splinters. Upon landing, the projectile started burning the destroyed shack.

"Cannon balls. They've got fucking cannon balls drenched in belleaf oil! No military prowess, my arse!"

"They've got cannons on their ships?" Keryon seemed surprised. "And they can shoot this far?"

Gimlore stormed back into her tavern as Pie was tying up Tavanar. She grabbed the foreign man by the neck and punched him square in the face. "Why didn't you say they had cannons, you fucking bastard? Were you trying to get us killed?"

"N-no! That's not possible! I didn't see any cannons! There can't be that many. He must have kept that from me."

Another crashing sound thundered.

Shit. It will wipe the entire town out.

"I don't care if it's one cannon or five hundred cannons, if my town is being torn to shreds!" she snarled, even scaring Keryon and Pie. "You better pray to God Himself or whoever you worship that my beautiful tavern doesn't get blown to smithereens or you'll be burnt to ashes along with it. If you don't die in the wreckage, that is. You three are coming with me."

"Where?" Keryon asked as another cannon ball landed in the middle of the high street, getting stuck deep in the mud. "Don't you see they have cannons that can destroy a town like this in minutes?"

"And I've got *you*, Mister Keryon. I'd wager you're better than a cannon or two. You didn't think I was going to keep you here while everybody else fought, did you? I hope you still have your herbs with you."

Keryon stared at her, speechless, and Gimlore produced a quick victorious smile, then turned back to Tavanar. "You piece of shit. Anything else I need to worry about in the ships?"

Tavanar swallowed. "Yes. There might be."

"What?"

"Doi always has this woman with him... She's devoted to him. And she's a smokesmith."

"How strong?" Keryon asked.

Tavanar shrugged. "I have never seen her fight, but Doi trusts her with everything."

Keryon looked dead serious. "It's the woman who snarled at you down at the beach. The smokesmith, remember? I told you."

Gimlore recollected the woman dressed in dark. She looked freakish and gave her shivers, but Keryon didn't seem bothered by it.

"One minute ago, you looked shocked that I wanted to jump into the ocean to blow up the ships and now you're all excited about facing this smokesmith woman."

"Nonsense."

"Sure, sure. Let's go!"

And off they went, leaving the tavern and looking into the sky, doing their best to avoid more cannonballs along the way. Gimlore panted as she ran, with Pinesy in front of them. He could have run much faster, even with the entire box of greasy bombs he carried on his back.

They had to find a way not to be seen by anyone.

"Wait!" Gimlore said as she picked up a dark grey blanket a merchant had left outside in their rush to leave the town.

This is where Edmir would come in handy. He thrived in these situations. He kept his cool in moments of panic. And he was the best with greasy bombs. Gimlore left the thoughts of her old friend aside and focused on the escape route. The descent down to the south-eastern beach was rocky and slippery, although the elevation of the terrain wasn't too high. Pinesy led the way and let the others figure out the best way to place their feet.

So, this is the "emergency" exit they talked about, she thought, glad she had told them to prepare it. Multiple exit plans were necessary.

Except this time, instead of escaping, they were marching straight into the monster's den. A powerful smokesmith inside the most powerful fleet in the world. Nearby was a man who may or may not have the power to break the earth open.

THIRTY-FOUR
SABOTAGE

GIMLORE - KERYON

I *infused dreams into their veins, smoke into their lungs. I gave them one more opportunity.*

— From *Mother's Memories*

"Watch your step." Foloi extended his hand as they descended a rope into the southeast beach from the slippery ravine, out of sight of all the enemies on the battlefield. The dark sky and lack of moonlight made it hard for Gimlore to figure out where to put her feet on the way down without slipping into oblivion.

She took Foloi's hand after hesitating. He had become too protective, almost possessive, after she hadn't let him fight alongside Rednow and the Leeth. But that was why she was paying the mercenaries. None of her people should die.

Keryon and Pinesy went on ahead of her and prepared the small rowboat for the four of them to head out into the sea while Foloi helped her get down without tripping.

"How come you didn't let me fight? Am I just your bodyguard now?"

"You're my enforcer and you collect the money I'm owed. That means you work for me. You're not a soldier."

"I used to be a warrior in my clan," Foloi said, but Gimlore wasn't having it.

"I don't care what you used to be."

"What about the warden? I see how you look at him."

"Are you serious right now, Foloi?" Gimlore asked. "You and I fuck sometimes, that's it."

"You know, people usually enjoy it when others show they care."

"There's a difference between caring and being almost obsessed."

"As you wish, *boss*." Foloi's words seemed final. He looked away from her as they reached the beach and jumped on the small rowboat.

Gimlore sighed. She didn't need a man as big as a marcruncher acting like a child. Not in the middle of battle.

The cannon balls crash-landed on top of the shacks of Heleronde. Her town... what was the point of paying that much for the Leeth's protection if the enemy had cannons?

As they jumped on the emergency rowboat, Pinesy and Foloi took over the oars while Keryon and Gimlore remained seated in the front and back. She covered them with the dark blanket in case an enemy scout was paying close attention despite the darkness.

"Row slowly," Gimlore said.

The sea was mild, and the wind had almost stopped. Even oars pulling water would be an undesirable noise. Pinesy rowed with ease, exerting no effort despite the heavy weight of the boat, making Gimlore wonder how strong the pinehead was.

After they circled the rocky side of the peninsula through their right, Gimlore saw the entire battlefield. The townsfolk had not yet put the fires out. The beach had hundreds of corpses piling up, and there was one vessel from where all the cannon balls were being fired, leaving a trail of fiery oil as they ripped through the air towards the town. Gimlore counted five cannons.

Shit. Maybe there was a warship hidden in the Floating City Fleet, after all. There must be at least three hundred paces between the vessels and the town, and yet the cannons could reach it with ease.

Gimlore glanced at the vessels. The larger one, painted black with red highlights, was the one where all the cannons were. The false god would be inside that one. If she took any longer, she would lose this battle. The Leeth were already on their last legs and the cannons continued to shoot dozens of greasy cannonballs.

"Pinesy. How many greasy bombs do you have with you?"

Instead of responding, Pinesy opened the wooden box he had carried on his back. Gimlore counted at least thirty. They were rudimentary, but they would have to do. The citizens of Heleronde weren't like Edmir, after all. No one was. Those would have to be enough.

"Listen. We're going to split up into two groups. Pinesy, I know you don't fight, so I won't ask you to do it. All you'll have to do is row the boat and hand out the greasy bombs to Foloi. Foloi will throw two bombs on each ship. You hear me, Foloi?"

"Two greasy bombs per ship," he nodded. He looked cranky and annoyed but trying not to show it.

"Yes. Make sure that when you throw them, you do it in a place where they will explode and damage the ship beyond repair. If you can sink it, all the better. Do this for as many ships as you can without getting caught. If they find you, escape. Can you do that?"

"What if we get caught? What do we do?" Foloi asked.

"You wanted to fight. So, you fight! Don't you dare die on me! And don't let Pinesy die either. That's an order."

Foloi swallowed but gave her a nod. "What about you two?"

Gimlore looked at Keryon first, then at Foloi. "We're going inside the large ship to stop those cannons. If we're lucky, we'll take out the cult leader too, or we sink the ship with him inside."

"That's too dangerous! You're jumping into an unknown ship while hoping for the best?"

"People do crazy things when they are desperate, Foloi," Gimlore said. "And I don't know about you, but I'm pretty desperate."

There was a moment of silence as her words echoed in their minds, interrupted only by another shot from the dreadful cannons, many words left unsaid, engulfed by the silence, overwhelmed by the dark night. All Gimlore could think about was to act before the cannons destroyed the Maiden's Hall. That building meant more than her life. It was her legacy. Her past and her future. A symbol of her perseverance. Her ability to resist even the worst tyrants. She couldn't let it go without doing everything in her power to protect it. And the town. If it was destroyed, everyone would leave. What would happen to them? They'd be enslaved again.

Pinesy and Foloi started rowing.

"Drop us close to the hull of the ship. We need to be as quiet as possible while rowing between the ships."

The clouds covered the night sky, and it was dark enough that they could paddle the oars in plain sight without being seen. Gimlore hoped the sailing crews would focus on the battle ahead of them so much that they wouldn't see their small boat approach.

It was so quiet they could hear the ins and outs of the ships as the rowboat sailed between the hulls. Sailors bragged about surviving the massive storm, others longed for their loved ones. All Gimlore could do was stay silent and hope none of them looked down at the water from the decks.

Pinesy and Foloi rowed with caution until they reached the large vessel's hull from its left side. It was like taking a stroll around Heleronde, circling a good dozen shacks before turning on the next street. The monstrous ship was a true marvel of the sciences that no current ship maker could replicate.

Keryon and Gimlore reached the rope ladder on the hull and Foloi and Pinesy continued forward on the rowboat, headed to other ships. Most ships were empty, operating only skeleton crews. The bastard had really sent everyone he had into her town.

Gimlore climbed the ladder after Keryon and waited until there were no sailors on that side of the deck, and then they got on, minding their steps.

After stepping on the deck, two sailors appeared. Keryon grabbed Gimlore and pulled her into hiding behind a few barrels and nets. She felt his breath at the back of her neck and his heart beating on her back. But then he released the firm grip of his hands and both continued down the passageway, taking a few stair steps to the lower deck.

They continued forward, and the voices of the crewmen became louder. Just in case, Gimlore produced a few small throwing knives from inside her vest. They kept walking towards the cannon but stumbled upon three sailors exiting a door.

"Hey! What the—" a soldier said, before one of Gimlore's throwing knives hit him in the throat. Keryon silenced the other two with a short dagger of his own, produced from under his shirt sleeves. But the first shout of the sailor was enough to alert others who saw them and started shouting in Sirestine.

"Intruders!" the sailors shouted. Their uniforms were dirty and ragged, and their bodies looked frail and so malnourished that Gimlore almost felt bad about the knives she stuck in their throats.

"Run!" she commanded, and Keryon followed her. They ran on the lower deck and lost count of how many sailors and crewmen they had behind them. But they didn't look like warriors or soldiers. They were men and women brought along to operate the ship, as broken as those she had back home.

Then they found the cannons.

Cast iron magnificence likely kept in secret even among the top brass of Sirestir.

A hint of sulphur entered her nostrils. But this time it wasn't Keryon's smoke. There was another smokesmith guarding the cannons as the sailors fired them and others prepared the greasy cannon balls.

Gimlore locked the door to the cannon room from within, preventing the pursuers from entering.

"I'll deal with him," Keryon said before jumping to face the man. One of his kin.

For a moment, it was hard not to look.

Keryon's smoke ignited, and he commanded it, using it to burn the enemy smokesmith. The Sirestine smokesmith concentrated enough smoke in a specific point to protect himself from Keryon's blasts. But then, on his right hand, the concentrated smoke hardened and formed a dark blade that looked as hard as steel.

Gimlore forced herself to focus on the scattered enemies. Aware of her presence, they had stopped firing the cannons, but they were all trying to corner her, swords and hatchets in hands. Gimlore threw a few more knives and two of them landed.

Three bastards left.

Gimlore used the space to evade them as she found more knives to throw inside her vest. She kicked over a box and the grease from the cannon balls spilled onto the wood floor. She threw one more knife, and the soldier fell, but she was almost out of breath. The smell of sulphur was strong and pungent. Keryon ignited his smoke and created flashes of light, blinding everyone in there. The heat produced by his fire gave her a feeling that she could burn too if he wasn't careful.

His opponent was fast, fighting with a smoke sword and smoke shield that shifted and moulded to the wielder's needs. Keryon relied on explosive power. And almost everything in there was flammable.

She wasn't fit for this any longer. All this fighting. All the times she barely avoided the underworld. But she couldn't let herself go there. Not yet.

She threw two more knives and one of them found a victim, but a bastard hid behind a wood pole, where the knife landed. Gimlore was almost out of knives too.

Shit.

She found Madam Mazi's blade inside her left boot and pretended like she was defenceless. Like she was about to run out. And when the sailor came, she threw it with all the strength she had left.

With all the enemies gone, there was only the smokesmith left. Keryon was the pursuer. The one exploiting weaknesses in the enemy's stance. Gimlore threw a knife at the man, forcing him to summon a small smoke shield to protect himself.

The distraction worked.

Keryon entered the man's range and ignited his smoke, burning him to a crisp. The man bellowed in agony before losing consciousness. Gimlore stood there, astonished. How Keryon could stay so collected after doing such a thing, she didn't understand.

"Well done, madam Gimlore," the Warden said, out of breath. "Very well. What's the plan now?"

Gimlore stopped for a second and took a deep breath. "Let's find the bastard and sink this piece of shit."

Keryon produced a quick smirk. His face showed exhaustion and was full of sweat and soot, but he was still way too handsome for his own good. "In that order?"

"What do you mean?"

"Well, can I destroy the ship?"

Gimlore smiled back. "Be my guest."

Keryon nodded. Just as the man was turning back, a large flash of light lit up the sky. Another flash right after that. Keryon and Gimlore peeked through the window where the cannon used to be shooting from as the commotion formed inside the ship. The Floating City Fleet had one of its vessels attacked.

Finally! She hoped Foloi and Pinesy were smart enough to survive that.

"That should be enough distraction," Keryon said. "Let's set the entire ship on fire and then we'll find the bastard. With the ship burning, he won't be hiding for too long."

Gimlore gave him a nod and saw him blow a breath into the oiled-up leaves in his hand once again. The herbs turned into a small constant flame he preserved, and a deep white smoke came from them. When he inhaled the smoke, its remnants stayed with him again, as if tracking his movements. It couldn't be good for him to do it so often, but he did it anyway.

They better find the fucker. If Tavanar was telling the truth, a knife in the throat should be enough to kill this false god.

....

Keryon ran with Gimlore on his tail. He ignited the smoke that circled him enough to spare her the heat that it created. He touched the sides of the lower deck with his hands and the fire glued itself to the wood at his command.

There was no way anyone could put out that much fire.

Keryon shook his head. What was he even doing?

Sabotaging a war vessel like a pirate.

Destroying private property.

Vandalising the livelihoods of hundreds of people.

He looked back at Gimlore. *All because of her.*

It was only the circumstances that forced him to lower himself, to lower his standards. He was a man of justice and always would be. When this entire battle was over, he would be a wealthy businessman. A man of honour. And he would take advantage of Gimlore's exploits as well, like Piesym suggested.

He moved past the pestilent sailors he found in his way. They were the weak-minded followers of a man who claimed to be a god. Smokesmiths were the closest beings to gods. Underappreciated, and even hated. But the ones that everyone turned to in their times of despair.

"Slow down, Mr Keryon," Gimlore said, gasping. The soot and sweat covering her face made her look like a coal miner. "I can't keep up with that smokesmith speed of yours."

Keryon nodded. Of course, she couldn't. He continued to leave his traces of fire along the ship and, with a quick glance behind his back, he realised how much damage he had already caused. This was his second time wreaking havoc on the dreadful woman's behalf. Had she been that persuasive, or had he been too easy to sway? Oh well, he enjoyed being the warden and had always enjoyed that sense of responsibility.

"I want a commendation after all this, madam," he said, appearing calmer than he was.

"If we survive, you can have two," Gimlore said. "Now focus!"

He continued running and went even deeper into the inner decks. Then a loud bang came from a nearby vessel, followed by a second explosion, as loud as the first.

"The giant brute and the pinehead aren't dead yet. Good for them," he said.

Gimlore nodded and she grimaced. Could it be that she actually cared for these people?

He searched all around the lower levels of the ship for something he knew would get the job done even quicker. He saw food, supplies, weaponry, and ammunition. Then he found several wooden barrels of black powder.

Aha!

"What are you doing, Mr Keryon? I don't like this."

"I'm doing you a favour, madam."

He removed the lid of a barrel as the crew tried to deal with the fires he had started on the upper deck. With Gimlore's reluctant help, he lifted the heavy barrel and walked with it, leaving a trail of the powder running on the ship's floor for about forty paces. He took the half-empty barrel back to where he found it and jogged to the end of the room. Then to the stairs to go up to the lower deck. Before he walked up, he knelt and ignited the black powder that continued burning all the way until reaching the barrels.

"Shit! Let's get out!" Gimlore yelped as they ran out of there as quickly as they could. "And I thought I was the crazy one."

By the time the barrels exploded and dug a hole in the ship's hull, Keryon and Gimlore were already running away from it.

"I'd call it... efficient," he said, looking everywhere for signs of the crazed cult leader.

Upon seeing Keryon, most sailors flinched and ran away. They screamed "smokesmith" or "monster," which were two different things and only showed their utter ignorance. It made him feel better to let them sink inside the giant wooden coffin that the ship had become.

"That pagoda over there," Gimlore said. "The tall one! I'm sure he's in there. Let's go."

The problem with such a prominent, tragic ship like this one was that they had made no efforts to hide the whereabouts of the high-ranking officials. That would be the god pretender. So he started running towards the tall pagoda, with multiple eaves.

Everything he touched burned.

The smoky fire helped him run faster as it burned inside him too, eating at him. His least favourite part of being a smokesmith.

Keryon climbed the stairs from the lower deck to the main deck, where most sailors had gathered, choosing between jumping ship, or fixing the vessel. But he turned into a walking nightmare of fire and smoke in their eyes. Another two loud bangs emerged from another ship right next to that one.

"They are lasting longer than I thought they would..." he trailed off.

"Desperate people make fearsome opponents, Warden."

How true that was.

Keryon glanced at the pagoda from up close. That gracious building should be for people like him, not pretenders. It should be for officials, captains, and other diplomats travelling on board. In another life, perhaps he would have been a diplomat himself. He had an effortless charm and poise that drew people to him.

A group of retainers guarded the place, giving away the man's location. They carried silly weapons like halberds and spears, none of which would work against him.

"What are your plans, madam?" he asked, his eyes still fixated on the enemy. The poor bastards were too scared and confused by the fire and the chaos in the ship to realise his presence. "Should I blow them up to draw the little sneaky fellow out?"

Gimlore's lips stretched far wide.

There.

The woman's smile showed her devious nature.

"Do it," she said.

He inhaled the smoke. He needed to poison himself with it as much as possible to ignite the entire place in a blast.

As soon as he walked towards the retainers, they noticed him and drew their halberds at him. Keryon jumped into the air and, lifted by the smoke he commanded, he spun upon himself, turning himself into a whirlwind of smoke and fire. He spun faster and blasted all the fire he gathered, destroying the honour guard, and tearing a hole in the pagoda's wall.

But he was tired after using such power as that, and collapsed onto his knees for a moment, before Gimlore came back and lifted him.

"It's getting hot in here," she said.

"My, my, Madam Gimlore, you're so forward."

Gimlore gave him a look of disgust and rolled her eyes. "Don't flatter yourself! I was talking about your abilities."

"Perhaps there were two meanings."

What am I even saying? Did I wish there were two meanings?

"You men always think we have the hots for you. You all think you're so charming, and..."

Two figures appeared out of the pagoda, lured out by the fire and the explosion. Keryon recognised the lunatics. He knew *crazy* when he saw it. He used to chase crazy. And those two were it. The man was frail and bony, and the surrounding destruction covered his face and clothes in soot and sweat, but the red orb hanging around his neck was still bright and unaffected. The woman looked concerned. But it wasn't self-preservation.

She feared for him. Keryon could see it. He was her life.

"We came to say hello," Gimlore said.

Upon seeing them, the frustration in the blonde woman's eyes turned to pure vile hatred, her love for the false god overpowering even her temptation to rush in and attack them.

"We were hoping you'd have time for a quick chat," Gimlore said, goading her into charging, but the woman didn't bite. Orberesis took cover behind her.

"We must escape, Highest One. For your protection," the blonde woman said.

"We can't let you do that," Keryon said. "Madam Gimlore and I are doing this experiment, you see? We're trying to find out if gods can bleed. They have tasked me with gathering evidence."

THIRTY-FIVE
SHATTERED

ORBERESIS - SOLVI - GIMLORE

I see a glimpse of light now. I hope you'll see it too.

— From *Mother's Memories*

The smoke blurred Orberesis' vision. The scalding heat made his body swell and his head dizzy. But it was seeing the flames all around the *Stormbane* that hurt him the most. Memories of a childhood gone with the ashes, followed by a life of nothing but misery. Mud, shit, and hunger plaguing him. Crimes he was proud of and crimes he wasn't. They all started with his family being turned into fodder, burned to a crisp in front of him in flames not too different from those around him now.

Panic took hold of him, and he struggled to breathe.

For years, he tried to stay away from the fire, and now it had come for him.

It was only fair.

But Orberesis didn't want to go yet. He was still young. Powerful.

Yes, powerful.

He found comfort in the thought as he faced the dreadful woman and her henchman. He was a smokesmith, too. His power differed from Solvi's, but just as devastating. Perhaps even more so.

"You... will pay," Orberesis said, tying his long hair up, shoving the terror inside him deeper and deeper so it wouldn't incapacitate him.

"Highest One, we must go now. The ship is sinking, and the surface is burning," Solvi said, ever sweet, but not taking her eyes off the intruders.

But Orberesis had already dipped his feet in anger and vengeance. He was God Himself and gods didn't cower. "Can you handle the smoke-smith?"

Solvi looked confused. "Yes, but... what about you?"

"I will be fine. I have the orb, so I'll escape by myself. But you have to kill him." She hesitated. "Do it, Solvi."

In a secretive motion, Solvi blew into a handful of herbs. The greased dried leaves started burning in a tiny blue flame and the white smoke it produced followed her. She breathed it in, then gave him a nod.

Orberesis ran.

He forced his way out of the room and kicked open one of the burning bamboo boards that made up the wall of the pagoda to the deck, leaving Solvi to deal with the smokesmith. But he heard someone else chasing him. With a quick glance, he saw the savage woman in pursuit. She didn't look like much of a warrior.

Perhaps he could handle her.

When he reached the deck, reality startled him. It was far worse than he had realised. Curtains of fire burned almost every wooden surface of the *Stormbane*, including boards on the deck floor. The ship's sails were long gone and the other half of the *Stormbane* was already underwater. Crying, sailors kneeled and prayed for him to help. In desperation, they reached for his feet, trying to kiss them and almost tripping him as he shoved them away.

But there was nowhere to go.

The less devout sailors were already jumping ship, with tears cleaning soot from their faces. Poor folks were too far away from home to die like that. They yelped concerns for their lives and wishes for their loved ones, because even throwing themselves overboard was dangerous and not guaranteed survival.

Orberesis looked to the horizon and saw the world had turned into his worst nightmare. All but two of the vessels were gone, burning in large flailing flames that stretched to the top of the masts.

"You have nowhere to go," Gimlore said from behind him.

He turned back to face her, envisioning her head on the edge of a spear and her body being blown to smithereens. She walked towards him, unfazed by her surroundings. Wasn't she afraid of the fires?

Shit.

"I am God Himself. I will kill you," he said, but even he didn't believe it. His voice lacked both conviction and strength. His hands trembled and his legs shook like wild reeds on the riverbank. Why wouldn't the orb react?

"Let's see you try."

······

Solvi bonded with the smoke from the *Tangled Twins* herbs and the more she held in, the faster she became. She willed it to shroud her, and it offered her a few seconds of hiding in plain sight, so she used that time to leap sideways and catch the pompous tall man from the side with a stab of her dagger.

She had no time to waste.

Find the Highest One.

Run.

Keep him safe.

Producing a dagger from her robe again, she jumped towards the man but then he started spinning, and all his built-up smoke lifted him into the air before it ignited into a large fire blast that exploded and burned the entire room. It forced Solvi to retreat and recall her strike.

Her eyebrows rose as she understood his power.

He can ignite smoke.

That explained how he had burnt *Stormbane* so fast. She would have to tread with caution.

The fires caused by the explosion subsided, but there was still a terrible heat between those four bamboo walls, and the room's ceiling could collapse at any moment after it was bit by the flames. She needed to defeat this man fast and join the Highest One. Her love.

"My, my," he said, coughing and spitting blood. "I wasn't planning on using so much smoke, but that... invisibility? I've got to be careful around you."

Solvi wouldn't honour him with a response.

She held the white smoke in again and jumped.

One breath.

One jump.

One death.

Her dagger lunged at him as she landed behind him, shrouded in the smoke. The sharp edge of the blade thirsted for his blood. But the man did not die. He parried her strike and forced her back as if it was a regular strike from a common opponent. His own daggers were barely a threat, but he was a master at using them defensively.

Who is this man?

She clouded herself again, making herself one with the smoke. It raged inside her, striving for control of her body. She disappeared for a few moments and forced the enemy to blast the room again to find where she had gone. She would get him tired like that, force him to burn his insides with his smoke until he couldn't continue. *Annoying bastard!*

"That is quite a neat little ability," the man said, jumping at her with two daggers, propelled by a cloud of smoke and fire. She fended off his blades with her dagger easily. His voice trembled, but he did not shy away from pressing her forward with the blade. "Show me again,"

Solvi's anger flared. She couldn't waste time with him, but he was truly troublesome.

How is he keeping up?

"Which herbs are you burning? Show me." His dagger flew with power towards her. He got close to her before she could evade the blow, so her only option was to parry it. Barely.

"I will show you nothing but death," she hissed, countering his strike, and pushing him back with a flurry of blows.

The man smiled, as if he enjoyed the challenge.

"I can't let you and your friend threaten the people of my town. They've been through enough. They want to be left alone. You're a smokesmith like me. Haven't *you* had enough too?"

Solvi's lungs flared in pain, and she struggled to keep up, to have her strikes match his.

"They can go somewhere else, but they can't occupy land that belongs to the Highest One. They cannot exploit his resources."

The man chuckled as he pressed his dagger against hers. They were so close she could smell his breath. "That is where we disagree, my lady. This land belongs to no one. It's a free land. We want to keep it that way. Sorry."

Lady?

Solvi forced herself out of his way with a downward strike and a jump back, just as the man created another fire blast that left him spitting blood once again. The heat engulfed Solvi every time. Sweat built all over her, as if she was almost burning inside and out.

"What's your name?" he asked while trying to stab her, as if he was dancing with her, or courting her. "And where are you from?"

Solvi stayed quiet, clouding herself in smoke and gathering her thoughts. He was trying to distract her. Then he would take advantage and stab her in the heart. No. She wouldn't let him. But the man kept talking as if they weren't trying to kill each other. As if she didn't have to protect the Highest One.

"I'm from Mosendel, if you can't tell by my accent," the man said.

Solvi remained silent. There was nothing attractive about the man's sharp jawline or bony face. He was filthy, working for the enemy. Working for the fiends of the underworld that dared stand against her love.

"Shut up!" She charged at him with a stabbing motion. Her hand was fast and her dagger thrust to find him, but the man was faster yet.

"I'm a lawman. I'm sure you were one too, were you not?"

Solvi feigned a stab to set up a punch with her left hand that caught him right in the face.

He seemed surprised at first, but then smiled, shaking off the blow, charging her with a power she could not suppress. "Why do you follow this man?"

"That," she said as she disappeared again. She reappeared right above him, on his blind side. Her blade stabbed at him again. "Is none of your business."

The heat was palpable there. It was everything. If the lungs weren't the end of her, that heat surely would be. She had to finish him off quickly.

"I'm a smokesmith," the man said. He took a second to breathe and recover from her blow, bleeding from his shoulder, where her dagger had reached. "I know how much pain it causes you to do this and how much pain they have taught you to endure. Only I truly understand you."

He struck again and Solvi scowled, dodging the blow.

"Does your god know how much blood you spit? Does he know all the leaf teas you drink to soothe your spirits after all the years of self-poisoning?"

Solvi's mind blanked, but her body kept fighting. A flash of guilt went through her as she found herself considering his words.

"I do. Join me. You can stay here. We can live in peace or get the appreciation we deserve. Out here, with no master, you would be a hero. You could help people. Save them. They would respect you, not hate you like they do on the mainland."

She did her best to keep her face flat and unreadable, but inside, her foundations were shaking. She burst into a rage, appearing and disappearing from the smoke to strike him, forcing him to push her off with his blasts. To take back his words. Her loyalty would always be with the Highest One.

"You're strong," he said, gasping. "So why follow him?"

Solvi screamed.

She flew around the room as smoke became indistinguishable from fire. She leaped and spun, avoiding his blasts, but not the heat. The man got weaker every time he tried them, but his relentless strength made him push forward.

How long can he continue?

The heat was immense, and fiery wooden beams started collapsing. The man pressed on as if the heat did not matter, as if hunting her down was his only goal.

"Why don't you die?" she snarled.

"Because you don't want to kill me. Because I'm like you. I know your pain."

....

Fear of fire paralysed Orberesis. He scrambled, ridding himself of the woman that pursued him like a predator.

No, *he* should be the predator.

He was no longer a child from the sweat provinces of Sirestir.

He was God Himself now, but his legs were still shaking.

In sheer desperation, Orberesis lunged at her, imagining her neck between his hands, and hoping the orb would aid him.

A blow to the right side of his face and ear interrupted his thoughts. The woman had a wide, devious smile as she fiddled with something in her hand.

Orberesis reached for his chest, but the orb was no longer there.

His heart raced and his chest tightened, making breathing harder than it already was amid all the smoke.

The orb had not protected him this time.

⋯⋯⋯

The red orb was lifeless. There was nothing special about it.

"So, this is it?" Gimlore asked. "*This* makes you powerful?"

Orberesis rushed at her with a fury she had only seen a few times. But his wild eyes also showed confusion, or perhaps despair. He did not seem to understand how she took the orb from him.

He did not know that she had spent her entire childhood picking things. Misdirecting and deceiving.

If what Tavanar had said was right, the man was just a man. Perhaps she could study the sphere and harness its powers. Maybe that was all she needed for other monarchs to leave her town alone—a petty show of strength. What she needed to restore the lost peace.

The conman's charge was frail but forced her to shove him away while she held the orb. She just needed to end the man. No one would worship a deceased god, would they? They would realise he had never been a god.

Maybe she could still do everyone a favour.

Gimlore hadn't understood Madam Mazi's words back then.

You need a knife, child.

She had been with the mistress for four winters and she had never once needed to use a knife. As if sensing her doubt, Madam Mazi had pulled a very thin and sharp stinger from her sleeve, wiped it, and handed it to her.

This belonged to my grandmother. Then to my mother. Now it belongs to me. I was supposed to hand it down to a daughter, but I never had one until you tried to snag my purse, so I want you to have it. Here, take it.

The gods had protected her on the day, and she had found Madam Mazi by chance. She had taken the knife and assessed its weight. But it was more than physical. The weight of responsibility being passed down to her.

Those who carry knives are bound to use them, child. Remember that.

Gimlore was pulling Madam Mazi's knife from her boot when Orberesis tackled her, desperately trying to reach the orb. Gimlore moved her left hand away from the filthy man, but his right hand grazed the orb, prying it from her hand.

Both Gimlore and Orberesis fumbled to grab the orb, which now dwindled like a wickplate jumping out of the water to tease starving fishermen. Gimlore lunged forward to catch it, and so did Orberesis. Two extended arms and hands reaching for the rogue red orb, without success. What would happen if it broke? Would it even break?

As if answering her questions, the orb bounced once, twice, on the ship's wooden deck. Then the bouncing became too much, and it shattered, showering both Gimlore and the madman in red broken crystal. For a moment, they were both paralysed, looking at nothing but crimson shards that covered them and the surrounding deck. The sounds of the battle echoed around them as the flames consumed the ship.

"Y-you broke it," the man said.

His ire seemed to surface. Gimlore wasn't too pleased either. That was supposed to be her way out of this, her way to protect the town. Now she no longer had use for the man. With no orb, he couldn't even pretend to be a god. He had no powers, he was nothing.

She reached for her boot again and pulled out Madam Mazi's dagger, small and reflecting the orange flames. "You have nothing else that I want now."

But this time, Gimlore wouldn't throw the knife. No. Madam Mazi's knife forced its wielder to face responsibility for using it.

She lunged at Orberesis, aiming for the neck.

And then there was light.

THIRTY-SIX
SWALLOWED

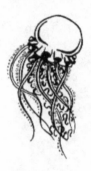

ORBERESIS - GIMLORE - SOLVI

Forest of lights, forest of souls. It still flows on me. Through me.

— From *Mother's Memories*

There was so much light Orberesis had to close his eyes. And even with his eyes closed, it was too much. It was blinding him, incapacitating him. He would give up his body to make the light stop. But after a while, the light subsided. After a few moments, he recovered enough to open his eyes.

He was no longer in the destroyed *Stormbane*. He was back at the beach where it all had started.

The place of his nightmares.

Shaking, he was almost too scared to move, but he did so anyway. As the waves washed his feet, he looked to the horizon and flinched as he saw *him* once again. The enormous figure towering in the horizon, breaking the clouds. The man still had Orberesis' face, but this time, it stared at him, aware of his presence.

Frightened, Orberesis started running from the beach and onto dry land. He couldn't stand being there, looking at the figure. But even though his feet moved, he stayed in the same place.

"It's pointless to run," the giant man said inside Orberesis' head.

Orberesis jumped from where he stood.

"Who are you? And where is this?" he asked. He squatted, looking for protection. "The ship. And the enemies..."

The enormous figure sighed. "You're safe here. We're inside your mind, if that comforts you."

It didn't.

"Am I dead?"

The figure laughed. "You've only just been born, boy."

"Who are you?"

"I'm more ghost than man, Doi. We both are."

"What do you mean?" Orberesis asked. He didn't like this at all. "And how do you know my real name?"

"We've been together for a long, long time. You and I are very similar," the man said, using the most soothing and paternal voice Orberesis had ever heard. "We're both thieves, in a way. We were also both rejected by a world that gave up on us."

"The orb... Are you..?"

"You've understood, but not entirely. I'm not *the orb*, but I was inside it until you freed me. Now I'm free."

The pain in his head subsided. He looked up at the figure, wide eyed. "It was you!" he said. "All the migraines, the nightmares, and everything else. It was you, trying to break free."

"It was necessary. You'd understand it if you were trapped for centuries."

"Fuck you," Orberesis hissed.

The giant man was a torso with nothing below his abdomen. Legless, he floated towards Orberesis through the ocean, and shrank until he was of about his size. He just stood there, floating, arms and head next to him. It all gave Orberesis chills.

This was impossible.

"You've climbed the mountain, but there are other peaks ahead of you, Doi. Higher ones."

Orberesis understood nothing. How was this possible?

"I will hand you my ladder to the heavens. If you help me, that is."

Orberesis almost believed him.

"You talk in riddles. Tell me who and *what* you are and what you were doing inside that orb. And what power do you own? How is this all possible? And how are you inside my head?"

The man sighed.

"They used to call me the Old One. I am as old as that land you walk on. As these waves bathing your feet," he said.

Orberesis raised his eyebrows, paralysed by a mix of curiosity and sheer fear. "You're one of the Ancient Ones."

The Old One shook his head. "Older than them. I was a... scholar. I found herbs across the land and studied their properties. They grew wild, and yet, one day, while burning them, I discovered one of them opened a curtain between worlds. It was an arcane science that I called temporal exploration. And you know what, Doi? I was the first of my kind to do it, to go into the void, to achieve temporal exploration. To make a fold in the air and slip between the curves. Now... Now, I'm nothing."

"None of that makes sense," Orberesis said. But the Old One wasn't listening.

"I surfed through dimensions. I found other worlds. Other... people. I became their leader. And I brought them here. You've seen them."

"I have?"

"You have. Some still live among you, for better or worse. But you only know the non-intelligent ones: Bloodsleuths, shadesgrowls, hearthspears, marcrunchers, wickplates. I brought them here, but my efforts at giving refuge to all these species weren't... welcomed by the Ancient Ones."

"What did they do to you?"

"That, my friend, we will have an eternity to talk about."

"What?"

The Old One looked so sad that Orberesis almost wanted to comfort him.

"Part of me is lost forever. Destroyed. But another part of me lives in *you* since the Awakening. Since you picked up the orb. Do you understand?"

Orberesis was even more confused. This was the strangest nightmare he had ever had. "Awakening?"

The Old One nodded. "Right here, on this beach. Ten years ago, or the blink of an eye for someone like me who lives outside of time. You woke me when you grabbed the orb and asked for help. I woke up to help you and nearly broke the world while I was at it. But with that, I also broke myself. Most of my powers left me then, and they have been fading away since. I only exist in bits and pieces now. I have no other choice but to cling to you. Oh, but what I can give you in return..."

Orberesis could not believe this. He knew the orb had powers, but this story sounded ludicrous. This had to be all a dream. An illusion. He would play along with this false version of himself.

"So, you're a parasite clinging to survival."

"I think we both are, Doi. But you're right. I won't deny it."

Orberesis scowled. "How do I get out of here?"

The Old One grinned. "Is that what you want? Humanity has put you up against the walls since you were born. They had you defeated and humiliated for years, as if you were not one of their own."

"Where else would I go?"

"To the heavens. The *real* heavens. I told you. I can't take you there yet, but I'll show you what it looks like."

The Old One placed one hand on Orberesis' shoulder. He tried to avoid the hand. But as soon as he was touched, the environment changed.

Instead of the beach, they were... nowhere. In darkness. They were floating in the nothingness, as if they were in the starry night sky. But they could sway.

"Feel, Doi," the Old One said. "The best way to travel is to feel everything to the most extreme."

He could feel.

He knew it wasn't real, but that lightness, the weightlessness, was addictive. There was a perfect balance in him, his surroundings, everything. In that moment, he was not a false god. He was a true god, living in the heavens.

It was all made worse when he was brought back to the beach. His humanity felt tired and dirty on him, and he was almost disgusted with himself and with how filthy it was to be of flesh and bone.

"Once you know the feeling, you can't let it go, can you? It was like that with me, and it will be like that with you. One day you can take my place, Doi. We'll be together, in the heavens. I can take you there. I can show you other worlds. But you must stay with me for now. There is much you need to learn. About this world, in particular, and about those working against me. Against us."

"But the battle... Solvi..."

"What are those compared to true holiness?"

Nothing.

"They'll win the battle, but you'll win eternity. Leave it behind for now, Doi. They won't forget you. You've already left your mark on the world. You will come back stronger."

Nothing mattered. Not the lands, or the borders, or the wars. Or the people. None of them mattered. Orberesis had found a greater purpose. A real purpose. He would turn into a real god this time.

"I will be your host, then?" Orberesis asked.

"If you so wish."

"And what do I need to learn?"

"Much, my dear Doi. All in due time."

"What's in it for you?"

The Old One smiled. There was something cheeky and devious about that smile. There was something the Old One was hiding from him. "With your help, I might help some friends of mine. And they'll help you back."

Orberesis considered it. No more migraines or nightmares. And a new-found power. He had won, even if his armies were to lose. "Will I be a real god, then? Will I be able to seek revenge?"

The Old One sighed. "Humans and their petty grievances. Sure. Revenge, if that's what you seek. But once you've got the power, Doi, you will crave more of it instead. I know this. I've been with you for some time. What do you say? Are you coming with me?"

"I am," Orberesis said.

The world warped into a fold, and he lost his consciousness.

....

Gimlore stopped as the light took over. A beam so strong she closed her eyes and then it got so bright she had to cover them with his hands. Was she blind?

She had attacked the man who claimed to be God Himself, but she never thought she would end up in the underworld.

Around her, sailors screamed in pain. Was it because of the light?

She tried her best to walk. To find a way out of the cursed ship, but flames surrounded her. The heat was immense and disorienting. A false step and she would walk to her death.

Two children waiting back at home. She would crawl all the way to them if she had to, one move at a time, but home was on dry land.

She started opening her eyes.

Where am I? Where have I walked to?

The vision was still blurry, and the flames still ate at the ship. She was trapped between an ocean, a known gateway to the underworld, and flames that feasted on the wood.

I need to run.

One mast dropped and crashed onto the deck, creating a forest of flames and tiny sparks her blurry vision could see.

Gimlore escaped.

Where was Orberesis? The fucking charlatan. A man with the nerve to fool the entire world. And the entire world foolish enough to believe him. Eager to believe, even. To believe life amounted to something more than sitting somewhere and waiting to die.

She kept walking around the dead mast. This must be her punishment for the wrongs of the past.

Gimlore had to fight for her life. She had to make it home, so she walked. She walked. Would she jump into the water and drown? Would she let the flames turn her into charcoal? No, she had to live.

Amid shouting and screams of despair from the crew, it was everyone for themselves. She abided only by her own survival instincts. All the first officers trying to rein everybody in could go fuck themselves. She wasn't one of them anyway.

And where was Keryon?

There was almost no one near the charred pagoda. Good. Maybe she could find a small raft before the ship turned into little more than floating ashes. The little false god would probably have a life raft ready for him.

Not if Gimlore could find it first!

She glanced left and right but saw no life raft. Instead, her stomach turned.

Orberesis sat on the deck, motionless, in a vast sea of thick, viscous white tentacles that were wrapping themselves around him. The slithering things crawled around Orberesis, covering his eyes, circling his head, his arms, his legs, his back. If they didn't move at all, they would look like exposed roots of an ancient white tree, coming out of nowhere, trapping Orberesis to the deck. It was as if they... came from *inside* him.

The creature's white slithering tentacles grabbed Orberesis and enveloped him. Gimlore almost felt like vomiting, such was the stench of death. The tentacles lifted the inanimate body from the deck and dragged him into the sea waters.

Gimlore had never heard of a creature like that, with hundreds upon hundreds of tentacles. She knew how much danger she was in.

Run. I need to run now.

....

Solvi woke up, still drowsy. Her whole body was wet and covered in grains of sand. Her tongue tasted like paper and her lungs hurt every time she breathed. She realised she was no longer aboard the *Stormbane*, but at the beach on the new continent. Someone had tied her hands and feet. She realised the predicament and scrambled to break the bonds, but the ropes tying her were strong and every time she contorted her body to move, it ached in a blinding pain that almost sent her into shock.

She noticed two figures in the distance coming towards her. With eyes still blurry, she closed her eyelids, remained motionless, and pretended to still be unconscious.

"Are you alright?" a voice said. *That woman Gimlore...*

There was a squishy sound of spit hitting the sand. "Yes, I am," the man said.

"You're spitting blood!" the dreadful woman shouted. Her voice was disgusting. If only Solvi could free herself...

"It's nothing..."

"What about her? Tell me the reason you kept her alive."

"No more killing, madam," he said. "That fool brainwashed her. She deserves another chance."

"I'll be the judge of that."

"No, madam," the man said. His voice was firm. "We're together in this, now, remember? You can't make unilateral decisions anymore."

"Fine, fine. But keep her bound and out of my sight. At least for now."

There was a silence between them, interrupted by the crashing waves and the white birds flying in the distance and cawing at each other. Why was he keeping her alive? He couldn't be telling the truth... Was he defending her from the vile, savage woman?

The man broke the silence again. "And what happened on that ship? Where is the impostor?"

"One second he was in front of me and the next, he wasn't. There was this massive blast of light that almost blinded me when the orb broke, and I opened my eyes. He was nowhere to be found. The ship was sinking, so I had to be quick in searching for him, but I couldn't find him," Gimlore said, though her voice hinted at something she was withholding.

Highest One! My love... I will find you.

"Do you think he is dead?"

"I don't know, but I'm alive and we won the battle. We live to see another day, Mister Keryon."

Keryon. That's his name. The man I couldn't kill. The man who let me live.

Thirty-Seven
Rite of Passage

Rednow - Gimlore

Find them. The ones you wished you could be. I still hear your voice. I will care until you die.

— From *Mother's Memories*

It was a beautiful sight.

The burning ships lit up the dark sky and the sea reflected the flames in shades of red and orange. Observing from the swamp, Rednow could barely move, but he needed to continue. The ships burned, but the Red Orb soldiers he faced had not surrendered yet. Rednow had been spitting so much blood that it wasn't too different from bleeding out. He would be lucky to even breathe after this.

He continued to hold on to the foul smoke left of his lungs, loving its power, hating its power.

His sword hand moved across the enemy soldiers, cutting them. But he was only a shadow of what he used to be. By now, those men and women had likely abandoned all faith in their false god and believed the monster Rednow was. The last thing they saw before they died.

No mercy.

But Rednow was dying with them. Even in that monstrous form, the pain would come later. It would take years of recovery, if he was to recover at all.

A column of light erupted from one of the burning ships far in the distance, illuminating the sky, as if the Sun had descended upon the land. It froze him and the rest of the enemy soldiers for a moment, before they realised they were still on the battlefield.

He's back, Rebma's voice said inside his mind. *I knew it. He's back.*

Rednow did his best to ignore it and focus on the battle. That voice made little sense. It was evidence of his sickness spreading, his age reminding him he was useless.

REDNOW!

It startled him, as it was now louder than usual.

"Stop it!" he said to himself, knowing how silly he looked—like a senile old fool, speaking to himself.

He's back Rednow. He's back. The voice talked to him now.

"Rebma?"

HE'S BACK!

Rednow flinched and retreated. The soldiers seemed puzzled by his sudden step back. The brave ones took advantage of it by entering his space, probing him with swords.

"Who is back?" he whispered.

The Old One. The Deceiver. He's back.

None of it made sense. Rednow was insane, dreaming of his sister's last words. He remained silent and shook off the voice from his mind yet again. Madness. He was going mad.

Pretending he was normal, Rednow pressed on against the enemies, but shouts of retreat echoed across the front lines and the Sirestine bastards started turning back, retreating.

"No dawn for these hounds!" Merey shouted, starting the pursuit. "Their heads will hang from our hands!"

Those of the Leeth that could still run followed her and chased the enemies. They tripped them and killed them with no hesitation, but Rednow did not pursue. Merey struggled to go on as well, limping forward with her jaw clenched firm and pain almost pouring out of her eyes.

Rednow willed himself back to his normal self and the pain flooded every bit of his body. He dropped to his knees. It was too much. He felt every bit of aching he had expected. In his arms, legs, torso, neck, and head.

He was dying.

I can save you, Rebma's voice said.

Rednow fell and let himself lie on his back on the swampy ground. "No, sister. I will die here."

I will save you.

Rednow should not have believed the voice, but he did. Somehow, his insanity made sense, and those words were true. But he did not want salvation. He wanted to perish and let his remains feed the trees for ages to come. He wanted to die in battle, like the demon he once was. What was the point of dying like an old man, frail and weak?

I will save you, the voice repeated. *Embrace me.*

"Leave me alone," he pleaded on his deathbed.

An invisible weight took over his chest, and he closed his eyes. That was it. He would go now. He would see the underworld. The darkness. He would meet his ma and pa's spirits.

But then, the weight was gone, and he felt lighter than he deserved.

I take, but I also give.

Rednow opened his eyes again. He was still there, in the swamp, but most of the pain was gone. He got up from the ground and looked into the horizon of dead soldiers, where the Leeth was still chasing its enemy. When he tried to use his left arm for balance, he realised it was no longer there.

"My arm?!"

I took it. In exchange for your life. I give but I also take.

"Who are you? I told you to let me die! Get out of my head!"

I am not your sister. I'm everything and everywhere. The sum of all things.

"If you're not Rebma, why do you speak like her? Who are you?"

There was a moment of silence, but the voice returned.

I'm the Essence, Rednow. Your sister was my embodiment. And you, my dear stubborn child, have been carrying me this entire time. Surrounded by me. Aided by myself.

The bloody sword next to Rednow started glistening in a bright crimson red. The red stains took over the entire blade.

Rednow shook his head as he moved over to the side, without taking his eyes off the glowing blade. He dared not touch it. Then the red glow flowed out of the sword and into the air and materialised into the figure of a woman who looked like Rebma.

"She tried to tell you, so many times," the Essence said, appearing before him in near-complete human form, though there was nothing human about her. Divine was more appropriate. "Your sister. She begged you to pick that bloodied sword and was stubborn enough to convince you. I've known her since she was a child. I've told her plenty about this world. She understood what I was and cared about what I did. That is why she lent me her presence when I needed it most. She knew to take care of people. She knew not to judge."

Rednow remained quiet at first. A tear dropped from his face. "I don't understand..."

The Essence smiled using Rebma's face.

"I'm ancient, Rednow. It's alright. You wouldn't understand. It took your sister a lifetime. Those whom your people call the Ancient Ones used to worship me. They called me Mother Nature, if that makes it easier for you. They didn't understand me either, but at least they respected me. Now here I am, crippled and dying after clinging on to your sister for survival. After trapping a bit of myself in the sharp edges of a piece of steel. For centuries I called, but no one listened. Not until Rebma, that is. I borrowed life from her and now I'm using the last of my strength to heal you. To talk to you and warn you, but you are stubborn, aren't you?"

Rednow nodded like a child, listening to his mother.

"If you know anything about the myths told by the Ancient Ones, you'll know there's... somebody else. Someone else."

Father Time...

"Yes, they called him Father Time, although he goes by many names. I call him the Old One. I used to care for the world and grow it. Then he would come with his slow, yet firm hands and give its end to everything and everyone. I liked this monotonic melancholy, but it bored him. So, of course, he found a way to travel between planes, and left for a time. But when he returned, he brought with him nothing but disgrace to this world, which I couldn't take. I couldn't let my brother destroy the world we were supposed to watch over. So, he and I fought for ages, well before your Ancient Ones. We destroyed this world. I realised we had both failed. So, in my last gasp of life, I implanted a part of myself into the world itself, but also sealed bits of my conscience inside this weapon, that was supposed to be passed only among the warriors that had fought alongside me, that wanted to fight for me. Of course, over time, they abandoned me..."

Rednow gasped.

Flashes of his purchase of the sword came back to him. Memories of a much younger Rebma gripping his arm.

Brother! That sword. I want this one. This one. Get this one! It has to be this one!

She had insisted so much, Rednow had to get it from the merchant. The sword had spoken to Rebma and asked for her to take it. He had thought it was the musings of a child, but no. She had heard the Essence's calls for help.

"But when I gave myself up for your Ancient Ones to defeat the Old One, I gave them herbs that produced powerful smokes you know so much about. With those powers, the Ancient Ones defeated my brother's minions, but he still lived. So, I sealed him off, using every bit of strength I had. I stuck him inside a red orb that the Ancient Ones hid deep inside a dungeon."

Rednow remained quiet as his heart raced, but he said nothing.

"Do you understand it now? The Old One is back. I don't know how, but he's found a new host. Even inside the orb, my brother can be persuasive. He has been manipulating that poor soul this entire time," the Essence said, regret and frustration on her face. "He's biding his time, gathering his strength. You do not know how frustrating it is to see him get what he wants and not be able to stop him. I tried to throw him into the depths of the ocean with that storm, but the ship wouldn't go down."

"You manipulated my sister like the Old One manipulated Orberesis, didn't you? Used her to do your bidding, so what makes you better than him?"

The Essence grimaced, as if this had long been on her mind. "I still need you."

"But why? What can I even do? How can I even stop a god? I'm an old man. A pawn of fate."

The Essence smiled, but it didn't look real. That was the face of someone burdened by duty, by rules created an infinity ago. The face of someone bound to protect and with little ability to do so.

"Old man? You are a child, both dead and alive. You have breathed the smoke from the soil, which makes you more ashes than flesh. And you know how much I weigh. I'm a heavy load to bear. You're the only one prepared to carry it, Rednow. The Old One is weak now, so he will hide. But he will come back. You must be ready when he does."

"I refuse to fight a proxy war between two... deities," he said, his reverence fading. This Essence was no better than all the monarchs he fought against, using the powerless to do their bidding. "My sister would never agree to it either."

The Essence laughed, a hint of arrogance now showing. "Are you certain? Because your sister spent her life dedicated to me. She wasn't writing songs, Rednow. She was writing *scripture*. She wrote everything I taught her. Remember her bag? She told you to keep it safe. Then read it! See it for yourself. You have much to learn before the Old One strikes, Rednow."

And just like that, Essence smiled in a way that only Rebma could have. It was as if he was looking at his sister one last time. The red glow covered her and flowed back into the blade, returning the thick red stains back to where they belonged.

Rednow dropped to his knees and sobbed like a child, then picked up the sword.

....

"How is Tellwoon doing?" Rednow asked.

"She lives, but she's still asleep. The smoke worked. They were saying she was reckless, and that's why she got caught. Reckless, Rednow! Tellwoon being reckless! What a load of shit."

Rednow agreed. Merey was the reckless one. She was the one that always charged into battle while Tellwoon remained behind, cool and calculated. She was often the one hesitating in the name of doing things the right way.

Rednow walked with Merey through the swamp. It was hard to find his footing when bodies filled the entire place. Merey's leg was flaring and bleeding, so she needed to lean on him.

But her pain had nothing to do with the leg.

It was hard for him to say something when he had concerns of his own. He did not tell her about the Essence or about Rebma serving a deity her entire life, though he was sure Merey would believe it, as would everybody else in his army. Rebma had been almost a deity herself. Maybe with good reason. His hand reached inside Rebma's bag and found the folder she had left behind. He still hadn't had the time to read any of it.

He didn't even tell Merey yet how he lost his arm and how the wound had closed so cleanly. She would assume it had something to do with his smokesmith abilities, but for now, only an unconscious Tellwoon occupied her mind.

They walked through the swamp for a little longer, with soldiers around them walking in the same direction. Rednow might be alive, but he was so bloody tired. It felt like he had come out of the Seven Peaks ages ago, now. He thought about his little encampment, facing a dreaded winter. With the gold from Gimlore on the way to them, they could survive until spring.

When they reached a clearing inside the swamp, there were three Sirestine soldiers kneeling in the middle of the Leeth warriors. Their uniforms were dirty with blood and ragged from the battle. They had wounds and cuts all over their body and their eyes poured a fountain of tears.

Rednow helped Merey towards the centre of the clearing. There was no good time to do this, but Merey still deserved it.

"Gather around!" Rednow said and his soldiers who were nearby came closer in a huddle. "My friends! We have won this battle!"

Cheers and war cries echoed. "Leeth! Leeth! Leeth!"

Rednow calmed them down with his hands, asking for silence. "We will celebrate our victory later. But we will also weep for our fallen brothers and sisters. It was their effort and their loyalty that allowed us to win and to live to see another day."

Rednow looked around and the Leeth warriors nodded. Everyone there had lost a friend, or a loved one. They knew it came with the job. They could only move on from there.

"We still have a matter to settle. I call this a rite of passage," he said, and the warriors exchanged glances. "As you can see, I lost my arm, so I can no longer be the Leeth's leader. Thank you for fighting alongside me in my last battle as a Leeth warrior. It's time for me to make way for someone well deserving of it."

Warriors gasped, but others had already been expecting it for a while. It was unusual for someone at Rednow's age to still be fighting alongside them.

"I will retire today, but first, let's have ourselves a little ritual for generations to come. I have chosen Merey to be my replacement. She will be the new leader of the Leeth."

"ME-REY! ME-REY!" the warriors shouted, welcoming her with taps on the back and shoulder. She did her best to be nice about it. She would give that up in a heartbeat if that meant getting Tellwoon back.

"Alright, alright. Calm down," Rednow said again, then turned to Merey. "Are you ready for this?"

Merey swallowed and gave him a short and courteous nod. "I am."

"Unsheathe your sword. And do it."

Merey turned to the three prisoners of war dressed in dark and red and adopted a stance that made the pain in her leg visible in the grimace that took over her face. She unsheathed the weapon as quickly as she could and, in three quick blows, her blade caught the necks of all three soldiers. Their heads rolled on the muddy ground and the bodies fell on top of each other.

"May your strength guide them!" Rednow said, letting the warriors hear it well. They cheered. "May your wisdom protect them! May your bravery inspire them!"

Merey wept as he lifted her sword hand up. What a bittersweet feeling that must be. Winning and losing at the same time. Rednow knew what that was. How would Tellwoon come out of that illness? He fought off a few tears of his own. But it wasn't about him anymore.

It was time to settle down and turn into a one-armed farmer, taking on the land Gimlore had promised him. He knew a few of his warriors would want to stay there as well. Perhaps he would have company, or he would sit down by the candlelight at night and read everything Rebma had been writing all those years. The so-called scripture. Just the thought alone left him sweating, but the weather made it worse.

He walked over to Merey and placed his arm around her shoulders. "Now it's up to you."

Merey wiped the tears off her face and nodded. "Thank you. How does retiring feel?"

Rednow shrugged. "I'm ready."

"With Gimlore around, you won't be bored."

That much was true.

⋅⋅⋅ ⋅⋅ ⋅⋅⋅⋅

Gimlore had cuts, bruises, and a gash on her left arm, but as she stared at the Maiden's Hall, the pain increased tenfold. The beautiful three-storey building, once the tallest in Heleronde, was now reduced to a ground floor and a half-burned second floor.

She sat there for a second, contemplating the disaster, lost and defeated. Her eyes welled, but she held back the tears as much as she could. A hand rested on her shoulder, and her first instinct was to shove it away, but she stopped herself from doing it.

"You did well, dear," old woman Eshof said, passing her hand from Gimlore's shoulder to her face and wiping off the tears from Gimlore's eyes. "We won't forget, you know?"

"Huh?"

"We won't forget about what you did to save this town," Eshof said, then looked at the ruined Maiden's Hall. "We won't forget how much you've sacrificed."

Gimlore scowled. "They'll still find reasons to hate me."

"Maybe so. But you never let that stop you, did you?"

Gimlore produced a smile and nodded to Eshof, embracing her. "Thank you."

"A few destroyed buildings are nothing, dear. We can rebuild. Think of all the lives you saved."

That was easier said than done. She would spend every bit of gold she had in rebuilding the Maiden's Hall, making it better and bigger. But she also had to invest in strengthening the town's defences and in training people to fight.

Nork and Nosema came running toward her. "Boss! Come with us."

"What is it?"

"It's Foloi and Pinesy," Nork said as he ran towards the beach.

"I'll be back, Eshof!" Gimlore said, and she ran, fearing the worst. But then she realised Nork and Nosema did not seem worried or angry. They looked... amused.

The walk down to the beach allowed her to see the entire battlefield again in the aftermath. There were craters all over the muddy ground caused by her little seeds of war, but no one had yet removed the dead bodies, which were already decomposing. In the swamp, the Leeth soldiers gathered in a ritual she didn't understand.

At the beach, the scenery was even more grim. The constant pull of the waves washed off more bodies as the tide surged. It was as if the sea was claiming them and healing the beach by moving the sand around to cover the craters.

As she walked upon it and caught up to the twins, Nork pointed at the sea. Besides the pieces of burnt wood floating in the waves and being washed to shore, there were still two colossal ships in the distance, one behind the other.

Nork and Nosema giggled, but it took Gimlore a second to understand what was so funny. Then she saw it and chuckled. In the first ship's stern, an enormous man stood, waving at them. Gimlore smiled and waved back at Foloi, before noticing a tiny figure in the stern of the second ship mimicking the big man. It had to be Pinesy.

"They kept the ships, boss."

"Beautiful bastards," she said. "Do you know how to navigate something like that?"

Nork and Nosema shook their heads. "I can row, but for something that big, we're going to need navigators and astrologers."

Gimlore hardly listened to Nork. Upon seeing the ships, all she could think about was how much money she would get back by having them. It would open trade routes and help them in battles if they could build cannons. If it all failed, she could sell the ships, too. It was like sitting on a gold mine.

Building the Maiden's Hall back up would be easier now.

Thirty-Eight
Four Graves

Gimlore - Rednow

*E*ven upon his return, you still have a chance. Collect what's left of me. *Wear a mask of bravery and suffer in silence. Don't say goodbye too* *soon.*

— From *Mother's Memories*

The scalding sun gave way to the pouring rain of winter, making the days a bit more bearable, but forcing Gimlore to use clothing that was too damn hot and made her sweat buckets.

The sharp raindrops hit Gimlore in the face, forcing her to squint or cover her eyes just to see where the hearthspear was going. Tinko's arms were tight around her as she rode. Next to them, another hearthspear rode with the same relentless momentum, with Keryon sitting on the saddle and Thata holding on to his back.

Ugh. We look like a family.

She pushed those dreadful thoughts aside as the four of them reached their new farmstead. It was a wooden shack stable enough not to fall with the wind, the construction poor. She expected that, since the owner of the property built it alone and with no help from carpenters. But the trails around the farmstead were all well-established, and the unwelcome bushes had been removed. It would soon be a good place to raise mossbacks. It had only been a week since the battle ended, but Rednow had already got a lot done for an old man with one arm.

Gimlore still wasn't sure how he could survive the battle while losing one arm, but it must have had to do with his abilities, being the Blood Collector and all. If anyone survived that, it would be him. After his warriors marched back to the mainland, he stayed behind and rarely showed up in town. The old man was a true loner, a scary one at that.

When the hearthspears stopped upon reaching Rednow's lands, there he was in the rain, holding a shovel, digging enormous holes. He stopped when he saw them coming.

"Welcome," he said.

"Hi, uncle!" Tinko said from behind Gimlore, jumping off the hearthspear and running towards the older man.

"Mama says you are a crazy, powerful warrior," Tinko says.

"Your mama is very generous, then."

"But are you?"

"Enough, you little pests. Leave the man alone."

"No need for that. I grew up around children. I raised many on my own... Anyway, come," he said.

Rednow walked towards the rough front porch to get protection from the heavy rain. Gimlore and Keryon followed him and at every step, they were left with mud above their ankles. Rednow always walked barefoot and didn't seem to mind the rain or wear any protection for it.

"What brings you here?"

"There's a favour I'd like to ask, Blood Collector,"

"Please, don't call me that. I'm Rednow."

"Right."

"What is the favour?" he asked as he watched Tinko and Thata play in the rain, chasing each other and wrestling in the mud.

"Well," Gimlore looked at the kids as well. "Mister Keryon told me he thinks my kids could have... abilities as a smokesmith. But he says his way of uncovering those abilities would be far too dangerous for them. He says you might have a safer way to awaken their abilities. Much less traumatic than what happened to him."

"Did he?" Rednow assessed the children as they fought. "Are you sure you want *me,* of all people, to watch after your kids?"

"Yes," Gimlore said. "As long as they don't die, they'll be fine. They need discipline to use whatever abilities they might have."

"It will be tough."

"They will be fine."

"I mean *really* tough. Being a smokesmith is painful. It's a self-inflicted disease and the training that comes with handling the smoke is gruesome. The moment I take them, I will only let them go back once I consider them ready."

Gimlore swallowed and hesitated. "Sure."

"And you're alright with me using them as child labour here at the farm too?"

Gimlore shrugged. "Why not?"

Rednow nodded, amused, as if it almost impressed him. "You're the first person I've ever heard say 'I want to see if my children can be smokesmiths.' I appreciate your trust. And I'm surprised your man over there recommended me, since we started off on the wrong foot."

"Oh, he's not my—"

"I was wrong about you, old man," Keryon said.

"It seems like I did too."

"Okay, enough with the romance," Gimlore said after clearing her throat. "Will you see what you can do with the kids?"

Rednow chuckled. "Yes, I will. They are... vivacious. This will be interesting. I'm sure they already have tricks up their sleeve."

Gimlore cringed.

"You know, Gimlore. I wasn't expecting you to let me settle here at all. I thought you would stab me in the back to keep this piece of land."

"I considered doing that. But well, it all worked out for the best."

"Come on, you can admit the only reason you didn't go through with it was so that you could still call the Leeth in the future if you needed. You know there will be more invasion attempts."

Gimlore grimaced. "I guess that's true."

Keryon frowned and gave her a serious reproving glance. She gave Rednow a nod and turned around towards the rain, but the old man hadn't finished.

"A piece of information... for your scheming..."

Oh?

"With Orberesis unaccounted for and the Sirestine army in tatters... the crown of Sirestir and Yab is weakened. There will be a focus on that. I suspect the Leeth will get involved in skirmishes. But there's something else."

"What?"

"Gasho is in peril. Succession crisis and civil war. There will be other forces at play."

"The pierced faces?" Gimlore lifted her eyebrows.

"The less you know, the better. My point is you should have some time with no invasions, with all the greedy hounds of the mainland fighting for the same bones. I would recommend you shore up your town and your land. And do it quickly, while you can. Now is the time. They will need resources to set themselves apart to win more battles. And where do you think they'll find those resources?"

Gimlore swallowed. "Here," she said.

Rednow nodded, then his eyes moved to the children, who were now covered in mud. He got up and walked towards the kids. Then Gimlore noticed the holes the old man had been digging were not simple holes.

They were graves.

Three of them were already full of dirt, but there was still an empty one where the rainwater was filling.

"Hey, Rednow," Gimlore called. "Who are these graves for?"

Rednow turned to her, and his face changed from amusement with the kids to a solemn grief. "The first two are for my parents. They were from the south and in the south is where they should rest. The third is for my sister. You would have become friends if she were still alive. I'm sure of it."

Gimlore eyed the dirt on the grave. "Well, she's here, now."

"I think she will be for quite some time." Rednow said, nodding, as if there was something Gimlore didn't know.

"What about the fourth grave?"

"That one is for me."

Gimlore frowned. "Did you... dig your own grave?"

Rednow nodded. "It's a reminder that we always have to answer for what we do. I'm quite happy to dig yours as well."

"We'll get out of here," Gimlore said. She then turned to the kids. "You are staying here with Rednow. You will do whatever he says. He's in charge of you two now."

"You heard your mother. Now, whoever rips out the most weeds from that side of my farmland wins," Rednow said.

All three adults stayed back as the kids raced each other to the right side of the fields.

"You should show up in town more. At least get a drink. Whenever the Maiden's Hall is back up and running."

"I've never been much of a drinker."

"Maybe you can find yourself company there..."

"Not much of a lover, either."

Gimlore didn't understand the man, but she nodded and left him alone. A legendary killer who lived his life in hiding, depriving himself of things most people wouldn't go without. Not a drinker. Not a lover, but a killer. And even if he was old, even if he only had an arm left, he still was a killer.

Her skin prickled just thinking about him in that monstrous form. At least she had him on her side now. She would have never guessed, but good things happened when she started trusting people more.

⋯⋯⋯

"And what now?" Keryon asked Gimlore as they arrived in Heleronde and jumped off their hearthspears. "What happens to me?"

Gimlore gave him a side glance. She trusted him now, as much as she could trust anybody. She didn't like how smart he was. Smart men only led to trouble, but she needed to trust someone. "Well, you're the warden, aren't you? It's your job to keep the town in line, so do it."

"No sham?"

"No sham."

Keryon nodded, smiling with the cocky look that pissed her off so much. "What about Piesym's laboratory? The elixir?"

"Look. All I'm trying to do right now is rebuild the Maiden's Hall as quickly as possible. Without that revenue stream, I'm fucked."

Keryon smiled.

"What?"

The Warden pointed to the distance. "It looks like they're already taking care of it for you."

Gimlore looked around and saw a large group of villagers. Carpenters, builders, and even other people in a commotion around the decrepit Maiden's Hall. She recognised a few faces, but she didn't know some of those people. At first, it looked like they were destroying the building's ruins with hammers and hatchets. Her stomach turned, and she hurried her steps. As she got closer, she realised what it was and her eyes watered. They were demolishing the building. They were helping her start fresh.

"Why are they doing this for me? They hate me."

"It seems like they don't. I don't think they ever did. Either that or they can't wait to have a place to get drunk again."

Gimlore smiled as they approached the crowd in front of the Maiden's Hall. Nork and Nosema came running towards her.

"Boss, they said they wanted to help... We didn't know what to do," Nosema said.

"It's... It's fine..."

When the crowd noticed her, they turned towards her and started clapping. Old men and young children. Older women and young maidens. They clapped.

For her.

"What did I do?" she asked.

"You kept your promise, madam," a toothless old man said. "You protected us."

Gimlore wanted a place to hide somewhere. She was no saint, no protector of the poor and hungry. Just a taverner. They knew it too, but maybe they didn't care.

It didn't matter who she was. It mattered what she did.

"There might be other news..." Keryon said right after the clapping broke. The townsfolk returned to their demolition work.

The Warden looked beyond the crowd and Gimlore gasped as she saw it. She crossed her arms and stayed there for a moment, looking at Foloi and another man kissing on the street, impeding the traffic of people and wagons looking to cross it.

"He's doing that to make me jealous. Who am I going to fuck now, then?" she asked with a sigh.

Keryon cleared his throat. "Well…"

Gimlore frowned and looked at him. "Not you! You're a lawman and I'm a rascal."

"I think by now we've both realised how bad of a lawman I am and how bad of a rascal you are," Keryon said, his lips unfolding into that irritating, beautiful smile.

Gimlore scowled, rolled her eyes, and continued forward to help the folks with the demolition work.

·····•·····

Rednow watched as the kids fought each other and grabbed the weeds with their bare hands. He smiled. They would soon learn oak ivy was not to be touched like that. He glanced to his right side, to the track that would lead to the swamps and then to Heleronde. Perhaps one day he would have his own hearthspears as well, but there was no rush now.

He was retired.

Well, not if the Essence's words were true.

After a long sigh, he shifted his attention back to the children and sat on an improvised chair he had built. They were lively enough but turning them into smokesmiths would take a long time, especially if they were not to risk their lives. He had sworn never to do to others what they had done to him unless they were about to perish, but this was their mother's will. Perhaps he could still be useful. Perhaps his days of mentoring weren't over yet.

He reached into the forsaken bag he never lost sight of these days. For months he had put off opening it. He didn't want to believe anything the Essence had said, but if it was Rebma's handwriting on those paper sheets, then everything must be true.

Rednow swallowed and pulled the folder out of the leather bag, letting it fall on the mud by his side. He rested it on his lap and took one last glance at the children to make sure they wouldn't interrupt him.

He opened the folder, and a loose, small piece of paper almost fell from the first page. Rednow picked it up.

Brother,
You've always loved my songs. Here is the most important one of all.

Your dear sister,
Rebma

Rednow couldn't contain his watering eyes. He imagined his sister with her beautiful long red hair flowing in the wind, kissed by the mountain breeze. He imagined her watching over him, out there. Wherever she might be.

Cleaning up the tears with the sleeve, he put Rebma's tender note aside and took a better look at the heavy stack of paper sheets. Scripture, the Essence had called it. He flicked the first white page on top and big, heavy inked letters marked the title.

MOTHER'S
MEMORIES

Mother... he thought.

Not his mother.

Rebma had recollected sparse and loose memories of the many years of the Essence's existence and tried to organise them in a way that made sense. His sister's handwriting was beautiful and made him want to read more.

She deconstructed many of the legends known to humankind about Mother Nature and Father Time, two murderous deities eager to be served by the Ancient Ones. She even wrote about the power they got in return.

For what seemed like hours, Rednow read like he never had. Rebma's prose was compelling even when describing the pain the Essence had felt and endured over centuries. How she had tried to protect humanity from the deviations of the Old One. She had long suspected her brother was awakening again and would soon break the shackles she had built for him. And if she was to be believed, he would be back now and somehow Rednow had to do something about it.

And then he started believing.

Rebma had written about the origins of the smokesmiths and how they harnessed their power in a level of detail that she would never have been able to have. There were extensive details about the powers of the Old One, whom she also called the Deceiver. Too detailed to be fantasy.

With the children now panting by his side, waiting for new instructions, Rednow froze, focusing on the last few lines that seemed almost directed at him.

Read it again and again. And always keep fighting.

THE END

Thank you! Please Read!

You've made it!

Thank you so much for dedicating your precious time and love for the genre to *Seeds of War*. Without readers, there would be no point in telling stories. It is only with your support that I carry on with *The Smokesmiths* series.

So, if you enjoyed *Seeds of War*, please leave a rating or a review on Amazon. Please. Thousands of books are published every day, millions every year. For *Seeds of War* to have a fighting chance among them, it needs all the help it can get. That means ratings and reviews from readers like you. Leaving a review is one of the best things a reader can do.

Writing *Seeds of War* was quite the bumpy journey. This was a story I've wanted to tell for a long time. I've tinkered with parts of it in my mind for years and some bits even came from unfinished manuscripts. I've always wanted to tell stories about non-conventional families and single parents who thrive on their own despite everything thrown at them. About older people, who are often told to stay in their lane. I also wanted to tell stories of displacement and the feelings that come from being forced out of your reality one way or another.

Writing is my passion. I intend to do it forever, and count on you for support. It truly means everything to me!

I promise I'll keep writing and always sharpening the writing tools in my satchel.

Stay strong and persevere,
João F. Silva

JOIN THE SMOKESMITHS

Sign up to João F. Silva's mailing list at www.joaofsilva.net and read his short story 'A Dead Man' for FREE. You'll be the first to receive all the news, writing updates regarding *The Smokesmiths* series, any other projects or special offers and discounts.

ACKNOWLEDGMENTS

This book is for everyone who is struggling under the surface. I see you.

Seeds of War would have never seen the light of day if it wasn't for a very special group of people. I have to thank my parents for buying me books when I asked and even when I didn't. They wanted me to be an avid reader, and now I am a *little* more than that. I must extend my thanks to Claudia and Steffen for gifting me a copy of the *Name of the Wind* all these years ago and ending my decade-long dry-spell of fantasy books.

My editor, Sarah Chorn, turned a less-than-polished manuscript with issues into something that I'm excited for people to read. Without her, this book would have been very different.

There are many fellow writers who have followed my journey. The feedback given by my alpha readers Lara and Lena has been a tremendous help. They read some of the earliest drafts of *Seeds of War* when maybe no one should have. Massive thanks to all the other amazing beta readers whose feedback helped shape this book into its final form.

And of course, I had the support and encouragement of my wife, W, who has long been the rock that keeps me grounded when my mind is plotting imagined worlds and creatures. If I had the perseverance to finish writing this book, it was because of you.

There is no looking back now!

About the Author

João F. Silva was born in a small town in Portugal but now lives in London, with his three feline co-workers/bosses. He writes Epic Fantasy, Science Fiction and Horror and has been on the jury for the 2020 and 2022 editions of the "Best Newcomer" Award at the British Fantasy Awards. His short fiction has been published in Grimdark Magazine and Haven Speculative.

Get in touch by filling in the form on his website (www.joaofsilva.net), by emailing him at joao@joaofsilva.net, or by following him on social media

GLOSSARY

Alarkan – A newly-discovered continent, emerged from the depths of the ocean.

Ancient Ones – Ancient Lost Civilisation which disappeared without a trace.

Belleaf Oil – Highly flammable oil extracted from belleaf flowers. Doesn't require a spark to start burning. Often used by smokesmiths.

Bloodsleuth – Blind reptilian hound with a three-way muzzle with a keen sense of smell for blood.

Cerro – Fruit tree which produces bittersweet berries.

Crimson Wars – A bloody period that lasted years and during which humanity was plagued by hordes of monstrous creatures like bloodsleuths.

Floating City Fleet – A fleet of hundreds of massive-sized maritime vessels owned by the Two Kingdoms of Sirestir and Yab.

Greasy Bomb – Explosive consisting of a sack of black powder doused in belleaf oil. Thrown at enemies like a knife.

Hearthspear – Agile, reptilian creatures used as mounts.

Heleronde – The busiest settlement in all of Alarkan.

Marcruncher – Furry carnivorous mammal. Inhabits cold areas.

Mossback – Reptilian creatures found in Alarkan. They produce a coveted liver elixir.

Ominous Kas – A rare herb that grants abilities to smokesmiths when burned.

Leeth – Legendary and covert mercenary group.

Pinehead – Sentient humanoid species with a child-like appearance and size.

Puncturing Ceremony – Tradition in Gasho during which a member of nobility pierces their face dozens of times as a symbol of power and wealth.

Smokesmith – Person who is able to breathe smoke and has the ability to manipulate it.

Shadesgrowl – Large yet slow herbivore creature used as a mount in cold climates.

The Miracle – The event during which Orberesis broke the world, slayed the monsters that plagued humanity, and ended the Crimson Wars.

The Two Kingdoms – A political alliance between the kingdoms of Sirestir and Yab.

Twisted Twins – A rare herb that grants abilities to smokesmiths when burned.

Wickplate – Giant maritime creatures with durable scales. They are fished and their scales are used to build breastplates.

DRAMATIS PERSONAE

Doi "Orberesis" Sonoda – Cult leader who goes by the moniker 'God Himself'

Gimlore – Businesswoman, owner of the Maiden's Hall and de facto ruler of Heleronde

Rednow – Leader of the Leeth, brother to Rebma. Known as the Blood Collector

Keryon – Former lawman and smokesmith.

Solvi – Orberesis' most trusted aide and protector

Edmir – Gimlore's most trusted companion

Rebma – Rednow's younger sister

Merey – Brash and confident general of the Leeth

Tellwoon – Thoughtful general of the Leeth

Tavanar – Orberesis' oldest friend and confidant

Foloi – Big and strong cage fighter. Gimlore's lover

Nork – Gimlore's henchman

Nosema – Gimlore's henchman

Zatak – Lead houndsman of the Leeth

Piesym – Keryon's business partner and shopkeeper

Doemus – King of the Two Nations

Thura – Queen of the Two Nations

Taishay – Main political advisor of the Two Nations

Pinesy – Pinehead in Gimlore's crew

Tinko and Thata – Gimlore's infant children

Eshof – Old woman, citizen of Heleronde

Clafa – Peasant farmer in Gimlore's farmlands

Basa Akan – Herald from Sirestir sent to Heleronde

Rednalf – Rednow's long-deceased nephew

Caligo – King of Gasho

Printed in the USA
CPSIA information can be obtained
at www.ICGtesting.com
JSHW020633291223
54424JS00037B/524/J